TIDE OF DARKNESS

BOOK I

AMARAH CALDERINI

Copyright

This is a work of fiction. All of the characters, organizations, places, and events portrayed in this novel are either the products of the author's imagination or used fictitiously.

TIDE OF DARKNESS
Copyright © 2022 by Amarah Calderini

All rights reserved.
No part of this book may be reproduced in any form or by any electronic or mechanical means, including information storage and retrieval systems, without written permission from the author, except for the use of brief quotations in a book review.

Cover Artwork and Design: Sarah Hansen of Okay Creations
Interior Formatting: Tiarra Blandin
Editorial: Tiarra Blandin of Allotrope Editorial

Dedication

To Shannon—for always being a light in the darkness.

CHAPTER ONE

Mirren

The world is dark beyond our Boundary. One step outside the towering fence and electricity flounders. Light is swallowed by inky black night, extinguished forever. Normally, the lights of Similis calm me. But today, I wish bitterly for some of that ancient obscurity, if only to douse the eerie blue glow of the machines attached to my brother.

The Healing Center is cold. The antiseptic indifference of the place permeates my overcoat. Wrapping my arms tightly around my middle, I stare at the Healer who speaks to us, not seeing a person at all, but rather, a physical manifestation of facts.

My brother is dying. I am going to be alone.

The Healer has moved beyond the facts that matter and onto the ones that don't, like the cause of Easton's disease and the treatments that have failed, but I hang on to the last word of his first sentence.

Dying, died, dead.

I try to grasp them. To roll them around on my tongue and make sense of them, but ultimately, I fall short. 'Dying' has always been an abstract word. It's what happens when you grow old. Your belongings are given back to the Community, goodbyes are said, and then you die. Surely, the word cannot be applied to a boy who has barely had time to say his hellos, let alone his goodbyes?

"Dying," I say out loud, hoping the word will make more sense in my own voice.

The Healer abruptly stops talking, eyeing me warily. Easton turns to me in concern. I attempt a reassuring smile, but must not succeed, because the line between his brow doesn't smooth. He's my little brother and he is dying, and he should not need to be the one offering comfort. He accepts what the Healer has told us the way he accepts most things in life—with a pleasant face and a self-deprecating smile. There is no denial or obstinate arguing, like I would be doing if I was able to wrap my mind around the meaning of any of it. He doesn't throw himself on the ground and cry at the unfairness of it all, something that has also crossed my mind.

Instead, he is smiling politely at the useless Healer and comforting his mess of a sister. I glare at the Healer, though being willfully rude is against the Keys. Hitting him until he takes back his proclamation is also against the Keys, so I'm settling for the lesser of the two offenses.

"The only way to combat the illness is a transplant," he says, as he unhooks a variety of wires from Easton, "but unfortunately, your sister isn't a match."

The Healer's long face becomes longer. It's an expression I recognize well, one I've become intimately familiar with. Pity. "It is an anomaly, I'm afraid. With the balance of our society and the precise way we match life partners, we have a 97% success rate at avoiding these genetic malformations. The other 3%, we have always been able to combat with the help of parental unit donation. In your case, unfortunately..." his voice fades into an uncomfortable silence. He won't finish his sentence because it would be intrusive. Unharmonious.

I almost laugh at the absurdity. As if there is anything harmonious about this moment. "Our parental units were Outcast," I finish for him, my voice razor-edged.

Easton's disappointment is palpable, though the only outward sign is the slight purse of his lips. I should not be making the Healer feel uncomfortable with these things. It's unkind.

The man has the decency to drop his eyes and I feel, at once, victorious and completely ashamed for the way my words have affected him.

"We can make you comfortable while the disease runs its course, but unfortunately, that is all we can do," he says to the sterile white floor. I stare at the top of his head, hoping to burn a hole through his shiny blonde hair.

"Thank you for your time, Healer," Easton replies, his voice light. "We won't take up any more of it. I know your daughter is being Bound today and we wouldn't want to make you late."

The Healer nods and exits the room, all the while avoiding my gaze. He shows kindness by not reporting my flagrant disregard of the Keys, but I feel no gratitude.

I round on Easton. "We wouldn't want to make you late to the Binding?!" I say, incredulous. Easton always allows me leniency in my tone of voice when we are alone, and he does so now. "Who cares about the Binding?"

"*You* should," he says pointedly. He glances at the clock above the door. "You're going to be late, too, if we don't leave right now." Hopping off the exam table, he begins to gather his things.

"I'm not going!" The word 'dying' has rendered everything else, including the Binding ceremony, meaningless. "It doesn't matter who I'm Bound to if I don't have you."

Easton shrugs into his overcoat and turns to me, his face serious. "You know, Mirren, anyone would be lucky to be Bound to you."

A lump forms in my throat, constricting my breathing. His life has been completely overturned in a matter of minutes and still, he puts my feelings above his own. He speaks to the fears of my heart, knowing them without judgement and attempting to assuage them. I cannot lose the only person in the world who knows me—really knows me—and doesn't hate me for it. "Easton," I begin, but he shakes his head softly.

"We can talk about what we learned tomorrow. Today is about you."

He leads me gently from the exam room, his steps soft and sure. I don't want to talk about what we learned today. Shoving it down and hiding it deep in the recesses of myself will surely keep it from being real. At the same time, the need to talk about it threads through me. To spill my words and fears and wrap them around the truth until it changes into something more malleable.

I look up at my brother as we walk the long hallways of the Healing Center and wonder again at how different we are. Despite being two years his senior, his willowy frame towers a good foot over my stockier one. He has my mother's light hair and hazel eyes, while I inherited my father's deep chestnut and sea-green. Easton has always floated through the Community easier than I have. Perhaps because his face doesn't remind everyone of our Outcast father like mine does. Or maybe, it's simply because he is better than I am. Our Community Keys have always come naturally to him. *Kindness before trust. Fairness before prosperity. Community before self.*

Easton never needs to be reminded to be kind because he always is. He doesn't have trouble guarding his tongue, because he is always concerned about how his words affect others. When people look at him, they don't see an Outcast's son; they see a genuinely good person who uplifts those around him.

I don't know what people see when they look at me, other than someone who doesn't deserve Easton.

I push open the glass doors and we step outside, the spring air heady with moisture and the scent of new blooms wafting in from the agricultural fields. As if the earth itself is mocking me with its promise of new life when mine has just unraveled. Worry gnaws at my stomach as Easton keeps pace with me. Has the illness already taken hold? The Healer said he would have months, but he also said it was unprecedented. What if he was wrong?

"The Covinus doesn't make mistakes," Easton says confidently, and I stare at him for a moment before realizing he still speaks of the Binding. "You will be Bound to your perfect partner. One who doesn't care about the past. One who only cares about the future."

I scoff. There will be no partner who doesn't care about my past. As far as everyone in our sector is concerned, and probably every other sector in Similis, my family is guilty of breaking our sacred Keys. The fact that I had nothing to do with the offense—don't even *know* the nature of it—has seemed to matter little in the eyes of my peers. Whispers follow me like an icy wind and have for most of my life. Over the years, I have learned to duck my head and weather the storm. Most days, the gossip no longer brings a hot wave of shame to my cheeks.

My thick skin doesn't translate to days like the Binding, when I am to be paraded in front of the entire Community. In less than an hour, every eighteen-year-old will be Bound to their life partner. Classmates have been analyzing and giggling about it for ages, but I've always kept it in the corner of my mind, an intangible date to be dealt with somewhere far in the future. Now, it's arrived and brought with it an acute sense of dread. That is, until Easton's appointment at the Healing Center, when all my other worries were diminished by the massive one now looming over me. It's difficult to see shadows when your entire world has turned to night.

The Community center is located in the central metropolis, same as every other important building, so it only takes a few minutes of walking to reach it. It's a large structure, practical and plain like most everything else here. The entirety of the Covinus is housed within, along with the amphitheater where the Binding will take place. Tall and rectangular, it casts everything but the cobbled square in morose shades of gray.

The square is the only colorful part of Similis, a splash of crimson in a sea of taupe. In a world of uniformity, it is almost an affront to the senses. The stones spiral out like ripples in a pond in every shade of red imaginable. I often wonder about the square's creator and what they meant in adding such a riot of color in an otherwise monotonous world. Maybe it was meant as a reminder to Similians that the square, and our Covinus encased within it, is the heart of our Community. I doubt the artist meant to make viewers feel rebellious and anxious and full all at once, the way I do when I see it.

On a different day, the square reminds me of all these things, but today I can only see blood.

Easton's and mine, intwined. Blood means little here, no Community member above another, but it means something to me. The same life force runs through both of us, so that no matter where we go, we are always connected through it. Until he goes somewhere I can never follow.

Easton smiles at me gently and I have the urge to grab his hand. To squeeze and feel its warmth and make him promise to never let go. But touch is not something taken lightly, and he would be horrified if I attempted it in such a public place.

I am still staring at his hands, at the elegant fingers and perfectly shaped nails, when the first explosion rocks the ground beneath us.

The activity in the square comes to an immediate halt, a horrified hush descending over the red bricks.

We are a quiet people. Screams are rare. But they sound now, loud and anguished, from the direction of the Boundary gate. The gate that separates us from the Dark World and keeps the monsters from overcoming our Community, ones both human and beast in nature.

Everyone around me is frozen, their eyes blinking wide and uncertain. They are rabbits in a wild field. When faced with a predator, their best hope is to melt into their surroundings. This time, the predator isn't even the explosion itself. It's the novelty of it. A jagged tear in the smooth curtain of scheduled monotony.

My heart beats wildly and my muscles tense. The need to move, to do *something,* races through me but before I can bend to its call, Easton lays a soft hand on the sleeve of my coat. The contact, so rare and unexpected, shocks me into stillness.

"Trust in the Covinus. They will keep us safe."

His eyes are imploring, and a sharp wave of shame

pierces my chest. *Don't go where I can't follow.* Did I not just issue the same silent plea to him?

I dig my teeth into my lip, allowing the stinging pain to settle me. When our parents were Outcast, I promised myself to stay with Easton, to mold myself into whatever the Community wanted me to be in order to stay with him. And yet, twelve years later, I still struggle with calming whatever lives inside me.

Covinus vehicles race out of headquarters, dark vans with sirens as bright as the square. The Dark Worlders have made many attempts to breach the Boundary, but they've never succeeded. Easton is right. The Covinus always keeps us safe.

I force myself to turn away; to calm the racing of my heart and follow the crowd that has already started moving toward the Community Center.

Easton removes his hand, but his touch lingers even after I am seated with my year.

CHAPTER
TWO

Mirren

The air is chilled on the roof of our quarterage. I shiver against it, peering out at the same squat gray buildings that stretch for miles around me. Quarterages give way to agricultural fields and beyond that, the lights of the Boundary. I'm too far away to see the Boundary men patrolling the wall, but I know they are there, warding off whatever threats exist on the other side.

One was gravely injured in the explosion, his burned body escorted to the Healing Center in a rush of sirens. No culprit was named in the attack, but it wasn't necessary. Everyone knows it was a Dark Worlder. Our Boundary is what keeps us safe from the curse that shadows their land; a curse so dark and depraved, it infiltrates everyone who lives under it, twisting them into unrecognizable evil.

They say it's our lights, shining against the stygian sky that keeps the curse at bay. The lights serve as a reminder of the prosperity that comes when you reject selfishness and embrace kindness and fairness. The lights of the Similian boundary shine at all hours of the day, a beacon of hope in an otherwise cruel world.

They don't feel hopeful to me now. Instead, I feel numb.

I have been waiting to feel something else, something heated and powerful; something that could change the circumstances Easton and I have been handed, but the numbness remains. The lights only serve as a reminder that what was once bright is now dark. What once was full is now empty.

I've often sat up here and wondered what those living in the Dark World see when they look at our lights. If they see them as a beacon of what peace is possible, as we are taught, or if they are simply a cruel reminder of all that we have in Similis that they lack.

Most Similians don't spare more than a passing thought for our lights or the Darkness that lay beyond, but I am not like most Similians. Most don't have parents that were Outcast.

On nights like these, I often climb to the roof and squint into the Darkness, picturing my father's green eyes. In all my memories, they are always twinkling as if in the midst of some great laugh, but I can never remember the sound of it.

Maybe it's because I never actually heard it. We are a muted people, always keeping such things to ourselves.

I look at the lights and imagine my father's eyes and wonder if the curse has taken the souls of my parents. Or if they even survived long enough amongst the Dark Worlders to be turned. There are no laws in the Dark World except one—do not kill. But there are plenty of other depravities that can be inflicted upon a person.

It doesn't matter much either way, I suppose, but still, I wonder. And tonight, when my heart aches and I can't catch a full breath, I allow myself to imagine what my life would be like if they had never been Outcast. If they were here to shoulder the weight of Easton's sickness. To figure out how to fix it. To tell me I'm not alone if they couldn't. Dangerous thoughts. But thoughts I can't help.

"There you are."

I turn and smile at Easton. He smiles back and something in my chest eases. Even if our world must change, it hasn't changed yet. "I was starting to think you'd run off to avoid being Bound," he says wryly.

"I was just up here thinking. And besides, there's nowhere to run."

Easton situates himself beside me. Though we don't touch, his body is a warm comfort next to mine. "So," he begins amicably. "Harlan Astor."

My shoulders tense. When Harlan was announced as my life partner, there'd been an explosive boom of collective scandal that sounded eerily reminiscent of the one that shook the square. When Harlan climbed the stage, all creamy skin and golden hair, it was all I could do to look him in the eye and try to appear sorry for the way my stigma was already affecting him.

They pressed the Binding mark into our skin and as soon as we were dismissed, I threaded my way through awkward-looking partners toward the exit without so much as a backward glance.

"What about him?"

"You certainly could have done a lot worse for a life partner."

"Well, I don't think the girls in my year agree with you."

"Ah, so you noticed that did you?" Easton says lightly.

"It was hard not to."

"Did you consider it was out of jealousy?"

I frown. No, I hadn't considered that at all.

Easton rolls his eyes. "Of course, you didn't. I'm sure you were certain it was some all-encompassing statement about you."

I glare at him, even though he speaks the truth. I rarely get out of my own way long enough to see that not everything has to be about being an Outcast's daughter.

"Harlan is a good person," Easton continues.

I shrug noncommittally. "I'm sure he is. I don't really know anything about him."

This is both the truth and a lie. I've never said so much as 'hello' to Harlan, but he's been in my year for as long as I can remember, so I've gathered a few things. He's eighteen, like me. He smiles easily, unlike me. And many of the girls speculated who he would be Bound to. I doubt any of them guessed it would be the girl with Outcast blood running through her veins.

"The Covinus doesn't make mistakes," Easton says confidently, and I can't help the incredulous scoff that escapes my lips.

"The Covinus doesn't make mistakes?" I repeat with disgust. "What about you, Easton? You don't think what's happening to you is a mistake?"

At the Binding Ceremony, a member of the Covinus had addressed the crowd, speaking of the perfect balance of our society and how Similis has eradicated war, poverty, and disease through upholding the Keys. I squeezed my eyes shut to keep from screaming. Disease has not been eradicated; it is alive and ravaging through my brother like a tidal wave only I can see. And if disease is living in our Community, when the Covinus says it is not, what else is thriving in the parts of Similis no one can see?

Easton looks at me with pity and I know immediately,

it's pity for me. Not himself. "Mirren, you can't blame the Covinus for what's happening to me. The Healer explained quite clearly that in usual cases, they can use the parents as a match. It's not the Covinus' fault our parents aren't here."

He's right. It isn't the Covinus' fault that our parents chose breaking the rules over protecting us. It's *their* fault they aren't here to heal Easton. My father's eyes flash in my mind once more and I want to claw them out.

"You are going to go on to have a wonderful life with Harlan."

I shake my head. "I don't want to *go on* anywhere, Easton!" my voice is raised, and he eyes me with alarm. Anger could earn me sanctions, and while Easton has always given me grace when we are alone, his Similian upbringing still shines through. "I don't want to just accept this or come to peace with it. I don't want to do anything that confirms it's real. That I'm going to be here and you're not."

Easton shrugs. "I can't come with you when you're Bound anyway, Mirren, and you shouldn't want me to. You're going to have your own life, with your own family. And if things were different, I'd have my own life, too." His face grows tight for a fraction of a second, before it releases into its usual geniality. "You'd only see me at Community events. How is this much different?"

It's different in so many ways, but they are ways I don't have words for. Words don't encompass the way someone feels like wrapping yourself up in a soft, worn blanket; in the way that they know you, fit around you. Easton is the only person in the world who knows me, and if there is no one to remind you who you are when the world makes it hard to remember, how do you hold on to yourself?

I don't say any of this because it's jumbled and ridiculous and I'm sure it'd make Easton uncomfortable. You aren't supposed to rely on your family to tell you who you are; that's what the Covinus is for. They will tell you that you're a Similian citizen and that is the first, and most important, part of your identity. But Easton has always known the other, smaller parts of mine, and that seems to matter more.

"Get some sleep," he says. "It will all feel better in the morning."

He turns to go inside. After one last glance at the lights, I follow.

The next day is never ending, each interaction more unbearable that the last. Everyone at the Education center smiles politely and listens kindly, and none of them can see the black hole that has opened up inside me, threating to swallow everyone in my path. When the last bell rings, it's all I can do not to trample over the throng of students that file patiently out the door. When I finally reach the exit, I gulp down the thick air as if I haven't sucked in a full breath all day.

"Mirren," a voice calls from behind me and I look longingly across the square, the brightly colored paving stones winking in the afternoon sun. I could run across them right now, run until my breath comes in painful puffs and my muscles tingle with exhilaration. Run far, far away from every other pair of eyes.

"Mirren, you forgot your notebook."

I cringe and turn to Harlan, who holds up my tattered notebook, golden hair and eyes sparkling in the afternoon sun. *I am the dark and you are the light. I will ruin you.* "Thank you," I say, plucking the notebook out of his hand. I swing my bag off my shoulder to stuff it in.

"It's a very nice day. It finally feels like spring," he says, watching as I struggle to zip my overstuffed bag. Our guardian, Farrah, has been trying to get me to carry a new one for an entire year, but I stubbornly told her that I *liked* the way the fabric has worn, and the zipper has warped. It's an irritating time for her to be proven correct.

"The air seems freshest in the spring," Harlan continues, apparently undeterred by my huffing and puffing.

The air is never fresh in Similis, obscured as it is by a thick cloud of coal from our power plants and factories, but I don't say this to Harlan. Instead, I keep my lips firmly closed and yank at my zipper, pleading with it to finally give in so I won't be forced to have an actual conversation with my life partner. He's a good person. He won't want to make me feel uncomfortable, so I know he will push through.

Finally, the zipper gives way and I almost cry out in relief.

I haul my bag over my shoulder and turn toward my sector. Despite the crisp breeze, the sun is warm against my cheek, its ray a gentle tease of the summer to come.

"Did you hear about the explosion at the Boundary?"

"You don't have to do this," I interject irritably, beginning to walk and hoping that if I'm fast enough, it'll save us both the humiliation of trying to have a conversation.

Harlan follows me, those amber eyes round and innocent. "Do what?"

I grind my teeth. "Talk to me, be nice to me, be *anything* to me."

I stop and face him. He is not very tall for a boy, but I still have to tilt my chin in order to speak to him. His frame is stocky and though our jumpsuits are made to fit loosely, I can see the curve of muscle beneath it. "I am under no illusions that you being Bound to me makes us friends. Don't feel obligated." I turn on my heel and speed-up my pace.

"Friends seems like a good place to start, don't you think?" He falls into step beside me.

"No," I mutter at the ground. I shouldn't be so willfully unpleasant to him, but it seems to be what I default to, against the Keys or not. I'm trying to help him, in my own twisted way, since he doesn't seem to be aware enough to help himself. We won't move into a quarterage until the end of spring; he has three months of blissful living, away from the mess of rumors around me.

Harlan doesn't acknowledge my objectionable countenance. For him to respond would be an unkindness in itself and he doesn't seem the type to chafe against the rules as I do. Instead, he walks beside me in silence, keeping pace with a small, contented smile on his face.

"Isn't your sector the other way?"

"Yes," he replies simply, but he doesn't turn.

"Look," I struggle to keep my voice low. I remind myself to breathe, to keep my voice soft and my face passive. Harlan doesn't deserve to be made to feel inferior because of my own insecurities. I don't know why I'm not better at this, after all these years. "I am trying to help you."

Harlan adjusts the strap of his bag, his face still unbothered. I wonder if that's what my face would look like if my parents hadn't broken the rules. If they'd stayed with Easton and I and raised us to thoughtfully exude the Keys. If there were no whispers or anger poisoning my heart, making it better suited for the wilds of the Dark World than for the brightness of the Community. Have I always been cynical and restless, or have I been made into what I am?

I've felt the way I have so long, I can't remember feeling any different.

"I don't need help, thank you," Harlan replies, polite and pointed.

I huff a frustrated sigh and keep walking. Fine. If he wants to commit social suicide in the last few months of freedom, who am I to stop him?

We walk past the buildings of the metropolis and into my sector. The few trees that are planted along the walkways blow in the breeze, the rustle of their leaves the only sound that breaks our silence.

Finally, we arrive at my quarterage. I turn to Harlan, feeling inexplicably like my hands are too big for my body. "Well, this is it."

"I know." His voice is warm. Like honey.

Of course it is, I think darkly. *All honey and gold.*

"I'll see you here tomorrow before school," and with that he turns back toward the main square.

I stare at him dumbly, watching his silhouette disappear into the afternoon sun. It isn't until much later that I wonder how Harlan knew which quarterage was mine.

I was seven when my parents were Outcast. My father dropped Easton and I off at the Education center, the third floor where all children not of schooling age go during the day while their parents are at their assignments. I remember his gait being easy as we walked, telling us a joke about a lobster that five-year-old Easton thought was hilarious and that I, in my seven-year-old wisdom, knew was cheesy. We'd wished my mother a good morning before setting off and my father had kissed her on the cheek, an action so foreign it still brings a heat to my skin when I recall it.

I've thought about that morning so many times, trying to pinpoint something I must have missed. There had to be an anomaly I didn't see—something that would point to what was about to happen. My parents must have said something, given some sort of sign, that would clue me into their decision to break the Keys. To alert me to their decision to uproot my entire existence.

Hard as I try, the morning remains the same, frozen in memory like ice on a pond. Routine, uneventful, and worst of all, happy. Aside from my father's peck on the cheek, there's nothing about it that stands out from any other morning. Except, at the end of the day, when all the other parents came to collect their children, Easton and I peered through the window, waiting for a father that would never come.

Instead, a man dressed in Covinus-issued navy came and told us of our parents' banishment. He took us to our new housing assignment, the home of a middle-aged couple that had a deficit of children we were now expected to fill. We were never even allowed to return to our former quarterage; instead, another man in blue was waiting at our new home with a small box of our things. An entire box wasn't necessary; nothing is really ours in Similis anyway. It all belongs to the Community.

Even then, as a boy with pudgy little fists and even pudgier cheeks, Easton took the news in stride. He was pleasant to our escort and charming to our new host parents. I, on the other hand, was anything but. I screamed my head off. I tried to slug our Covinus escort in the mouth until he took back his words. I held my breath until I turned blue, demanding to see my parents. I suppose, in that regard, I haven't learned much.

In the end, none of it mattered. Our new guardians, Jakoby and Farrah, injected me with some sort of medicine they claimed would heal the rift in my mind and I fell into oblivion. I woke up hours or days later in my new bed with a headache and a throat raw from screaming.

I held on to my parents for a long time, through the whispers and stares. I'd slip their names into conversations and then glare defiantly, daring anyone to say something back to me. I would ask our guardians about them repeatedly until Jakoby's endless patience finally wore thin and he admonished me for preying on Farrah's nerves. He said that I, too, would be Outcast if I didn't shape up.

Eventually, I stopped talking about them for Easton's sake. Jakoby was right. I couldn't be Outcast too, or Easton would be entirely alone. I decided to be better than my parents. I would choose my family over selfishness; I would follow the rules and I would follow them so well there would be no chance we would ever be separated. I never managed to do it well, but I did manage.

And what was it all for? I stubbornly kept my place in the Community instead of throwing myself to all my destructive urges so we would be together. And now, he's dying. What will happen to me when he's gone? Have I learned anything in the eleven years since my parents left? Or will I ravage myself the way I did when I was seven, screaming and railing against the Covinus until I'm finally Outcast? It will serve me right.

"Do you ever think about the day Mom and Dad were Outcast?" I ask.

Easton, who is perched on a threadbare chair in the living area of our quarterage, looks up from his homework in astonishment. I haven't spoke of them since I vowed to follow the rules and we have nothing left to bring them to mind. All their clothes were reused, all their belongings never really theirs.

"Why are you speaking of such things?" His tone is reminiscent of Jakoby's; scolding. I purse my lips in irritation that he favors Jakoby, but quickly push it away. It isn't Easton's fault he aspires to be like the only father figure he's really known.

I shrug as if this conversation is casual even though it doesn't feel that way. Maybe Easton really never thinks of it. Maybe that's why he's had an easier time; he accepts things as they are. "I've been thinking a lot about being alone. It calls them to mind." The truth.

"Mirren, you aren't going to be alone. You will have Harlan. You still have Farrah and Jakoby," There is a crinkle between his brows that only appears when he's worried, which is generally only when he's talking to me. It emerges now, his face a mixture of anxiety and consternation. I hate that I cause him that, but I also can't help myself.

"They aren't my family. You are."

Easton shakes his head, loosing a breath of frustration. "They are your Community," he replies firmly and looks back down at his school work. Conversation over.

I stare at the top of his head, at the way his chestnut hair swirls around a cowlick at the back. It has always endeared him to me; that no matter how old he gets, he can never quite tame the childishness out of his hair. His cheeks and hands have thinned and angled, but he will always be a pudgy toddler in my mind, sticky fingers threaded through mine. Before he learned such things are unacceptable.

"Their hands," Easton says quietly, as if I have somehow spoken my thoughts aloud.

"What?"

"Their hands," he says again, meeting my gaze, hazel brown to emerald green. "I remember that morning, their hands…"

Easton's voice trails off and the world slows around me. It's as if it takes hours for me to realize something isn't right, instead of the few milliseconds that actually pass. My little brother's face freezes and his eyes roll sharply to the back of his head.

"Easton!" I cry, leaping from my seat and lunging toward him. I reach him just as he slides from his chair and begins to convulse on the floor.

I grab his hand. It feels wrong to the touch, cold and clammy. His body wrenches and shakes, as if something otherworldly controls his movements. They don't seem natural, don't even seem human, and I gather him to me, trying to keep him from tearing himself apart.

And then I am screaming. I know it because I can feel it, even if I can hear nothing but the labored pains of Easton's breathing. I am screaming for help. For someone, anyone to come save my brother.

The convulsions cease as quickly as they began, and Easton lays still on the floor.

Hours later, I collapse on my bed, fully clothed. My entire body aches, either from trying to drag Easton's unconscious form to get help or the sobs that consumed me afterward. The afternoon comes in flashes: the heaviness of Easton's body as I tried heaving his weight out of the living room. Running into the street, my eyes streaming and my throat burning. The eyes of my Community watching another fall from grace for Mirren Ellis.

By the time the Healer mobile arrived, Easton was unconscious for more than fifteen minutes. They weren't able to revive him on the street and when we arrived at the Healing Center, I had retreated so far into myself I could no longer even scream—no longer do anything but stare at the eerie glow cast across my brother's face from the blue lights of the machines keeping him alive. He looked as if he wasn't quite real. As if none of it was.

My mattress feels stiffer than this morning and my body feels twice as heavy. But I force myself to sit anyway, if only to buy some respite from the way the linen sheets scratch at my skin.

Dying, dead, died.

I stare across the room, uncertain where to go to make myself more comfortable, while at the same time knowing there is nowhere to go. This room, which just this morning could be recognized as mine, no longer feels familiar. It was Easton that made the quarterage home, and without him, there is nothing to connect to. The thought crashes against me, breaking against my heart and pounding at my ribs.

Before I consider why, I run into Easton's room. I burst through the door and inhale the air as if it is his, and his alone. The room is tidy and well kept. There's a bed, a desk and a small dresser, all plain and functional. The walls and surfaces are all bare and a lump forms in my throat. There's nothing in this room that belongs to Easton, nothing any different from my room or every other bedroom in Similis. Easton could die tonight, and I will have nothing to cling to. Nothing to remind me of his small smiles and patient kindness.

Desperate, I rip open his dresser drawers, yanking all the folded jumpsuits out and discarding them carelessly on the floor. I do the same with the next drawer, and the next, until the entire dresser stands empty. Farrah will have a fit when she sees the room in ruins, but I move to the desk anyway, emptying its drawers as well. It's mostly writing utensils and loose paper, but as I reach my hand into the back of the final drawer, my fingers brush against something different. Foreign. Metal.

I yank the drawer out unceremoniously and peer into the far corner. There, where the back and bottom of the drawer meet, sits a small, circular shape. I pry at it with my fingernails, but it's wedged so neatly that it doesn't budge. I scan the room, the mess I've made of it, until my gaze lands on Easton's scissors. Opening them up, I leverage the blade until the little piece of metal pops out of the crack and lands on the concrete floor with a crisp *ting*.

I cradle it between my thumb and forefinger, running my fingertips delicately over the bumps of cool metal. I've never seen it's like in Similis, but I have seen them in our lessons of the Dark World—money. A coin.

There's never been a need for coins in Similis, currency being something that was outlawed by the Founders. Fear slithers up my spine, fear that someone will know that Easton has broken a Key. Wonderment edges my worry. What is my brother, a rule follower and Key believer, doing with contraband?

It's not as if he's hoarding extra rations or clothing, something that would get him a minor sanction. Money is what caused the fall of the Dark World. From it, greed, hatred, and jealousy were birthed. Wars waged that were so terrible, a queen sacrificed herself and all her power to bring down the curse upon the land. It's said that Similis was spared only because of our dedication to selflessness.

And it's this continued self-sacrifice that keeps the curse at bay, even today.

So, possession of something such as a coin will not get Easton a slap on the wrist; it will get him Outcast.

The sharp cold of the concrete floor digs into my knees, but I hardly feel it as I examine the coin. Etched in the red metal is the picture of a majestic looking mountain, its snowcapped peak stretching toward an open sky full of stars. Vertical rocks surround the base, shooting up into the sky like some sort of natural crown. And underneath are the wild waves of a sea.

I stare at the coin, imagining a place where an ocean like this exists, cradled between towering mountains. Imagining how far this coin must have traveled to end up here, stuck in the back of Easton's drawer. Easton is immaculately organized and there have been various times when I've seen him take everything out of his desk to reorganize it. There's no way he would have missed it. This little coin, or perhaps whoever gave it to him, means something.

I rub my thumb over the back, and though it should be smooth, it bounces under my skin. Flipping it over, I bring it closer to my face. The metal is glossy, its many ripples fanning out from the center, but there are two words carved crudely into the back. *Here, love.*

My breath catches in my throat. I spend a full minute suspended like that, knees pressed into the concrete and the coin raised above my head.

Here, love.

Is it a message from whoever owns this coin? Could that sea be a real place? Every map I've ever seen always shows the Dark World as a black stretch of land, gaping and blank. But there must be *something* still there, something that lives and thrives, if there have been breaches to the Boundary.

Love. Heat floods my cheeks. A word never uttered here, much less written down. Love is said to have driven Dark Worlders mad, responsible for as many tragedies as money and war.

How would Easton have gotten the coin in the first place, when he has never even been close to the Boundary and none of us has ever seen anyone outside of Similis?

My heart pounds and my breathing hitches.

Anyone outside of Similis.

Except for two people who used to be *inside* of Similis.

My parents.

And if my parents are alive, that means...that means that Easton has a chance.

Parental donation.

The coin falls from my hand and rolls across the floor, the sound as loud a clap of thunder.

CHAPTER
THREE

Outside the Boundary

The hole is bigger than I expected. It gapes like the open maw of a creature that roams the Nemoran wood, hungry and grotesque. For a wall that has stood as long as man's memory, that has never once even been dented, it crumpled easily enough beneath the force of my explosion.

The Boundary men have been scurrying around it since yesterday, the way rodents do when smoked from their burrows. And isn't that just fitting for a people who blindly follow a false god, comfortable in their prison while the world around them burns? My lips peel back from my teeth in distaste.

The little lemmings search in vain. There is no remedy for the wall, no earthly material that will repair the damage. Whatever magic was used to construct the Boundary has long since been extinguished. Power courses uncomfortably through my veins and for once I allow it to fill me. I have crumbled something timeless, infinite. Now the people of Similis will finally feel the agony of the Darkness, it's sharp edges and unforgiving waves. They are no longer safe from its influence.

This was a necessary violence, but it is satisfying, nonetheless.

"Tonight, then?" My companion asks from his place next to me. Weapons line his chest and legs and a large bow peeks from over his shoulder. A warrior, just as I trained him to be. Who will not balk at what comes next and the blood it will most certainly reap.

I nod, quick and terse. Words aren't needed.

Tonight, I will meld into the Darkness, dropping into its twisted depths until it is all I am, all I can feel. Tonight, blood will rain at my hands and I will get back what is mine.

CHAPTER
FOUR

Mirren

"Mirren, are you dressed? Breakfast is getting cold." Farrah's harried shouts rouse me from a sleep that evaded me most of the night. I'd snatched the coin from Easton's room and carried it back to mine like it were made of glass. After tucking it safely under my mattress, I'd laid in bed, but sleep wouldn't come.

Images of my parents flooded my brain, of my father's twinkling eyes and the wry set of my mother's mouth. And Easton.

Long after I stopped speaking of my parents in public, I still spoke of them to my brother. I'd sneak into his bedroom after Farrah and Jakoby were asleep and tell him everything I remembered about them. Most of it was mundane, quiet as most things are here. It made me feel better to speak of them. To remember they were real. To make sure that neither of us would forget them, and by extension, forget what bound us together.

But when Easton was seven, he turned to me, his eyes rimmed with silver and asked me to stop talking about them. Remembering them hurt, he told me, and he didn't want to hurt anymore. I was horrified, both at the fact that I'd caused Easton pain when he'd already gone through so much and at the thought of never being able to speak of my parents to anyone again. But I respected his wishes. That night was the last time I spoke their names out loud.

And the whole time, Easton had a way to find them.

Here, love.

"Mirren, you have five minutes until you need to leave for the Education Center," Farrah calls from the kitchen. I pull myself out of bed. There's no need to get dressed, because I never changed out of my khaki jumpsuit, so I settle with splashing some cold water on my face. I stare at my reflection, the mirror in the bathroom being the only one I'll see for the rest of the day. Similians don't give much thought to physical appearance, beyond the uniformity of it. My eyes are rimmed red and puffy from tears and lack of sleep. My face is pale, and my dark hair is a riot of curls and tangles.

I run my fingers through it and quickly braid it back.

It'll have to do.

Going to the Education center feels ridiculous when my heart is still pounding from what I learned last night. But it isn't possible to go barreling over the Boundary in broad daylight. And I haven't told Easton my plans. Even if he's unconscious, I can't leave without saying goodbye.

I jog through the kitchen and toss my bag over my shoulder.

"What about breakfast?!" Farrah looks positively scandalized that I'd skip a meal.

"I'm not hungry."

She opens her mouth to scold me, but I bolt out the door, straight into a solid, but very warm wall.

"Oh, I'm very sorry," Harlan immediately apologizes, rubbing his chest where my nose just collided. "I didn't think you'd be rushing out so quickly."

I rub my nose irritably. I forgot Harlan said he was going to be here this morning. I don't know how him walking me to school complicates my plans, but it feels like an unnecessary obstacle. Trying to make conversation with him. Trying to act like everything is normal when it definitely isn't.

"It's my fault," I reply, picking up the bag I dropped on impact.

"Are you hurt?" Genuine concern lines his face. I resist the urge to roll my eyes.

"I'm fine," I say, trying and failing to keep the bite out of my voice. "Let's go."

I begin walking before he has the chance to ask me anything else.

"How was your night?" A polite, usual question that no one is ever looking to actually hear answered.

My whole life changed, how was yours?

"Fine."

"I heard about your brother," Harlan says slowly.

"I don't want to talk about that." My voice is anything but pleasant. I'm dangerously close to breaking a Key and all Harlan needs to do to get me reprimanded is report me to the Covinus. I take a deep breath through my nose. I won't be able to cross the Boundary if I'm stuck doing sanctions all night.

"I will trust in the Covinus. The Covinus knows what's best for Easton," I say in a lighter voice that doesn't sound anything like mine.

"Mirren, I'm sorry about what is happening to Easton. And if you do need to talk, I'm here to listen."

I stop walking and turn to stare at Harlan. He looks much the same as yesterday, all golden hues and pleasant smiles, but his eyes are more earnest. Maybe I am simply imagining what I want to see in them. "Talk about *what*, Harlan?"

The challenge hangs in the air. *How I am feeling.*

I shouldn't be feeling anything other than complete trust in my government and Harlan shouldn't be assuming I do. We are on a precipice, only a step away from free falling into treason. Will Harlan make the leap? A leap I've made so many times, but always unspoken and always alone.

"I'm here to listen," he repeats carefully, "Trust in—

I huff in annoyance and begin walking again. "The Covinus. I know. Thank you, Harlan," I say tightly. I shouldn't be so abrasive. He's only doing what he was raised to do, what we've *all* been raised to do. Emotions should be kept to ourselves. History has proven they must be reined in or even the most solid of foundations are at risk of cracking beneath them. It's a logical Key, to limit our feelings, and until today, I've always considered it a benevolent rule.

But if the world isn't crying out at losing someone as kind and good as Easton, then it isn't a world I care to be a part of. I can't stay here—not when there's still a chance, even a slight one, that Easton can be saved. I can't pretend to trust in the Covinus, when the Covinus is so willing to wash Easton's life away. Nothing belongs to us in Similis, not really, but Easton belongs to me. And I will hold onto him as long as I can.

"Did you hear about the Boundary?"

My heart thunders at his question, as if Harlan can somehow see into me, cataloguing all the treasonous thoughts that entangle themselves around me like black ribbons. I force myself to breathe. He's only making conversation, just like yesterday when I cut him off.

"I was in the square when the bomb went off," I tell him neutrally.

"There's a hole in it."

I stop once more, turning to stare. "A *hole?*"

The Boundary hasn't been breached since the days of the Founders.

"A hole so large a child could fit through it."

I look around wildly. Foot traffic is still sparse at this time of morning, and no one pays us any mind. "How do you know that?" I hiss.

Harlan shrugs. "I saw it." He begins walking once more and this time, it's me that follows.

"How?" There have been plenty of attempts on the Boundary before. While bombs are rare, I can recall a handful of times one has gone off in just my lifetime. All other manners have been tried, from grenades to good old fashion sledgehammers. Nothing has ever even made a dent. To blow an actual hole through it—I can't even imagine the kind of fire power needed.

Or what kind of person would wield it.

"They haven't been able to fix it," Harlan continues. I lower my brow. How does Harlan know so much? The Covinus has said nothing about the attack, other than to further damn the Dark Worlders who committed it.

I hum noncommittally, but my blood suddenly feels hot running through my veins.

For the first time in our history, the Boundary has been breached. For the first time, there is a clear way into the Dark World. A clear path to find my parents and force them to come home. Force them to save Easton.

It has to be tonight. Before the Boundary men can figure out how to repair it.

Harlan and I reach the Education Center, the red heart of the metropolis fanning out beneath our feet. Today, I'm not reminded of blood. I am reminded of rebellion.

∼

The machine lights throw shadows across Easton's face and sap what little color remains in his cheeks. He doesn't look like a real person, but a carved wax figure, lifeless and wan. Is this the natural order of things, to be so vibrantly alive one day and then fall so quickly to a muted version of yourself?

I sprinted out of the Education center as soon as the bell rang, pushing my way past stunned looking classmates. I'll get sanctions for behaving so carelessly, but I won't be here to complete them. I needed to leave before Harlan could insist on walking me home.

I had to see Easton before I cross the Boundary. To explain where I'm going and why, just in case. It seems prudent, considering what I know of the Dark World. I'm not guaranteed to survive. It isn't even a high probability.

But now that I'm here staring at him, words fail me. Am I really going to leave him when these could be his last moments? Shouldn't I cling to the few I have left? I glance at the door before taking his hand. His skin is cold and clammy against mine and though I have not held hands with anyone since my parents' banishment, I know his skin feels wrong. As if whatever was inside him that made him Easton is gone.

The door opens with a quiet squeak, and I jump back from my brother as if I've been burned. It's silly, considering I won't be here to be reprimanded anyway, but it's been ingrained beneath my skin and burrowed into my very being—touch is wrong.

The Healer from the other day comes in the room, his white-blond hair reflecting the machine lights. "Hello Ms. Ellis," his voice is pleasant, but he eyes me as if I am a tiger that will strike him at any moment. "I trust you are well."

I bite my lip to keep from hurling my true words at him. Easton isn't here to keep me in check, so I need to restrain myself. At least for the rest of the night. "And you."

"As you know, we were never sure of how much time Easton had and it seems that it is drawing to a close quicker than we were expecting." He says this succinctly, no trace of the apologetic Healer that first gave us the news. As if then it was a terrible tragedy, but in the span of a few days has become routine. "Easton must remain in the Healing Center for the remainder of his days. The Covinus would ask that you gather his belongings and bring them with you when you report to the Education center in the morning."

I stare at him, feeling suddenly like I am being dragged beneath the waves of a stormy sea. "Why?"

The Healer stares at me in alarm. No one ever asks *why* because the why is always the same—because the Covinus asks it of you and the Covinus knows best.

"I—"

The Healer stammers, at a loss for words. I stare hard at him. What does he think of a young boy's life being so easily erased? That one day you are a valued member of the Community and the next there is nothing left to remind anyone you existed at all.

He shifts in his seat. "Because the Covinus has asked it of you, Ms. Ellis." He meets my gaze. Surprising, that he is willing to show I've flustered him.

"The Covinus has also asked," he pauses, looking down to his fidgeting fingers. My eyes follow his, to his square cut fingernails and nailbeds that have been picked to the point of scabs. "They have also asked that you limit your visiting hours to thirty minutes per day. It isn't right to lock yourself away in here and ignore your responsibilities to your Community."

"What?" My cheeks flush. "What do you mean it isn't right? He's my brother!"

"And we are your Community."

It's only the thought of being Outcast that forces my teeth to bite together roughly, trapping my words inside my mouth. I may be planning to run, but I cannot be Outcast—there would be no chance of return. If I choose to leave, I can choose to come back. At least, I'm hoping so. As far as I'm aware, no one has ever chosen to leave. Why would they? We are fed and cared for. No one has any more or less than anyone else. No sane person would willingly give that up to take their chances with the vile beasts and ancient evil that thrives in the Dark World.

I watch Easton, taking note of the way the color has been sapped from his lips, leaving them dry and pale. "I do this for you, brother. Please forgive me."

With that, I leave the room, my last thoughts pounding in my head with a violent sort of rhythm. We are all valued members of the Community. Until we are not.

~

It's night when I step out of our quarterage, but not dark, never dark. I'm armed only with my standard issued backpack, stuffed with a change of clothes and a rations bar. I own nothing else.

The Dark World coin hangs at my neck. It seemed too valuable to shove in alongside my khaki jumpsuit and it's too easily lost in a pocket. In the end, I tore a small strip of fabric off my pillowcase and threaded it through as a makeshift necklace. I'm almost sorry I won't be around to witness Farrah's look of horror at the destroyed Community property.

The streets are empty, but I stick to the shadows cast by the quarterages anyway. Curfew rang in thirty minutes ago, but I don't make the mistake of assuming this means I'm alone. There are always eyes. I know the feeling of them better than most. The sting of them on my skin, the rage at otherness possessed within them. Eyes have followed me my whole life and it would by folly to assume they aren't with me now.

The air is crisp, but winter's bite has faded substantially. I'm thankful it's spring. If Easton had gotten sick in the winter, I would have to deal with freezing temperatures alongside everything else that is trying to kill me beyond the Boundary.

My feet feel heavy, like the pavement beneath them snaked its way around my ankles, attempting to hold me back from what can barely be described as half a plan. I don't know where I'm going beyond the Boundary; I have no supplies, no survival skills, and no sense of direction. The odds aren't even low—there are no odds. Nothing that would indicate I'm going to do anything other than die.

I push the thoughts from my head. Doubt won't help Easton, and neither will staying safe behind the Boundary.

I turn into the neighboring quarterage. It mirrors our own, the squat gray buildings all standing in perfect unison. It would be faster to traverse through the metropolis, but it felt too vulnerable. A lone figure crossing the sea of red in the middle of the night would most certainly raise alarms. So, I take the long way around, through the quarterages and to the farmland on the other side.

Beyond that, lies the hole. The idea firmly implanted in my brain when Harlan spoke of its size. *Large enough for a child to crawl through.* I've always been small in stature and fitting through that hole is my best chance of slipping into the Dark World without being seen.

It isn't just fear of being caught that plagues me. It's the fear I'll turn back. If I'm forced to explain, or to consider for a moment the danger I'm getting myself into, I will lose my nerve. I'll turn around and go back to the bedroom that isn't even mine with the family that isn't mine either. I'll gather up Easton's things and resign myself to a future that doesn't include him, in a place that doesn't care.

One thought drives me forward.

For Easton. This is all for Easton.

I let it force my feet to keep moving, taking me through another quarterage.

Because the Dark World doesn't bear thinking about. I know nothing of it, really, nothing concrete. Only what we have been told in the Education center which has always seemed too terrible and fanciful to be real. The videos played are old, the pictures warped, and the sound warbled in places, but the images have been clearly burned in my mind anyway. War, famine, rape, torture. Things that have been eliminated in Similis but run rampant there without the Covinus to keep the violence at bay.

I've watched them through squinted eyes, not wanting to fully open them to the horrors human beings are willing to inflict on each other. But there has always been a deeper part of me, shameful and dark, that has been morbidly drawn to them.

The Dark World has no laws, save one: thou shalt not murder. A place with no rules, no Keys, where a person is only answerable to one's own conscious is both terrifying and alluring.

"Mirren," the whispered sound of my name is so unexpected that I nearly fall over, my heart jumping suddenly into my throat. I whip around, a cold sense of dread sinking low in my stomach. Nothing moves as I peer into the shadows.

I should flee. I've always been a good runner, something I've prided myself on during our fitness time, but I'm not sure I can outrun a Boundary guard. Or the Covinus. And besides, there really isn't anywhere to run.

"Where are you going?" A muscled frame topped with a shock of golden hair steps forward.

"Harlan," I breathe in a mixture of surprise and irritation. Of all the nights for the golden boy to break curfew, for some reason he chose this one. "It's none of your business where I'm going," I hiss, turning on my heel. My heart flutters in my chest. *Please don't ask me again.* My nerve has grown thin as water and one challenge will cause it to leak out.

Harlan reaches out and softly catches my hand in his. The touch is so shocking that I freeze immediately. If Harlan were to do this in the daytime, he would receive a reprimand. Touching, especially in public, is not allowed.

His skin is soft and warm against mine, his fingers thick and strong. I can't remember the last time someone touched my bare skin willingly. "You can't do this alone, Mirren."

"I...do what alone?" I say, distracted. His skin against mine makes my head feel fuzzy, my thoughts tangled up.

He steps closer to me, close enough that I can see the

color of his eyes, the lights casting them in a soft yellow. "I know about your brother."

"I know that," I say slowly. Once again, we are dancing at the edge of a ravine, but now, in the stillness of the night, it does not feel innocent. It feels dangerous. "You told me this morning."

Harlan grips my hand tighter, his pale skin sparkling in the moonlight and his face deadly serious. "You can't save him alone."

I stare at him, my mouth agape. How has Harlan come to be in an alleyway so far from his sector on the very night Easton is pronounced doomed?

Maybe he is part of the Covinus. It isn't unheard of for members of the younger generation to be participants. Not full-fledged members, but as eyes. Harlan has already seen enough to get me sanctions. Possibly enough to see me Outcast.

"I'm not going to save him," I say, keeping my voice light. I relax my face and widen my eyes. "I am trusting in the Covinus. The Covinus knows best."

If he truly is a Covinus member, it's probably already too late for me. But saying what's expected can't hurt.

Harlan drops my hand and shakes his head, something like sadness flashing briefly across his face. "Mirren, I know you're going into the Dark World. Let me help you. We are life partners, Bound for eternity. Don't start your eternity without me."

If he is Covinus, this seems an odd thing to say.

It doesn't feel Covinus fed though. It feels like...like Harlan. Exactly the kind of obtuse, self-flagellant thing the golden boy would say.

I turn away from him and begin walking, quickening

my pace. "They will find you a new life partner. One that won't make everything so difficult for you."

Harlan doesn't respond to this. Instead, he falls into step beside me just like he did the afternoon after the Binding. He lets me set the pace but never falls behind as we walk for what feels like hours through one sector and finally, through the one closest to the Boundary. My shoulders hunch with every step, the weight of what's to come bearing down upon them.

Finally, we reach the last quarterage. The only thing between the Boundary and I is a large, empty plot of land. The dirt is overturned, ripe with new planting.

"Mirren, I—

I brace myself for whatever he's about to say, but he cuts his words off abruptly and whips his head to the north. Toward the sector we just came from.

"Harlan, you have to—"

I fall silent at the shake of his head. He motions for me to follow him, around the quarterage and down a small sidewalk that connects to another residence. The squeal of a siren rents the air. The sirens of the Covinus.

Someone has broken the law.

With a delayed deference, I realize it's me. I'm the one the Covinus is coming to punish.

"Harlan," I cry, desperate. I try to push him away, but his chest is solid beneath my hands. I want him to leave and keep himself safe. I want him to stay and tell me what to do.

But he can't tell me what to do. What I am doing is beyond the bounds of what Harlan, or any Similian, is familiar with.

He shakes his head at me again and peers around the corner. The swirling lights of the Covinus vehicles are visible now, casting oddly shaped shadows dancing across the gray walls. "The hole in the Boundary is across that field. You'll never be able to outrun them."

The sirens grow louder. People have begun to peer into the street from behind their curtains, hoping to catch a glimpse of the Key-breaker, Community-traitor. Oh, their glee when they realize it's me. Every suspicion of a defect in Ellis blood clearly confirmed. "I have to try, Harlan. I can't go back. I...I need to do this. For Easton!"

Harlan looks at me patiently, and though it's hardly the time, I admire his composure. Even as the weight of the Covinus bears down on us, his face is untroubled, and his breathing is even. Perhaps he is not a willow blowing beside the pond; perhaps he is the wind that blows it. "You can't outrun them, so they need something else to chase."

It takes a moment for his suggestion to register.

Himself. He is suggesting himself.

"Harlan, no!" I cannot let him do this, sacrifice himself for me. It's untenable, unbearable. He's done nothing wrong, other than having the bad luck of being Bound to me. What will his punishment be if they think he's trying to betray his Community and leave them forever? Will he be Outcast? I'm willing to bet my own future on a loophole of leaving willingly, but am I willing to bet Harlan's as well?

"The hole is on the right side of the gate. I am going to take them through the sector and toward the other side of the Boundary. The Boundary men have had personnel shortages this month. If I cause a big enough commotion, there won't be anyone to stop you from slipping out. Once you're out, get to the trees as fast as you can."

"Harlan, you can't do this. What if they—

"It's the only way to save Easton," he says, his words final. Strong.

Before I can utter another word, he takes off running and I am left alone in the shadows.

In seconds, the Covinus overtakes Harlan; vans with angry red lights swarm around him, the squeal of their brakes sounding so much like the injured screams from yesterday's explosion. Harlan leaps through a small space between two vans and a mass of people in navy jumpsuits hurtle after him, their black helmets glinting beneath the Similian lights.

Violent trembles run up my spine, causing my teeth to clack together. I want to run after him, to grab him by the collar and pull him back into the shadows with me. I want to curl up into myself, to sit down and close my eyes and pretend that I'm safe and my brother is safe and that none of this ever happened. But I force myself to move.

I plant my feet firmly in the pavement. With a rallying cry, Harlan leads the Covinus away from me and toward the front gate of the Boundary. The four Boundary men who guard the hole do exactly as Harlan said they would and race toward the commotion, determined to stop the defector.

So, I run.

With a speed I didn't know I possessed, I sprint toward the now empty hole. This close to the Boundary, the lights are bright as day. If any of the Covinus or Boundary men look my way, there will be nowhere to hide. But I run anyway. I run for Easton. And for Harlan, the nature of whose sacrifice remains untold.

My heart pumps roughly in my chest, but my breathing remains steady as I will my legs to move faster, to carry me further. I don't dare look over my shoulder, but the commotion surrounding Harlan follows me. Yelling and anger, sounds so rarely heard in Similis. But I don't look. The hole is so close.

When I reach the Boundary breach, I almost cry in victory. The Boundary gapes like a decrepit wound, seeping and raw, as if the wall is made of flesh rather than metal. A hole made from violation and hatred, but I am thankful for it nonetheless.

I am about to climb through when a loud crack echoes through the silence of the night. Reflex has me whipping my head toward the noise and a sharp pang of fear sizzles through me.

The Covinus points what is unmistakably a gun at Harlan. And then shoots.

Another crack echoes and I shove my fist into my mouth to stifle the scream building in my chest. Harlan's eyes flash in my direction for only a moment before they roll up into his head. He collapses to the ground and the golden boy is still.

The Covinus and Boundary men swarm him, blocking his body from my view. Orders are shouted and more sirens scream. I only have moments before the entirety of the Covinus descends on the front gate. Only moments before one of them looks up.

I am shaking so violently that when I crawl through the Boundary, the broken shards tear at my jumpsuit, scraping my hip. The hole is only big enough for me to slide through on my belly, so I claw at the damp ground, dragging my body through the opening.

I scramble to my feet. My shoes slip on the loose gravel. I throw my hands out in front of me as I fall, scraping those, too. I need to move. I'm a sitting duck here in the open, beneath the lights.

I can honor Harlan in the one way I have left. I can

escape and make sure his sacrifice wasn't in vain. It's the only thing my brain clings to, the one thing that keeps shock and terror from freezing me in place and letting the Covinus shoot me, too.

I push myself up and stand tall, the Boundary a solid presence behind me. Under the grief that threatens to overwhelm me, under the fear and confusion, a grim determination settles deep within me. I've crossed the Boundary. Home lies behind me and only the unknown lays before me.

I am in the Dark World.

CHAPTER FIVE

Mirren

Three breaths. That's all I allow before forcing myself to run. The dull slap of my feet on the dirt sounds in rhythm with my heart and fear grips me that it's all too loud. That one of the Boundary men will spare a glance over his shoulder and they will come after me as they came for Harlan.

Panic, hot and sharp, squeezes my chest as I think of the way his eyes rolled back in his head. The smacking sound of his body hitting the ground.

Dying, dead, died.

Could Harlan be dead? I've never seen a gun, other than in the old Dark World videos, but there is no mistaking that cold glint of metal.

Relief washes over me as I pull myself into the cover of the trees, my fingers scrabbling against the rough bark. I lean against one as I catch my breath, watching the flurry of activity unfold beneath the lights. I wonder what they've done with Harlan. Surely they've moved him by now.

Bodies in the middle of streets do not represent a peaceful society.

Rage fills me. To the Covinus, Harlan is the same as Easton. Disposable. A nuisance. They are no longer people at all, only problems that undermine the Community.

I turn away from Similis, instead facing the darkness of the forest, welcoming it. At least the darkness has never pretended to be anything other than what it is.

The lights that have comforted me since I was a child falter beneath the thick branches, and it only takes a few minutes of walking before they are enveloped completely. I am practically blinded, groping through the trees as if a handkerchief has been tied over my eyes. There is no electricity outside Similis. No lights, street-lamps, or flashlights. It's the root of the land's name, both a moral and literal description of the place. It was once called something different, but it's been lost to time.

I expected the darkness. I didn't expect that it would be so disorienting; to feel both enveloped and desolate. The same shroud blankets us all, but it is pulled so tightly over our eyes, we could wander alone forever.

I should have brought a lantern. I should have brought a coat. I should have brought some semblance of a plan.

The darkness settles around me and with it, the reality of what I've done. Left everything I've ever known and run blindly into a place I know to be dangerous. Whatever blasted a hole through the Boundary lurks beneath this same dark sky. Leaves rustle and branches crack. I swear I can hear the scrape of claws and the tormented howls of some forlorn beast off in the distance.

I have no rations. Nothing to barter with. I've no sense of Dark World geography, or if there are even any cities left standing after their multiple civil conflicts. How did I ever expect to find my parents with nothing but a silly coin?

The world suddenly feels unsteady as if the darkness itself will open up and swallow me whole. Lost in my own sense of panic, it takes a ridiculous amount of time for me to notice that the night has begun to flicker, casting odd, distorted shadows around me. They dance across the trunks of the trees, creating the illusion that the trees themselves are alive and dancing. It only compounds my feeling of unmooring, but I venture forward anyway until I discover the source—a fire.

I freeze, acutely aware of the loud crunch of leaves beneath my boot. Masses huddle around the fire. People.

Dark Worlders.

Dread fills my stomach like leaden ice. In all my time staring out into the Dark World, I've never once seen anyone in these trees. Or *anything*. And all this time, there have been people living minutes from the Boundary? It seems impossible.

And yet, here they are. Arguing and guffawing.

Dark Worlders are an angry people. Violent and ruthless, only beholden to their own twisted souls. Anyone who tries to bring light is torn down or mutilated. But not killed. Never killed.

It's been drilled into us since we were young, the kind of people that reside outside the Boundary, but I've never taken it to heart. Maybe it's because my parents *are* living outside the Boundary or maybe it's simply that I've always thought that people are just people, no matter where they live. Now, though, it isn't just my heart that will be tested. Am I willing to lay my life on the foundation of people being inherently good?

Something cold presses into the back of my neck.

"What do we 'ave here?" The voice is gruff, his accent harsh and distinctly foreign. I make to turn around, but the man thrusts what I ascertain is a knife more roughly into the back of my neck. "Don't move, girl," he growls, and I don't. I couldn't even if I wanted to.

For another thought has crashed over me like a thunderstorm. The reason these Dark Worlders are so close to the Boundary is *because* of the Boundary. They're the ones who destroyed it. And if they were capable of blowing through an unbreakable wall, what will they do to my entirely breakable body?

"Where you from?" he asks warily.

I don't reply, instead, biting down into my lip so hard it bleeds. Admitting to being Similian would be foolhardy, but I don't know enough of the Dark World to make up a convincing lie. "No one comes this far into the Nemoran wood 'less they plan on getting shot."

My eyes widen. Shot? By who?

The man pushes me forward suddenly. I stumble on the uneven ground but manage to regain my footing before toppling over completely. He is herding me toward the fire —toward his companions.

"I...I was just out for a walk and got turned around. My brother is surely looking for me by now," I blurt out. I don't know why I say it, other than wanting desperately to not appear alone.

"A walk, huh?" the man muses, shoving me forward once more. "I know where you from running like that," he leans forward and says directly in my ear, "pretty little thing." His breath is hot and sour, his face rough against mine.

"I could fetch a good price for someone with skin like yours." He laughs, the sound grating and humorless. Any thoughts of appeasing this man dissipate instantly. There will be no reasoning with him. There will only be surviving him.

"Maybe I won't turn you in. Maybe I'll sell ya and retire somewhere nice and warm. Let's get a look at the rest of you in the light." He chortles to himself as if he's made a clever joke, but in my terror, it's lost on me.

My fingertips go cold as he pushes me forward.

If we reach that fire, I will be his. I'm outmatched now, but it will be worse when it's one against seven. The decision is made so quickly, I'm not even sure it *is* a decision, so much as instinct. As the man makes to push me again, I duck to the ground. Tucking my knees to my chest, I roll out of his path.

He roars in frustration, the force of his own momentum causing him to stumble, but I don't pause to see whether he regains his footing. Instead, I take off in the opposite direction of the campfire. Angry shouts ring out behind me, the man alerting his companions to my presence.

Faster, Mirren. Faster.

I force my legs to carry me further, but they already feel heavy after my earlier escape. My pace is slowing. I need to find somewhere to hide. To become invisible.

Something catches my ankle and I let out a terrified scream as I tumble roughly to the ground. I kick out frantically, working to disentangle myself from whatever has a hold of me. Desperation grips me, certainty that Dark Worlder is only moments away from catching me once more and dragging me to whatever hell he has in store.

But the more I struggle, the tighter I'm ensnared. I peer through the darkness, and with no small amount of horror, realize it is not a root or vine that holds me in place. It's a *hand.* One so large it swallows my entire ankle within its grasp.

I cry out, in fear and furious anger that I've allowed myself to be caught not once but *twice*. I made it ten minutes outside the Boundary before stupidly running into capture; what chance do I stand in the rest of the Dark World?

Harlan gave his life and instead of honoring his sacrifice and saving Easton, all I've done is gotten myself killed. Or worse. For an absurd moment, I feel like laughing at the irony of it all.

Bright fury burns behind my eyes. Harlan didn't even hesitate before running toward danger, sacrificing everything for a boy he barely knew. As long as I'm still breathing, is it not within me to do the same? I will give everything I have, escape ten thousand captures until there is no strength or breath left in me. I refuse to give Easton up because of my failure.

I channel all of my fire and anger and grief and pull back my arm, swinging with everything I have at whoever is connected to the hand that holds me. There is a satisfying thud, followed by a stream of curse words and the pressure on my ankle lessens.

Heartened, I kick out. A sickening *crunch* sounds as my foot makes contact with flesh and bone. My ankle finally free, I spring to my feet, but my attacker recovers enough of their senses to throw themselves at my legs. I scream as we crash to the ground in a tangle of limbs.

I writhe desperately, unable to tell which way is up in the fray.

"Good gods, woman," hisses a fierce whisper. A man's voice. "Will you quit screaming?!"

He presses a large hand over my mouth to illustrate his

point. I thrash against him, trying to work my teeth around his finger to bite it, but I may as well be throwing myself against a solid brick wall for as much as it seems to faze him. "It's a wonder you haven't brought the entirety of the Similian Boundary men on us with the noise you're making."

His body is a solid mass against mine, heavy and immovable. His voice is still whispered, but its tone is deep and soothing. Casual, as if he is ruminating on the state of the weather. "We're going to have to make a run for it, I suppose."

I stop struggling long enough to narrow my eyes at him. He is only shapes in the darkness, sharp and angled. Who, exactly, is he planning on running away from? Between the Boundary and the dangerous men who hunt outside of it, this man's loyalties remain dangerously unclear.

To my satisfaction, he rubs his jaw as if it pains him. *Good. I hope it hurt.*

"You nearly broke my jaw," he says, but he doesn't sound angry. Instead, he sounds faintly amused.

I don't know how I can tell in the darkness, but I feel the moment he turns his eyes on me. As if he can somehow peer straight through the pitch black.

"If you promise not to scream again or try to punch me," the man pauses thoughtfully. His hand still presses against my mouth, and I decide immediately that I *will* punch him the first chance I get. "Or *kick* me, for that matter, I'll let you go. Do you promise?" He presents the question innocently, the way a child might demand an agreement to a pinky promise. But it isn't innocent. There are lives at stake. Easton's, and I am too belatedly realizing, my own.

Seeing no other choice, I nod my head mutely.

The man must be pleased, because he lifts his hand from my mouth and proceeds to disentangle himself with surprising dexterity. The moment the weight of his oppressive limbs lightens, I jump to my feet. With another muttered curse and lightning-fast reflexes, he grabs my wrist and yanks me to the ground. I swing at him, my fist connecting with his face. Hot, agonizing pain shoots up my thumb.

"This is undoubtedly the *worst* rescue I've ever been a part of," the Dark Worlder remarks dryly, grabbing my other wrist. "Your form was terrible, but at least you packed some power. I think I'm now going to have a black eye to go along with my bruised jaw."

The lights of the Boundary swing toward us, bathing the forest in dancing shadows. In my panic, I must have run back toward Similis.

I stare at the man, trying to ascertain the details of his face. All I can tell is that he is tall and angular and topped by a wild mop of hair.

"Hasn't anyone taught you to punch with your thumb out? You probably broke it," he tells me haughtily, "which really just serves you right."

"Serves *me* right?!" I hiss indignantly.

"Well, you did promise not to punch me," he points out.

"You tackled me to the ground and smothered my mouth and told me not to scream. Of course, I'm going to hit you!" My voice rises a few hysterical octaves, and the man shushes me fiercely.

"Are you *trying* to get us caught? Because if you are, you're doing a turn up job," his voice drips with arrogance and I consider punching him again. Only the poor state of my thumb keeps my hands pinned to my sides. "But if you'd prefer to stay out of the hands of the Similian infantry and the Boundary hunters, we need to move in about 15 seconds. As soon as the lights move on."

I shake my head, trying to hold on to a clear thought. Whoever this Dark Worlder is, he apparently isn't associated with the men at the campfire, but that doesn't mean he isn't dangerous. All Dark Worlders are dangerous. "I'm not going anywhere with you." My body tightens in anticipation, waiting for the moment the man grabs me and forces me to move, but he only shrugs.

He opens his mouth, but before he can shoot off whatever obnoxious comment he has ready, two men appear behind him like specters. They haul the Dark Worlder to his feet and shove a gun roughly against his temple. It is the Boundary hunter, but he is no longer alone.

I scream and scramble to my feet, backing away from the gun in horror. I've never seen a gun before today, and now, I've seen two in less than an hour.

A set of arms snake out from behind me, wrapping tightly around my throat. My breaths come in painful gasps. I struggle, looking around wildly. Five men surround me and the Dark Worlder, the hatred in their eyes clawing through the darkness.

The lights sweep over our clearing once more. The Boundary hunter's face is twisted into a thoughtful scowl as he eyes the Dark Worlder with apparent interest. "Well, look it here, Eulogius," he says to the man restraining me. "Wonder what kind of price we can get for the little Similian if we throw in a wretched Ferusian, too."

Eulogius' arm tightens against my throat and then loosens once more, in time with his cackle of laughter. Blossoms of color begin to swim at the corners of my vision as I struggle to take shallow breaths. "Come on, Murph. Ya know they ain't gonna pay us for a Dark Worlder, less he's dead."

The lights pass, darkness lying thickly over the clearing once more.

Another man raises a lantern and I watch as the man called Murph shoves the gun harder against the Dark World man's temple. Murph laughs humorlessly. "You hear that, boy? You ain't worth nothing to this world 'less there's a bullet in your brain."

Desperation is a hard knock against my rib cage. My air is running out. With every sweep of the Similian lights, my chance for escape drifts farther out of reach.

I claw at Eulogius' arm, digging my fingernails into his skin until I feel blood bloom beneath them. He lets out a surprised cry, but his arm remains a hot iron bar across my windpipe. The lights sweep the clearing again. His other arm presses against my chest, pinning my arms to my sides.

I twist my body, kicking and thrashing in his grip.

My thoughts are repetitive and panicked. *Get out, get out, get out.*

In contrast, the Dark Worlder seems perfectly poised as the lights sweep over him, as if he has guns pointed at him all the time. He stares at the men, each in turn, his face blank. He is all chiseled angles and planes, appearing all at once both younger and older than I imagined. His gaze flicks to mine, and though his eyes are impossible to see from this distance, my heartbeat slows as if he has willed it.

He looks away from me quickly. "Typical of the Covinus' finest," he spits, his tone harsher than it was when he was speaking to me, "doesn't even know the proper way to point a gun at someone."

My jaw drops and that odd wave of calm dissipates completely. Taunting me about my punching skills is one thing; taunting a man with a gun pressed to your head, and five others to back it up, is entirely another.

He's insane. I've gone and shackled myself to an absolute mad man.

Murph's eyes narrow, his face lined with cruel malice. Leaning closer to the man, his voice is dangerous. "Whenever my gun is pointed at a Dark Worlder brain like yours, it's in the proper place."

"That's the problem with guns," the Dark Worlder replies conversationally, and I wonder what's happened to him prior that he's able to keep his voice so nonchalant. "They make cowards feel brave."

And then he moves, so quickly it takes my brain a lagging moment to catch up to my eyes. He twists, swatting the weapon deftly out of Murph's hand. Latching on to Murph's wrist, he leverages the Boundary hunter's weight against him and in one smooth movement, flips him to the ground. Murph lands with a thick thud. The gun skids across the forest floor.

His face still terrifyingly calm, the Dark Worlder levels a blow to Murph's head, knocking him unconscious. The move is neat and methodical; undoubtedly used many times before. The man flies toward the next hunter, throwing a kick to his gut before any of the others have even managed to draw their weapons.

"Now would be as good a time as any, Cal!" he yells out, sounding only slightly annoyed, as he dodges two well aimed blows to the head and retaliates with a sweeping kick. He knocks two hunters' feet from under them.

I have no idea who he is talking to, but I don't take the time to ponder it. Taking advantage of the momentary confusion, I throw a well-aimed kick at Eulogius' kneecap. He bellows in rage, and I wriggle out of his grasp. I take off at a sprint, my lungs burning as I gasp for air. My clouded vision finally begins to clear as I force down oxygen.

The Dark Worlder has knocked another man unconscious, or perhaps worse, the hunter lying in a crumpled heap beside the fray. The two remaining hunters attack him with renewed vengeance for their fallen companions. They slash out at him with knives, but he ducks and weaves with a mesmerizing grace. All of the fighting in the Dark World videos has always appeared dirty and savage; this, though still brutal, looks like an exhilarating sort of dance.

One hunter brings his knife down in a vicious arc, catching the man's arm. Blood spills, but he doesn't even hesitate. He ignores the injury completely, his face calm and assessing, his actions smooth and efficient. But he will only last so long against these odds.

Feeling an unwarranted sense of comradery with the arrogant man, I scan the ground for the gun. If I can keep it away from them, we will stand a better chance.

As I run, my toe catches on a tree root and I tumble to the ground. Ignoring the flash of pain that shoots up my wrist, I claw my way over the underbrush. A hand grabs my ankle for the second time tonight, this one calloused and clammy against my skin. I scream, struggling against Eulogius' grip. I kick as hard as I can, my fingers reaching across the damp ground, scrabbling in the dirt until my nails are caked with it.

The cool, alien metal of the gun feels almost merciful when my fingers finally wrap around the hilt. I spin around, the weight foreign, but victorious in my hand.

Eulogius blinks at me, his attempt to yank me toward him abandoned. I can see the details of his face now. The way his eyebrows curl toward his forehead and the way his skin is discolored in large, unseemly patches. His thin lips twist in an ugly sneer, revealing several missing teeth and gums that have turned an unappetizing shade of gray. "You don't even know how to shoot that thing," he says confidently. "You don't even know where the trigger is."

He's right. I've never witnessed how the mechanisms work or how to even tell if it's loaded. But it doesn't matter. I won't give up. For Easton. For Harlan. I don't know how to shoot a gun, but as long as there is *something* in my hand, I will continue to fight.

"You're right," I tell him. While he is still trying to figure out my sudden acquiescence, I throw the gun as hard as I can at his head. It cracks against his skull with a sickening thud, the sound of metal colliding with skin and bone, and he slumps over in an unconscious heap.

Fire burns through my veins as I scramble to my feet. The Dark World man has disarmed another of the hunters and done significant damage to the other's shoulder, his arm dangling uselessly at his side. The hunter throws a punch at the man's head, which he promptly ducks to avoid, kicking out at the other hunter's legs.

His movements are no longer too fast to track and his eyes flash toward me, wide and telling. He is tiring. He won't last much longer by himself.

Run, his eyes seem to tell me.

The same as Harlan's.

Determination settles in my stomach. I won't leave. Not when the man is only entangled with the hunters because of me.

I spot the knife lying on the ground and make to grab it, when I am lifted off my feet. The hunter's grip tightens around my throat. My face heats as I choke and sputter. I kick out frantically, but my feet only slice through air, useless. A gunshot cracks through the forest.

No, no, no. Not again.

My vision swims as the hunter drags me backward with a grunt, away from the scuffle and the Dark Worlder. A prize claimed. I claw at his skin until I feel blood, but his grip only tightens. He crushes my windpipe, and it burns, burns, burns.

Through a haze, I make out the man's form duck and roll as another shot rings out. Relief plunges into me, cool and sating. He's still moving. It hasn't happened again, another life to be sacrificed for my prideful determination.

He dances sideways, kicking out at a hunter's knee. I want to scream out, to warn him of Murph, who has risen behind him, wielding another pistol. No sounds come from my mouth except breathless squeaks. Desperate wheezes for oxygen.

I think of Easton and wish desperately I could hold his hand. That I could hear his guffaw of laughter, illegal and yet, undying. It seems a shame that we are both going to die so far divided, that I didn't at least think to die next to him, our fingers intertwined.

Two figures streak out of the woods, tackling one of the hunters to the ground in a furious flurry of limbs. The Dark Worlder throws a sharp hook and the hunter in front of him stumbles to the ground. The man whips his head over his shoulder and shouts, "Max! Get the girl!"

With a detached sort of comfort, I realize I'm the girl he's referring to, but it hardly matters. The burning in my throat has finally subsided and the world floats before me in waves, waves of an ocean I have never seen. The Dark World man is tackled to the ground, and I want to help—I *always* want to help and never can—and it is the last thing I see before the world goes black.

Chapter Six

Mirren

"Wake up, Lemming."

My first conscious thought is of the rodent we've read about in school, but I have never seen. The second is that I can feel my feet, and people who can feel their feet cannot possibly be dead.

I open my eyes, regretting the decision immediately as my retinas burn in the midday sun. A sharp ache throbs in my skull, keeping time with my heartbeat as the events leading up to this headache come back in bright, anxious, flashes. Escaping Similis. The Boundary hunters. The strange and irritating Dark World man apparently saving my life.

"Ah, there you are," a familiar voice says from nearby.

As my vision sharpens, I see the Dark Worlder clearly for the first time.

My breath catches in my throat. The man can't be older than twenty and he is, without a doubt, the most beautiful person I've ever seen, male or female. His face is made up of angular planes, as if chiseled delicately by a sculptor, with a layer of smooth, caramel colored skin stretched artfully across them. His jet-black hair sweeps effortlessly across his forehead in thick waves, curling at his temples. His lips are full, the corner tilted upward as if in the constant throws of a smirk.

But it isn't his beauty that leaves me breathless. There's little use for attractiveness in Similis and I haven't come so far as to see its point now. It's his eyes that give me reserve, that make me forget momentarily that he saved me, that he may be an ally.

They are the lightest shade of blue I've ever seen, so at odds with the rest of his deep coloring. They are ice in the moonlight, and they churn with an otherworldly power. They crash against me, so cold that they burn or so hot that they melt, and I want to rear away, to hide, from their intrusiveness.

I force myself to remain still but can't help the gape that widens my mouth. Whatever it is that burns in that gaze, I know instinctively, I would do well to stay away from. A destructive power that consumes not only itself, but everything in its path.

The man stares back at me so intensely that heat rises to my skin. I shake my head. *He is just a man. A person like you or Easton.* But even as I think it, it rings false. The way he disarmed Murph so easily, as if it is something he has done his entire life, proves his otherness. Even the cold metal of a gun pressed against his temple hadn't seemed to bother him. He is comfortable around violence in a strange and terrifying way, and though he may have saved my life, I'm right to be wary.

"You can't kill me," I blurt out suddenly, trying to wrench myself away from him, from the strange heat of his gaze. I quickly realize that I am on some sort of makeshift cot, tangled up in a pile of thickly woven blankets.

The man tilts his head, an odd expression clouding his handsome features. "And why's that?" he asks, in the tone of one inquiring about the weather.

"It—it's the rule."

I have no idea why I say it. He's the one so obviously from the Dark World, and probably well aware of their one law. After seeing the way his eyes burned, perhaps I felt compelled to remind him of it.

I wish I had done so slightly more eloquently, because now he examines me as if I am an interesting sort of bug.

"It's the Dark World rule. You can't kill me."

At this, the man narrows his eyes. "There are worse things than death, Lemming," he says, his voice low and serious.

I think of Easton. Of the way his face looked lit by the lights of the machines keeping him alive. But not forever. The machines will only last so long. If I die, Easton will too. "Not for me," I tell him, staring up at him with wide eyes.

I'm terrified—of him, of my journey, of succeeding and seeing my parents after so many years—but it all pales in comparison to the terror of losing the only person in this world who truly knows me.

I take in my surroundings surreptitiously. We are in an outcropping of rocks, surrounded by forest in either direction. The trees here are older, three times as wide as the ones in the forest that borders Similis. Roots snake under the ground, the size of small trees themselves, roiling under the soil like large snakes. We must be much deeper into the forest. Though how we got here, I don't think I want to know.

"What do you want from me?" I ask him, sounding braver than I feel.

The Dark Worlder stares at me a moment longer, his gaze oddly hungry, before his face relaxes and he smiles. The effect so wholly transforms his features that for an absurd moment, I feel like smiling back. "Relax, Lemming," he tells me, and I wonder why he thinks that's my name. "If I wanted you dead, why would I have gone to the trouble of rescuing you?"

I'm not entirely sure I *have* been rescued, but it seems silly to point this out. I glance around the clearing, suddenly remembering the man's two companions, but we appear entirely alone. I don't know whether to be comforted or terrified.

"Please just tell me what you want. I'll give you anything, but I have to be on my way as soon as possible." I bite my lip to keep from saying anything further. I doubt pleading will get me very far in the Dark World, and certainly not with someone capable of taking out five armed men single handedly.

The Dark Worlder narrows his eyes and tilts his head slightly, a raven piece of hair falling haphazardly over his forehead. The tendril reminds me of the silk of a bird's wing and for one wildly inappropriate moment, I wonder what it would feel like if I ran it between my fingers. Ridiculous. I shake the thought away quickly.

"You really shouldn't be promising someone you don't know whatever they want. What if I want your kidneys? Are you going to give them to me?" he asks blithely.

I swallow roughly. "Do you?"

"Do I what?"

"Want my kidneys?"

The man waves me off impatiently. "Of course not! I

have two of my own that work perfectly, thank you very much. I was just pointing out it was a stupid thing to say."

My fear slowly dissolves into something closer to annoyance. Though I should be practiced at hiding such things, my voice reflects my irritation. "Just tell me what you want," I demand loudly. If I were home, I would correct myself. Use a lower voice and utter a humble apology.

But I'm not home. And I have no time for a boy who amuses himself at my expense.

He ignores my demand completely. "Why is it so important that I not only refrain from killing you but also let you go?"

"What does the reason matter to you? If you were going to kill me, you would have done it already." I almost rear back at my own voice. It does not sound like a girl that hides behind corners to keep from having to speak. It sounds like one who isn't afraid of speaking or anything else.

"You're right," he agrees cheerfully, "but I did go to an awful lot of trouble to save you to not receive some sort of payment."

Trepidation clutches at my throat. I should have known he'd want something even if he did save me. No one in the Dark World does anything that isn't in their own self-interest.

I stand up and abruptly wish I hadn't. My head swirls and my throat aches as if the Boundary hunter's fingers are still stretched around it. I ignore the pain, focusing instead on the trees behind the man. If I can only figure out how far we've traveled, I might stand a chance at guessing which direction I need to run.

I've seen what he's capable of and I'll have no hope of

overpowering him. But maybe, if I move fast enough, I can disappear into the dark before he can find me.

"I have nothing to give you," I tell him primly. My hands clutch at my neck, and I breathe an audible sigh of relief when my fingers touch the cool cotton of the makeshift coin necklace.

The man's eyes follow my movements with an unsettling pervasiveness. "Oh, there's always something to be bartered with, Lemming."

"Why do you keep calling me that? It's not my name." It's an obvious way to stall, to buy time to find a way out of this situation. The man seems more humane than the Boundary hunters, perhaps he will let me leave freely?

He rolls his eyes. "Well, obviously it's not your actual name, but it is what you are, isn't it?"

"I'm a small, arctic rodent?"

He breathes a loud, impatient sigh and his eyes flick skyward. "I guess it's true that Similians take everything literally," he says offhandedly, but as his eyes settle on me, my urge to run grows exponentially. That gaze misses nothing. He knows exactly what I am. "Lemmings are what we call those living behind the Boundary."

Sweat coats my palms. I've learned quickly, thanks to the Boundary hunters, that Similian is a dangerous thing to be in the Dark World.

The man still studies me, his face an unreadable block of stone. I don't have much practice at reading emotions, as outward displays are so rare at home, but even if I did, his angled features give nothing away. If he is planning on capturing and selling me, he is certainly taking his time about it.

"You're the first one I've ever met," he remarks levelly. I wonder briefly what he thinks of this. What he thinks of *me*.

"If you've never met one, what makes you think I'm Similian?"

The Dark Worlder lets out a startling laugh. "Even someone half as brilliant as I could figure out what you are. Those Boundary hunters back there probably have one brain cell between them, and they obviously caught on pretty quickly."

His eyes rove over me, running from my hairline to my toes. My skin tingles.

"Even if you were dressed normally, you give yourself away as soon as you open your mouth."

I frown down at my jumpsuit, the standard issue khaki now smeared with dirt and a substance that looks suspiciously like blood. He's right. Clothing never occurred to me in my frantic run out of Similis and I foolishly thought I'd be able to pick up Dark World mannerisms quickly enough to avoid attention. Foolishly thought they wouldn't be much different from Similian habits. I assumed the Boundary hunters only knew what I was due to my proximity to Similis, but maybe there was more to it than that.

"Also, your skin," he adds, almost an afterthought, "you're really quite pale."

"So?" I retort, glaring at him. He's made his point, there is no need to insult my looks while doing it. "There are people of all colors in the Dark World."

But Murph had also said something about my skin, hadn't he? I can change my clothes, and perhaps fake my way through Dark World customs, but changing my actual biology is unlikely.

The man laughs again, and it skitters under my skin. I see why it's against the Keys, with its way of belittling. "All colors, yes. But no scars, no callouses, no windburn, no sunspots? We work hard for everything we have here, and our skin tells the story. Your skin says you've never worked a day in your life."

My cheeks feel hot. I forget that he's violent—that his face is made of stone. I forget to be afraid of him. Instead, righteous indignation surges through me. How dare he arrogantly assume that just because he knows a few generalities of Similian life, he presumes to know me? "You don't know anything about me. You don't know if I've worked or what I've done with my life. You don't even know my name. So, you can take your assumptions and shove them—"

"What is your name?" he interrupts. His voice is low, and his eyes are bright, and for some reason, I tell him.

"Mirren."

"Mirren," he says my name like a breath and a shock of warmth shoots through my stomach. I look down, embarrassed and uncertain, but if he notices, he thankfully ignores it. "It's unwise to give your name away so freely in the Dark World."

Irritation ripples through me again. "Are you saying I can't trust you? You did save my life."

"Maybe you can't. It's too soon to tell, don't you think?"

This is not an answer, and I am about to tell him so, when his two companions stride into the clearing. One, a girl, is shockingly tall, all legs and elbows with full lips and a regal-looking face. She blows at a piece of curly black hair that has escaped her bun, while the second, a lanky young man with a smattering of freckles and a shock of copper hair, lectures her.

"If I have to hear one more word about flower arrangements, I am swearing off her bakery for life," he is saying as he hops lithely over a fallen tree. "Especially with everything that's happened. I swear, I'm never getting married."

"You'd have to find someone to marry you first," the girl

replies smartly. "Besides, Evie doesn't *know* what's happened, so she can talk about her wedding if she pleases." The girl's dark eyes land on me and go wide.

"Well, if I do, we're jumping over a broom and calling it—"

The copper haired man watches the girl's face go slack jawed and follows her gaze. He gives a quick yelp and runs toward me. I throw my hands up over my head, squeezing my eyes shut but he doesn't touch me. Instead, he stops short and stares at me in abject wonderment. "You're awake!" He exclaims excitedly, before turning toward the Dark Worlder. "She's awake!"

"So it would seem," the man replies lazily.

"She really gave you that bruise?" the copper haired one asks incredulously. He eyes my feet, which I now realize, are bare. "*And* a black eye? She's all of five feet tall."

The Dark World man rubs his jaw. "Well, I didn't expect a frightened little Lemming to haul off and kick me in the face," he answers acerbically. Indeed, a deep purple splotch spreads out along his jawline and a matching ring circles one of his eyes. I assumed it was from his scuffle with the Boundary hunters and an odd sort of pride fills my chest as I realize it was from me. Proof I fought back. That I left a mark.

"Besides," the man continues, "she's not as delicate as she looks. She knocked out Eulogius with the butt of a revolver."

The copper haired man looks impressed.

"Did you find out who she is?" The girl directs toward the Dark Worlder. Her voice is abrasive, and her eyes are demanding. Her velvet black skin shines in the midday sun that pours through the canopy. "If she's a Lemming?" She spits the word with distaste and if I had any question before, her reaction confirms it is most certainly derogatory in nature.

The Dark Worlder nods, which seems to incense the girl and further excite the other man. "A real one?" he chirps, "where did you even find her?"

"I have a name," I mumble irritably. I've never liked being discussed as if I'm not in the room, something Farrah and Jakoby practice quite often. Talking about how well I'm faring in the Community as if I'm a piece of furniture, rather than a living person.

The copper haired man rounds on me, his warm hazel eyes as wide as saucers. "Of course, you do! I bet it's something weird. Similians are always naming their children weird names," he says knowledgeably to the girl. She sighs and pointedly ignores him.

I look to the Dark World man, but he seems in no hurry to provide his companions with the information I foolishly bestowed on him. Maybe I really can trust him with my name.

"I'm Calloway," the copper haired boy announces loudly, "but you can call me Cal."

He sticks his hand out toward me. I stare at it, uncertain what he's intending on doing with it, which seems to greatly amuse him. He bursts into laughter, a wild guffaw of the variety most often heard from children. The kind of laugh that has never learned to be self-conscious. In spite of everything, I have to work to keep myself from smiling back.

Calloway's face is open, his gaze friendly and inviting in a way I have rarely seen directed at me. Apparently not every Dark Worlder is made of stone.

"Is it true you aren't allowed to listen to music?" he asks with great interest.

I've never heard music, so I suppose it's true. I see no harm in telling him so, though my voice box seems to have disappeared somewhere inside my stomach. I settle for nodding awkwardly.

Calloway looks delighted by this information. He furrows his brow and opens his mouth, no doubt to voice another inquiry, but the girl interrupts him.

"Enough, Cal," she says forcibly, "she's a person, not a science experiment."

The sentiment is kind enough, but her eyes are vaguely threatening as they fall on me. She may think I'm a person, but she certainly doesn't consider me a trustworthy one. She looks to the Dark Worlder, her dark eyes meeting his light ones. Something unspoken passes between them.

Calloway still grins at me, making me feel awkward and light at once.

The girl determinedly avoids my gaze, an impressive feat, as I'm unable to stop staring at her. She is clad in the most outrageous outfit I've ever seen, with ripped trousers so tight they appear painted on and a shirt that ends in a ragged hem far above her belly button. Black ink tendrils only a few shades darker than her skin circle around her hips and climb up her ribcage, disappearing under her cropped shirt. I tell myself to look away, but I've never been able to control my reactions in the face of curiosity. It's always been like the pull of a magnet.

"She can't stay," she says to the pale-eyed man. Her voice is strong, edged with a power not used to being disobeyed, but he appears unbothered by her tone. Throughout the entire exchange, he's remained still, leaning against a tree like he's in charge of holding it up. His eyes have hardly wavered from me. I fidget once again underneath them, my skin tight. I may not be tied up, but somehow, I feel chained, nonetheless.

"I don't want to stay," I say quickly. If they aren't all on onboard with whatever nefarious plans the man has concocted behind those icy eyes, perhaps I can turn the girl to my side. "I want to leave."

The Dark Worlder's eyes finally flick to the girl. Their absence is like being doused in freezing water and I shiver in relief.

"Look at her eyes. She's the key, Max. We can't turn back now."

I spot my pack in a nearby pile of supplies and move toward it quickly. I don't know what he means about my eyes or what I'm the key to, but I don't care to find out. "Thank you," I say, forcing myself to look him in the face. The heat of a wildfire rushes over me and my instincts roar to throw my hands up and shield myself, but I hold still. "For saving my life."

The man only watches as I sling my pack over my shoulder. His body is set tightly, coiled and tense; a predator ready to pounce. His voice, however, is relaxed as he says, "Where exactly do you think you're going, Lemming?"

Calloway has fallen silent, watching the exchange with trepidation. With something like regret. The girl, Max, is still, her jaw set in determination, and I understand her dissent was short lived. Whatever the man says, they will both abide by.

"I have somewhere I need to be," I answer calmly, even though tremors of fear wrack my fingers. I clench my fist.

The side of the man's mouth pulls into a wicked grin. "I'm afraid I have somewhere I need you to be as well."

I take a step away from him toward the safety of the

forest. If I can just make it to the cover of the trees, I can lose him. I'm small, practiced at becoming silent and invisible. Surely there is some place to disappear that his hulking frame cannot follow.

The thought feels hopeless before it's complete. Max and Calloway stand between me and the woods. And even if they didn't, I've seen the wildness in the Dark Worlder. I won't last a minute against that tempestuous determination.

"I need to go. Please," the desperation lining my voice is repugnant, but I cannot be above begging. For Easton, I will get on my knees and ravage my pride an infinite number of times.

"Why do you think I saved you?" the man asks, finally rising from his perch. He walks toward me slowly—as if he is ensnaring an animal. He towers over me, his head at least a foot above mine. His frame is lithe but solidly muscled and he moves with the terrifying grace of a feral cat.

I don't answer him, only back away further. The undergrowth rustles behind me. Max and Calloway have moved closer, rounding me up as wolves do with their prey. Fear and anger billow through me.

"Did you think it was out of the goodness of my heart?" He is close enough now that I can see the sunlight glint in the blue of his pale eyes. His head is cocked, and a piece of raven hair falls over his forehead. The effect is almost boyish in nature, but there is nothing innocent about the way he looks at me.

"I'll tell you something, Lemming, something that every other fool who's ever met me knows but seems to have eluded you. There *is* no goodness in my heart. I was born into the Darkness, and I am the Darkness. There is no room for anything else in this soul of mine. I've come too far, torn apart too much of this terrible world, to give up now."

Realization settles over me, cold as hoarfrost. I assumed the Boundary hunters were the ones who blew up the Boundary. But it wasn't them. It was *him*. The man who saved me from slavery is the same one who blew a hole through a millennia of safety and put a man in the hospital. Terror sluices down my throat.

"It was *you*. You blew up the Boundary!"

He grins lazily, his chest rising and falling in a slow rhythm. "I saved you because I have need of you. And you will come with me, whether you wish to or not. Though it is up to you whether it will be of your own volition or if I need to tie you up."

No.

The word powers through me like a hot tide. Red spills over my vision and my blood pumps as though it's at the very surface of my skin. I've made it past the Boundary and escaped enslavement. I refuse to be waylaid by a violent, selfish *boy*. It's too much, too unfair.

Angry as all hell, I spit in his face.

The look of shock that passes over his features mirrors my own. Who knew a 'Lemming' has a backbone?

Who knew I have one?

The man's shock fades quickly, replaced by icy determination. He grabs my wrist with those lightning-fast reflexes. "Tied up it is, then," he growls, pulling my hands behind my back. My wrist barks in pain and I remember hitting the ground last night, fleeing from Eulogius.

The Dark Worlder brings his face close to mine, deadly serious as he taps the Boundary hunter's revolver now strapped to his belt, alongside a startling assortment of knives that hang from an ornamented band of leather across his chest. "A word of warning," he says softly, "if you try to escape, I do not miss."

A scream claws its way up my throat, but I force it down. My body twitches, demanding I set it free to attack the man, to kick and bite and tear at his skin. But I hold still as he wraps rope around my wrists, binding them tightly together behind my back. Let him think that's all the fight I have. When the time is right, he will learn differently.

"We've still got half a days' worth of light," he says to Max and Calloway. They've watched the exchange with guarded faces, but they showed me enough. They don't agree with his plan. When the time is right, I will leverage that against him like a battering ram. "Let's go."

The man picks up my sack and throws it over his shoulder along with his own. He gives me a gentle shove forward and I force my feet to move. I'll bide my time like the good Similian I am. And then, the Dark Worlder will learn he is not the only one with Darkness inside of them.

∼

Dark Worlder

The girl is the least graceful creature I've ever seen. I've always heard Similians don't spend much time outdoors, coddled as they are in their electric homes, but witnessing it is an entirely different matter.

I watch in mild distaste as she trips over another root, the same as she has done with every root prior. Which is saying a lot, as the Nemoran Wood is thicker and more gnarled than most on the continent. Thick enough for beasts and criminals to disappear within its depths and never emerge again. I've been inside this forest more times than I can count, but I'm not foolish enough to feel safe under its trees. First lesson of Ferusa—there is always *something* more dangerous than you.

The girl goes sprawling and Max catches her by the neck of that ridiculous jumpsuit, hauling her upright with a look of pure fury. Max has even less patience for ineptitude than I do, but with her steel-edged eyes and the twin swords strapped to her back, she is well suited for keeping the girl moving.

"Do you think *all* Similians are this clumsy?" Cal remarks from where he walks beside me. His bow, Xamani made and beautifully carved, peeks from behind his shoulder. His footsteps are silent, though it hardly matters with the amount of noise the girl makes a few paces ahead. "It's almost like she's never seen a tree before."

I grunt in acknowledgement, but know better than to assume this will quell Cal. He's never been one to be deterred by someone else's rancor. Especially mine.

"Do you think all Similians are as beautiful as her?"

I scowl in annoyance. "I hadn't noticed," I bark out. A lie if I were to examine it too closely. Which I won't.

Cal scoffs in utter disbelief. "I don't even prefer women and I noticed. Those cheekbones and those lips and especially those eyes..."

I let out a huff, turning to him with a furious glare. "*What* is your point?"

Cal ignores my ferocity with maddening poignancy. "My *point,*" he says slowly, as if I'm obtuse, "is she is a real person."

I watch as the girl hooks her toes in a scraggly bush, flailing her body as she struggles to keep from face planting. Max shoves her back upright with all the gentleness of an angry bear. "Obviously."

"It was one thing when we spoke of this in concept. Like

a story, with characters that had only outline and no substance. It's entirely different when it involves a living, breathing person with emotions and dreams."

A heavy steel wall slices down somewhere inside me, as unbendable as the Boundary used to be. "Enough, Calloway," I bark, rounding on him. "That girl is the key to saving Denver, no matter how real she is," my lips twist in a feral snarl. "I will sacrifice as many strangers as needed to get back what's mine."

Cal doesn't shy away from my savage anger. He only frowns. "You've never put stock in magical nonsense before."

His unspoken words hang in the air between us. *You must be desperate.*

I don't dispute it. Desperation flows through my veins, wafting off my skin in stinking clouds. It's what drove me across the continent, what I poured into the explosives that conquered the Boundary. There is no point denying it to Cal, who knows the inside of my heart as well as his own.

So instead, I glower at him silently and move to relieve Max at the Lemming's side. Max looks down her nose at me, a wonder, considering I have a few inches of height on her, and pushes a sigh through her nostrils. As if to say she should be congratulated for reigning in her patience and not pushing the Lemming into a bramble bush. I shoot her a grateful smirk and she turns on her heel with dramatic flair, taking her place next to Calloway.

The Lemming takes her eyes off the path in front of her just long enough to shoot me a furious glare, as if trying to set fire to me with only her eyes. With interest, I note her pale cheeks have been colored a flush shade of pink, even though we've been walking at a turtle's pace for less than an hour.

It takes me only a moment to determine the cause of her clumsiness. She doesn't look at the path in front of her, doesn't take in any of the obstacles that obscure the forest floor. Instead, her eyes scan the forest relentlessly. Searching.

Looking for an escape.

I set my jaw in a grimace. It seems my threats have whistled by her rather than sinking their claws into her skin. The determined set of her lush mouth and the hatred that burns in her eyes tells me that even harsh words won't deter her. Only actions.

I turn from her abruptly and she glances at me in wide surprise. "Keep walking," I growl, heading toward Max and Cal.

The girl nods slowly, arranging her face into one of innocence, but it's too late to shield what I've already seen. I wonder if she's aware of the way every thought she has splashes across her face.

Max raises a brow at me but keeps silent as I give her a slight nod.

It takes only a moment for the girl to take the bait. She sprints off the path, her bound wrists bobbing behind her, her small legs pumping furiously. I don't go after her, watching as she plunges into the depths of the forest.

My stride doesn't change when her scream rings out a moment later.

Cal presses his lips together in a thin line of disapproval.

I shrug sheepishly. "I don't want to be chasing her the entire journey to Nadjaa."

I take a few steps forward and yank the pistol out of my belt.

The girl is a few feet into the trees, her eyes wide and

her face pale in terror. I don't blame her. I was terrified, too, the first time I faced a Ditya wolf. Though I'd been five.

The wolf snarls, stalking toward her. It is not a wolf of old faerie tales, of beautiful fur and majestic head. Instead, it possesses a distorted jaw, so wide it covers most of its face. Its eyes are squinted and red and instead of fur, scales dripping with a rubbery green substance coat its powerful body.

With no use of her hands and no weapons, the girl is a sitting duck. Or rather, a sitting *Lemming*.

The revolver's weight is distasteful in my hand. Guns have never been my weapon of choice, impersonal and as expensive as they are, but that doesn't mean they don't have their uses. I pull back the hammer and lift the weapon with a steady hand, lining the sights smoothly.

The wolf pounces at the girl and they go down in a flurry of scales and slime. Her scream is agonizing, pulled from the depths of terror and, oddly, it pierces through me with alarming furor.

Heart racing, I squeeze the trigger. The wolf slumps.

I take my time ambling over to where the girl lays trapped beneath the beast's significant mass. I heft its carcass off of her in a smooth movement, expecting to encounter a trembling Lemming, but instead, coming face to face with a furiously spitting house cat.

The girl's emerald gaze is absolutely outraged as she shoves herself to her feet and turns accusing eyes on me. She spits hair out of her mouth, her face beet red. Green slime covers her body and fresh blood wells at a small scratch on her arm, but she appears mostly unharmed.

I have the distinct feeling if her wrists weren't tied, *I* wouldn't remain unharmed for long.

"You did that on purpose!" she shouts with righteous indignation.

I level her with an unamused glare, but in her anger, she doesn't even flinch. Just meets my wall of stone with her own powerful wave of fury.

"You knew that...that *thing* was in the trees, and you let it almost eat me!"

"You were never in any danger," I tell her calmly, which only seems to incense her further. I force the corner of my lips down. Since when is angering someone so much fun? "I told you. I don't miss."

She lets out a cry of outrage, looking as if her wrath might tremble its way right out of her small body.

"It's better you learn early," I say with the arrogant shrug I already know sets her blood to boiling.

"Learn what?" She grits out.

"That the Darkness bites back."

CHAPTER
SEVEN

Mirren

My fingers and toes have all gone numb by the time the Dark Worlders stop for the night. We come to a clearing and the pale-eyed man must see something that pleases him, as he nods to the others and they begin to make camp.

He pulls me to a nearby tree. "Sit," he orders, pointing to the ground like there is any way I misinterpret what he means.

I do as he says, my eyes burning and my body rebelling against his commandment. It has been commanded by others for far too long.

"Do I need to tie you to this tree, or can I trust that you now realize staying put is your best option?"

I bare my teeth at him, but I don't move.

Shivers slither up my spine remembering the stench of that beast's dripping maw. It's an image I'm not likely to forget any time soon. Covinus only knows what other creatures have bred and twisted within the Darkness. Aside from the one grinning back at me, of course. I am becoming all too familiar with his breed of beast.

The Dark Worlder smiles arrogantly at my silent compliance. "Good. You seem pretty smart. For a Lemming."

I withhold my biting response, preferring instead to appear unaffected, but the man doesn't appear to need one as he saunters away.

Max and Calloway have already built a fire, the latter throwing root vegetables into a large pot that hangs above it. The trio spoke little to each other during the day's journey, but their relationship appears to be beyond words. I watched closely as they communicated with minute ticks of their head and squints of their eyes, but unfortunately, couldn't decipher what any of it meant.

The firelight flickers, casting shadows that dance across the rock wall like eerie waves of night. The three of them sit around it, speaking in hushed tones and filling their bellies with hot stew. The delicious scent wafts over and despite my stubborn will to hate everything about them, my stomach growls loudly, betraying me.

I put hunger from my mind, shifting my body on the hard ground. My arms are sore from the position of the ropes and my injured wrist sends jarring pain shooting up my arm with each movement. My skin, rubbed raw to the point of bleeding as I tried to free myself from the bonds, stings with an unrelenting ferocity and has become almost unbearable in combination with the frozen ache of my extremities.

It was stupid to run out of Similis without an extra layer of clothes, but I hadn't considered how cold the elements would feel when exposed to them for more than a few minutes time. There are no furnaces here, pumping hot air whenever one wills it.

I hadn't considered much beyond Easton's dying. Now, miles away from the Boundary, with hunger gnawing at my belly and cold biting at my skin, I have plenty of time to ruminate over all the aspects of this terrible plan I didn't consider. It's a merciless game I've been playing all day, one in which there is no winning, because the past isn't malleable. My decisions are set in stone. There is only living with them.

I eye the Dark Worlder, my salvation. My damnation. He doesn't engage in the playful banter of the other two, but instead, stares idly at the fire. Though he is cast in shadows, I can still clearly see the planes of his face, cut sharply, like pieces of the rock cliff behind him. And indeed, if I'm ever to move forward, I need to find a way over the mountain he presents—rough, sharp, and utterly unyielding.

As if my thoughts have cast into the air, he suddenly turns his pale eyes on me. I meet them with as much hatred as I can muster and he gives me something equally heated back, until I'm finally forced to look away. I'm not accustomed to such raw forms of emotion, hateful or otherwise, and it brings an unwelcome heat to my skin.

"Are you hungry?" his voice is gruff. I jump, gazing up at him in alarm. He's somehow moved from the fire and stands in front of me, staring down with a face of stone. It's unnerving--how he moves with such unearthly quiet.

"No." He can't kidnap me and then do something humane, like try to feed me.

He cocks his head, something like a smile playing at the corner of his lips. The only sign he gives he's even heard me. "Are you cold?"

Desperately so. But I would rather eat nails than admit it to him. I grind my teeth. "No."

At this, he really does smirk and I want to lunge at him, to scrape that smile off his self-satisfied face.

"Are your wrists sore?" he presses.

"What do you care?"

He shrugs, stuffing his hands into his pockets. "I don't, really. But it's a bad plan."

"*What's* a bad plan?" I growl, infuriated I have to ask what he's talking about. That I am always a step behind when it comes to him.

"Starving yourself. Freezing to death. If you're planning on killing yourself to teach me some sort of moral lesson, I'm afraid you're wasting your time. I've got no morals."

"I've noticed," I snap, wondering how he has managed to replace fear with pure irritation in a matter of seconds. It has to be some sort of talent.

The smile still plays at his lips, lips I'm enraged to notice, are full and well-shaped. At least Eulogius and Murph reflected the darkness inside of them. This man is pure evil wrapped in a deceivingly beautiful package. It makes him all the more dangerous.

He shrugs again. "Suit yourself," he says, making to turn back toward the fire.

"Fine," I say to his back. It's easier to admit this small defeat when I don't have to see his smug face.

He turns, looking at me inquiringly. "Fine?"

I nod, a quick and rough gesture, but one that can't be mistaken. Though I'm ruefully irritated at admitting weakness, an unfailing sense of relief floods through me that the ache in my stomach is about to be sated. I've never been hungry before and never wish to be again.

The man wedges a hand under my armpit and pulls me gently to my feet as if I weigh no more than a feather. I watch with morbid curiosity the way the muscles of his arms coil and relax beneath the fabric of his shirt.

"I can't very well eat with my hands tied behind my back. Or are you planning to spoon feed me like a child?" My words are biting and ungrateful, but he only raises an eyebrow and motions toward a blanket spread by the fire. I imagine he's heard much worse. Said much worse.

"Cal, would you get our guest some stew?" he says, raising a brow in challenge.

I am nowhere near a guest and we both know it, but I remain silent. I can mouth off after I fill my stomach.

He helps me sit without falling over and then brings his face so close to mine I feel the heat of his breath. "Remember, I do not miss."

And with that, he runs one of his knives through the ropes, setting my arms free. I almost hear the joints of my shoulders cry out in relief, finally able to stretch and the cool night air soothes the sting of my broken skin.

Calloway brings me some stew, placing the bowl carefully in my numb fingers. He shoots me a furtive look that seems a mixture of apology and warning, but I ignore it pointedly. I have no use for apologies when they will not rectify what's been done.

"Eat and then we can tend to your wrists," the Dark Worlder says, taking a seat across the fire.

I glance at him in surprise, but rather than contemplating why someone who's abducted me would tend to my wounds, I dig into the stew feverishly. It burns my tongue, but I don't slow until my belly stretches with fullness. I can't even remember the last time I ate. Did I really decline the breakfast Farrah offered me?

The food clears the fuzzy edges around my thoughts, honing them into clear lines.

Calloway fills my bowl again without my asking and I devour that one, too.

I feel the Dark Worlder's eyes on me as I finish the last few bites. "Thank you for the food," I say softly, without looking at him. It's more comfortable not to look at him.

"You dying of starvation doesn't serve my best interests," he replies.

Now, I do look, square and direct. "And what are those interests, exactly?" I ask, my mouth tight. It feels odd, to be in a place where my anger doesn't make people uncomfortable—if anything, it seems to spur the man on.

"Don't worry about it. I have need of you, and when I'm finished, you'll be let go."

I stare at him. "Let...let go?"

He rolls his eyes skyward. "It was a bit hard to get a word in edgewise with your spitting antics, but yes, I've always planned on letting you go."

It can't possibly be that easy, especially if he refuses to name what exactly his need of me *is*. Something he can't get anyone else to do, obviously, or he wouldn't have resorted to kidnapping. "Why would you do that?"

He cocks his head and I swear, his eyes sparkle. "Would you rather I didn't?" The tone of his voice conveys something unspoken, something untamed, and I immediately shy away from it, despite the thrill that roils through me.

I don't respond, just watch him from beneath my lashes. The way I would watch a dangerous animal. A leopard or a tiger. His body is no longer tense and coiled, or ready to pounce in that wild manner of his, but there is still something about the way he holds himself that leaves me feeling uneasy. He is too still. As if he has singular control over every muscle in his body.

He clears his throat. "It looks like you fractured your wrist."

My eyebrows knit together as I look down at the aforementioned wrist. It does look unnaturally swollen, but I've never been interested in a Healer's track and therefore have no real knowledge of what injuries look like.

I set down my stew and wrap the blanket tightly around me. My teeth have finally stopped chattering and I suddenly feel as if I could sleep for days. No matter that I will most likely be sleeping on a hard, dirt floor surrounded by violent heathens.

"I should splint it, so it heals properly," the man says.

I eye him skeptically. He only waits, his face unreadable.

I hold out my hand. After digging in his pack for a few moments, he tosses a wad of thick fabric in my direction. A cloak.

He waits until I wrap it around myself before settling beside me. His body is warm and solid next to mine. The slight scent of woodsmoke and spice tinge the air, and I wonder abstractly whether it is him or the cloak.

He carefully places a few sticks at strategic points around my wrist and then begins to bind them together with thick cloth. He is careful, his skin never brushing mine and I wonder when I became so aware of the *lack* of someone's touch rather than the touch itself.

I take the distraction of my wrist to watch him unabashedly. His dark brows are furrowed, and his lashes are a sweep of black across his caramel skin.

He makes quick work of the splint, tying it off with a neat knot. "Take it easy and it'll be as good as new in a few weeks." His eyes travel slowly to my throat. "That too. Though the swelling, at least, should go down in a few days."

"Are you a Healer?"

The Dark Worlder makes a rough sound that could be a laugh and begins to carefully roll the remaining cloth. "No. But I am intimately familiar with a slew of injuries." He hands me a tin. "Put this on your wrists and on your arm where the Ditya scratched you. It will help with the pain."

I think I imagine his wince as his eyes sweep across my injuries.

"What's your name?" I blurt out suddenly. "You know my name, it's only polite to tell me yours."

He flashes a wry grin. "Were your last kidnappers overly concerned with manners?"

I chew at my lip. Though he is utterly infuriating, pummeling him would probably only hurt my wrist.

"It isn't wise to be giving your name away to strangers," he repeats his sentiment of earlier.

I let out a huff of frustration. "Fine—"

"It's Shaw," he interrupts with a lazy smile. His pale eyes sparkle in challenge. "I don't think you're really in a position to do much with my name. Or know what to do with it if you were."

Shaw. It seems so...ordinary. Though I don't really know what I was expecting. Maybe something less human? He's insulted me with his confidence I can do nothing with the information, but gaining his name feels like a small victory, nonetheless. And something of a relief. A relief to name the danger sitting beside me. Shaw.

∼

Shaw

The man is exactly where I left him. A relief that I don't have to spend the entire evening hunting him down in whatever run-down taverns exist in whatever paltry Boundary town is closest. It's already been one of the longest days of my life, made longer by the fact I will have to relieve Max from watch when I return to our camp. Sleep, it seems, will elude me for another night.

He is wrapped in a large overcoat, a ridiculous choice for the warmth of the evening, but not uncommon for the Boundary hunters that prowl these woods. Cloaks like that afford plenty of space to stash weapons. I smile assuredly. "Why, hello there. Eulogius, was it?"

The hunter bares his teeth as I approach, snarling against the wad of fabric Max gagged him with. I take it from his mouth, resisting the urge to laugh that the gag is bright pink, probably the remnant of some old dress of hers. She's never been one to resist a little humiliation when it comes to the scum of slavers.

"You're either brave or stupid for messing with me!" His voice is higher than I would have guessed. He must be younger than he looks. Though the Dark World has a way of doing that to people, prematurely aging those by the measure of what heaviness lies in their souls.

"It's a fine line," I reply indifferently, scanning the forest. Aside from the stray howl of an angry creature in the distance, it appears deserted.

"I told you, I ain't talking without payment. You have what I asked for?" he demands, shifting his weight from foot to foot. He's clearly nervous, but that's to be expected. This isn't the kind of thing he does every day. Most of the men that inhabit these Boundary hovels only work as hunters to make ends meet. He's merely a farmer, only advantageous to me in what he turns a blind eye to. The kind of activity that happens in the barn on the edge of his property and the kind of 'merchandise' men darker than him move through it on a monthly basis.

"That depends," I drawl, "do you have the information I need?"

"I'm not telling you nothing until you pay up," he blurts out, his voice wavering slightly. He narrows his eyes and thrusts his fist into his opposite palm. A warning. "And you better pay up. I'm not risking my arrangement to get nothing."

I almost laugh that the boy thinks I can be threatened but bite my lip instead. There's no need to provoke him. Yet.

"There now, Wayland Rutger is a man of his word," Probably. "And I brought what I promised." I pat the pocket of my cloak.

The boy's body visibly relaxes. His shoulders slump, as if holding his head high, even for only a few moments, has exhausted him. I don't judge him for it. He has a farm on the brink of ruin and a family on the brink of starvation and being proud won't save either of those things. Holding onto his morals and stopping the horrendous merchandise that's trafficked through his property won't feed his family. It might even get him killed for land so close to Similis. It's a natural progression, to start providing some of the *product* himself.

I understand him, even if I hate him a little.

Because I'm no better. Conscience is a luxury afforded only to the comfortable and safe.

I toss the small leather pouch at his feet. It's coin that could fuel weeks' worth of Denver's outreach programs in Nadjaa, feeding the poor and educating them to own their voices. I push the thought to the side. If it keeps me from breaking my vow, it's money well spent. I'll deal with the treasury deficit later. *After* I get Denver back.

The boy hunches over and weighs the bag in his hand. "Yen Girene is always looking to buy," he says.

I already know this, but don't say so. I'm supposed to be a simple farm boy, after all, not a wraith that collects shadows like currency.

"If you got something...*unusual,*" his voice is rough as he says the word. Perhaps giving voice to one's sins, instead of closing your eyes and refusing to see them, is taxing.

"The Achijj is looking to add to his harem and will..." he stutters and presses his eyes together, his mouth twisted in disgust. I resist the urge to grab him and pry them open. To make him look upon the filth he associates himself with, even if it is by simple negligence.

I take a deep breath and stretch my fingers wide, before balling them into a tight fist. The moon has already risen to its full height and Max will be exhausted. There isn't time to open anyone's eyes to their own personal brand of darkness.

"He's offered a high price if you find a beautiful Similian. Rumor has it, he's looking for one to complete the Gireni rite," the man shoves the pouch of coin roughly into the pocket of his cloak and glances around furtively. I frown in disgust. The Gireni are a brutal people and their leader, the Achijj, is the cruelest of all. Every spring he takes a woman from his harem and has his way with her atop his towering wall. Then pushes her off it, supposedly as a way to keep his lands fertile. "Whispers say that he has a long-term guest, a political adversary he is looking to impress."

It's the information I came here for. When Denver was captured, I wondered why no ransom was ever sent to the city's council. Now I'm thankful it wasn't. The council would never officially sanction some poor girl's murder, even if it would save their Chancellor. I still don't know *why*

Denver was taken, but I'm further than I was when he disappeared. At least I now have a clear idea of where he is and how to bargain for him back.

I should feel relief, that I haven't sold my soul and kidnapped an innocent girl for nothing. The way to save the Chancellor is clear, but the abyss within me writhes furiously at the cost. I narrow my eyes at the man. "And is the Achijj who controls your warehouse? Of *merchandise?*" My lips form a sneer around the word, a reminder to the farmer that we both know the extent of what happens here.

The man blanches. "I—I—"

"Answer the question," I demand. Though I make no move toward my daggers, the majority of which are strapped across my chest and hidden under the depths of my cloaks, the man tremors as if I've threatened him. And I suppose, in a way, I have.

I simply uncloaked the fury that burns in my gaze, proof of the chasm that roils inside me. Empty and wanting, broken apart piece by piece. Killing comes at a steep price in the Dark World, a price I have paid over and over. A piece of your soul. It was in the First Queen's curse, the one that plunged Ferusa into darkness. With every life taken, the curse demands payment.

It is why no one can meet my eyes. Because in them, one can behold every piece missing. Empty and swirling with nothing but Darkness.

"It—it isn't the Achijj," he barely manages the words. His hand inches toward the shot gun he has concealed under his cloak. I resist the urge to roll my eyes. If I'd wanted him disarmed, I would have done so when he was out cold, but it wasn't even worth the energy it would have taken. By the time he manages to pull the lumbering thing,

I could already have snapped his neck. It really is extraordinary how safe guns make people feel.

"It's the Praeceptor. He's controls everything from the Boundary to Nadjaa, now."

My mouth goes dry. The last I knew, the vicious warlord known as the Praeceptor had been beaten back to his territory in the north. The result of bloody war and an alliance between four other warlords, brokered by none other than Denver himself.

"What happened to the Blood Alliance?" I say, my voice deathly cold.

The man shakes his head furiously. "I don't know!" he cries, shying away from my gaze. "It was quiet, not a war. One day the warlords ruled and the next, it was only the Praeceptor's men. I don't court death by asking questions."

So he isn't entirely naïve. I'm well acquainted with the kinds of things the Praeceptor does to those who ask questions. Things that still bring a wave of nausea whenever they come unbidden to my mind.

And now, he controls all the territory on this side of Nadjaa, the moon city. The *free* city. The place Denver built as a haven of prosperity and safety. Of education and enlightenment. The very antithesis of everything the Praeceptor stands for.

The desperation in me is a knife twisting in my gut. If the Praeceptor is going to make a move on Nadjaa, he's going to do it while its Chancellor has disappeared. Determination rises up in me. I need to get Denver back to Nadjaa. Now.

My desire to save him began as a selfish need, but now, it is all that keeps Ferusa from utter destruction.

"Thank you for your time," I say, not bothering to cloak the menace that lines every word. I watch with a feral grin as the boy backs away, slowly at first, before breaking into a lumbering run.

I turn toward the woods, toward my family and the watch they keep over the Similian. The girl whose shoulders the fate of the Dark World now rests. The Lemming who, according to the prophecy that drove me here, will save us only through her utter ruin.

CHAPTER
EIGHT

Mirren

I wake the next morning with a groan. My fingers drift to my throat, aching and sore where Eulogius wrapped his fingers around it.

"Today will be the worst for the swelling."

Shaw's voice makes me jump, dread pooling in my stomach. My dreams were so blissfully blank, I almost forgot about the horrible degenerate who holds me hostage.

He sits in the same position he did last night when exhaustion finally overtook me, his pale eyes wary and watching. Perhaps he didn't sleep. Perhaps he never sleeps. I'll never be able to escape if he's some sort of night creature that never needs to close his eyes.

I push myself up to sitting and run my hand over the back of my hair. Horrified, I quickly pull away from the tangled mess.

"You can speak fine, so I don't think there's any permanent damage to your larynx," Shaw continues knowledgeably. I shoot him a glare. He either knows a lot about the human body or a lot about injuries. I can probably guess which one.

"Where are you taking me today?" I ask, succinctly ignoring his attempts at humanity.

"That is the question, isn't it," he replies vaguely. It isn't an answer, and he doesn't bother to look at me as he says it, digging instead into his pack.

"Of course, it's the question," I say hotly, "you've kidnapped me, and I deserve to know what you plan to do with me." The words are sharp and, quite possibly, stupid. There's no telling how much disobedience Shaw will put up with before deciding to be rid of me permanently. And with no law to guide his morality, I only remain unharmed on the whims of his limited mercy. And yet, just the sight of his face sends words careening out of my mouth.

He pulls a wrapped package out of the pack and tosses it in my lap. I stare at it dumbly for a moment before Shaw mutters, "breakfast. Unless you're going back to starving yourself. And anyway, I thought Similians are supposed to be agreeable. Isn't your attitude against the law?"

I grimace, ripping into the package which turns out to be a nutrition bar. I take a large bite, the crumbly texture odd against my tongue. "I'm not in Similis anymore," I reply tartly though a mouthful.

Shaw's eyes flash. "No, you're not," he agrees, his voice low. "Why is that?"

"That's none of your business."

"Usually those outside the Boundary were forced. Outcast, I think you call it. But they leave with nothing. Not even the clothes on their backs," he runs his eyes from my head to my toes, leaving a heated trail in their wake. "And you appear to be fully clothed."

I scowl at him, my cheeks heating. Attempting to keep

the horror from my face, I fidget uncomfortably. Outcasting members of the Community has always been touted as necessary, a benevolent punishment intended for the greater good. But leaving someone outside the Boundary with no clothes or supplies only seems cruel. Especially when I have witnessed firsthand those who wait outside it.

"So, the question is then, what made a small, unskilled Lemming scurry from the safety of her home? From a world that feeds her, clothes her, and thinks for her?"

I hate him. I've never even thought the word 'hate' before, not even in the depths of my shunning for being an Outcast's daughter, but it's all that's appropriate for the man who's kidnapped me and then belittled everything about my existence. "No one thinks for me," I reply through gritted teeth.

Shaw's face breaks into a wickedly decadent smile. "You didn't answer my question," he points out. "Why did you run?"

"Why did you blow up the Boundary?"

"To give you a way out."

His face is utterly unreadable as we stare at each other. Shaw couldn't have known of my brother's plight and even if he did, there was no way he could know I was going to escape. *I* hadn't even known I was going to leave. There is more to this than he lets on and I resolve to figure it out before I free myself of him.

At that moment, Calloway appears at the edge of the clearing, his cheeks flushed with exertion and his bow strapped across his back. "Looks like a storm to the west. We can probably avoid it if we head north, but I think we should leave sooner rather than later so we can make it to Havay and gather the horses..."

His voice trails off as his russet eyes settle on me. "Oh, Mirren! You're awake. How did you sleep?"

It's an odd question, considering the fact that he's holding me hostage in the middle of nowhere and that we all slept on the cold, hard ground, but I appreciate the polite exchange nonetheless. It feels familiar, something that tethers me to a world that now seems so far away. "Well. Thank you, Calloway."

He waves a hand dismissively. "Call me Cal."

It feels intimate to call him the same name his friends do, but Dark World definitions of intimacy are markedly different than mine. Like the way my skin sparked when Shaw held my hand before the Boundary hunters found us, but he didn't seem to notice at all. What a strange way to live, being so accustomed to things like touch and private names that you don't pay them any attention.

"Thank you, Calloway, but I'd prefer to use your given name. We aren't friends, after all. I'm here against my will."

His eyes are grave as he nods and glances at Shaw. Something passes between them, something spoken without being vocalized. They did that a lot on the journey here, spoke without speaking at all, as if they can read each other's minds.

"You're completely right," Calloway agrees, his face pained. Guilty. I tuck that away, to be used later. "But as Shaw said, we have no intentions of hurting you."

I don't meet his eyes, choosing instead to focus on my hands. "Unless I try to run."

The color leeches from Calloway's face. Whether it's horror at what he's been a party to, or horror at the truth laid so bare, I will never know as Shaw chooses that moment to interrupt us.

"Go get Max. Let's get on the road. We need to reach

Havay before sundown. I don't relish the idea of being on the old road after sunset this time of year, especially with no horses."

Calloway gives Shaw one last meaningful look and disappears into the trees, swift as a gazelle.

"For someone so concerned with manners, that wasn't very polite. He was trying to be kind to you."

I frown, my fury rising once again. "I have no use for kindness when freedom is what I need. And I'm not going to be polite to someone who has tied me up and stolen that."

Shaw's eyes flare. "Cal wasn't the one who tied you up," he says neutrally.

I raise my chin. "He watched you do it and said nothing. Some would say that standing by and doing nothing while evil is committed is just as evil."

I expect Shaw's anger. I do not expect the appraising look he fits me with, as if I have somehow passed a test I didn't know I was taking.

"Some would," he echoes, before turning to gather his supplies.

∽

I hate these woods. I hate the trees, so large even Shaw wouldn't be able to wrap his arms around their trunks. I hate their gnarled roots that run underfoot like giant veins. I hate the sickly-sweet scent of them and the way the very air clings to my skin, pasting my curls to my forehead and neck. I hate the uneven ground and ache of my muscles.

My toes hook under a root and I screech loudly, stumbling over a log. My wrist barks in pain as I shove myself back to my feet with a furious huff of breath. Shaw doesn't even break stride, his face as unruffled as ever.

Most of all, I hate *him*.

The reason I'm stuck in these Covinus-forsaken woods. Only a day earlier, hate was a foreign word, one I never spoke, let alone felt. But with his smug smiles and handsome face, Shaw has opened up a gaping chasm of it within me. I hate him so fiercely I feel I'll burn with it every time he sets his eyes to mine.

We've been walking for less than an hour, during which time he's amused himself with belittling everything about my existence. Only determination keeps my rage buried deep. That and the absolute refusal to grant him the pleasure of knowing he's gotten under my skin. He may be in control of my physical person, but I'll be damned if he controls my mind as well.

If only we were out of these horrible trees, I'd be able to think clearly again. I could ignore Shaw's taunting and come up with a plan of escape, but something in the thick foliage clouds my mind and leaves me feeling disjointed.

Low hanging branches sting my face like whips and insects buzz unpleasantly around my head, darting into my ears and pricking my skin. Finally, Shaw throws up his hands and begrudgingly announces that we're taking a break.

I collapse to the ground and swear I can hear my bones cry out in relief. My throat is dry and swollen and I can feel every muscle with an agonizing clarity. It's like my body has aged twenty years in only a few days' time.

You don't look like you've fought for anything a day in your life.

I scowl at Shaw's words and mutter a curse under my breath. I am fighting now, and it isn't a pleasant experience.

"Didn't take you long to pick up our colorful vocabulary," Calloway notes.

The leaves rustle beside me and though I would rather continue to stare at the canopy and contemplate just how far off kilter my life is at the moment, I look over to see him situating himself next to me. "Thought you might be thirsty," he says by way of greeting and hands me a canteen.

I don't even bother to sit up before I gulp greedily, the cool water spilling into my neck and hair. My mind instantly sharpens. I take a few more sips before reluctantly handing the canteen back to Calloway.

"Keep it. I've got another one in my bag." He waves me off.

He stretches his thin body next to me, cradling his head in his interlocked palms and staring up at the trees. His red hair is bright against the dim light of the forest and his freckles practically jump off his tanned skin. When he feels my eyes, he turns his head and shoots me a kind, lopsided grin.

It isn't an expression directed at me often, and in spite of myself, I smile back at him shyly. "Thank you," I say and find that I mean it.

Shaw and Max stand a few feet away, having an animated discussion in hushed tones. Judging by their furtive glances in my direction, I am clearly the subject.

"It's hard to get used to hiking through the woods, isn't it?" Calloway asks genially. He takes some dried fruit from his bag and offers it to me. I tear into it without hesitation, remembering my earlier conversation with Shaw. I may hate him, but he's right about starving myself getting me nowhere. I'm going to need all my strength to escape.

"Yeah," I admit, taking another bite. It's leathery, but pleasantly tangy.

"It's something that takes practice, like anything else."

I raise a brow doubtfully. There is no amount of practice that would award me the complete control over my body Shaw seems to employ. When I wasn't falling, I watched him move between the trees. He held his head high and moved over the lush grounds as if he was born to do just that. Even when I watched the ground as hard as I could, I still slid on the gravel or tripped over tree stumps.

Cal smiles. "It really is. Max grew up in the southern isles and she had a really hard time when we first took her into the woods. And look at her now."

I steal a furtive glance at the girl. She hasn't spoken more than two words to me since that first day and I can't decide whether or not it's a blessing. But Calloway is right. She moves like Shaw, effortless and powerful.

As if sensing she's the topic of conversation, Max saunters toward us suddenly, the defined muscles of her abdomen rippling in time to her strut. "I would appreciate you not selling information about me to a *Lemming*," she says, her full lips twisted in distaste. I drop my eyes to the ground and bite my lip. Words seem to fight their way out of my mouth around Shaw but retreat far down my throat in her presence.

"You're just sensitive about tripping over that rock and almost falling into the ravine in Dauphine," Calloway fires back. My eyes widen. He must be far braver than I to provoke her.

When I dare raise my eyes, Max's face isn't angry at all. In fact, it's considerably lighter as she throws a hand on her bare hip. "At least I didn't almost get us all killed stealing a *cookie*," she shoots back.

Calloway winces. "That was one time—"

"If you two are done reminiscing about your inadequacies, we need to talk about a change of plans."

I jump at Shaw's voice. I was so caught up watching the exchange between Max and Calloway, teasing and yet kind at the same time, I almost forgot he was here. Almost. It isn't possible to forget him entirely, not when his presence raises the hair on my arms.

Calloway grins at me conspiratorially and my heart swells. "He just doesn't want us to bring up the time he almost fell out of the window of the Council house because he leaned too far back in a chair."

Shaw crosses his arms. "The floor was slanted," he deadpans.

Calloway's laughter rings out into the forest and for a moment, I feel like laughing along with him. Like I belong somewhere, as these three belong to each other.

"As I was saying," Shaw says pointedly, "I think we need to split up. At this pace, it's going to take three weeks just to reach Havay."

His eyes slide to me, and my face reddens.

"If you don't wish to be inconvenienced by a slow, clumsy *Lemming,* perhaps you shouldn't have kidnapped one," I intone, my voice saccharine.

Calloway coughs loudly into his sleeve, a half-hearted attempt to cover what is clearly a laugh. Shaw's jaw twitches, but his face remains as unreadable as ever as he replies, "*Perhaps*, I should just knock the Lemming I have unconscious to be spared her thoughts."

"You're a brute!"

Amusement passes over his face. "And you, my dear Lemming, walk slower than a turtle."

My mouth drops in hot indignation, but before I can reply, he turns away, succinctly dismissing me.

"If we miss Havay, we miss the horses. Which means the journey to Nadjaa takes a month rather than a week. We can't afford to waste that much time. I need you guys to go ahead. Gather the horses, freshen the supplies, and meet up with us near Shadiil Pass."

Max's lips pull into a frown, her eyes serious as she studies Shaw. "We shouldn't split up. Not with who's controlling this territory now, Shaw."

I wonder at the worry that tinges her voice. Who could possibly be dangerous to a man like Shaw?

"You shouldn't be alone."

Shaw's eyes land on Max, but instead of hardening with anger, they soften. I had him pegged as the unchallenged leader of the three, but maybe I was wrong. "We'll be fine, Maxi. Won't we, Lemming?"

His voice is light, and he smiles in a way that transforms his face from terrifying and cold to warm and charming. I press my lips together, keeping my face neutral. Losing Max and Calloway will only tip the odds in my favor. Shaw may be a formidable foe, but one is certainly better than three.

Max's eyes narrow. "I don't like this at all," she looks to Calloway with a plea in her eyes.

Calloway's gaze has been volleying between Shaw and I, and I get the distinct feeling he sees far more than he lets on. That perhaps his cheerfulness is meant to conceal the shrewd mind beneath.

He shrugs. "We do need horses," he says slowly, watching Max closely. "The faster we can get out of this territory, the safer we'll be."

They've either forgotten I'm here or think so little of me they feel no need to censor their words. But I hoard them as if they are precious weapons. Whoever scares them is someone I need to find.

"Max, we're all doing things that are uncomfortable. But it's what has to be done," Shaw says. It's an answer, but also a command.

Max relents. She nods once, her back strong and straight. "Be careful," she says, her voice laden with unspoken words.

Calloway envelops Shaw in a hug. He claps him on the back twice before pulling away, his face serious. "Do not take unnecessary risks, brother."

I can't take my eyes off them as Calloway and Max shoulder their packs. My breath is short. I've always thought Dark Worlders cared only for themselves, but it isn't just violence that ties these three together; there is something soft between them, tenable but fierce. Something I know no name for.

As they disappear into the woods, Max with one last pointed look, I feel hollow. It isn't until much later that I pinpoint the feeling. Jealousy.

∼

Shaw

Silence presses against my ears. The forest, with its thick canopy leaves blocking all but miniscule slivers of sunlight, makes me feel as if I'm wrapped inside a cocoon. An effect that can be both comforting or disconcerting, depending on the day. At the moment it's the latter. This wood is raw and ancient. It doesn't matter how many times I've been in the heart of the Nemoran, there is always something that lingers just beyond my line of sight that sets my teeth on edge.

Something darker than me, darker than even the Praeceptor.

The departure of Max and Cal has only served to further sour my mood. Their absence is a dull ache in my chest, pressing somewhere close to my heart. We've been separated many times before, but it never gets any easier. I should take strength from the pain and recognize it for what it is; the ache for home, something I wouldn't have dared imagine only a few years ago.

I glance at the girl beside me. Her cheeks are flushed with exertion and her breathing is heavy, but she has yet to complain. Maybe that's the Similian in her? I know little of the inner workings of their society, but from what I observed in my time at the Boundary, complaining is probably an Outcast-worthy offense. Just like everything else that requires individualistic thinking.

Or maybe, her lack of complaining has more to do with her innate stubbornness. Based on the fiery glares she's been shooting my way, it's not a bad guess.

Her toes hook on an overgrown tree stump and she sprawls forward with a sharp cry. I thrust my arm out before she hits the ground, steadying her as gently as I can manage. Which turns out to be not gentle at all as I haul her twisting body up by the scruff of her jumpsuit, like a mama cat with her kittens.

How anyone has survived this long being so clumsy, I have no idea. "It's no wonder the Boundary hunters caught you so easily," I remark dryly, unable to keep the mocking look from my face as her eyes snap to mine, "You can barely walk properly, let alone run."

Her eyes narrow, that stunning shade of green roiling like a storm at sea. "I can walk just fine, thank you." Her words are clipped, but soft.

That softness is maddening, from her lilting words to her smooth, unmarred skin. It invokes a war of emotions within me: thrilling curiosity battling an unfettered rage at the unfairness of it all. I want to reach out and stroke her skin, to wrap myself in the tender tone of her words. I want to scream at the injustice of it all, that there is someone in this world who has been allowed to move through it untouched.

Everything about her is like velvet, from her lush lips to her pillowy soft curls to the curving roll of her body. Except—that moment, when she realized I was not letting her go, just before she went pliant—I saw something else. Her eyes sparked and her delicate jaw set, and I'd *known* there was something harder beneath her surface. Similians may have outlawed emotions, but they haven't been successful in breeding them out entirely. At least, in this one's case.

I've already spent an untold amount of time wondering what, exactly, it would take for the girl to release whatever crawls beneath her surface. And what it would look like. If it would share the same edges as what resides beneath my skin.

"Are you always so polite when being insulted?"

She purses her lips. "There is no need to be unkind just because you are," she replies tersely. She pushes a sweaty tendril of hair off her forehead and takes another huff of air.

I slow my pace. "I think you'll find there are plenty of reasons to be unkind when someone else is."

She looks up at me, meeting my gaze for just a moment before dropping her eyes to the path in front of her. She does this a lot—refuses to meet my eyes. At first, I assumed it was out of the same fear that drives most people away from my gaze. It's a natural instinct to avoid the darkness inside me, but since the first night, I haven't seen anything resembling fear on the Lemming's face. I'm intimately familiar with the emotion, the taste of it and the shape it takes. The way it coats a person's mind until their entire being is slick with it, but there's been no trace of it on the girl.

Anger and rugged determination, yes. A wish to do violence to my person, certainly. But no fear.

"I don't believe that's true."

I raise an eyebrow.

"Just because I'm in the Dark World, doesn't mean my values automatically align with yours. We are all human and I will treat everyone as such."

I scoff. Loudly.

Ridiculous Similian nonsense. "Some are less human than others," I tell her, an edge creeping into my voice. She's been kidnapped, *twice,* and somehow still thinks there is good in everyone? "You'd do well to learn that quickly. The faster you stop assuming everyone can be trusted, the safer you'll be. You're going to be severely disappointed if you go around thinking everyone has the same heart you do," I pause, then add brightly, "Or severely dead."

The Lemming purses her lips, biting back a barrage of responses. "You know nothing of my heart."

It's an odd thing for a Similian to say. A direct reference to the part of themselves capable of feeling something as traitorous as love or hate.

I stop, allowing her a moment's rest. She takes a deep swig from Cal's canteen and settles herself rather ungracefully on a low boulder.

"Is your heart what drove you out of Similis in the middle of the night?" My voice is low. Rough. I watch her intently. The small flick of her braid over her shoulder, the bob of her petite foot. "Because that doesn't seem like something your brain would do."

She looks up at me through a curtain of dark lashes. If it were possible for a girl to spit fire, I have no doubt she would. Soft hearted or not, she would scorch me, cleansing the earth of my sins. "You know nothing of my brain either."

"Do Similians even have them? Seems a waste."

The retort flies out of my mouth and I wince slightly. What's the matter with me? I've already caused the girl enough pain. Am I really that desperate to reveal the ugliness inside me? To watch the familiar film of fear coat her features until she can no longer stand to look at me?

Her face flushes a deliciously vibrant color, lips pressing hard together. I find myself leaning forward, eager to hear whatever words would pour unbidden from them.

But she reins her temper in with enviable control, a perfect example of Similian restraint. I run a hand roughly through my hair, as if the feeling of my fingertips against my scalp will rein in my own.

"Where are we going?" her voice is level.

I swallow roughly, shooting my gaze to the sky and pointedly ignoring the way her fingers pass over the corner of her lips, wiping away the small droplets of water gathered there. The forest has a way of suspending one in time, but I've been crawling my way across its floor for as long as I can remember, fluent in the language of the trees. The tiny slivers of sun have disappeared so it must be past midday.

I heave a sigh. Too slow. We are going far too slow.

The thought makes my heart race uncomfortably, but I force air into my lungs. We will reach Nadjaa by the week's end if I have to carry the Lemming across the entirety of Ferusa. It doesn't occur to me to contemplate what will happen if I fail, because I *don't* fail. If my father's training has granted me anything, it's the ability to succeed at all costs. It's already carried me this far.

"Does it matter where we're going?" I finally answer, "you don't know where we are anyway."

The Lemming grinds her jaw. "It matters because I want to know how many days you're planning to keep me."

Keep me.

The words send a wave of nausea, hot and acidic, roiling through my stomach, but I keep my face neutral. I don't have time for this now, to sink into the void and blanket myself with shame. I will it away, smothering it until the hot coals disintegrate to ash.

"It depends how fast we can travel."

Her eyes widen, surprised I've conceded an honest answer.

"At this pace, it's going to be awhile. Normally, Nadjaa is about four day's journey from the Boundary."

Her lips twist into a snarl. "Perhaps you should have kidnapped someone better suited for hiking through the woods."

Delight, as pure as if I watched a flower bloom, threads through me. "You're right. Before my next kidnapping, I'll take that into consideration."

Her eyes remain on mine, the longest she's ever held my gaze. There's no way for her to know I'm mostly joking; that I intend for her to be the last person I have to force into subservience, but even so, there's no fear in her eyes. Nothing soft or pliant, only a flash of raw anger that calls to me on a primal level. A thrill shoots through me. Perhaps whatever is coiled beneath that smooth Similian skin is not easily leashed.

We walk on in silence.

I grow still when sunlight filters through the trees once more, every muscle coming to life. The old road. A relic of an ancient civilization that runs from one side of Ferusa all the way to the Shadiil mountain range. The easiest path from the Boundary to Nadjaa, but a gamble, even at the best times, because it's usually teeming with thieves and highwaymen. And that was before the Praeceptor took over this territory.

Now—now, we need to get far, far away from it. Even if the way around takes three times as long.

The girl eyes the road wistfully.

"Let's cross," I tell her tersely.

She blinks at me in bewilderment. "Cross? Why can't we take the road?"

A muscle feathers in my jaw. "Because we can't." The road appears deserted, as do the trees that line the other side, but that means nothing here. The shadows are deep and the Praeceptor's reach is far.

She plants her small feet. "You said we were headed west. That's west," she insists stubbornly.

I glare sidelong, unable to help the irritation that rises. I hold a breath, reminding myself she doesn't know better. She's lived her life safe behind the Boundary. Things like warlords and their reigns of terror are entirely unknown to her. "The road isn't safe," I say finally.

She mulls this over for a moment. "I have such a hard time traveling through the woods," she says and my eyes snap to hers. This is the first she's acknowledged her weakness directly, and certainly the first time she's sounded *apologetic* about it.

"I'm trying to hurry," she presses on. I narrow my eyes. If anything, the Lemming has only walked *slower* since my proclamation that our journey was taking too long. "But the road would be far faster."

Her voice is pliant, as soft and smooth as butter, and for a moment, I'm struck dumb. Her face is open and innocent, no sign of the restlessness I glimpsed earlier. And she's right. The road would shave off at least two days of traveling. We would be able to meet Max and Cal by tomorrow morning and ride to Nadjaa quickly after that.

Time is the one thing I cannot bend to my will, no matter how hard I try. It does not fall beneath my command, and I am helpless to stop its trudge forward. The month will come to an end. And if Denver has not returned to lead Nadjaa, the Praeceptor will come to claim the free city.

"From the way you handled those Boundary hunters, I doubt we're in much danger on the road," the girl adds, gazing up at me through a curtain of dark lashes. Like two emeralds sparkling through black ash.

"You know nothing of the dangers of Ferusa if you think I'm the most dangerous thing here."

She merely purses her lips delicately and shrugs. "If you say so. The woods it is then. I hope whatever is in...Nadjaa, did you say?" The name of the moon city sounds funny and foreign on her lips. "I hope it doesn't mind waiting."

I curse roundly, both highly impressed and irritated she's so acutely observed my weak point. I've never thought her the meek, simpering girl she pretends to be, the one I *expected* her to be, but for someone unschooled in the art of emotions, she is an unnervingly quick study at wielding them as one might wield a sharp weapon.

Which doesn't change the fact she's right. I have no time and the road would buy me a reprieve. Room to take a breath for the first time in a fortnight.

Anxiety threads through me, turning my stomach to lead. "Let's go then. The road," I practically snarl at her, but she doesn't balk. Only nods demurely and takes a step onto the pockmarked pavement as if she's merely following my orders.

I follow her with a growl. I know full well who has ordered who and there's not a damn thing to do about it.

CHAPTER NINE

Mirren

As it turns out, I'm not much faster on the road than I was in the woods. Much of the pavement has crumbled, giving way to the tendrils of nature that have forced their way through. As if the woods themselves are determined to overtake all signs of civilization, ancient and cunning as they are.

I spend the better part of the afternoon jumping over large plants that have sprouted through the cracks and skirting my way around gaping potholes where the pavement has buckled completely.

To my infernal irritation, Shaw moves with the same lithe grace he had in the forest, though his mood has soured considerably. He no longer teases me with that arrogant smile dripping across his lips and as the day wears on, doesn't deign to speak at all.

In fact, he's hardly looked at me since we started on the road, his eyes moving everywhere *but* me. His gaze is restless, and his body is coiled tightly as a spring. It's unnerving, how he constantly seems poised for an attack, as if at any moment someone will jump from the trees and accost him.

I can only hope.

No matter how I slow my pace, Shaw matches it, never allowing me to fall behind him. I don't mistake it for an act of kindness; he doesn't trust me at his back. I may have overplayed my hand by pressing into the one weakness I saw, but I don't regret it, not when I realized Shaw's avoidance of the road was an avoidance of *people*. People I can possibly convince to help me escape his grasp.

Shaw halts suddenly. His fingertips press into my skin like a hot brand, gripping my upper arm and pulling me still. His whips his head behind us, his eyes narrowing on the empty road.

I open my mouth, but before I can find words, he hauls me by the arm and pulls me roughly to the side. "What are you—"

"Hurry," he hisses, before shoving me unceremoniously into a small ravine that borders the road. I awkwardly tumble forward into a prickly set of wildflower bushes. The branches pull at my hair and sting my cheeks as I scramble to get my feet beneath me. Before I can even protest, Shaw jumps into the ravine after me.

"Are you mad?!" I seethe, but he presses a finger to my lips. A warning. The unexpected touch shocks me into silence.

He shimmies closer, pressing his body against mine until the bushes hide us both from the view of the road. My heart beats wildly against my chest, and for an absurd moment, I wonder if Shaw can feel it. I've never been so close to another person, unless you count our first meeting, when he tackled me to the ground, which I do not. We're close enough the warmth of him radiates through layers of clothes, as if he burns twice as hot as a normal person. Or maybe it's my own skin that feels like fire? Like I am branded with the touch of him.

This close, the scent of peppermint and woodsmoke is much stronger than the lingering hints on the cloak I wore last night, but it's the other scent that swirls around me now, the one I wasn't able to place. It is subtle and pleasant and its—its *him*. How strange for a person to possess a scent unique only to themselves. Perhaps everyone has one and I never realized, having never stepped into their personal space.

I shake my head, clearing away thoughts of Shaw and what he smells like. It doesn't matter if he smells like fresh baked pastries, he's a morally corrupt fiend who's abducted me. And he just pushed me into a ravine without so much as a barked warning.

Still, there is something about what flickers in his eyes that keeps me quiet. Something like *fear*. And if there is something that makes this fearless Dark Worlder hesitate, maybe I should hesitate as well.

Moments drag on, and still, Shaw remains crouched behind me. The planes of his chest press against my back, hard and unrelenting. He's unnaturally still, his breathing tempered, even as I shift and fidget in front of him. My joints ache fiercely, and I am just about to damn the consequences of his wrath and jump back onto the road when I hear it.

Thunder.

As the minutes pass, the roiling growl of a storm severs into individual beats, as varied and powerful as the rhythm of a drum. "What is that?" I mouth at Shaw.

He gazes fiercely in the direction we were headed only moments earlier. "Something spawned in the Darkness," he answers, a grave whisper so soft it is more of a susurrus against my ear than a sound.

The sound moves closer, the pavement vibrating with each beat. It isn't thunder or drumbeats. It's the fall of footsteps. *Hundreds* of them.

My breath catches. People are coming. Hundreds of people I can lose myself within.

They appear over the small incline of the road, men and women clad in khaki uniforms much like my own. Thick soled boots lace up their calves and large guns are tucked under their armpits, moving in time with the sway of their synchronous bodies.

They aren't just people. They're soldiers.

I've never heard of a Dark World army, or anything that would denote any semblance of order. But here they are, plain as day and marching toward me.

I hazard a glance at Shaw who hasn't moved a muscle. He doesn't look anything like the casual, arrogant man I've come to hate. Any trace of bravado has given way to an abject wariness. His lips, too lush to be fully masculine, are set in a tight line and that muscle feathers in his jaw. The Dark Worlder who is not afraid of anything dreads whoever is in that army.

And if Shaw doesn't wish to be seen by them, I do. I know from his predatory stillness and the shortened temper of his breath that if I can get to that army, he won't follow. It isn't just hesitation that lines his body. It's fear.

Because an army means order and what could possibly be more directly in contrast to the wild cacophony that is Shaw's barely controlled chaos? Whether he's afraid of punishment for one of his numerous crimes or of being drafted into the army itself, I have no idea. It hardly matters. Whatever it is that keeps him leashed, that mutes his burning flames, I have to bet on.

I slowly let out a breath as the front of the army passes. These soldiers are shabbier than those who come after them, denoting some sort of rank. I've no intention of rousing the leaders and potentially being taken once more, so I need to move when the middle marches by. Slip into the crowd and disappear as fast as I can. Hide myself away until Shaw gives up.

The massive cloud of noise shakes the ravine. My shoulders tighten, readying for the right moment.

Not yet. Not yet.

Three, two...

I freeze when a distinct coolness presses into my throat.

I hadn't even felt Shaw shift to pull the blade. He presses it into the bruised and swollen skin of my throat, just above where my life's blood thrums. "Don't move," he breathes into my ear, his words pebbling my skin.

If he keeps me here much longer, my chance will be lost. If there is a time for risks, it isn't when I'm alone in the vast woods with him, miles away from anyone that will be able to help me. It's now, only a few feet from the only people he shies away from.

I spin so quickly that Shaw barely has time to wipe the startled expression from his face, but his knife doesn't waver as I face him. I pour all my anger, my hatred, into my stare; not only the anger I've felt toward him, but the mad darkness that's inflamed me since my parents left.

I dip into my rage and will it to become bravery. To face him without quivering.

"If you were going to kill me, you would have done it already." I raise my chin in challenge. My voice is steady and fierce, and I feel the truth of it in my bones. Whatever Shaw is, he is not my murderer.

His face twists into a humorless grin. He presses the knife further into my skin, until I gasp. A hot trickle of blood runs down my neck. "The minute you become useless to me is the same minute you become dead to me," he snarls quietly.

Whatever truth I felt instantly turns to dust. Whatever hope for Shaw's humanity that I've nurtured somewhere in the back of my mind, the true belief he is just as human as anyone else, vanishes. But I do not tremble. And I do not relent. "I don't imagine being stabbed is a very quick way to die," I tell him. My voice is no longer a whisper, but a powerful force. I watch as his eyes dart to the road, panicked that someone will hear me.

I'm suddenly aware of just how close we are. His squatted knees press around my body, and I can read every detail of his face. I haven't allowed myself before, but now, I take it in. The cupid's bow of his upper lip. The thin, white scar that dissects his right brow. The razor-sharp peaks of his cheekbones. The bruising of the shiner I gave him contrasting against the lightness of his eyes. "I will scream. It will only take one to bring the weight of that army down on you and all you've done."

Shaw stares hard at me. Considers.

"I will scream," I say again, louder. In this moment, I am Similian no longer. I am not meek or powerless. I am a someone to be reckoned with and will be quiet no longer. Something inside me shimmers, powerful and ancient as I stare down Shaw.

One of the soldiers glances toward the sound of my voice, and it is only by the mercy of those prickly wildflower bushes that Shaw remains hidden.

His face is flushed with fury as he watches me, a rage more intense even than when the Boundary hunters were actively trying to kill him. I force myself not to balk, not to consider the consequences his rage will rain down upon me if I should fail. Not to consider that he may not even allow me to survive long enough to feel it.

"I will scream!"

I shout it with all my might, one last, desperate attempt to force his hand.

The rage disappears from Shaw's face, cooling to an icy calm. "No. You won't," he whispers, raising a hand toward me. I flinch, steeling myself to run, but the world goes black.

Chapter
Ten

Mirren

I wake with a dull ache in my skull and an unrelenting rage roiling in the pit of my stomach. It's the second time I've awoken in the Dark World from the depths of unconsciousness but unlike my first experience, no time is needed to place where I am or what happened. I know exactly what happened.

Shaw.

I push up to sitting, perturbed to find myself wrapped in the depths of a down sleeping roll. Did he actually knock me unconscious and then find me a comfortable place to sleep? Absurd laughter bubbles within me.

I prod gingerly at my throat until the pads of my fingertips scrape across a small scab, no larger than the point of a pen. The size itself isn't vexing; in the grand scheme of injuries I've acquired in the last 48 hours, it barely warrants a mention. It is that it's there at all and who was so willing to inflict it.

I will not harm you. I will let you go.

I've never trusted Shaw, but somewhere deep down, I trusted the truth of his words. And why? He's never shown himself to be anything but ruthless.

I untangle my legs and roughly shove the blankets away in disgust. Like everything else, it smells of peppermint and woodsmoke, and the thought of breathing Shaw in makes me feel sick. I was so close to escaping—close enough I could have reached out and wrapped my fingers around it, taken it for mine. But I didn't. Instead, I bet on some shred of humanity in Shaw. A sliver he's never even alluded to, but some stubborn part of me believes exists in everyone.

How surely I've been proven wrong. At the expense of my freedom. And my brother's life.

"I made breakfast," Shaw says in a chipper voice.

Gritting my teeth, I whirl to face him. My skin suddenly feels as though it's been immersed in hot coals. "I'm not hungry."

He looks up from the fire, his long fingers curled around a dagger he's using as a cooking utensil. His face is as indifferent as ever. I wonder vaguely where he got the food and if it was before or after he knocked me over the head. "Going back to starving yourself?"

I could hit him. I could damn the consequences and throw myself across the campfire and claw at his eyes and kick at his ribs until he finally forces me to stop. Which he's already proven more than willing to do. Violently.

My blood pulses, pooling in hot waves at my temples and cheeks and neck. "Does it make you feel good to have to knock women over the head to get them to do what you want? Does it make you feel tough and powerful?"

Shaw raises an eyebrow, the only sign of surprise he'll give. I know that now—that all I've learned about him has only been exactly what he intended. Every so called 'weakness' I've spotted have all been purposeful. Carefully designed to make him appear more human. Less monstrous.

Didn't he warn me it was dangerous to assume everyone has the same heart I do? Why did I refuse to listen?

"Dark Worlders really do get off on violence. On inflicting their pain on others."

Shaw's eyes flash. Not with shame, but with unfettered rage. A moment later, it's gone, replaced by that same arrogant smirk that drips from his lips. "You were going to get us both killed," he replies, his voice low and even.

I shake my head, stomping toward him. All thoughts of appearing meek and compliant have eddied from my head, driven by the pulsing heat that has always lived inside me, but I've never had a word for. Anger. Anger at my parents, at the whispers, at the universe itself—anger I've always held close to my heart, buried underneath a Similian exterior. Close enough that it twisted into something that crashed and crashed and crashed, terrifying in its depth. Now, it sparks beneath my skin and ravages through my brain until I am staring out at Shaw from beneath an ocean of it.

"You were going to get *yourself* killed. All you had to do was let me go and we would both be safe."

Shaw laughs, the sound humorless and ringing. "You know nothing."

"You're a hateful, disgusting creature! You couldn't stand being outsmarted by a Lemming, couldn't stand losing your precious *prize!*" My voice rings in shouts now. I have the odd sense of stepping outside of myself and not recognizing the wild, savage girl that stares back. As if I've allowed the beast within me to take form and now it will never be caged.

Shaw stands up and it's only then I realize how close I've moved to him. He towers over me, his frame lithe and powerful. Every bit the predator I first imagined him to be. "You know *nothing*." There is nothing of the teasing arrogance that usually laces his voice. Now, it is only icy wrath. "Do you have any idea what army that was? *Whose* army that was?"

I stare back at him, refusing to relent even as my mind whirls. *Whose...*

Shaw's grin shapes itself into a condescending sneer. "That's right, Lemming. An army does not mean peace. An army doesn't mean order or lawfulness. An army means money and power and who has the most of it. And trust me, you do not want to know what the man who leads that army does with pretty young girls like yourself. You don't want to know what that man does to *anyone*." Shaw's features are a mask of glacial rage, remote and terrifying in its intensity, and I suddenly realize that the Darkness Shaw purports lives within him is not a metaphor—it is a living, breathing, horrifying thing that is barely contained beneath his human skin.

Though I am standing directly in front of him, he looks through me, as if I am nothing more than a mirage, whatever he sees far more corporeal to him than I am.

A moment later, he thrusts a hand through his hair with a labored sigh and settles back into himself, but a moment is all I need. I was wrong about Shaw's humanity, but I was not wrong about this—whoever leads that army terrifies Shaw and not in a distant way. Shaw's fear is intimate. Known.

"You may think whatever you wish, but I will never

apologize for keeping you out of that army's way. I have enough respect for life that I would work to keep a dung beetle from that man's path."

"Enough respect for life?!" I yell incredulously, throwing my hands on my hips. "You respect life and yet you find it palatable to abduct me? Force me across your Covinus-forsaken land?! Tie me up and pierce my skin and knock me unconscious?!" The words tumble out in a violent fervor, my voice rising higher and higher with each tally of Shaw's wrongs against me.

Shaw presses his lips into a thin line of disgust. "Of course I don't find kidnapping to be 'palatable'," his tongue twists sardonically around the word, as if it is almost too ridiculous to repeat. "But this is Ferusa, Lemming, and I will do whatever I have to do to keep the ones I love safe. I will steal and lie and hurt as many times as I need to, because there are things in this world that need doing and sometimes, there is no one else to do them. I will tear myself to shreds, become exactly the monster you imagine me to be, and you don't get to judge me for it. You have no idea what it takes to survive. No idea that this world demands your very soul. And you would gladly give it, same as I."

"I would *never* do the things you've done. It is not the world around you that matters! It's your choices and values in the face of hardship that do."

Shaw laughs, throwing his hands up. "Oh, you think you have morals and values, do you?" His eyes are oddly bright, fervent and burning. "You have absolutely nothing! Morals and values are made so by challenges and you, my dear Lemming, have never been in a position to test them. What if you were starving? Would you sit back and die? Or would you fight someone else and take what they have?"

"I would starve rather than harm someone else!"

He tilts his head, reading something in my face that I'm afraid I haven't given freely. "What if someone you loved was in danger? What if they were the one dying?"

I feel as though he's stripped me bare.

Love.

The word feels dangerous and tempting, remote and yet intrinsic all at once. It is too full, too wild. It isn't a word allowed within the Boundary of home, and yet, isn't it exactly what drove me into the Dark World in the first place? My undying loyalty to Easton. Also called love.

And Shaw—gruff, violent, terrifying, Shaw—he loves. Loves fiercely enough that it drives him across every moral line he encounters. Can anything good come from such a powerful force? A force that upends everything you believe in.

Shaw circles my good wrist with his long fingers, holding it between us. The rope burn is stark against the pale inner skin. A stark reminder of everything Shaw is willing to do. "The truth is, you don't know what your morals are or what lines you will cross. And I know all too well there are no lines."

The heat of his skin against mine makes it hard to find the sharp edges of my thoughts; for a second, everything is frayed and blurry.

"Who is in danger?" I finally ask.

Shaw's breathing is heavy, and it takes his eyes a moment to focus, as if he is momentarily somewhere far from this clearing. "What?"

"Who is in danger that you've done this for?"

Shaw presses his lips together and shakes his head. "It doesn't matter. I've done it all the same. Knowing why won't make my choices less abhorrent or more forgivable," he meets my gaze, his face defiant. "Will it?"

It occurs to me that perhaps Shaw doesn't wish to be forgiven. That beneath the burning anger and hard exterior, lies a wounded boy who thinks he doesn't deserve it.

"It might," I tell him honestly. A weakness, to admit that after everything, I am soft enough to forgive.

Shaw scoffs angrily, abruptly dropping my wrists.

"Who did you do this for?"

His face is as cold as stone. "Rest assured, I'm as selfish as you imagine me to be. My reasons are only ever for my own gain."

Horrible, awful, repugnant *bastard*. "You're appalling. You hold yourself as morally superior to those Boundary hunters, and whoever runs that army, but you should know one thing: you are just as much of a soulless monster as the rest of them," I fling the words at him like a weapon.

Shaw pales, stumbling back as if I've physically struck him.

In truth, I've probably only paid him a highly received compliment.

He only turns toward the fire and says in a dangerously low voice, "I'm glad you finally realize that."

∽

Shaw

We walk for half a day, and I spend the majority of it alternating between cursing the girl's glacial pace and cursing myself for making such a monumental mistake and almost getting both of us killed. I knew she was manipulating me, wielding my desperation like a well-honed dagger in the hopes of seeing someone on the road. Knew and allowed it anyway.

Emotion has no place on a battlefield.

My father's words, hardened and cold, from a decade earlier. And though this battlefield has boundaries that are yet to be determined, the opposing side shrouded in mystery, it is a battlefield nonetheless. One that requires every bit of my focus if I'm going to win.

And now, because of my incompetence, time has slipped further from my grasp. By night fall, Denver will have been gone for three weeks and the fact that the Praeceptor's army was marching so openly across the old road doesn't bode well for Nadjaa. Carrying the Lemming across Ferusa is becoming a more definitive possibility with every passing minute.

She hasn't spoken a word to me since morning, when her eyes went wide and her lower lip quivered with rage. *Monster.*

She's not wrong.

A part of me sighed in relief when she spat the word. I've kidnapped her, hurt her and still, she looked on the verge of forgiving me.

Which was unacceptable. I don't deserve her forgiveness. Hers or anyone's.

So, when she called me a monster, I wanted to say *good, you understand. Protect yourself.*

If rendering her unconscious and keeping her from the Praeceptor is what it took for her to harden herself against danger, then so be it. Even if the irony of it makes me want to laugh. Or punch something.

The girl huffs an agitated breath beside me and abruptly stops walking. She perches her hands on her hips. "I'm exhausted," she announces.

I push down my annoyance once more, reminding myself it isn't her fault she isn't conditioned for such hard travel. Her cheeks are branch-stung, and her hair has escaped her braid in wild tendrils, all now plastered to her forehead with sweat.

Many things are wrong with my world, but I can't imagine one where I wasn't comforted by the forest. Since I was a boy, I've always run into the quiet womb of the Nemoran wood, jumping over felled trees and old stumps until I was far enough away from every other human that I could only hear my own breath. Even riddled with terrifying creatures like the Ditya wolf, animals twisted by remnants of old magic and the lingering effects of the queen's curse, the wood has always had a muted beauty. And the creatures that dwell here have never judged me for the monster I am, for they too are ruled by their primal instincts that allow them to survive the Dark World at any cost.

They're probably the only company I'm fit for.

The girl gulps the last few drops of her canteen.

I gesture to the small stream bubbling between the trees. "We can rest there and refill your canteen."

Her eyes blaze. "A few minutes is not enough. I'm tired, I'm dirty, and I can't walk anymore."

Nothing remains of her pliant Similian ruse. Now, there is only tempered steel. I can't decide whether to be thrilled or terrified at the abrupt change in her demeanor.

As if sensing my unease, her fingers travel slowly along her throat. I swallow roughly, telling myself to look away, but my eyes remain glued. Her skin is mottled and angry where Eulogius wrapped his hideous hands around it and hot rage surges within me. I should have peeled his skin from his body. Slowly.

"I need to rest," she insists. Her fingers linger on the point where I pressed my dagger, invisible from this distance. Her throat bobs as she swallows under my stare, but her eyes don't leave mine. A challenge. *Look what you've done. Soulless monster.*

A boiling wave of shame and rage wash through me. I choose the more manageable of the two emotions, the one that's granted my survival all these years. "Yes, I imagine being nearly murdered multiple times in two days must be exhausting."

She doesn't take the bait. Only blinks balefully at me, her eyes as green as grass and as wide as a fawn's.

I curse loudly and throw my pack to the ground. "We'll camp here for the night. You can bathe and rest," I glare at her hotly, "And in the morning, we'll travel without stopping until we find Max and Cal."

The last sentiment sounds more like an animalistic snarl than words, but she merely nods obediently.

I don't believe for a second that she'll do anything obediently, but I see no other way to persuade her west aside from physically dragging her.

I dig around in my bag and toss her a bar of soap. Homemade and unscented, but its new. "You can wash there," I grunt, motioning to the shallow edge of the stream.

"And where will you be?"

I cock an eyebrow. "Here."

Her eyes widen minutely. A wicked grin spreads across my face. "You didn't really think I'd trust you alone for a second after that stunt you pulled yesterday, did you?"

Irritation flashes across her face, telling me that she'd quite clearly thought that. I would tie her to a tree if it kept her from running back to the Praeceptor's army. Of all the things I've done to her, I can't bring myself to regret that one.

"But you can't...I mean, *I* can't..." she stutters helplessly. A delicious shade of rose flushes her pale cheeks that sends a thrill straight through the center of me.

I wipe the grin from my face. "Relax, Lemming. I'll turn around."

She clutches the soap to her chest and eyes me suspiciously. "You can't peek," she tells me haughtily.

"I won't."

"You have to promise."

"And what would my promises mean to you?" *After everything.* The remaining words don't need to be spoken because they hang in the air as if permanently nailed there.

She glances longingly at the stream, and I know before she says it that her desperation to be clean is victorious against her Similian sense of propriety. "Fine. Turn around." She glares at me expectantly.

Unable to help the sly grin that pulls at the corner of my lips, I do as I'm told. I lean against a tree, crossing my arms and closing my eyes. I try to focus on the sound of the leaves rustling, of the water pouring over stones, of pretty much anything other than the sound of that ridiculous jumpsuit scraping against her skin as she undresses.

I refuse to picture that skin. Refuse to spend one more moment pondering the probability of it feeling like fine silk if I pulled it against mine.

When I hear the sound of the water lapping gently against her toes as she wades into the stream, I feel as though I'll burst out of my own body. A hiss of pain escapes her and its only through sheer force of will that I don't leap to her side.

"Is everything okay?" My voice sounds strangled, even to me.

"I'm fine. I just cut my foot on a stone."

I don't like the idea of her blood running freely into the stream, but the sound of water lapping against her resumes, so I force myself to relax. To think of something else.

"Are you ever going to tell me why you barreled out of Similis as if you were on fire?"

"Are you ever going to tell me why you kidnap women and what you plan to do to them?"

"Wo*man*, singular," I correct primly, "And I'll tell you when its necessary for you to know."

"Likewise," she shoots back. She dips her head back into the stream and I'm thankful she continues speaking before I can begin imagining the way her fingers work through that thick mass of curls. "Who's in charge of that army?"

The sudden flash of the Praeceptor's face is more effective at sobering me than if I'd dunked my head in the cold water of the stream. Even years later, the mere sound of his name is enough to send a slimy shiver down my spine. The Praeceptor, or Cullen, as those unfortunate enough to be in his intimate circle call him, is not a man to be forgotten.

"A warlord."

The girl pauses her washing, mulling the information over. I don't need to wonder if she'll press more. She's proven herself insatiably curious, even if no one but me would notice it. It's refreshing that she's abandoned the act of pretending to be uninterested in the world around her, when I've watched the way her eyes spark, drinking in everything about Ferusa. "Is a warlord like the Covinus?"

"You mean like your government? No. There is no

government here anymore. No law except for one's own conscience. Which, in the case of the warlords, is nonexistent. They control territories, usually with militias, violence, and other unsavory means. They are rich and ruthless and always fighting with each other for more power."

The sudden sound of water rushing over skin as she submerges herself draws me once more from thoughts of warlords. Now, they're consumed by images of droplets clinging to generous curves.

I dig my fingernails roughly into the palm of my hand, the steady pressure calming me slightly. Gods, what's the matter with me? I've bedded plenty of women and have never once had my thoughts spiral beyond my control.

"Except murder."

"What?" I reply, distracted.

"You said there are no laws. But even the warlords can't commit murder."

My throat grows tight at all she doesn't know. There are so many things that grow in this twisted Darkness, things that plague dreams and live behind your eyes every time you close them. Things that even in my most ruthless goals, I hope to keep far, far away from her. Vindication burns deep in the chasm within me, brighter than my shame and disgust. I did the right thing keeping her from Cullen's army. I may not have done it the right way—is pressing on a pressure point until someone collapses in your arms ever the right way—but it was the right thing.

Because the thought of her innocent wonder being twisted and bent to satisfy the Praeceptor's thirst to wring pain, is nearly unbearable an entire day later. If she had ended up in his hands, there's no telling what I would have done. Probably something extremely stupid.

A shriek echoes through the forest and my skin goes cold.

I whirl around, facing Mirren. She yelps indignantly, her hands clambering to cover her bare body, but my eyes skip over her. Instead, they rest on the creature that now stalks the shore behind her.

Twice as tall as I am, the yamardu's eyes glow red even in the bright light of day. I keep my movements achingly slow as I creep toward Mirren. The creature must have scented her blood, but it's blind in sunlight and relies on its other senses to find prey. The water is the only thing keeping her invisible to it. Vicious and strong, the yamardu bleeds its victims out slowly until there isn't a drop left. Its shriek can cause permanent hearing loss. Another creature bred inside the Nemoran woods.

"Mirren, don't move."

She blinks at me, but something in my tone must alarm her, because she goes completely still. I pull a dagger from my bandolier in slow motion, not taking my eyes from the creature. It will take a hell of a lot more than one dagger to bring the beast down. Its skeletal wings are black and muscled, topped with a deadly talon used for shredding its prey.

I could really use Cal's skill with a bow about now, but my daggers will have to suffice until I can get Mirren to safety.

"Walk as slowly as you can toward me. Try to make no noise."

I might as well be asking her to breathe underwater for as loudly as she normally moves, but she nods in understanding and creeps forward.

The yamardu lets out another ear-piercing shriek and it takes everything in me not to drop my dagger and cover my ears. My ear drums ring, but I force myself to look at Mirren. Her eyes are wide and for the first time since I met her, her fear is palpable. I feel it as if it's my own, slick and viscid.

I reach my hand out to her. "Just move slowly and it won't be able to see you," my voice is calm and reassuring, the way I speak to the horses in Nadjaa. "It's attracted to blood. It smells yours in the water. But your foot isn't bleeding anymore, is it?"

She bites her lip and shakes her head. Her body trembles as she takes another agonizingly slow step.

"Good," I tell her, "Good. Keep going. The yamardu is blind. It won't see you if you keep moving slowly."

The yamardu shrieks again, plunging its taloned feet into the stream. Its beak sniffs the air, hunting for its next meal. Mirren gasps, but she doesn't rush her movements. My heart pounds in my throat as I wait for the killing calm of my chasm to overtake me, but for some reason, it is stubbornly silent. There is only adrenaline and Mirren's fear coating the inside of my throat.

Finally, her hand touches mine. I pull her against me, relief settling like a thick blanket. Water slides down her shivering body in thick rivulets as I wrap her in my cloak. I tug her along, moving as fast as I dare away from the shrieking beast. The stream will only confuse it for so long.

Mirren is silent beside me as we disappear into the trees. Her bare feet must be getting shredded, but there was no time to pull her boots on and she doesn't complain. My cloak parts to reveal her bare legs, the fabric swinging wider just as I look away. I dig my fingers into my palm.

The creature screams, the gut-wrenching sound closer now. Mirren stumbles, her terror fully realized as she claws at my skin to keep herself up right. But she doesn't cry out.

My forearm stings where her nails sunk in, but I pull her against me and we keep moving, ever so slowly.

When we are far away from the cursed stream, I finally release a breath. But I don't allow myself a moment to consider the plans that had unfurled in my head in the brief moments Mirren's life was threatened. Or why I had been ready to sacrifice everything to keep her alive.

CHAPTER
ELEVEN

Mirren

We are both panting by the time Shaw deems it safe enough to rest. He turns around as I slip into my spare clothes and then watches wordlessly as I inspect my feet. They sting, but thankfully, our slow pace prevented the skin from being broken. I tie up my boots, thankful Shaw had the forethought to throw them in his pack before our escape.

He doesn't seem to notice the blood beginning to crust where I scratched him and for once, his face is not a stone mask. Instead, he looks at me with a ragged sort of intensity that is thrilling and confusing. As if he wants to both hurt and protect me; angry and hungry and sad. I turn away, running my fingers through my hair and weaving it into a thick braid that hangs down my back.

I offer him his cloak, but he shakes his head. "Keep it."

The cloak smells like him, spice and woodsmoke and wild, open air, but it's thick and warm, so I only nod and wrap it around my shoulders.

"My father," Shaw says hoarsely.

I look over at him. His shoulders are hunched, and he is staring into the forest as if he can see through the miles of trees. "What?"

"You asked who I'm doing this for. I'm doing it for my father."

I stare at him in surprise. Shaw never allows information to slip without an intended purpose, but what can be his reason for telling me this? No matter how I look at it, it only seems like he's admitting a vulnerability.

His eyes are emotionless as they meet mine. "He would be ashamed."

I open my mouth to say something, though I have no idea what, when a crash and a shriek sounds from the trees.

"How—"

His words never get a chance to leave his mouth as the yamardu leaps at him, pummeling him to the ground. Something pulls tight in my chest as Shaw goes rolling, dodging slashes from the creature's razor-sharp talons.

Run.

The idea formed while we were escaping, quick and poignant. Admittedly, it was a long shot, one in which my own death was gambled. I clawed at Shaw and could only hope the creature smelled his blood and not mine.

The beast slashes, its muscular wings pulled wide and its shrieks rendering me nearly deaf. Shaw manages to pull a dagger from his bandolier and rolls to his feet. He twirls, slashing at the yamardu's legs. The creature lunges for him once more. It has eyes only for its prey and doesn't notice as I dive behind it.

I take off at a sprint toward the woods, but one of the creature's wings catches me in the chest before I'm free. My breath expels in a painful whoosh, and I'm tossed backward, landing hard on my spine.

I scramble backward as the yamardu suddenly turns toward me. With horror, I realize blood drips from a small cut above my brow. Shaw's eyes flash, taking the hesitation to lunge forward and stab the beast in the back. The yamardu rears up with another piercing scream, but his focus on me doesn't waver. He's scented his next meal and won't give it up easily.

"Mirren!" Shaw shouts and I look over just in time to see him toss me one of his daggers. I claw at it, lifting it just in time to see the yamardu crashing down toward me, talons flashing. Its beak is knife-edged and gleaming and it opens in a bellow of fury as I shove the dagger into its chest.

Hot breath buffets me as it shrieks. Blood coats my hands, sticky and viscous. Shaw grabs me by the waist, hauling me up and pulling me back. His heart beats wildly against his chest, but his face is calm and steadfast as he yanks me to my feet and pushes me behind him.

He brings up another dagger, slashing it deftly across the membrane of the yamardu's wing. The creature screams in rage and swipes at Shaw, battering him back with a powerful blow. Shaw struggles to get back to his feet, but his body buckles. Adversary defeated, the yamardu turns on me. I scream as it lowers its beak, black and gleaming.

An arrow sprouts from the yamardu's chest. It yowls in rage, as the first is followed by three more.

In the trees, a woman, dressed in the warlord's regalia, nocks another arrow. Shaw spots her the same time I do, but if he has a vendetta to settle against the warlord's soldier, the yamardu must take precedence. He rolls in front of me as another ear-piercing scream rattles my brain against my skull. I throw my hands over my ears, sure they're bleeding, and the scream will be the last thing I ever hear.

The yarmardu bears down on us as Shaw meets my eyes. Nothing remains of his soulless mask, panic and determination now burning freely on his face. Something passes between us, something unnamed and wild, but I don't stop to examine it. This is the Dark World, and Shaw has made it clear that it is me or him.

I choose me.

I slash out, running his own dagger over his forearm. Crimson blood blooms, but it is nothing compared to the fury that blooms in his eyes. Realization washes over him, that I led the creature here purposefully. Shaw lunges for me but I scramble out of his reach just as the yamardu crashes down against him once more.

Creature and man go flying in a tangle of limbs and wings, but I don't stop to watch. I run toward the woods, toward the soldier.

She lowers her bow immediately. "Let's get out of here, girl," she says, her voice direct and clipped. "I don't care to be around when that thing finishes with him and finds it's still thirsty."

I look over my shoulder once. Shaw fights for his life, ever nimble. His eyes flash between me and the soldier. "Don't! Mirren, don't go with her!" he yells. Blood streams everywhere now and his eyes are mad with panic.

Run, Mirren.

Shaw stabs the yarmardu once more and it rears up in agony. But instead of running, he takes the gun from its place on his hip. And points it at me.

His hair is wild, his cheeks streaked with blood and grime. His face is white with fury, and I remember that he is something to fear. He may be capable of love, but it only makes him more dangerous. "Don't go with her! Please!" His voice breaks on the last word.

Heart in my throat, I run after the warlord's soldier just as Shaw's bullet grazes my cheek.

CHAPTER
TWELVE

Mirren

My heart pounds erratically as I urge my feet to move faster. They've already failed me once. This time, I won't allow them to slow, not even for a second; not when Shaw's presence still lingers in every part of this wood.

Maybe the yarmardu has finished him off. It was only cowed when I took off, not defeated, and Shaw was covered in blood. There's no way he'll be able to outrun it. I have no idea what it takes to kill that creature, but I imagine it's something that not even Shaw possesses. At least not alone.

I refuse to let guilt overtake me, not when Shaw's voice beats in my mind to the rhythm of my breaths. *I do not miss, I do not miss, I do not miss.*

In that moment just before the yamardu attacked, I believed something shifted inside of Shaw. As if he peeled back the layers of stone around him to reveal a beating heart inside. And not just a heart. A soul.

But then, faced with the loss of his prize, the stone slammed down around him once more. I shudder as I recall the terrifying fury that burned in his eyes as he raised the revolver. As he pulled the trigger, knowing he never misses. Because if he couldn't have me, no one would.

I haven't been in the Dark World long enough to wish him dead, but I've been here long enough to not feel sorry if he is.

"Come on, girl," the soldier urges. Her gun is slung over her back, her blond hair clipped short against her skull. "Move faster. The quicker we reach camp, the better our chances of staying alive."

I don't know if she's referring to the yamardu or Shaw, but I don't argue. I only urge my feet forward, my mind whirling. She means to take me to the warlord's camp.

I remember Shaw's plea just before he lifted the revolver, the last word etched into my brain as thoroughly as a brand. *Please.* It's the only time I've heard the word on his lips and though he abducted me, and hurt me and shot at me, the word gives me pause.

I hate that even now he inhabits my thoughts. That he still twists them and shapes them until I no longer know what's real.

"What were you doing in the woods?" I ask the soldier as she pulls me along. The trees are thick here and I wonder briefly how she knows where she's going. How *everyone* seems to know where they're going in this Covinus-forsaken country, except for me.

"Patrol." Her answer is short. Perfunctory.

"For the warlord?"

At this, she turns to me, something glinting in her eyes. "Ah, so you've heard of the Praeceptor, have you?" she doesn't wait for my answer. "Then you know that nothing will touch us once we're inside camp. Yamardu or otherwise."

She says this not as an opinion, but a fact. For some

reason, it sets my teeth on edge. I have no wish to meet the infamous warlord, but if I want to avoid Shaw, the camp is my best bet. If Shaw manages to escape the yamardu, there's no way he will follow me into this camp. Not when he refuses to even speak the Praeceptor's name.

The sun has fallen well below the mountains when we reach the crest of the hill. I gasp, taking in the militia's camp. It is a sprawling, living thing. Canvas tents spread in all directions. Loud voices ring out from soldiers clustered around fires and as we approach, the smell of cooking meat and unwashed bodies wafts lazily toward me.

Armed guards line the boundaries of the camp and two of them eye us warily as we approach, raising their large guns. My soldier holds her hands up, shifting her fingers in a sign that they must recognize because the guards immediately relax.

The first guard nods. "Retiring from patrol so early, Dumi?"

"Got someone for the *legatus* to meet," Dumi replies airily, but I barely hear her words. A gasp catches in my throat as I realize what towers above the entrance to the camp. A pole, as large as any tree, rises two stories high. And staked to it is a man.

Or what I can only assume used to be a man. His face is bruised and mottled beyond recognition and his stomach has been slashed. I cry out in alarm as a breath rattles through the man's destroyed chest and Dumi's eyes flick to me.

There is nothing in them. It's the same deadened mask that adorns Shaw's face, the one he briefly lifted just before the attack. "Don't mind him. He's not long for this world." She doesn't spare the dying man another glance as she moves past the guards.

Think like Shaw. It's that man's life or mine. His life or Easton's.

I can do nothing for the man hanging, but I can still save Easton. The thought thoroughly wrecks me but I swallow down my nausea and follow Dumi with my head held high.

Dumi weaves through the various tents confidently, as if her feet have trodden this path thousands of times. I wait for the relief to settle in my bones, the knowledge that I'm now free of Shaw. One man would never be able to cut his way through this camp and then through the warlord himself. But relief doesn't come. There is only a pricking sense of unease as we travel deeper through the tents.

We come to a small clearing in the heart of the camp. There are no tents here, only a smattering of soldiers gathered in a close circle. While the rest of the militia looked at ease, these soldiers are straightened and alert. Their fingers clasp high powered rifles and swords.

In the center of the soldiers stands a tall, metal cage. And there is no mistaking what's inside.

People.

A gasp of horror stops somewhere in my throat. The warlord has *people* caged, pressed against each other as if they are nothing more than livestock. So many of them that their skin presses into the metal of the bars. Most so thin that their bones protrude at odd angles. Some lie down unmoving, and the sound of their keening is so unbearable that it takes everything in me not to cover my yamardu-ravaged ears against the misery. To close my eyes and block it out.

Dumi notices my hesitation and turns toward me, her eyes narrowed. She doesn't even look at the people in the cage. To her, they aren't a novelty. She is so well acquainted with the cruelty that it no longer registers as something inhumane. "Is there a problem?"

Oh, Covinus help me, there are *children*.

Children, dressed only in ripped trousers despite the cold nip of the evening. They are silent, the tracks of tears on their faces now dry. As if they have nothing left in them, even to wail.

"Do you wish to be safe?" Dumi implores with a tick of impatience, "because if you wish to earn the protection of this camp, it's only through the Praeceptor's will."

Earn. For the first time, it occurs to me that the cost may be too high. Too high to pay for even Easton's life.

Shaw said there were no lines, no morals that mattered when it came to saving those you care about. Is he right? Am I able to force myself past a cage full of battered children, if it will save my brother? The selfishness is shameful, but I force my feet to move. *Easton, Easton, Easton,* I repeat to myself until his name is a mantra in my head. I try to focus only on his face, but every time I blink, the sight of those children is branded into the back of my eyelids.

Dumi leads me away from the cage and toward the far side of the camp, her saunter as unaffected as ever. She stops in front of a canvas tent, neatly crafted and larger than the others. It is nondescript and I only glean its importance by the number of soldiers posted around it.

Eight. Eight men and women who refuse to meet my eyes.

The truth of it unfurls inside of me, like a serpent in wait. I misread Shaw's rage and fear as a vindication of his own guilt. Shaw may be a lot of things, but something evil crawls in this camp. It is the twisted Darkness of lore that mutilates and warps. Slithers and scratches. *Please.* It wasn't entirely for himself that he pleaded.

Dumi ushers me toward the tent flap. My legs have gone numb and only instinct keeps them moving. As I dig my heels in and open my mouth to protest, the cold of shackles bites my wrists.

CHAPTER
THIRTEEN

Mirren

Dumi delivers me to the hands of one of the guards and disappears between tents without so much as a backward glance. I want to scream at her for the betrayal, but it would be foolish. She owes me nothing. She lives by the same rule as every other Dark Worlder; every man or woman for themselves.

The heavy iron of the shackles bite at my skin as I struggle against them, and they are clamped so tightly that my shoulders already ache. The guard deposits me inside the tent, forcing me into a seated position against one of the support poles.

The tent is sparse but brutal in its efficiency. There's no furniture, save for a steel medical table in the center of the room and a small drink cart on the far side of the wall. It looks nothing like I'd imagine a warlord's accommodations would look, containing none of the luxurious comforts that would come with such power. Dread sinks low in my stomach along with Shaw's words about the Praeceptor.

You don't want to know what that man does to anyone.

The flap of the tent pulls back and a large man ducks in. It appears I'm about to find out.

Obviously someone of import, the guard immediately straightens his posture, avoiding the large man's eyes.

"At ease, soldier," the man says in a voice that sounds like the rumble the ground sometimes makes near Similis. Deep, dark and angry.

The man crosses the tent in less than two strides. He pauses in front of the tray to pour himself a generous amount of amber liquid from a carafe. "Dismissed."

The guard glances at me cagily before disappearing through the flap. Whatever hesitation he possesses about leaving me with this man clearly doesn't override his sense of self preservation.

"I hear you demand an audience with our Praeceptor," the man says. He stands with his back to me as he tips his head and pours the contents of the glass down his throat. He is tall, as tall as Shaw, but at least twice as wide. His body is wrapped in thick, gnarled muscles that are apparent even beneath the red of his uniform.

I clear my throat, trying to forget the images of the man on the pole. Of the children in the cage. I can't think of them and think of myself. There may still be a way to salvage this.

"I do. And I do not appreciate being made to wait in chains like a common slave."

The man turns to me for the first time. His eyes are gray, and they are like hard chips of slate as he examines me. His face is as gnarled as the rest of him, with weather beaten skin and a wide nose that appears to have been broken more than once. His cold gaze trails from my forehead to my toes, lingering overlong in places that bring an embarrassed heat to my skin.

Finally, he lifts his eyes back to mine. Something dark flickers in his gaze, fathomless and greedy. I shift in my seat, but don't look away. Thanks to Shaw, I'm practiced at staring down dangerous men without flinching.

"You are far from common, that much is apparent," he says as his eyes travel along my jawline. My skin feels oily where his gaze trails. I resist the urge to wipe at my skin. "I am Shivhai, the Praeceptor's legatus." He looks at me expectantly.

It isn't wise to give your name away freely.

My cheek still smarts from where Shaw's bullet grazed, and while I hate him with a ferocity that steals my breath, his advice was sound. "Ridley," I tell him, thinking of the girl who sat behind me at the Binding.

"Ridley," Shivhai repeats, rolling the word off his tongue in a way that makes me thankful I didn't give him my true name. He turns back to the small cart, pouring another finger of the amber liquid and downing it quickly. He plucks a small instrument between his large fingers and panic grips my throat. It isn't a drink cart. In my haste to get free of my shackles, I didn't notice the instruments that line its sterile shelves. Instruments that wouldn't look out of place in the Healing Center.

The one Shivhai selects looks like a large needle, thin, but strong and dangerously pointed. I wonder at the craftsmanship, having seen nothing of its like in the Dark World. It makes Shaw's daggers, even with their beautiful carvings, seem rudimentary. "What were you doing in the Nemoran wood, Ridley?"

It doesn't matter who crafted the needle if Shivhai plans to gut me with it. I force my voice to be soft. Even. To keep my face mild and pleasant. I've been trained since birth that feelings are a shameful thing, and even though they've run wild since my escape, shoving them down is like slipping into a familiar skin. "I was on a journey to Nadjaa and got turned around," it's the only Dark World city whose name I remember clearly. "I was accosted by that horrible creature while I was trying to find my way once more."

Shivhai tilts his head as if I've said something of interest. "And where are you journeying from?"

My throat is dry. *He knows, he knows.*

He can't know. Unlike when I first stepped past the Boundary, my skin is now marred with bruises and cuts and covered by a thick layer of filth. Shaw's cloak covers my Similian clothes and a layer of his blood coats the skin of my hands. If I can keep calm, there is no way for Shivhai to guess my origin.

"From my father's farm. My brother was escorting me back to the city, but we were separated. I wish to call upon your Praeceptor's mercy to shelter me until I can find my way back once more."

Shivhai lets out a rough laugh that sounds again like the scraping of ancient lands. He steps toward me, his large boots pounding the dirt floor. He weaves the needle between his fingers and in a few steps, there is barely a hairsbreadth between us. I squirm backward, only to find the support pole digging into my back. "Odd, that you would leave your *brother* to be bled out by the yamardu."

I pale. He's spoken to Dumi.

"That...that wasn't my brother. That was a highwayman who kidnapped me."

Shivhai ignores me, his greedy eyes drinking in my face. "Such a beautiful little bird," he murmurs. His calluses scrape the underside of my jaw as he runs his fingers over my skin.

I think of Shaw's calloused touch and the fevered ache it brought with it. There is nothing pleasant or aching now as Shivhai runs his fingers over my lips. There is only unrelenting cold. His hand travels toward my hairline, then dives into the thick strands, gripping and pulling with an icy air of ownership.

"I wonder if you'll sing for me." He tightens his fingers, pulling me up by my hair until tears spring to my eyes and I'm forced to stand on my tip toes.

I bite my lip to keep from crying out, willing my panic to smooth and calm as if it is rough waters and I am in the wind. "I wish to speak to the Praeceptor," I repeat.

Shivhai runs the point of the needle across my cheek. "I will ask you again, little bird. Where do you come from? And why are you in this wood?"

The hard crack of Shivhai's knuckles against my jaw stops the words in my throat. Stars bloom behind my eyes as I stumble sideways. With my wrists still clamped behind me, I am merely a passenger as I fall, my face catching the brunt of the impact against the compacted dirt floor.

Get up. Don't let him see you weak.

I bend and twist my body and finally, finally, get to my feet. Before I can steady myself, Shivhai's fist flies into my gut. The air whooshes out of me as I tumble once more, my head cracking against the ground.

"This is a new world, little bird. No one travels through the Nemoran wood anymore without the Praeceptor's say so."

He winds the point of the needle down the side of my neck, scratching lightly at my throat. "He's a methodical man. He believes neat, clinical torture is the best way to get one to spill their deepest secrets."

Shivhai presses the needle hard enough into my skin that hot blood wells at my neck. I press my eyes closed and bite my lip to keep anything more from pouring out of them. Something tells me that begging will only spur him on, quenching the thirst for pain that threads through his every move.

"The Praeceptor is an efficient man, and he always gets what he's after. I, however, find there are more *enjoyable* ways to get pretty little things like you to tell me whatever I want to know."

Shivhai removes the needle from my throat, and I greedily gasp for air. The relief is short lived, as he whips my cloak open and presses the needle to the leg of my suit. I thrash as he pokes through the material, ripping upward until the skin of my leg is exposed to the bite of the air. "He's not here, so I suppose we'll do this my way."

He grins, victorious and revolting.

By the Covinus, the warlord isn't even here. Whatever desperate hope I've been clinging to that the Praeceptor is more than the militia he commands, that he might save me somehow, evaporates. No one is coming to save me from the fate I've brought upon myself. The warlord is gone, and Shaw is dead, and there is no one else in the world who even cares where I am.

Shivhai shoves a hand through the opening he's created in my clothes, and I recoil as his clammy skin brushes mine. His movements are unhurried and assured, as if there is no doubt in his mind that he now owns me. To him, I am exactly like the people trapped in cages. No longer a person, just a vessel to be used as he pleases.

His fingers clamp painfully on my bare hip, and he

hauls me closer to him. His breath is hot as he leans over me, tearing my pants further.

"NO!" I scream frantically, searching for something, anything that I can use as a weapon. Anything to stop what's coming. Panic descends over me, the room only visible from behind a milky film of fear.

"I think by the end you'll be begging to tell me exactly why you're here," he growls. His hands are suddenly everywhere, and I am paralyzed. I can't move, can't breathe, can't get away from those greedy hands...

"I believe the lady said no."

My hearts leaps into my throat. His voice is smooth, melodic, and unbearably casual for the scene he's walked into, but it sends a full breath of oxygen barreling into my lungs. Shaw.

Shivhai freezes above me, whipping his head to the tent entrance, where Shaw is leaning against one of the support beams with his arms crossed. Dried blood is smeared across one side of his face and his shirt and pants are torn, but otherwise, he looks decidedly alive. His face is uninterested, and his body is relaxed, as if he regularly comes across shackled Similian girls in the middle of his enemy's camp.

I have no idea how he escaped the yamardu alive or how he made it through the vast number of soldiers to this tent without being killed, but his presence makes me want to cry out in relief. Whatever Shaw's flaws, he has never tortured me. Or forced himself on me. And at the moment, that's worth a lot.

Shivhai doesn't remove his hands from my skin, but in his distraction, the needle has fallen to the side. If I can just work my body slightly to the left, I might be able to reach it. To do what with, I have no idea, but being armed is certainly better than not.

"Who are you?" Shivhai growls, his eyes narrowed in irritation.

Shaw ignores him completely, addressing me instead. "Do you enjoy being chained up or something?" he asks me sardonically, tilting his head. My relief at his appearance is swiftly overtaken by annoyance. Of course he'd choose now, when I'm pinned to the ground by a mad man, to be a smug, arrogant bastard. "Because if you do, just let me know and I'll stop interfering. No judgements," he adds with a mischievous grin, and I vow to stab him as soon as we're both free from this wretched camp.

Only a few centimeters remain between my fingers and the needle. Shivhai watches Shaw warily, apparently trying to decide whether Shaw is incredibly dangerous or incredibly stupid. He seems to notice at the same time I do that there are no longer shuffles or grunts outside the tent. There is only silence.

Shivhai's face turns murderous. "Where are my guards?"

Shaw doesn't bother to look at him. "Well, Lemming. What's it going to be?"

"You're an arrogant *bastard*," I scream at him, wildly and without reserve. I use my outburst to shift my body, stretching my fingers a little further until they finally touch the foreign metal of the needle. "If you hadn't kidnapped me in the first place, I wouldn't be here!"

Shaw winks. *Winks.*

And then he nods, imperceptible to anyone but the girl who has been watching him and learning his every tick for the past week. He knows I've armed myself. I grip the needle in my fist.

"Who are you and how did you get in here?" Shivhai barks, unused to being ignored. He rolls off me, threading his fingers through my hair once more. Pain, hot and sharp, radiates from my scalp as he yanks me to standing. Tears stream unabashedly down my cheeks now as I work to get my feet beneath me. To keep hold of the needle behind my back.

Shivhai yanks a pistol from his hip and presses it roughly to the back of my neck. "And I suggest you speak quickly, or it will only be worse when I get back to your girl." He sneers. "Maybe I'll make you watch."

Shaw doesn't even flinch, his face pure stone as he finally draws his gaze to Shivhai. "She is no more mine than the ground we're standing on and I hold the same level of indifference about them both," he says, casually peeling himself from the beam. He holds his hands up, proof he isn't armed.

An *unarmed,* arrogant prick. Wonderful.

Shivhai shoves me down roughly in front of him. A shriek escapes my lips as the gravel digs painfully into my knees. Fingers still threaded tightly in my hair, Shivhai points the pistol at Shaw. It's the second time I've seen a gun pointed at him, but this time I'm privy to what was veiled by darkness the first night we met. It starts in his eyes, the ice blue blazing as if a true fire rages somewhere deep inside him. He says it's darkness that lives within him, but this is something different—something wild and uncontainable that burns. His lips are twisted into a grin, but it isn't a handsome one. It is barely bound madness.

Shivhai clicks the bullet into the barrel, having not taken notice of the transformation in Shaw. I wonder how he misses the predator that gazes out of the man, feral and hungry. I am no longer afraid, as if the darkness inside Shaw has somehow soothed my own. Transforming it from something suffocating into a weapon to be wielded.

"Do you know who's camp you've stumbled into?" Shivhai's voice is dangerous. He bares his teeth. "Do you know who I work for?"

Shaw's eyes flash. He takes a measured step toward Shivhai. "I really don't care." Quicker than Shivhai can react, quicker than my eyes can even track, Shaw launches himself toward us.

CHAPTER
FOURTEEN

Mirren

Shivhai's fingers loosen in surprise, and I duck with a yelp, as the two men go crashing into the metal table behind us. I scramble to my feet, just in time to see Shaw crouching on top of Shivhai, one of his daggers buried in the other man's neck.

Shivhai coughs, a wet, sloppy sounding thing. Blood coats his lips and pours from his wound, losing itself in the red of his uniform.

Shaw grabs the bottle of amber liquid from the cart and lifts it just as Shivhai's eyes widen. His face pales as if he's seen a specter. "You," he gurgles, his voice almost reverent.

Shaw brings down the bottle and Shivhai goes still. He removes his knife from the man's neck with a practiced flair and turns to me.

I stare at Shivhai, the mountain of a man now a crumpled heap on the ground, with my mouth open. I try to form words, something to encompass the cacophony that swirls through me. Anger and hurt. Shock and *relief*. But before I can say anything, Shaw grabs hold of my upper arm and hauls me out of the tent.

"Where are we going?" I ask desperately.

He doesn't bother to answer. He takes a hard left at the mouth of the tent and tugs me past the crumpled forms of all eight guards. I stare at the still-bleeding bodies, horror and awe mingling together.

By the Covinus, he did all this *himself*?

If he notices my hesitation, he doesn't acknowledge it. He glances over his shoulder and then picks up the pace as we race down a narrow row between tents. Hours must have passed since I was first thrown into Shivhai's tent, because the camp is quiet. A few spare soldiers are left stumbling here and there, but they are deep in the spirits and take no notice of us.

Shaw is moving so fast that I have to sprint to keep from being dragged behind him. My wrists burn, the skin beneath the shackles rubbed completely raw. "Shaw!" I yell at him, breathless.

It's all happened too fast. Horror and relief and regret mingle so furiously that I stagger to a halt, nausea overcoming me. I struggle to breathe, to keep the contents of my stomach down, but the air stings in my lungs.

Shaw shoves me unceremoniously into the darkness between a storage tent and a large tree, his hand over my mouth. His eyes flash with warning and I remember the way he talked about this militia and the warlord who commands it. I'm not the only one in danger here.

He's risked death or worse by putting himself in reach of the Praeceptor. Why? Was it still desperation to save his father that drove him? Or was it something else?

"I don't know whether Shivhai notified the Praeceptor

that you were here, but if he did, we need to get out of here before he finds out you're gone."

I have only seconds to wonder how, exactly, Shaw knows Shivhai's name. "I thought you said you didn't care who he worked for."

Shaw doesn't look at me when he answers. "I didn't then. I do now."

The glow from cooling campfires glints in his eyes, rendering them almost colorless. He looks like a wraith, terrifying and desperate. A far cry from the collected assassin he was just moments before. "We can argue later about my kidnapping you and then following you and what a bastard I am for it, but right now we need to move."

The need to laugh strikes me, staggering in its absurdity. "You *shot* at me."

He sets me with an amused stare. "If we're airing grievances, may I point out the fact that you set a yamardu on me and then left me for dead?"

I glare at him, though he makes a fair point. "That doesn't make us even. *This* doesn't make us even." Whatever *this* is.

He nods so enthusiastically that I'm positive he's just placating me until we reach safety. "I wouldn't dream of calling it even, Lemming." A soldier guffaws from a few tents over and Shaw stiffens. "We'll forge terms later. When we're safe."

I don't miss the use of *we*. Whatever happened before this is water under the bridge. For now, we're on the same side. I have no choice but to trust him.

I turn to move when a thought strikes me. "Shaw!" I cry out. A moment of my own pain and the memory of the others' is swiftly forgotten. "Shaw, they're keeping people here in a cage. We have to free them! They're keeping them like livestock."

Shaw pales. Something akin to agony washes over his face. "We can't. Those cages are kept in the middle of the camp, Lemming, and there are only two of us."

"We can't leave them locked in there. Covinus-knows what's going to happen to them!"

I watch the emotions swell over his face and then recede as quickly as a winter tide. Sadness, defeat, fear, and then...then there is nothing. Shaw's face hardens and whoever he was just moments ago, disappears behind the mask I've grown to despise. "It's not our problem." His voice is hard. Commanding.

Unfortunately for him, I'm not his to command. "I won't leave them."

My muscles tense, bracing for the moment Shaw decides I'm no longer worth the hassle. The moment it becomes apparent to him that it would be easier to overpower me, pull on my shackles or press on that convenient little spot behind my ear, but he doesn't move. He just watches me in preternatural stillness, his jaw clenched. His gaze travels to my neck, where blood from Shivhai's needle is crusted against old bruises creating a grotesque necklace.

"If you'd like to keep that pretty throat of yours intact, we need to move. Now."

My face heats, but I plant my feet and raise my chin. "I will scream and thrash and bring every soldier in this Covinus-forsaken camp down upon us unless you help me free them."

Shaw tilts his head, his face lighting with something like respect. "I really wish you'd stop threatening to scream all the time," he sighs. "We could be killed doing this, you know. Either now, or later, when Shivhai wakes up and they hunt us down."

He didn't kill Shivhai? Cool relief trickles down my spine, but I can't place why. Why should I care that Shaw spared that monster's life? "Which means whoever you traveled into the Dark World for will be lost as well."

How he guessed, I'll never know. Easton's hazel eyes flash before me, but there isn't a decision to make. Easton, with his easy grace and kind temperament would never choose his own life over those children. And though I have chafed and fought against the Keys my entire life, in this moment, I understand they are not all wrong. I can see the worth of Community before Self. "My life isn't worth more than theirs. Neither is his."

Shaw rolls his eyes and mutters, "Similian nonsense."

"Shaw, there are children in there." It's a fool's errand, to beg for mercy from the man who abducted me, who I've seen dance in violence and blood. He's proven he has no heart, and yet, here I stand, chained and desperate, trying to appeal to it.

A muscle feathers in his jaw and then his body relaxes, as if he's released the tension in every muscle with one decision. "Turn around. Let me see if I can pick the lock on those chains."

I release a breath I didn't realize I was holding and do as he asks. Disbelief keeps me silent, as if speaking out loud will break whatever spell caused him to agree to help me. There is a soft sound of metal against metal and then my shackles come loose. In addition to startling acts of violence, it seems Shaw is also adept at picking locks.

His fingertips brush the raw skin of my wrists gently and a spark of pain as well as something warmer and altogether more pleasant shoots through me. He rises behind me, and his voice is a whisper at my ear. "Mirren…"

I shiver, unable to decide if I wish to pull away or extend my throat so that his breath brushes more of the sensitive skin. It's only the third time he's said my name, and the thrill of hearing it on his lips, wrapped in his lilting accent only amplifies with each instance.

"You're going to be the end of me."

It isn't a malediction or an admonishment. His voice trails along my skin, sweetly reverent.

Like a prayer.

CHAPTER
FIFTEEN

Shaw

Aggie's prophecies are unreliable at best, but the night I came to her after Denver's abduction, her pronouncement was startlingly clear. *Break through the Boundary. Capture a Similian with green eyes.*

As I followed the prophecy, the rest of the plan unfurled before my eyes. Eulogius, the same Boundary hunter that attacked the girl, pointed me toward Yen Girene. The Achijj, leader of the stone city, is famous for his harem and his penchant for the unique is well known. If I could just overcome the small problem of my conscience, the way in seemed obvious. Blow up the Boundary. Get the girl. Trade for Denver.

A suicide mission to steal slaves from the most vicious warlord on the continent is not just a deviation. It's an entirely different path.

When I finally slayed the yamardu, my blood was heated magma coursing through my body and my breaths came in ragged puffs. It wasn't exertion, though I'd come close to death more times than I cared to count before the beast was finally felled by my blade. I've been trained to kill without tiring, to run without stopping. It was something else, something I refused to name. Something that will consume me if I let it.

Where is she, where is she, where is she.

The words reverberated inside my skull and against my ribs, a harrowing ratification of everything I'd done to deserve her disappearance. It wasn't losing her that I cursed—no, that, I certainly deserved. It was that she was headed straight into Cullen's twisted hands, and it was my fault. I showed her too much; the raw anger that barrels through me at any mention of his name. And Mirren, unschooled in the ways of emotion, plucked it from me as if I shouted it to her. As if I gave it willingly. If only I'd given her the rest.

It was terror that put that pistol in my hand. Pure fear that aimed it at her. Not to kill, but to stop her long enough for me to explain that it wasn't her death I feared. To explain how Cullen would systematically break her body, how he would relish cutting open her undisturbed skin; how he would make her beg for death long before he would ever grant it.

The thought of it threatened to undo me. It buried every fear of the Praeceptor discovering that I'm alive beneath it and drove me into this gods-forsaken camp after her.

"This is probably one of the stupidest things I've ever done," I tell Mirren succinctly. She's crouched next to me, wrapped once more in my cloak. Her curls are a wild halo around her head, having slipped from her braid during the scuffle with Shivhai, and her small hands are wrapped around the locks of the shackles.

She shoots me a wry grin. "Considering you've almost

gotten yourself killed countless times in the week I've known you, that's really saying something."

I raise an amused eyebrow. "More times than you have?"

She bites her lip, looking up through her lashes. "We may be even on that account," she concedes grudgingly.

I watch as she works the pick slowly, her brows furrowed in concentration. She's a quick study, her movements surprisingly clever and concise. After a moment, the mechanism clicks open and Mirren exhales a surprise gasp of pleasure, her cheeks flushing with pride.

I follow the flush with my eyes, down her mottled throat to where it disappears beneath the neckline of my cloak. It's oddly enamoring, the way the simplest things bring color to her skin. I wonder if it feels as heated as it looks.

I remember how every bit of color drained from her as Shivhai's hands pulled at her body like it was something he owned, as if it's possible to possess something as venerable as those curves. The chasm inside me roared open when I witnessed him try to take what she had not freely given. It was sacrilegious and I was half mad with rage by the time I leaned against that pole. It took everything in me to remember the piece of my soul that remains, to uphold my vow and not tear that man limb from limb. Even now, I have half a mind to burn my way through the camp and finish what I started.

Later.

I shove my rage down where it's useful, at the bottom of the hollow pit inside me. I am fueled by its fire, ever burning deep within, where it rages and toils in the space where my soul should be.

"Are you ready?" I ask, handing her one of my daggers.

Her fingers wrap around the hilt. I wish I had time to teach her how to wield it properly, but something is better than nothing.

She nods once, her soft lips pursed. Her eyes are alight with anticipation, and I notice, with surprise, her hand is steady on the weapon. Though woefully untrained, she's more of a warrior than I've given her credit for.

"As soon as the fighting starts, you do not hesitate. Pick the lock and run as fast as you can. Do you remember the directions to the cave?"

Mirren nods, her curls bouncing. I have the absurd urge to pull on one, to feel the silky tendril beneath my fingers and watch the way it springs back toward the crown of her head.

I shake my head. Thinking of curls instead of the death dance in front of me will only get us both killed. "Whatever you hear, do not turn back. Get them out and keep yourself out of the Praeceptor's hands. Those are the only things that matter. It's imperative that you—"

I stop talking at her haughty glare. "Shaw, I know," she says irritably, as if I'm a meddlesome mother. "I will get them out," her voice is determined, and it lifts my heart inside my chest. "Besides, Shivhai said the Praeceptor isn't here."

This should fill me with relief, but I don't allow it to settle. The Praeceptor has always kept his movements hidden, even from those closest to him. It would be foolhardy to assume we were safely out of his grasp. Not when it reaches through the Darkness, no matter where you are.

"Do you think you have enough weapons?" Worry tinges her voice. Worry that I won't be able to hold off the soldiers long enough to free the slaves? Or worry for my safety?

I shove the thought aside and pull my face into the arrogant grin that makes Mirren furious. "Don't worry, Lemming. I need no weapon. I *am* one." It sounds as narcissistic as I intend it to, but it's also the truth. It is what I was trained to be. Unthinking, unfeeling; hard, dangerous and uncompromising. To spill blood and reign violence. It's what I am good at. I will yield to no one except the Darkness' final calling—Death.

Mirren scoffs, the tips of her ears turning a delicious shade of pink. Her eyes haven't left the cages. The slaves are packed so tightly inside them that the chain wire digs into their soiled skin. Their bones protrude from their malnourished bodies. Some lie prostrate, never to get up again.

It's a sight I've seen many times before, but it never gets any easier. Anguish threatens to wash over me, and I know I would have found my way back here whether or not Mirren pleaded for my help. Rage claws at my throat as I watch a small boy cry out for his mother, a mother he will probably never see again. I will it down, down, down. I feed the abyss until it glows. *Wait,* I tell it. *A few more minutes and I will feed you with blood.*

Eight soldiers surround the cage. They laugh and joke, their eyes rarely glancing in the direction of those they guard, indicating they are low level. They've been trained to draw blood, but they have not been raised in it. Once Mirren leads them toward me, they'll be easily dispatched.

The problem is getting fifty malnourished people through the camp without disturbing the higher-level soldiers. Or worse, Cullen himself.

I wonder if he feels my presence here. I often thought as a child that the wind itself whispered its secrets to him, for how else could he have known the things he did? Things he never should have been able to know as a man and not a god. The hair rises on the back of my neck and for a wild moment, I expect him to walk out from behind the cage. To catch me with that cutting gaze and strip me bare.

A flash of a different camp appears before me. A camp set next to a village where homes burned, and children screamed, and bodies—so many bodies. It isn't now, I know that well, but the smell of burning skin and the coppery tang of blood seem to coat my skin and mouth nonetheless.

He is just a man. No more.

I've been repeating this to myself since I was thirteen. I don't know that I will ever really believe it.

Mirren's fingers tighten on my dagger. I should say something before we begin; something that shapes the way her bravery makes me feel like crying and the power in her makes me feel less alone, but I have no words. I simply nod and take my leave.

My feet make no noise as I prowl my way through the camp. I was made for shadows and darkness, and they draw me in like I'm one of their own. *Come,* they say. *Become us.*

I'm across the camp in no time. I staked out the most strategic place I could find for the fight, which isn't saying much in the wide-open expanse of the camp, but it's better than nothing. A roughly hewn storage shed on one side and the stables on the other, with the mountain covering my back. In the small space, the soldiers will be hard pressed to surround me and be forced to fight two at a time.

I pat the daggers that line my legs. Only six. I'd been forced to abandon my bandolier, along with my sword, at the edge of the camp in order to appear unarmed beneath my cloak. Despite what I told Mirren, not nearly enough.

I strain my ears, listening for any signs of disturbance,

but all is quiet. This should bolster my confidence since our plan depends on Mirren creating a convincing but *quiet* distraction, so as not to rouse the rest of the sleeping soldiers, but instead, discomfort settles over me. A twist of the stomach and a pressure on the throat, it feels similar to watching her disappear into the Nemoran wood with that soldier. I don't like being unable to see her. To know with certainty that she's safe.

A few seconds pass in disquieted agony and then a relieved breath flies from my lips as she rounds the corner. Her cheeks are flushed with exertion and her hair streams behind her like a gleaming flag as she tears through the darkness. She is sobbing, as she said she would be, but her acting is impeccable and though I know it as false, the sound of it tightens my chest nonetheless.

"Please!" She cries frantically, "Please don't take me back to him! He'll kill me!"

Her eyes meet mine, wide but dry even as the sobs rack her body. And trailing behind her are the guards from the gate.

Trained enough to know they need to bring this slave girl back to Shivhai or risk their necks, but not trained enough to know leaving their post is also a death sentence.

I take a slow breath, descending into my abyss. It is calm and dark, and the world recedes as its fire climbs up within me. It heats me from my heart to my fingertips until the only thing I can feel is its raging power. And then I move.

～

Mirren

There's no time to make sure Shaw has occupied all the

guards. As soon as I'm past him, I circle back through the camp, my breaths coming in short puffs. I move carefully, like Shaw told me to. I can't wake any other soldiers. It will be the end of this plan. And of me.

My heart flutters wildly as the cage comes into view. The people inside rear back from me, as if I'm another unknown horror waiting to be unleashed upon them. Their fear grips me, tangling with my own, but I force myself to keep moving. "I'm not here to hurt you," I say softly, creeping forward. I extract Shaw's pick. "I want to free you."

All the sounds of the cage have gone deathly silent as a hundred pairs of eyes gleam in terror.

The man nearest to the cage door shakes his head violently. "You cannot!" His words are heavily accented and the whites of his eyes glint in the darkness. "There is nowhere to go. They will hunt you."

"Then let them hunt me," I say and place the pick into the padlock.

"I cannot ask that of you, even for the sake of my people," the man insists. Everyone else has gone still, looking to him.

The lock is heavy iron, made the same as my shackles. Shaw's lesson in lock picking was short and rudimentary, and while I'd made progress, all locks are not the same. *Work slowly. Feel the mechanism inside. Once you know it, you'll know how it can be undone.*

Nonsense. The lock feels just as foreign to me as the rest of this Covinus-forsaken continent.

"What's your name?" I ask the man. He is young, his face unlined and perhaps handsome, if he hadn't been starved near to death. His brown hair is matted and drapes over his shoulders and his clothing hangs in tatters off his emaciated frame. The exposed skin of his limbs is mottled with angry burns, as if someone held him over an open flame. But his cheekbones are high and beautiful, and his slightly upturned eyes shine brightly with something I recognize. Hope. Defiance.

And pride.

"Asa," he replies softly, watching as I struggle. His eyes dart to the direction the guards ran, waiting for them to reappear at any moment. The same thought plagues me. I can only hope Shaw's skills are enough to keep them at bay.

"Asa," I keep my voice calm, speaking in a Similan tone. Polite and smooth. "I need you to make sure everyone is ready to move as soon as I spring this lock. We're going to go west, but we must move quietly."

I tell Asa the same directions Shaw gave me, the ones that lead to a complex cave system that wends its way beneath these mountains. Even if we are separated, if Asa can find the mouth of the cave Shaw spoke of, they will all be able to disappear from the warlord's grasp.

Asa stares at me, torn, but after a moment he nods. He whispers a message quickly to those around him and I watch as it's relayed around the cage. Suddenly, there is no more wailing. No more crying. Everyone stands silent and alert, as if the words themselves have brought them to life.

Hurry, Mirren. Shaw's voice says, deep and reverberating. *Once you know it, it can be undone.* I close my eyes and listen. I push away the sounds of the camp, of breathing and fear, and just feel. I keep my eyes shut until the lock is familiar, until I know the sounds of it, the smell of it, the small give of it when I push at its mechanism.

I feel, more than hear, a small click and a breath whooshes out of me.

I toss it to the side, savoring the dull thud of it against the ground. The same sound my shackles made. Freedom.

Yanking the gate open, I press my finger to my mouth. *Quietly. So quietly.*

I motion Asa forward and the group surges toward me. Terror keeps them silent as they file through the gate. A mother clutches her daughter's hand, blinking at the open space around them as if it will swallow them up. I wonder the last time they were able to move freely and anger washes over me.

When the last person is out, I close the gate softly. I don't look at the bodies that still remain, the ones who will never get a chance, instead moving to the front of the crowd, to find Asa. A boy, no more than four, clings to his neck and Asa grips him tightly as I approach. "What is your name?" he asks. People all around him wait for his command. He is their leader, I realize. And with the way he gathered each of them to him, helping them out of the cage as if every one of them matters deeply to him, they are lucky to have him.

"Mirren."

"Mirren," he repeats and in his heavily accented voice, it sounds like 'Murr-inn'. "Thank you, Mirren."

I smile shyly. "Don't thank me yet. We still have to make it to the caves."

He nods gravely, his eyes shining. "Even if we die now, I will forever owe you my thanks. Because my people will die free beneath the sky, instead of caged and shackled."

I don't know what to say to this or how to overcome the lump that's formed in my throat, so I just nod.

Because I think of Easton and wish desperately that he, too, could know the open sky before it's too late.

Shaw

I bring my dagger down hard on the first soldier's temple. He drops immediately and I allow myself one quick glance to make sure Mirren has escaped.

Satisfied she's made it to the other side of the camp, I dance backward, positioning myself between the tree and the shed. There are seven soldiers left. A rabid grin lights my face as two of them run forward. I palm another dagger, one in each hand and slice out with the blades. I catch the first across his weapon hand and the other at his knees. I spin as their howls ring in the night, throwing two more blades at the soldiers behind them.

The daggers land true and they fall, blades sprouting from their stomachs. The remaining three pick their way through the bodies of their comrades, their eyes glowing with a rage I know well. But they haven't been taught to hone that wild anger, to wield it like a broad sword, and so theirs crumple against mine. I unleash myself, sweeping my feet around and knocking the legs out from one before springing up to power my fist against another's solar plexus.

He gasps for air, but I don't stop. Don't think, just feel the fire burn its way out of the abyss. The next one comes at me, a long sword in his hand. A powerful weapon, but too heavy for tight combat. I use it against him, ducking beneath the blade and slicing at his wrist. He howls in agony, dropping the sword. My heart clenches. Too much noise. I need to end this quickly.

A blow to the head silences his wails. I yank my last dagger from my hip and hurl it at the remaining soldier.

Blood sprays in powered spurts from where it protrudes in his leg. I finish him off with a knock to the skull.

I survey the carnage around me, my breaths powered in my lungs. My blood runs like acid through my body and I take a moment to soothe the gaping emptiness inside me. To remind myself that I'm more than just a savage weapon, fueled by hatred. That a soul, however ravaged, still lives within me, fed by love. *Cal, Max, Denver.*

The list is short, but it grounds me. The fire in my veins recedes as I go to collect my weapons, leaving a cold emptiness in its wake.

A scream sounds from the other side of the camp.

Mirren.

My heart seizes. *Too long. I took too long.*

I bend down to yank the dagger out of the unconscious soldier's leg, desperation clawing at my throat, but I freeze as a sword presses to my throat.

I hear words from so long before. *Emotion is deadly. Fear, love, rage. You are a weapon and weapons do not feel. Weapons do not hesitate.*

Mirren's scream paused the very beat of my heart and in turn, I allowed myself to be ambushed from behind. A fraction of a moment's hesitation and I've doomed us both.

I stand up slowly, arms raised above my head. The soldier must be as tall as I am, if not taller, because the sword at my throat doesn't waver. Its blade is a cold, steady pressure against my windpipe. A revolver presses against the back of my neck and I force myself not to shy away from it, to remain completely still.

Mirren screams again and I don't even wonder how I know it's her, how its sound reverberates in my bones and radiates under my skin. I tense, weighing the chances of disarming my attacker blindly. Of the probability of accidentally slitting my own throat on their blade in the process.

"Ah, now, don't go running off. My men will bring the girl and then we can all really have some fun together," the deep voice rumbles and scrapes and just like that, the chasm inside me explodes. I grit my teeth, burning wrath cloaking everything around me in an alarming shade of red and all I can hear is that voice threatening Mirren.

Shivhai.

He presses his blade harder against my throat and I force myself to swallow against it.

"I wondered when you'd show your face here again. *Shaw.*"

CHAPTER
SIXTEEN

Mirren

Asa and I head west, toward the green mountains bordering the camp. It's where Shaw entered, silencing the two guards before anyone knew he was there. While he assured me he hadn't killed them, he was confident they would still be out of commission. Not in a position to debate the morality of it, I can only hope whatever Shaw did holds long enough for us to sneak past and disappear into the cave system.

The throng of people behind me is tense and quiet, but their footsteps are loudly discordant against the soft night. My heart beats in my throat, and for a moment, I swear the sound of their collective breath is as loud as a fall wind. At any moment, any of the hundreds of soldiers in this camp could wake. There will be no mercy, no cage. There will only be slaughter and it will be my fault.

A strangled howl rises from the other side of camp and goosebumps rise on my flesh. The sound echoes from where Shaw is and for a moment, I freeze, my heart clenching. Fear winds its way around my limbs, tightening uncomfortably. Fear for Shaw, or fear that the noise will awaken more soldiers, I don't know.

Asa touches my arm gently. The little boy he carries has fallen asleep and my heart lurches at the thought of someone like Shivhai hurting him the way he tried to hurt me. "We must hurry, brave one. The Praeceptor will return, and they will descend."

I nod and force my feet to move. To go faster. I won't let that little boy be trapped by my web of fear and self-doubt. We hurry forward in silence, going as fast as we dare. The edge of the camp feels miles away, but I tell myself it's close. I tell myself a lot of things in these moments: that Shaw is fierce and will survive to meet us at the caves; that I'm ridiculous—he kidnapped me and I shouldn't care whether he survives at all. I tell myself that I'm choosing the lives of these strangers over the life of the one person in the world that matters to me; and then, that Easton would be proud to know I did.

Finally, the edge of the camp comes into view. Three guards are crumpled unceremoniously on the ground, their legs sticking out at awkward angles as if they simply fell asleep where they stood. I wonder briefly if it's the same trick Shaw used on me or something more nefarious.

A sound rustles in the tent next to us, followed by a shout of anger and my elation swiftly dissipates. Someone has woken.

Asa turns toward the sound, his face leeched of color.

"Go," I mouth at him, gesturing furiously at the unconscious guards. "Run. Follow the stream to the west. There's a cave with a willow leaning over it. The caves go for miles. Disappear until you're well enough to move on."

He shakes his head frantically. The little boy is gripped tightly in his arms. "We can't leave you—"

"Cover your tracks. Don't disturb the forest branches. Disappear as fully as you can."

"You must come with us!" Asa cries desperately.

"You're responsible for these people. Save them!" Asa doesn't move. Everyone comes to a stand-still behind him. "I have a friend in the camp. He'll help me," I push him bodily until he begins to move. "Go!"

"I will never forget this. I will repay you in this life or the next. The Xamani always settle their debts."

I nod once and with one last meaningful stare, Asa finally moves. Their pace is achingly slow. There are too many to move any faster. I need to buy them time.

My heart leaps into my throat as I run toward the sound of the soldiers. Shaw explained that it takes time to mobilize a militia of this size and if the slaves can just get hidden, the trail will have gone cold. I can only hope he's right.

The soldiers run toward the edge of camp, so I tuck the dagger into my pocket and head them off. I veer directly in front of them, slipping into the girl I was earlier. The crying, traumatized victim of Shivhai isn't a stretch. I can already feel the bruises on my legs from where his hands gripped me, and I don't need a mirror to know that a nasty welt has arisen on my cheek.

I let out a sob, covering my face and trembling wildly. "No, no! Don't take me back to him! Please!"

The soldiers, three of them, slide to a stop in front of me. They glance at one another uncertainly. They are young, around Shaw's age, and I wonder if Shaw learned to fight somewhere like this camp. If his familiarity with blood and savagery was honed in a place just like this. The thought unsettles me. There's no way I will survive a camp full of soldiers like Shaw.

"Take you back to who?" one soldier barks, a man with overlarge teeth and a swath of yellow hair.

I let out an incoherent babble of sobs, angling my body. The soldiers move their bodies as well, determined to keep me in their line of sight. I glance surreptitiously behind them. Asa herds the group into the trees and they disappear one by one. Only a few more moments. I just need to keep the soldiers from looking to the forest for a few more moments.

And then what?

The soldiers shift uncomfortably as I drop to my knees and cry. A ruthless satisfaction rises within me. They're unwilling to look closely at someone's pain, which means they won't see my dry eyes. Or the dagger poking out of my pocket. Or the line of people I just freed from their grasp.

Another soldier appears from behind one of the tents and my eyes narrow in disgust. Dumi. The woman who brought me here and delivered me to Shivhai. There's no question she knew exactly the kind of things that happen inside that tent and gave me to that man anyway. There should be a special curse for the kind of woman that would deliver another to a fate like that.

"She is Shivhai's," Dumi snarls. "What did you do to him, girl?"

The blonde soldier eyes me skeptically. "You think this wisp of a girl could really do something to the *legatus*, Dumi?"

I cry louder, but Dumi isn't fooled. The last of Asa's people disappears into the tree line and something like relief settles in my stomach. Not for myself. I'm far from safe. But Asa, and that little boy, and the hundred others like him, are and that's worth something.

Dumi's eyes narrow and she withdraws her sword as she stalks toward me.

She stops less than an arm's distance from me. "Tell me where our *legatus* is, girl," she says, her voice low and threatening.

I scream as she slices the sword across my chest.

∽

Shaw

Shaw.

I wish to tear my name from Shivhai's tongue and then carve it from his memory until he can never speak it again. When I charged into camp after Mirren, I knew the risk of being recognized. The Praeceptor, after all, has an appreciation for those willing to get their hands dirty and who do so efficiently. He keeps his loyal followers close; he's pragmatic, among other things.

I was relying on the changes manhood had shaped in my face and body since the last time I was here to cloak my features. That, and the sheer stupidity of coming back into this camp. No one who knew me before would expect me to be dense enough to cross paths with the Praeceptor again.

You.

Shivhai's eyes had gone wide, and he'd spoken the word before I knocked him out and I knew he had guessed the truth. He was only a foot soldier the last time I was here, one known as much for his cunning as for his cruelty. It's the cunning that plagues me now; his uncanny way of noticing things that others deem unimportant and wielding them accordingly. I hardly knew him then, but apparently, he knew enough of me to put the pieces together now.

You should have killed him.

The thought rattles through me, but I know it isn't my own. It's the voice of the Praeceptor. *You left him alive because of a silly vow and now you and the girl will both die.*

I close my eyes tightly, willing away the voice that haunts me in waking dreams and terrifying nightmares. I focus instead on another voice. One that belongs to a man with green eyes that have never held judgement and gentle hands that have never been coated in blood. Denver's. My adopted father and the man whose disappearance was the catalyst to this journey. *Your vow will protect you, Shaw. Protect you from a fate worse than death. It is not weak to want that.*

Neither of those voices will save me now. It is only the abyss that can do that, the killing calm that burns from the inside out, so that is the one I choose to abide by. The voice that tells me to move. To cut Shivhai down before he can kill me. And then to hack my way through everyone else in this camp who stands between me and Mirren.

"I didn't think you'd ever come back here," Shivhai growls from somewhere over my shoulder. I mark where his voice is. Close. But close enough? "I thought you'd crawled in some hole and died, like the cowardly vermin you are. But *he* always knew."

I squirm, testing the strength of his hold. The blade is pressed so solidly into my throat that if I move forward at all, I'll cut my own windpipe. The revolver is shoved so firmly into the base of my skull the barrel feels as if it's branded there. Patience has saved me from as many situations as brute force and though my body screams at me to move, to get to Mirren, I command it still.

"I see you've finally worked your way up the Praeceptor's ladder. How'd you do that? Licking his boots clean?"

Shivhai growls and I mark his location again. Closer. "The only thing I licked on my way here were sweet smelling Similians, just like your girl's pu—"

His words falter as my boot collides with his kneecap. Shivhai roars and a shot cracks from his revolver, but I'm already moving. I roll to the ground, collecting my dagger. A paltry defense against a gun, but better than nothing. Before he can haul off another shot, I throw the knife at his hand, knocking the gun to the ground.

I hesitate for only a moment, warring with the need to leave Shivhai here and run to Mirren's aid. But Shivhai will follow, and I can't allow that.

I lunge at him, ducking under his gleaming blade. We go down in a flurry of limbs, his body as hard and heavy as a steel wall. My daggers are gone, so I hone in on where I stabbed him earlier and punch him as hard as I can, before I lose the small advantage of surprise I have. Shivhai grunts and brings a boulder sized knuckle flying toward my head. I roll off him before it can connect. We both scramble to our feet and he flies toward me, cracking a kick against my ribs. He goes for my face, but I bring up my arm and sweep a kick toward his knees, aiming for the one I've already injured.

He goes down, and I instantly realize my mistake as his hand grabs for the discarded revolver. He whips it up, pointing it at me once more. The bullet is already in the chamber, and we are close enough that one move will send me to the grave. But the Darkness won't claim me yet. Mirren is still in the hands of the enemy, and I won't succumb until she's safe. She is one mistake in a lifetime of them I can still rectify.

Shivhai cocks a lopsided grin. It pulls at his gnarled face humorlessly. "I wonder what the Praeceptor will say when he finds out you've come *home*."

The word reverberates through me, and a wave of nausea rises as I realize Shivhai's intent. He lowers the revolver so that it is no longer aimed at my heart, but at my knee. He has no intention of killing me. His plans are far, far worse.

"What kind of greeting do you think he'll give the boy who betrayed him? That tried to cut out his heart even as he cared for you? You've seen enough traitors' executions. Do you think he'll be so kind, to simply let you die in humiliation? I think you know better than that. Know that he'll drag out your miserable life for *years*, peel the skin from your bones just to wait for it to grow back and then do it again. You will never know the peace of Darkness."

I suddenly forget I'm still fighting; that Mirren isn't safe, and neither is Denver and they'll never be if I get myself shot and dragged in front of the Praeceptor. I only see the Praeceptor's cold eyes on the last day I saw him. The way they widened, ever so slightly, as my blade went through his chest. The way his hot blood mixed with my hotter tears as I yanked the blade back out. And ran.

I watch in frozen horror as Shivhai's finger squeezes the trigger. As the shot rings out, I brace myself for an impact that never comes. Slowly, so slowly, I see the pistol on the ground alongside a dagger. *My* dagger. And Mirren, face flushed, running full speed toward me.

While I was frozen, she must have thrown the dagger and knocked the revolver from Shivhai's hand. I don't have time to wonder at her aim or her courage as she collides into me. Her skin is hot against mine, her face covered with tears and blood and dirt, but she feels so alive, I am reawakened.

The red that spilled over my vision at Shivhai's voice clears. The Praeceptor's cold laugh fades into the background. Three soldiers tear after Mirren and my mission becomes clear once more.

I spiral, down, down, down into that abyss. The fire feeds me again, burning, until I am no longer someone concerned with the boy I used to be or the man I will be tomorrow. Now, I am only the weapon. And I will have my blood.

~

Mirren

Dumi's blade is like hot iron as it sweeps across my chest, but I manage to dance back before she can give me more than a flesh wound. Tears spring to my eyes and blood soaks my shirt. Anger lights her face, bright and deadly as she moves toward me. Lithe muscles line her arms and there's no doubt in my mind that she can take my head off with one more well aimed swing. Her pale skin glitters in the moonlight.

My face sobers and if Dumi is surprised by the abrupt end of my blubbering, she doesn't show it. Only continues to assess me as if I'm the threatening one in this situation. As if I'm the one holding the sword. And though I'm not, I'm not unarmed. I possess that which has always come so naturally to me. The bite of my tongue. "How wretched is your soul that you would deliver one of your own to that monster? To be used and beaten?"

Her face twists in rage. "*You* are not 'one of my own'. You are a Similian robot, raised only to follow orders and work your government's fields."

I raise my chin and straighten my shoulders. "I am a woman, like you. Like your sisters. Like your mother and aunts. How can you not see their faces when you look at mine? And you still fed me to him as if I were no more than cattle, and he, a lion. Just look at you. You stink of self-loathing."

Dumi snarls, but her sword arm drops enough that I know I've hit my mark. That I've unsettled her. It's all I need. I turn, sprinting toward the heart of the camp. The dagger bounces in my pocket as run, but I'm useless with it. I'll never be able to outmaneuver three trained soldiers. My only hope is that I'm fast enough to make it to Shaw. And that he hasn't left me behind.

Dumi cries out in surprise. Feet storm behind me. My breath burns in my lungs, but I can't take the short way across camp or they will know the slaves are gone. I wind my way through the catacomb of tents. It's only because I've made it personal with Dumi that she doesn't alert anyone else. She will be the one to make me pay for the insult. As if erasing me will also erase the sting of the truth.

Her determination to be the one to capture me spares me for the moment but will be worse if she catches me. I pump my legs harder and throw myself around the last tent. My heart bursts in my chest as Shaw comes into view. Alive and whole. My relief is a palpable thing as it floods my chest but it's short lived.

Shaw appears unhurt, but his normally caramel skin is leeched of color. And he is still. Not the normal stillness, a predator ready to pounce, but a heavy one. Like he is mired to the ground.

My eyes travel across the clearing and a cry escapes my throat as I see Shivhai. Bloodied and bruised, but very much alive. And pointing a gun at Shaw.

I don't stop to consider what's stopped Shaw in his tracks. Instead, I grab the only thing I have. The dagger. The soldiers' exerted breaths sound behind me. I don't break pace as I hurl the knife as hard as I can at Shivhai's hand. There's no hope of hitting his hand with the blade but knocking his trajectory off track will buy Shaw a moment to move. To fight back.

A gunshot rends the silence of the night. It can't have hit Shaw, can't have felled him. We are too close to the end of whatever this is. He survived the Boundary men and the yamardu, and it isn't possible that something as mundane as a bullet will slow him.

I crash into him, with a force borne of both desperation and momentum, but he doesn't go over. He is steady as he wraps his arms around me, keeping us both upright. My hands tangle in his shirt, searching him for injury. I cling to him, the camp a blurred whirlwind around us, praying that infernal grin of his will appear and he'll save both our lives.

His skin is fevered against mine. He glances down at me once, his eyes pale and bright through his thick lashes. His lips part in surprise and something unspoken sparks between us. Before I can consider it, Shaw throws me behind him.

He yanks a sword from one of the unconscious soldiers littering the ground and snaps it up just as Dumi slashes hers toward his chest. The clang of steel rings out and the sound frees Shaw from whatever bound him. He spins and arcs and weaves, his long limbs moving in a graceful dance of blood. He glances over his shoulder as he swings the sword in an elegant arc, succinctly disarming the blonde soldier, but his eyes hold no victory.

They are fixed on Shivhai moving toward the pistol once more.

I propel my body forward, my mind straining against me. *Hide, Mirren! Don't put yourself in his sights once again.*

But I can't, because if Shivhai reaches that gun, it isn't just Shaw that will die. It's both of us.

I reach it just before he does, the metal cool and foreign against my skin. He roars in frustration and swings his thick arm out in front of him. I dance backward, the gun trembling in my hand. The wound Shaw gave him bleeds freely and I wonder if it's too much to hope that he will just bleed out.

"You've caused me a lot of trouble, little bird," he growls, his body a mountain lumbering toward me. "Trouble that I intend to make you pay for."

I grip the pistol tightly, biting down hard on my lip. I should shoot him. After everything he's done to me, to Asa and his people, surely he deserves it. But who am I to decide who is deserving? A girl who betrayed my country, who left my dying brother; who let my life partner be shot for my choices; who left a man who once saved me to be mutilated by a monster. Am I any better than Shivhai?

My indecision costs me. Shivhai grabs me, circling his large hand against my mouth and dragging me backward.

"Mirren!" Shaw shouts, his eyes drawn from the battle. I shake my head frantically, because in his distraction he doesn't notice Dumi creeping up next to him. My eyes widen in horror as she shoves her blade into Shaw's shoulder. My scream echoes Shaw's roar of pain, but the sound is lost beneath Shivhai's massive hand covering my mouth. He grabs for the gun in my hand, but my hesitation is replaced by feral desperation; all thoughts of morality eddy from my mind and now there is only a primal need to survive. I curl my finger against the trigger and the gun kicks back roughly as another shot rings out.

Shivhai howls in pain, dropping his hand to clutch at his foot. I run toward Shaw. His left-hand dangles uselessly at his side as he fends off Dumi and the remaining soldier with his right. He doesn't take his eyes from the battle, the sounds of his exertion ragged and painful. "Mirren, take the gun and run! Now." His voice leaves no room for question. It is a command.

Blood pours from his shoulder. His lips have gone pale. The blonde soldier lays unconscious, but Dumi and the other show no signs of tiring. And I'm not foolish enough to believe that Shivhai has been felled. I cannot leave Shaw now, not when he risked everything to help me. When he pushed aside his own will to survive to help Asa and his people. "I can't—"

Shaw shakes his head wildly, unadulterated agony written all over his face. His arm trembles as he meets Dumi's blade once more. In a flash, his vulnerability is gone, replaced by the unfeeling mask of the man who abducted me. "You're a Lemming," he snarls. He feints left, avoiding Dumi's blade while swinging a wide arc toward the other soldier. With a sickening smack, he brings his sword down across the soldier's head. The soldier crumples.

"You're raised to be unthinking. To follow orders without questions. Follow mine now and save yourself."

Dumi rushes at him and just before he brings his blade up to meet hers, he breathes, "You owe me nothing, Lemming."

Nothing. I owe him nothing. He abducted me and shot at me and *hurt* me. Sacrificing my life for Asa's people was a worthy choice, one Easton would have applauded. But this is different. I touch the small scratch on my cheek and Shaw nods once. I cannot give up Easton for Shaw's life. He knows it well. Knows it better than I do.

I have scorned my parents for their choices to be

Outcast, for their willingness to leave, but in a cruel twist of fate, I am cursed to make the same ones. Easton. Harlan. And now Shaw. I choose to leave them behind, over and over again.

I glance one more time at the Dark World boy. Cruel and exhilarating. Violent and beautiful.

Something wrenches painfully in my chest as I turn and run.

CHAPTER SEVENTEEN

Shaw

I only watch Mirren long enough to be certain she's gone. Something cracked inside me when I saw the hesitation in her eyes; her better-self warring against the need to survive until the most primal of her instincts won out. That small moment of uncertainty burns at the back of my throat, proof of Mirren's goodness. I silently thank her for it. Darkness knows, I've done nothing to deserve it.

A hollowness descends over me as I bring my sword once more to meet the Praeceptor's soldier. She is well trained and inexhaustible. In contrast, my movements grow increasingly sluggish. Her face twists as Mirren disappears and she feints to the left, but I'm ready for it. She won't follow Mirren. I'll make sure none of them are well enough to do so.

My left arm is useless at my side. My strength leaches out of me with every pulse of blood from the wound at my shoulder. If I can staunch the bleeding, the injury won't be life threatening. I need to end this. Quickly.

A rustle from behind is the only thing that clues me to

Shivhai's movements, and I spin just in time to meet his blade with my own. Blood spills from his neck and his boot, but his movements are fevered and powerful, driven by pure venom. His eyes are murderous, and he no longer aims to simply maim—he wants me ended.

I block the woman's blade and stomp down hard on Shivhai's foot. He doesn't slow, cracking his fist against my jaw. My head flies sideways. Stars bloom behind my eyes and blood fills my mouth. I can't take both of them on. Not with my dominant hand out of commission and my strength waning.

"How do you think the Praeceptor will punish you when he realizes you lost an entire shipment of slaves?"

The soldier parries my strike, her eyes furious.

"Probably with something from his instrument cart, right?" I strike again, my voice denoting a casualty I don't feel. "Do you think it will be public or private? You know how he *loves* to use failure as an example. An entire shipment escaping right under your nose is quite the spectacular failure."

The soldier pales and she glances to Shivhai uncertainly, realizing for the first time that I may be taunting her with the truth. I smile wryly, even as shame washes over me that I'm unable to give the slaves more time. I hope they've made it to the caves.

Whatever Shivhai sees on my face must convince him of my honesty. "Dumi, go," he orders, moving to strike once more.

I block. The impact jars my bones and the muscles in my arms scream as I struggle to retaliate. With a snarl, I slice at his side, but it's only a flesh wound, and it isn't enough. My limbs feel as though they are moving through thick mud. *Too slow. You are moving too slow.*

Dumi hesitates, clearly uncertain about leaving Shivhai in his injured condition.

"Go, you fool! One girl is not worth the Praeceptor's wrath!" Shivhai roars. He spins, catching me off guard. Though I move to block, I'm too slow and his blade arcs across my stomach.

Dumi runs in the direction of the cage, but there is no relief to be had at her disappearance. I face Shivhai. Blood now pours from my abdomen, mingling with the blood from my shoulder and pooling in a sticky puddle at my feet. *End this, Shaw. End this or he will end you.*

Pushing for one last reserve of strength, I bring my sword against Shivhai's. I know before it is done that it's not enough. He knocks my weapon easily from my hand. He shoves toward me, swinging his giant fists. I throw my hands up in a feeble attempt to block, but his fist cracks against my jaw. Something snaps and I stumble backward. He deftly sweeps my feet out from under me. My wounds scream as I hit the ground and it's all I can do to throw my last dagger up before his sword comes down on my neck.

The larger blade clashes against my smaller one and it's a testament to Calloway's blade crafting skill that the dagger doesn't snap under the pressure.

"*You,*" Shivhai snarls, his face so close to mine that I feel the heat of his breath. I struggle against his weight, my mind reaching for any way to disarm him, but my thoughts come in disparate clouds, thin and insubstantial. My arms shake. I spit out a curse as Shivhai bears down, his mottled face slick with exertion. Blood, his and mine, seeps into the ground. It's only a matter of time before my strength gives out completely. I know this in my bones—in my arms that are so, so tired. Even my fire has faltered, the chasm inside me hollow and silent.

"*You,*" he says again. A smartass retort sits on my lips, but my mouth has gone dry, and my tongue feels too thick to speak. "You're the little urchin that murdered my brother. Nine years ago, you bled him dry like a pig at slaughter. Feral little thing, skin and bones, but it was *you.*"

Oh. *Oh.*

Shivhai isn't coming after me because I stole a Similian girl from him. He isn't even coming after me from some vague sense of loyalty to the Praeceptor. It is something squirmy and rancid that drives him. Something that has festered for years until it melded with his soul. It is vengeance and there is nothing more personal than that. Even if I can somehow manage to cut off both his arms, the vengeance will drive him. He will never stop coming for me.

I stare hard into the bottomless pits of his eyes—the hatred, the malevolence surely a mirror into my own soul. I deserve to die here, pooled in a reflection of my own misery. My own sins.

I've fought all my life. I have thieved and lied and killed and then clawed my way out of the depths, only to find myself free falling into them once more. My body hums with anticipation, the only thing left inside me to feel. The last ember of the fire that has kept me alive all these years drains into the mud along with my blood and suddenly, I feel tired. So very tired. As if my body is a thousand years old.

Shivhai's blade gleams, taunting me with the reprieve it will grant. To finally deliver what I am owed—death. It won't be enough, will never be enough, to repay the atrocities I've wreaked on the world. Whatever is left of my blood will never be able to wash away the stain of darkness my life will leave. But it's all I have left to give.

And so, I let my arm drop.

CHAPTER
EIGHTEEN

Shaw

The world slows and speeds up at all once. I watch the surprise flash across Shivhai's face at my surrender, followed by the glow of victory. I feel the cool blade pressed against my throat. But the punishment I so desperately deserve is not to be mine, for in the same instant, I see a flash of familiar chestnut curls behind Shivhai.

She came back. The stupid, stupid girl came back.

Panic courses through me.

She isn't safe. And you're too weak to save her.

I grit my teeth and throw my arms back up with some reserve of strength I didn't realize existed. The chant pounds through my head, a harrowing benediction. *Protect, protect, protect.*

But it grants me no reprieve. No way to keep Shivhai's blade from my neck and then hers.

Shivhai lets out a strangled cry of fury at my renewed fight, slicing at my arm. The cut is shallow, but my arm trembles wildly as we struggle. With horrified deference, I watch as Mirren creeps up behind him. *Leave me!* I want to scream at her, to beg her, but no sound comes.

My eyes widen as she jumps onto Shivhai's back and digs a knife, *my* knife, into his neck. Shivhai drops the sword, clutching at his throat as blood blooms around it like a horrible sort of necklace. Mirren stumbles back. Shivhai gurgles and I throw him off me with a snarl. I haul myself to my feet, grabbing the sword Shivhai dropped in his distraction. I knock the butt of it roughly against his head and he crumples at my feet, blood pooling beneath him.

Mirren's eyes are wide and glassy as she stares at his prone body. Something like panic flashes across her face. "Is he...did I..."

"No," I say quickly, watching as her shoulders relax and her breathing slows. "You missed his arteries and his brain stem. As long as he gets medical attention, he'll make it." He probably won't be able to speak properly again, but I don't consider that much of a loss. It's all I have to offer her, the freedom from the weight of someone else's life. It is a heavy one and she doesn't need to bear it any longer than necessary.

I stare openmouthed at her, unable to make sense of her being here, of her saving me, of *her*. Her cheeks are flushed, her full lips open and panting with exertion. Her hair blows in a wild halo around her face and blood wells at a wound on her forehead, running crimson lines over her brows and lashes. The emerald of her eyes burns even in the dim moonlight, and I wonder how I ever thought her weak. She looks nothing like a lemming. She looks like a warrior.

As if her appearance clears the fog from my senses, everything sharpens around me. We need to move. Now. And I need to somehow not bleed out on the way.

I tug my shirt over my head and Mirren's cheeks flame a luscious shade of red I don't have time to fully appreciate. I tear the shirt ruthlessly into strips and then wrap my shoulder. "Tie this as tight as you can."

I sense it's only her shock that keeps her moving as her hands work in robotic motions and my sense of urgency increases. We need to get out of this camp before the trauma renders her immobile.

Despite trembling fingers, her knot is firm. I grit my teeth against the wave of pain that comes with it. Shouts sound in the distance, other soldiers alerted to the disappearance of the slaves. We'll never be able to make it across camp to join them in the cave system. Our only hope is to head south and hope we can make it across the Breelyn plain before they find us.

I throw the remaining shreds of the shirt over my head. Threading my fingers through Mirren's, I pull her inside the stable. The horses, used to the cacophony of battle, pay us no mind. I sneak to the side of a bay mare, running my hands reassuringly over her flanks. "There's a good girl," I murmur. She lifts her head and gives me an appraising stare.

I look to Mirren. She nods her permission and without waiting, I circle my hands around her hips and shove her unceremoniously onto the horse. I throw a leg up behind her, a fresh wave of agony radiating from my shoulder. I breathe hard against the nausea, focusing instead on nestling Mirren securely between my legs. "You're going to need to hold the reins," I manage to bite out. There's no way I'll be able to manage the horse. Even lifting my uninjured arm causes the slash across my stomach to burn bitterly.

She turns to me, eyes wide in alarm. "I don't know

how," she whispers frantically. I can feel her panic growing in the tense coil of her muscles, the labored breaths that gasp from her lips.

"You've already done more than you ever thought yourself capable of," I whisper at her ear. "You can do this."

My words settle over her and she lifts her chin. Her fingers curl around the reins. It seems impossible that she is still unaware of what lives inside her: the brave, cunning thing that drove her to leave everything she's ever known to save someone. The unwavering fight that refuses to be defeated.

Something light blooms in my chest and I think how like calls to like as I click my tongue and we are free of the camp.

∽

Mirren

What have you done?

It's all I can think as we ride as far away from the camp as we can manage, which isn't far, considering Shaw's condition. Though the makeshift tourniquet has stemmed the blood flow, his face is still pale and his normally rosy lips, an alarming shade of gray. He sways on the saddle, his eyes half lidded, but so far, he's managed to keep himself upright.

I risked my life to save the man who abducted me, that's what I've done. I left him with every intention of saving myself, but as I ran, something tore inside me. I couldn't breathe around it. Could think of nothing but the unwavering determination on Shaw's face when he told me to run. It was a look I knew well, the same one mirrored on my face whenever I think of Easton. A willingness to give everything up to protect someone else. I knew then I couldn't leave him to die.

Wouldn't.

Therein lies the difference I've steadfastly refused to examine too closely.

I push the thought away for the millionth time, looking ahead. The sun has begun to stain the sky pink behind the mountains. When we tore out of camp, we crossed a valley, wide open and lush. The threat of the militia loomed and though I feared tumbling from the horse, I pushed her faster at Shaw's bidding. Shivhai wasn't dead and it was only a matter of time until he was in decent enough condition to send men after us.

As the distant mountains finally come closer, Shaw's instructions become more frequent. It's hard to keep my bearings in the expansive land, but I know enough to gather we aren't headed to the same cave system that hides Asa's people. These mountains are jagged and looming, and far larger than the ones that bordered the west side of the Praeceptor's camp.

My stomach clenches for the thousandth time as I realize how much hope I'd put into the proximity of other people staying Shaw's nature until I could figure out a new plan. We came to a sort of truce in the camp, but I'm under no illusions it extends beyond it. Once the adrenaline of our endeavor wears off, Shaw will still be Shaw: single-mindedly determined to get what he wants. And I am back to where I began. Unarmed and subject to his whims.

My thighs are wedged tightly between his and with every stride of the mare, his body rocks further against mine, as if the control he holds over himself is weakening. I shouldn't be surprised his chest is so hard, not when everything about him is sharp, but feeling it so closely lights a new awareness low in my stomach. I want to shy away from him in the same breath I wish to nestle closer. To feel the pattern of ridges I imagine etched across his abdomen.

You have no one to blame but yourself.

The thought churns inside of me. I wouldn't need a way to escape him if I had just let him die. I should have run far away and left him at the mercy of Shivhai's sword.

Even more unforgivable is my complete lack of remorse. I can't bring myself to regret saving Shaw. Anger bubbles in my throat, but it's anger at myself for *not* feeling sorry. I should feel sorry. I should feel terrified. I should feel *something* other than relief that we are both free of the evils of that camp.

Shaw clicks his tongue. The mare responds immediately, slowing her pace and huffing an impatient breath through her nostrils. I wonder if Shaw was simply lucky in picking such a fast horse or if he's practiced at such things. I watch in alarm as he stumbles off her with a groan. I've never seen him stumble. Not once.

He runs his fingers over the mare's silky mane, whispering something low that sounds like no language I've ever heard. He walks ahead, clicking his tongue once more and the mare follows. His gait is labored, but he makes no complaint as he leads us slowly into the trees. I shift in the saddle, thankful for the small movement that relieves the aching pain of my behind. Never having ridden a horse, I had no idea the toll it takes on one's body.

Shaw is silent as he walks further up the mountain. Sharp stones and boulders larger than Covinus vehicles litter the spaces between the trees, but Shaw wends his way deftly around them. Though there is no discernible trail, he moves with purpose, as if he knows exactly where he's going. Before long, he disappears behind a curtain of vines that hangs over a steep cliff face. I shield my face as the mare follows him through without protest.

As I thread my way through the infernal plants, I look around to discover we are in a cavern. One large enough to comfortably house us as well as the horse. Shaw reaches out a hand to help me, gritting his teeth in pain, but I pointedly ignore him. Instead, I throw myself off the opposite side of the mare. The impact throws me off balance and I land in an ungraceful heap on the ground, but it's better this way. I don't need his help or anymore reminders of his humanity. We are safe and he's Shaw once more, my abductor and my enemy.

He raises a brow at my refusal, but thankfully makes no comment about my spectacular fall. Instead, he leads the mare gently to the far side of the cavern where a clear stream trickles from the cave wall, winding its way gently through the rock. Shaw must have known of this place before. Somewhere perfectly suited to hide from a warlord's pursuing army. As if he's done it many times before.

He removes his remaining daggers from their sheaths and bends to the water, gently washing away the stains of the night. The mare drinks beside him and he whispers to her gently, his voice praising and kind. The mare deserves them, for carrying us so well to safely with an amateur at the reins, but anger rises in me all the same.

How is it that he speaks so gently to this creature, when hours before I watched him slice down soldier after soldier? And hours before that, he raised a gun at me without so much as flinching? I'm not so daft to believe we can hide happily in this cave and then he will let me go freely. He helped me free Asa and his people, but there is still a chasm within him, a divide between his goodness and his darkness. He was willing to kill me rather than let me go. He'll do it again.

"We can recover here for the night. We'll reassess in the morning."

My mouth twists in disgust, all the words I long to shout at him suddenly battering against my mouth like waves against a dam. Shaw may have saved my life, but he is the reason I was in the Praeceptor's camp in the first place. If he hadn't abducted me, if he hadn't refused to listen, I would never have been in Shivhai's path.

The crack of the shot he aimed at me gapes like an open wound, as if the bullet actually pierced my body instead of just grazing my skin. I want to whip it at him, for him to feel the sting of betrayal as acutely as I do. "I don't know why you're even bothering to tell me. It isn't as if I have any more of a choice here with you than I would have with the Praeceptor."

If Shaw is confused by my sudden change in demeanor, he doesn't show it. His eyes flicker and for a moment, I expect to see something like remorse. But there is only pure rage when Shaw's gaze meets mine. "A 'thank you' for risking my life and the fury of the most dangerous men in Ferusa for *you* wouldn't be unwarranted," he says through gritted teeth.

I scoff. "Thank you? You want me to *thank you*? For what, exactly, Shaw? For stalking me like the prey I am to you? For kidnapping me twice in a week's time? You only saved me because being tortured and killed would ruin whatever nefarious plans are in that twisted head of yours. And you only assisted me in freeing those slaves because I wouldn't come quietly otherwise and you didn't want to risk the Praeceptor's attention. You have done me no favors and I will not grovel on my knees in front of you as if you have."

Shaw shoves his knives back into their sheaths without bothering to dry their blades and stalks toward me. His pupils are blown wide, and his movements are charged. Powerful. Injured, but no less dangerous. He is not just angry, I realize belatedly. Shaw is *furious*. His eyes burn, not with the icy wrath that he focused on Shivhai, but with a blazing heat that sends warmth shooting to my cheeks and pooling somewhere deeper. Lower.

His voice is deathly quiet. "You think you would have been better off with them?"

Deep down, I don't. But his anger seems to sing to my own and it burns too brightly for me to think beyond it. I square my jaw and shake my mangled wrists at him. They are bruised and scabbed from Shivhai's irons, but it was Shaw's own ropes that made the first mark, and I won't allow him to forget it. "I would have been no worse off in the hands of those monsters than in the hands of the one standing in front of me!" I shout at him. His very presence charges my skin. It pricks at my throat and looses a wave of crimson from inside me that washes over everything else. How dare he act as if *I* have wronged *him*.

Shaw's eyes blaze and a muscle feathers in his jaw as he steps closer to me. He holds himself tightly once more, coiled as though he will pounce on me at any moment. A day ago—hell, an hour ago—I might have ceded a step. Backed away timidly. But he's awoken whatever it is that lives inside me, the dark creature I've always fought to keep quiet. There is no caging it now. So, I use it.

Let it heat my cheeks and my skin and my very heart. And then I take a large step toward him in an unspoken challenge.

His eyes widen fractionally, the only sign of surprise he will give.

"You brought me from their prison to one more convenient to you." I step toward him again. He doesn't move, but a warm thrill shoots through my center at the way he looks at me. As if he will burn straight through me with his gaze. As if he cannot look away. "There is nothing noble about that."

He bares his teeth. "Lucky for you, I have no interest in being *noble*," he spits the word like it tastes foul. "Because a more noble man than me would never have snuck into the camp like a ghost and gutted every one of those soldiers from behind with no hesitation. They never even saw it coming. There's no dignity in that, but you know what there is? *Justice,*" His eyes drift to my wrists and then lower, where a deep bruise blooms on my thigh, beneath the layers of my cloak. A bruise in the shape of Shivhai's fingers, an imprint of everything he tried to take from me. "For aiding what was happening in that tent. For what has happened in that tent countless times before."

Fast as lightning, Shaw grabs my hand and yanks up my sleeve, revealing the watercolor of bruising that plagues my wrist. The skin is raw and bleeding and I can almost feel the weight of Shivhai pressing me into the ground.

Shaw runs his thumb lightly over the tender skin and the claustrophobic feel of the *legatus* is replaced with something that shivers and burns in equal measure. Meeting my gaze fiercely, he snarls, "I savored every bit of their blood."

I shiver again. There is something chilling about his words, something both deadly and reverent. How can such raw violence live alongside whatever it is that allows him to touch me so gently? This close, I can see the way his thick lashes brush his cheekbone as he watches his thumb dance across my wrist. It makes me ache for something I can't even name.

I move my eyes downward, to his chest, rising and falling in ragged breaths as though he's been sprinting miles. So at odds with the stillness in which he holds the rest of himself. I wonder, for an absurd moment, what it would feel like to run my fingers down the lean muscles. To reach under his tattered shirt and confirm the truth of my mind's imaginings. Will his skin feel soft stretched over his stomach or will it be as unyielding as the rest of him? He's only a breath away. I need only to reach out a hand and I could discover if he's really made of marble and stone. I could run them down the ridges of muscle, down the sharp bones of his hips to his...knife.

Forgotten in my breathless haste, forgotten in his wash of anger, his knives are right in front of me. In their scabbard, only a hairsbreadth from my fingers.

Shaw lets go of my wrist gently, moving his fingers to my throat. I swallow roughly, sure he can somehow read my traitorous thoughts, that he will wrap them around my throat, but he only brushes over my old bruises lightly. His face is pained, and I shiver once more, though I am far from cold. My skin feels fevered and my blood rushes like lava through my veins. His calluses scrape gently across my skin, the friction deliciously unnerving. His eyes never leave mine, and something like agony flickers in them as he traces my jaw lightly.

I can't seem to look away, can do nothing but stare at him. I wonder if every touch feels like this or if it is only his that electrifies my skin and makes my heart feel like it will beat out of my chest. Is it only his that makes me feel such...*want?*

Shaw's fingertips trace the small cut across my cheek

and the heat in me is abruptly replaced by something much colder. Emptier. It doesn't matter if he truly is the only one capable of eliciting such a cacophony of emotions. He isn't to be trusted. The gentleness inside him will expire, giving way to that horrible mask of stone and he'll hurt me once more. I owe him nothing.

I wrap my fingers around Shaw's knife and while he still touches my skin, I plunge it into the nearest part of him I can reach.

I yank the knife out as Shaw lets out a string of words I don't recognize but are surely a curse. Gripping the blood-soaked handle, I turn to run, but he sweeps my feet out from under me. I shout angrily, the irony of being snared by the same movement cuttingly cruel. I tumble to the ground, spinning myself around just in time to see Shaw throw himself at me. Even injured, he is terrifyingly fast.

Our bodies tangle as we grapple for the dagger. Shaw emits a sound more akin to a wild animal than a man. His body is heavy against mine, pressing me into the cavern floor. I know nothing of self-defense, or apparently where to stab someone to incapacitate them, but I did grow up with a brother. I bring my knee up as hard as I can between Shaw's legs.

He lets out another curse and his hand loosens fractionally. I bring the knife up again, slicing at his chest. The makeshift tourniquet flutters from his shoulder to the ground, a forgotten white flag, as Shaw roars in pain. My feet slip against the limestone as I slither out from under him.

I leap over him as his hand grapples for my ankle. Missing his fingers, I don't get far before one of his long legs catches me. I sprawl forward and it's only the cushion of Shaw's arms that keep me from cracking my skull against the rock. I yelp as he climbs over me, shoving a hard thigh between my legs. He pins my wrist to the ground with his good arm, squeezing until the knife spills from my fingers. I slam my other fist into his injured shoulder, but he doesn't even flinch. Just grits his teeth and pins my other wrist to the ground in a perfunctory manner.

Blood pours from his shoulder wound once more and wells where I sliced him in the chest. It feels scalding as it drips onto my chest and neck. How much pain has he endured that he's able to move through it so well?

I squeeze my eyes shut and let out a scream of rage. He's going to finish what he started and kill me. If he didn't plan to before, stabbing him will certainly have tested the limits of his limited mercy. Maybe I'll get lucky, and he'll bleed out before he can. A girl can hope.

"There it is," Shaw says. His voice is rough and so close that his breath is a warm whisper against my throat.

What?

Unable to quell my incredulity at his sudden change of tone, I open my eyes. He doesn't look angry any longer. He looks almost...amused? He grins, but if his previous smiles were lanterns, this would be a firework. It lights his entire face and for a moment, I can't breathe. I stare at him dumbly. "What are you talking about?"

Does he truly find me attempting to murder him amusing? And if he does, what in Covinus' name is wrong with him?

He tilts his head, his eyes meeting mine. If I were able to move more than an inch, I would rear back from what shines there. Hunger. Wild, frenetic hunger. As his eyes rove down to my mouth, he looks absolutely ravenous. "I thought I saw it when I first met you. But then you were so *willing* to let the world brutalize you, to allow it to blow you around as if you're no more than a leaf in the wind, that I thought I imagined it. But there it is."

I huff impatiently but realize immediately it's the wrong choice as it only further presses my breasts into the unrelenting stone that is Shaw's chest. The friction brings heat to my cheeks. "You thought you saw what?" I grind out, attempting to shimmy one of my legs from underneath his grasp.

Also a mistake. One that brings heat to more than just my face. "Quit talking in riddles and get off me!"

At this, Shaw grins wider. "Make me, Lemming."

"My name is Mirren!" I scream wildly at him.

I try to bring my knee up to his groin once more, but he holds me so tightly, the movement only serves to move our bodies closer together. Every part of me is pressed against every part of him and acute awareness threads through me. I shift, trying to quell the restless agitation that suddenly plagues me, reminiscent of heat lighting on a Similian summer night.

Where did the knife go when Shaw forced it from my hand? It must still be close. If I can distract him long enough, I can—

"If you're thinking of stabbing me again, might I suggest aiming for the neck?" Shaw suggests lazily. "Or the heart. Or really any major organ. You didn't even manage to hit a kidney." He releases the hand pinned by his injured arm. As if daring me to do something with it, he traces a finger across my jaw in a sizzling line of electricity.

I snap my teeth at him and he laughs loudly.

"What is wrong with you?" I huff, thrusting my hands against his chest. He moves off me easily, as if letting me know it is only by his grace he's moving at all. "Are you honestly telling me how to stab you better?"

Shaw shrugs, leaning back so he's perched on his ankles. He twists and yanks up what's left of his undershirt, examining the wound I gave him. After a moment, he says, "You should learn to protect yourself. Especially if you're planning on continuing your suicide mission after we part ways."

I glare at him. "You say it as though it's going to be something amicable. As if I'm still going to be in any condition to leave once you're through with me."

The amusement fades from Shaw's face and something flashes across his features too quickly to place. Embarrassment? Anger? "I told you before, I'm not trying to hurt you."

"Your word is worth nothing. You've already hurt me, Shaw. You *shot* me! The only reason I'm still alive is because you missed!" The violence that was running rampant through me moments before returns with fervor. I hoist myself up and shove him bodily. He stumbles back and I know it's only because he allows it. He's already proven that I won't be able to move him if he doesn't wish to be moved.

His eyes are wide, and he holds up his hands like he comes in peace. As if a man like him can ever come peacefully. "I told you, Mirren, I don't miss."

The sound of my name on his lips is a song, but I force myself to focus beyond it. I narrow my eyes. "What are you saying?"

"I am saying that I *do not miss*," Shaw draws out his words as if I'm being intentionally slow and I have the distinct urge to stab him again.

My fingers wander unbidden to the slice across my cheek. "Are you saying that you...that you grazed my cheek on purpose? That's..." I pause, bewildered. "That's impossible."

He shrugs. "Think what you want, Lemming," he replies, bending to retrieve the dagger from the ground. He swipes it against his pants, clearing the blade of his blood, until it gleams once more. By the Covinus, I actually *stabbed* him.

He pinches the blade between his fingers and holds it out to me, handle first. I watch it warily, as if it's a poisonous snake poised to strike. Shaw laughs dryly. "It's not going to bite. Take it."

I do no such thing. He never does anything without an ulterior motive, even if at the moment, I can't see what it could possibly be. "Why would you give me a knife?" I ask dubiously.

"Well, Lemming, let's see. You've been kidnapped, nearly sold into slavery, and then kidnapped again. Then you were nearly tortured and raped and then, once again, kidnapped. So, it would seem, you are in need of a weapon. And the knowledge of how to use it."

"Half of those things were done to me by you," I point out irritably.

Shaw only shrugs in agreement. He peels my fingers back gently from where they've been clutched in a fist at my side. I ignore the scorching heat that blazes inside me as he places the dagger in my palm. I know nothing of weaponry, but even I can see its beauty. The hilt is curved and though it feels strong, it looks delicate; crafted from ivory and carved with an ornate, trailing design. I allow him to curl his own fingers around mine until the knife is tightly in my grip.

"Why did you come back?"

The question startles me. When I glance up at Shaw, he is watching me intently, the corner of his mouth turned down. "Why didn't you run? I told you to run."

His natural assuredness has given way to abashed quiet. As if the question was pulled from his throat against his will when he isn't even sure he can bear the answer. I wonder again what kind of world has shaped him into what he is, what kind of history makes the worth of his own life something to be questioned.

The answer pours from me, unbidden. "I wouldn't leave you to die."

Shaw considers me for a moment longer, then drops his head and nods. He sucks in a ragged breath, stepping away from me. I feel the lack of him as intensely as his presence.

"I owe you a life debt."

I'm unable to keep the startled gape from my face. "You owe me nothing." Which isn't exactly true, but how does one even begin to tally what the things Shaw has done are worth? Not his life, surely. I already decided no one's life is worth their sins back in the Praeceptor's camp, even if I didn't intend to.

"I have need of you and then I will let you go. And," he hesitates, as if the words pain him. "And once I do, I cannot add another death to my conscience."

Another? How many deaths does he already carry?

"I'll help you do whatever it is you came here to do. To find who you came to find," his eyes plead, for forgiveness or penance, I'm not sure, but I find I can't look away. Because he's offered me the one thing I can't refuse in spite of everything that's happened between us—a way to help Easton.

It's too good to be true, especially coming from Shaw's mouth that is more adept at spewing wry barbs than speaking with any sort of sincerity.

"I'll teach you to use that dagger to protect yourself so that when we do part ways, I'll know that you won't be forced to do anything you do not choose. I will have you safe, Mirren."

Why do I believe him? And why does my name sound so wonderful in his mouth, resonant in that lilting accent of his? Like a breath of Dark World air, clear and sweet. "And what if I choose to use this dagger against you? What if *you're* what makes me feel unsafe?"

Shaw grins so wickedly that blood rushes all the way to my toes. His eyes rake down my body and back up again, lingering overlong on my mouth. I jam it shut quickly. "Feel free to use it against me anytime you like, Lemming."

CHAPTER NINETEEN

Shaw

Wouldn't. The word reverberates through me, bringing with it a wave of awe and relief. And underneath it all, a flash of anger. Mirren said wouldn't, not *couldn't*. It wasn't a result of her Similian conditioning or some misguided sense of altruism ingrained in her since birth; it was her *choice* to throw herself back into danger. And for what? To save the life of the man who brutally abducted her? What kind of person *chooses* that? I still can't decide if it was the height of honor or stupidity.

Mirren peers at me through narrowed eyes. Perhaps it's the blood loss, but I feel lightheaded as I meet her gaze, like my feet aren't quite settled on the ground and my stomach is floating somewhere near my throat. I've already waited far too long to stitch up my shoulder, but bleeding out suddenly doesn't seem nearly as terrifying as Mirren refusing my help.

Let her go.

I should. A decent man would, but I've never had any claim to decency. I want to grip her to me, the way a child selfishly clutches a blanket until it disintegrates. I want to push her away so that she's safe from people like Shivhai and the Praeceptor; from people like *me*. But what I want doesn't even matter, because the fact remains that if I let her leave, Denver will die and all we have worked for will die with him. Nadjaa will fall to the Praeceptor or to Yen Girene and Ferusa's only free city will be no more.

"Why would you help me?"

I lick my lips. They are bone dry.

The iron that's been clamped around my heart since Mirren's scream echoed through the camp has yet to fully lift, even as she stands before me. Alive. Relatively unharmed. Well, unharmed enough to stab me anyway. "I owe you a life debt," I tell her again.

My shoulder has gone numb. It's only a matter of time before the wounds at my chest, stomach and side follow suit. Soon, the shock will set in completely and the shaking will be so bad I won't be able to hold a needle. But I'm alive and that's more than I expected. And it's thanks to the girl standing in front of me, eyes burning with a fire that feels familiar. That feels like home.

She nibbles on her bottom lip, eyeing me doubtfully. I can almost see the wheels turning in her mind, trying to uncover whatever trick I've spun. Something like pride wends through me, that she finally, *finally*, knows I am not to be trusted.

"I can't let you go into the Darkness owing you a life debt."

"You owe me nothing," she says again, her voice brutal.

But I do. More than she knows. After a lifetime of inundation, of scraping and crawling, I almost gave up. I was seconds away from surrendering what little resolve remained and yielding to the Darkness once and for all. The relief I was denied still aches within me, but now, it's accompanied by a deep wave of shame. I almost gave up knowing that Denver is still in the grips of the Achijj, probably being tortured as we speak; almost gave up knowing that Max and Calloway would then be the ones to risk their souls to save him. I was so close to foisting my burden on to them, my friends who have loved me when I've done nothing to deserve it. The selfishness would have been unforgivable. And Mirren—she kept me from it. She ran in, hair streaming behind her like some sort of avenging angel and kept that mistake from being added to a list too long to remember. If not for my life, I owe her for that.

"You owe me nothing but my freedom and I demand no less."

She straightens, my cloak billowing around her in the soft cave breeze, my dagger still clutched in her fingers. It's the knife Denver gifted me after I took my vow and I've never been parted from it. The feel of it is as familiar as my own limbs, an extension of myself. I think of the soft velvet of Mirren's hands as I wrapped her fingers around it and feel comforted knowing that a part of me, at least, can keep her from danger.

"You're right. I do owe you freedom."

Her brows lift in a surprise that mirrors my own. Until the words spilled unbidden from my mouth, I still had every intention of taking her to Yen Girene and using her to free Denver, even though I know I would never be able to live with myself after. Maybe this is a different sort of survival instinct, one that strives to protect not only my life, but the pieces of my shattered soul.

"Help me and I will give everything I have to help you in return."

Her eyes spark, wild and hopeful. They are like *home*.

I shake my head. I have no home.

I turn to the far wall of the cave, cradling my left arm gingerly. I run my fingers along the wall, until they scrape across a familiar dip, and then I yank. I grimace in pain as the rock tumbles away, revealing a large hole. This cave was my escape for so many years and I was pleased to discover it hasn't been disturbed. That Cullen never found it.

I stumbled upon it when I was seven by pure chance, injured and desperate for somewhere to hide. Somewhere to nurse my wounds privately. It seemed like the mountain itself opened to me, led me to its heart and from then on, I always kept it stocked for whenever I needed the safety of its womb once more. I haven't been here in nearly seven years, but there are still a few supplies covered in a thick layer of dust. An old pile of bandages and a few jars of herbs. A spare bandolier and a few weapons. A couple canteens.

I reach for the bandages and herbs. For a moment, I am seven once more. On the brink of bleeding out and refusing to give in. I ignore the black that scrapes at the edges of my vision, the cold that descends over my limbs and focus only on the task at hand. I fastidiously grind the herbs into a paste, feeling the weight of Mirren's eyes as I work. The questions in them rub against the back of my neck.

I motion for her to sit and with a haughty glower that makes me bite my lip to keep from laughing, she settles onto the cave floor. I sit facing her, crossing my legs so that we're close enough to touch but aren't. I cradle the pestle gently in the crook of my bad arm. The icy numbness has spread from my fingertips and moves toward my chest. I'm running out of time.

I take a scoop of the herbs onto the tips of my fingers and hold them out to her. A question and an offering.

Will she accept my help? I've taken away her agency since the moment we met, and while nothing I do will ever fix that, I no longer have a desire to make any moves toward her without her permission. The decision lays with her now and it makes me feel lighter than I have in weeks. Like I am finally doing something Denver would approve of.

Mirren watches me for another moment in that peculiar way of hers. Curiously observant, mildly angry, but never scared. Even now, when I betrayed her and *shot* at her, there is still something soft in her face when she looks at me. She nods her assent and extends her hands toward me.

I take her mangled wrists gently into my lap, cringing inwardly. I've seen plenty of injuries in my lifetime, most gruesome enough that they could never be repaired, but these—these are the mark of enslavement. The evil remnant of subjugation. Of stealing someone's life from them. They are raw and swollen and she should never forget it is me who first put them there. I certainly won't.

A wave of nausea roils through me. It's amazing, really. Every time I think I'm as deep into the Darkness as I can fall, I manage to dig deeper. I press my eyes closed until the thought recedes.

I dip a clean rag into the stream and begin to gently dab Mirren's wrists. She sucks in a soft, pained breath and my gaze flicks to the way her teeth worry at her plump bottom lip. Suddenly, my mind is a confused toiling of heat and shame. I force my eyes back to the task at hand.

"Who are you trying to find?"

Mirren doesn't respond, only fixes me with a withering stare. I move to her other wrist, the one that she broke on her first night outside the Boundary. Her skin is warm and soft against mine and I remember how it felt to have my entire body pressed against hers. Soft and yielding, like falling into a warm bath. "My guess is your father."

Her mouth drops open and she inhales sharply, her shock overruling her determination not to speak with me. "How did you—"

I shrug, dipping my fingers into the herbal paste. "If you had parents in Similis, they never would have let you run off into the Dark World by yourself. And I've seen enough people Outcast to know it's almost always adults. Rarely children." I hold up my fingers. "This is going to sting for a moment, but it will ease the pain and prevent infection." I glance up at her to be sure she understands. Her face is still coated in dried blood, and I have the absurd urge to take the cloth and run it over her skin until it shines like moonlight once more.

She hisses through her teeth, but I make quick work of it as I wrap her wrists in bandages. "So, the question is why?"

"Why, what?"

"Why did you break out of Similis and run into the Dark World? No one has been Outcast recently, so it stands to reason your parents were banished some time ago. So, I suppose my question is, why *now?*"

Her tongue darts across her lips as she determines how much to tell me. "My...my brother is ill. Very ill. I need my parents for a donation to save his life."

"Like an organ donation?"

She nods and I let out a hearty laugh that startles us both. "Ha! And you accused *me* of being after your organs! When, really, you're the villainous harvester of peoples' insides." I wiggle my eyebrows and she rolls her eyes ruefully.

Her lips press together as if she is trying not to smile,

and I wonder what it would look like if she did. Or what her laugh sounds like. In our time together, I've never seen so much as an inkling of either. Not that she's had much reason to.

Focus.

I try, but it's becoming difficult. The cave has turned a rosy shade of pink that sparkles where I know shadows should be. I turn from Mirren and cup my hands in the stream, gulping down a few greedy sips and splashing the rest across my face. The icy temperature shocks my system, and the cave returns to its normal hue once more.

"Doesn't..." my voice is hoarse. I'm fading quicker than I thought. I clear my throat and try again. "Doesn't Similis have unparalleled medical care? Isn't that what the whole Binding ceremony is for? To prevent these kinds of things?"

At my mention of the Binding ceremony, Mirren's face flames. I would give anything to know why, but I don't have the strength to press her. Now that I've treated Mirren's injuries, I need to tend to my own. I gather supplies from the cavern wall, a thick needle and sturdy thread. Some alcohol and a few strips of linen. Tremors rock my hand as I attempt to thread the needle. One, two, five tries and it finally goes through. I want to cry out in victory, but the worst is yet to come. I've stitched myself enough times to know that keeping from passing out is the most trying part.

I rip the filthy sleeve of my shirt open and a drunken giggle spills from my lips as the blush on Mirren's cheeks grows deeper. "See something you like, Lemming?"

"I don't see anything," she hisses indignantly, turning her red face from me.

I splash some of the alcohol over my shoulder wound with a snarl and then tip some down the back of my throat. It burns in both places, but I relish the pain because it's all that keeps me conscious. I grind my teeth roughly and shove the needle in.

"The Healer said it's an anomaly. That it happens sometimes and usually they're able to treat it with parental donation, but Easton and I...we don't have any parents."

I focus on her voice as I pull the needle out and push it back in. On the way her tongue rolls the sharp edges of some words and soothes the hard consonants of others.

"They wanted me to give his things back to the community. Like he's already dead," her voice breaks, "as if he never existed at all. And I couldn't—I can't let them do that. I won't." The pure will in her voice warms me to my core. No wonder she's never cowed in fear before me; she has already learned that there are far scarier things in life than dying.

Halfway. I'm almost halfway done. Fresh blood streams from the wound once more and I wonder distantly how much more can possibly be left inside me. It's not the most I've ever bled, but I've never made it this far consciously either. The wound is two to three inches, and I can only hope the soldier's blade didn't damage anything more than muscle. I'm lucky it didn't pass all the way through, or I'd have passed out long before this.

"I will not be collecting your life debt, Shaw."

I meet her fevered stare. Her eyes are so green. It was the first thing I noticed about her in the daylight, for all the wrong reasons. But now, with the entranced haze of blood loss lingering about me, I think I notice them for the right ones.

"But Easton will. I will collect it on his behalf."

I nod, because it's all I can manage. The needle is halfway between out and in and for a moment, I can't remember which way it's supposed to be going. Darkness blurs the edges of my vision.

"Shivhai said you killed his brother."

I jump at her voice, balanced as I am between this world and a land of dreams.

Her words are direct. Brave. And not a question, so I give no answer. I pull the needle back out and a wild snarl erupts from me. I would give my good arm to know what she thinks about Shivhai's words and realize distantly that I only need glance at her face to know. Her emotions are always splashed there, loud and vibrant and impossible to ignore. Shame keeps my eyes downcast. Her thoughts are not for me.

"You would have only been eleven," she says in disbelief. Even in my haze, I know what she seeks. Assuagement that it's impossible, that I'm not the monster who ended that man's life. That she hasn't made the decision to accept the help of a man no better than the gruesome beasts of the Nemoran wood.

I'll give her no such thing. I don't reply, only breathe deeply against the burn of my shoulder.

"You don't have to tell me, Shaw."

Gods help me, I want to. I want to tell her the whole goddamn story, ending with how my soul became fractured enough to kidnap and hurt and ruin her. I never want to tell anyone anything; why do I want to tell her? To earn her forgiveness or scare her away forever?

"I don't care what you've done. And honestly, I don't care what you need me to do to help you, because I'll do anything to save my brother."

Don't say that. Don't ever promise anyone anything. *Especially me.*

I want to tell her this, but the words are lost somewhere

on my tongue. My blood coated fingers fall away from the needle.

"But I need you to tell me something true. Something honest. I need to know you are capable of being sincere. That you will do anything and everything you can to help me find my parents."

My eyes snap to hers and the openness in them guts me. Even now, after everything I've done, she doesn't shy away. Instead, she offers me another opportunity to prove my worth. It makes me so angry I want to shake her; how can she not know that creatures like me will always destroy beautiful things like her? It makes me so light I want to kiss her; how can she know I will give everything I have to become worthy of her faith?

My words float into the blackness before I can say them, but it doesn't matter anyway, does it? I can't remember.

"Tell me something true, Shaw." A command, not from a weak Similian, but from a mighty queen.

My body responds as if she has reigned over me my entire life.

"Anrai." It's hardly a word, and hardly one that matters anymore, but it's all I have left to give her.

Her eyes widen and her lips part. "What?" she breathes.

"Anrai," I repeat hoarsely, "My name is Anrai Shaw."

And then I pass out.

∼

Mirren

It isn't wise to give away one's name so freely in the Dark World.

It's one of the first things Shaw told me when we met, and it was sage advice. It's advantageous to move anonymously through the treachery of this world. If you can't be seen, you can't be hurt. Shaw has gifted me with his anonymity. He's no longer an unknown specter of the night, but something concrete that can be *seen*. After taking so much, he's found a way to give back some of my power and I see it for what it is—an act of contrition.

And then the stubborn ass had the audacity to pass out. Thank the Covinus he was sitting when it happened, because with the way he toppled backward, he would have taken us both out if he'd been at his full height. As it was, his eyes rolled into the back of his head and his tall body crumpled into an unceremonious heap. It's the most ungraceful thing I've ever seen him do.

I dance uncertainly on the spot, hedging glances at his vulnerable body. If even a small part of me doubts Shaw's word, now is the time to leave. He's lost enough blood that he might never wake up and if he does, he'll be in no condition to hunt me down. And this time, I have a horse, even if I barely know how to ride it. I could be long gone by the time Shaw wakes up.

Anrai. By the time *Anrai* wakes up. I say the name out loud, testing its weight in my mouth. Then I flush hotly. How ridiculous. Thankfully, he isn't conscious to witness my insanity.

Shaw is ruthless. He's violent and selfish. He tears his way through every moral boundary he comes across as if they don't exist at all. He's more than capable of finding my father and getting me back to Similis before it's too late. If I can only trust that when it comes time, he won't betray me for his own gains.

There was agony in his eyes when he asked to help me— when he asked *me* to help *him*—a desperate sort of hunger that seemed genuine. It was wide open and vibrant, different than the dispassionate mask he usually dons. He's done horrible things, things I will never begin to understand, but deep down, there is something about him that calls to me. Something I understand in those places I've kept hidden, where the dark and gnarled vines of abandonment and anger live. He is doing this for his father as I am doing it for my brother.

Undoubtedly, Shaw's version of help will require something terrible. But to have his fight, his determination, his *willingness* to do whatever it takes on my side for once—well, it seems like exactly what Easton needs.

The weight of indecision flutters from my shoulders like a bird in flight. My gaze falls on Shaw's prone form and a wave of irritation washes over me. Of course the stubborn ass would rather fall over unconscious than admit he was weak. I consider kicking him for good measure, but instead, walk carefully to his side.

His breathing is labored and uneven and I wish I paid more attention in my volunteer rounds at the Healing Center. Or any attention, really. Luckily for Shaw, I also volunteered at the seamstress. Stitching skin can't be much different than stitching canvas.

I pull Shaw's legs out from under him, setting them straight as if he's merely fallen asleep. I settle myself next to him, eyeing his shoulder warily. Though small in width, the wound is deep and gaping, exposing fascia and muscle. I swallow down my nausea and pinch the needle between my fingers. Before I can reconsider, I plunge it into his skin.

He doesn't even stir and fear presses against my chest. What if he never wakes up?

I work quickly, watching the wound close beneath my ministrations. I tie off the thread with a neat knot. Hitching a breath, I examine which injury to sew up next. The gash across his stomach from Shivhai's sword or the stab wound inflicted by yours truly. The tattered remains of his shirt barely cover him, but they'll need to be removed if I'm to reach the wounds properly.

I hold a deep breath, my lungs feeling oddly devoid of air, and work the fabric up gently. I curse the heat that creeps up my face as my fingers brush Shaw's skin. He is like ice. Worry twines through me. On the few occasions I've touched him, he has always burned. Steeling myself, I tear his shirt, pulling it apart to reveal the planes of his chest and stomach. The slash from Shivhai's sword spreads from his sternum to his ribs, but it isn't deep.

Old scars litter his body, but it's the one that sits on the left side of his chest, gnarled and angry that snags my attention. The man without a soul has a heart.

And at some point, he was stabbed through it.

"So you *did* see something you like!"

Shaw's voice sounds as though it's been dragged over hot coals and is so unexpected that I nearly fall over. My face flaming, I avert my eyes toward the stream, but not before missing the look of pure delight that crosses over his blood crusted features.

"In that case, Lemming, you should light that lantern and get a better look," the haughty tone has returned, but it's edged with exhaustion. As if he doesn't quite have it in him to maintain his obnoxious persona. It would probably take death for him to abandon it completely.

"I am not getting a better look at anything," I snap, failing to keep the scandalized tone from my voice. It's silly that skin has such an effect on me so far out of Similis. Considering the things I've seen in the Dark World, skin should be positively trite at this point. But I can't help but think of it the same way I always have; as something intimate. Private.

Shaw's fingers wander over the needle I discarded in my shock. He raises an eyebrow. "If we don't stitch and wrap this, I'm likely to die of exsanguination. Or at the very least, infection. Seems silly, after all the trouble you went through to save me earlier, to let me die now because of your attraction to me."

I jump and snatch the thread from his head, getting a good look at the victorious glow on his face. Even minutes from unconsciousness, and maybe even death, he's still a bastard. "You can spare me your overblown soliloquy," I mutter. The cool cave air suddenly feels stifling. Shadows dance across the carved planes of his abdomen and I feel a foreign tightening in my own.

"I don't think anything I say is overblown," Shaw replies thoughtfully. He takes a large swig of whatever is in the canteen and then pours it over his wounds with a hiss.

"That's because you're an arrogant ass."

He grins wickedly as I set the needle to him. "I do like the colorful vocabulary you've picked up in your time here."

I shoot him a withering look and pull the needle back out. Stitching a conscious person is much different than an unconscious one and I try not to wince as the wound spills more blood. But Shaw's face is set in stone. A slight twitch of his jaw is the only indicator he feels anything at all.

I work slowly, trying to keep my stitches neat, though I get the feeling Shaw doesn't care either way. His body is a mapwork of scars, all leading to the giant knot stamped above his heart. My mother used to say that every scar is a story. If that is true, Shaw's is a story of pain.

He grunts, startling me from my thoughts. His lips are white, and I wonder if he's going to pass out again. How much blood can someone lose before it can't be replenished? I work quicker. There will be no accolades for neat stitches if he dies before they can be completed.

"You've picked a hell of a time to be silent," Shaw says through gritted teeth, and I realize what he's asking for. A distraction from the pain.

"Why did you kidnap me?"

He lets out a rough laugh. "Going straight for the heart, eh, Lemming?" I only push the needle in once more. "Very well," he agrees as I tie off the final stitch.

I sweep my hands to his side, where the small stab wound puckers. I still don't feel badly about it. Shaw waits, his breath bated with my touch. I press the needle in once more and he lets it out slowly.

"There is a warlord who rules the mountains of the West. They call him their *Achijj*. He's taken someone I care about, and I needed a way to get him back."

"And I'm the way?" I ask doubtfully, meeting his gaze. He studies me somberly and then nods.

"His territory is small, but well-guarded. Yen Girene is surrounded by a stone wall, taller than Boundary and there's no way to sneak in. The only insiders granted permission to enter are traders with...*unique* wares."

I shove the needle in far more roughly than needed. Shaw growls, but there is nothing contrite in my movements as I yank it out and shove it in once more. "Hey!" he cries but falls silent at the mutinous look on my face.

"You were going to *sell* me? That's your plan? Because if you think I'm just going to allow myself to be sold like cattle—"

Shaw shakes his head wildly. "No! I was never planning to sell you and I'm most certainly not going to now. But I need to *pretend* I'm there to sell you. The Achijj has a harem, and he prizes rare women. You will spark his interest and grant me access to the city."

I shake my head in disgust. "The way human life is treated here is despicable. Is this because of the curse? Is that why everyone in the Dark World thinks that lives are a meaningless commodity to be bought and sold?"

Shaw watches me sadly. "It's because in every society, there are always those who value profit over humanity. And stop calling it the Dark World. It's Ferusa."

I look at him in surprise. "What do you mean?"

"Do you honestly think the entire continent is called the Dark World? We may have lost our light, but we haven't lost our history. Similis isn't the center of the world as they teach you to believe. There are places in Ferusa, and beyond that breathe and thrive, even without electricity."

I mull this over as I tie the final knot and lean back to inspect my work. Rough, but the wounds are closed and that's about as much as I can ask for. Pleased, I dip a new cloth into the stream and gently begin to wash away the dried blood around the wounds. Shaw flinches back, staring at me as if I have three heads. "You don't have to do that," he says awkwardly.

"And I suppose you can do it yourself? Rip your stitches open and pass out again? A lot of help you'll be to either of us," I bark. Shaw swallows roughly but allows me to continue without further argument. "Who was taken by the Achijj that you're willing to sell me for?"

"I would never sell anyone. His name is Denver."

I find my rancor slightly soothed at the pronouncement that there are at least *some* lines Shaw isn't willing to cross. "And he's your father?"

Shaw is silent so long I don't think he'll answer. Finally, he says, "Not by blood. But he is important."

I open my mouth to retort that this is obvious, what with his willingness to kidnap me for the sake of this person, but Shaw shakes his head. "Not just to me, but to Ferusa. He can bring light. He might be the only person who can."

Shaw shivers as I run the cloth absently over his chest, considering his words. I've never thought of the Dark World as a living thing, as something that could change and grow. Something that could be better. I've only considered it from beneath a Similian lens, as something different and therefore as something wrong. But what if, just like people themselves, it is capable of so much more?

With a start, I realize that Shaw's skin has been clean for a few moments, and I am still staring at the wound.

Or more accurately, where Shaw's wounds *were*.

I gasp, dropping the cloth in alarm.

I run my hands impulsively over the expanse of his caramel skin, blinking in disbelief. Because where only moments before angry wounds mottled his shoulder and chest is now only smooth, unmarred skin.

CHAPTER TWENTY

Shaw

My shock is reflected in Mirren's eyes. In the drop of her lips. Minutes before, I wasn't even sure I would survive the night, never mind the exceedingly high chance of infection and the probability of never regaining the full use of my shoulder. But now, my shoulder is whole and unblemished. It doesn't even smart as I roll it. The only sign that anything was ever amiss is a pale sliver of skin where Mirren stabbed me.

Because it's new skin. Somehow, I actually *grew* new skin.

I must have lost more blood than I thought.

Mirren closes her mouth, gathering herself. Under other circumstances, I'd enjoy the avid way she stares at me, but as I follow her gaze to my chest, all words die on my lips. It isn't just my shoulder that's healed. It's *every* injury. I extend my leg and my knee no longer smarts, something that has plagued me since I was ten when a fellow soldier shattered my kneecap during a sparring lesson.

Mirren lifts her eyes from my skin, bright emerald

through sooty, dark lashes. They remind me of the sparkling southern seas that surround Tahi Okua, Max's home.

"Where...how..." Mirren appears to have lost her words, a miracle, considering the way she usually struggles to keep them from battling their way out of her mouth. "How do you feel? Do you still feel dizzy?"

I shake my head. The threat of blackness that's edged my vision since we left Cullen's camp has faded, along with the nausea and tremors. I feel better than I have in months. Or maybe ever. "I feel amazing. Better than before."

Her eyes narrow suspiciously. "Are you—" she hesitates.

"Am I what?"

"Are you...can you use magic?"

I bite back a laugh at the absurdity of the idea and instead, just shake my head, still staring at the smooth skin of my side. An odd sense of regret threads through me. My body is decorated with scars from years of pain, but I think I would have enjoyed the scar from Mirren's knife. I could have pictured the flush of her skin and the way it felt to have her pressed against me every time I looked at it.

I shake my head. She is not for me and the sooner I remember that the better off we'll both be.

"No one can *use* magic, Lemming. It doesn't work that way."

She crinkles her brow, her fingers trailing over the space of skin I was just examining. I shiver, and then curse myself for such nonsense. They are only fingers, same as anyone else's.

"The magic of the Dark World," she shakes her head, "of Ferusa," she corrects with a ferocity that brings warmth to my chest. I like the name of my world on her lips. "It's just a myth then?"

"No, it's true. It just...well, it hasn't been seen in a very long time. Since the curse."

"So the curse is real," she mulls this over, dropping her fingers into her lap. I feel the absence of them so acutely that I clear my throat and stand up, just to give my body something to do.

"The curse is very real. It's why nothing electric works outside the Boundary. But magic was never something that people could just wield as they wanted. It comes from the elements, from the earth itself. It's in the sky and the trees and the water. And it chose when it would come and who it would come to. Rumor has it that it was attracted to the strongest emotions—love, hate, sadness. But no one really knows anymore. The land was cursed, and magic disappeared along with the light."

Mirren appears to be somewhere far away from this cave, and I wonder where it is. Then she asks, "Who cursed it?"

I shrug halfheartedly. I'm sure in all Denver's research, he's come across the name, but I've never thought to ask him. The name has never been as important as the repercussions of her decisions. "The name's been lost with time. This land was called something else then, but it was already a wild place before the curse—there were no limits except for one's own conscience. Magic and technology mingled freely, bringing wealth and abundance with them. But where prosperity lives, so does greed. Some stories say the great queen was grieved by the evil that pervaded the land. Other versions say she herself was after power and she wished to curse all those who challenged her. Whatever the reason, her curse doomed everyone to live in Darkness and everything electric in the world went out."

I shove my hands into my pockets. A shiver slides up my spine. I speak of things that don't wish to be spoken of, things ancient and slumbering that would be better left undisturbed. But Mirren soaks up my words as if they are sunshine, basking in them. How she's lived her whole life in a place that shames her thirst for knowledge, I'll never understand. Like Denver, her curiosity is a never-ending appetite that demands to be sated.

"No one can seem to agree on whether she meant to eradicate magic as well, or if magic was even something that *could* be eradicated. Maybe it was a side effect of the curse. But magic isn't the same as it once was. It no longer roams freely. It doesn't frolic with humans or anoint its choices with power."

"It's gone?"

I consider her question. Normally, I'd be the first to say I've never seen any trace of magic, but it isn't the truth. Aggie, my friend, and the woman who made the prediction that led me to Mirren, has always known odd things. Though until I was desperate, I'd always written it off as the harmless ravings of a lonely old woman. I wonder if in a different world, the world of the old gods, she would have been revered. If her visions would have been fully formed instead of the ragged snippets she receives now.

"There are traces of it. But it's muted. Like it's also lost its light."

Mirren stares at the bloodstained cloth she used to clean my wounds. My heart stutters in shame. I shouldn't have allowed her to care for me as she did. Not as I confessed how I planned to use her. As I purposely didn't tell her the entire truth of how I came to find her and what I intended to do with her. I didn't deserve her ministrations and know better than to accept them, but there exists a selfish part of me when it comes to her. A part that clings to whatever it is she deems fit to give. A primal urge, to clutch at the small scraps and declare them something like *mine*. But nothing about Mirren is for men like me.

"Shaw, I think the water healed you."

Her words drag me out of my never-ending cycle of self-flagellation with a start. I eye the cloth she grips in her hand. I vaguely recall her dipping it in the stream, the same stream I've used to clean my wounds since I was a terrified seven-year-old. It didn't heal me then, not even when I was closer to the brink of death than I cared to admit. A child, cleaning burns and slashes. Setting broken bones with dry eyes because there was no one to cry for anyway. No one that would care.

So why would the water heal me now?

"I cleaned all your wounds with it, and you said there was magic in the elements," she presses. She stands, waving the bloody rag in front of her. Her expression is animated and shy all at once, as though she is used to being shamed for her excitement.

"I also said it was attracted to emotion. Is there something you want to tell me, Lemming?"

She glowers, setting her lips in a line. "Maybe it couldn't resist the intense bloodlust that rises in me any time you open your mouth."

I chuckle but fall somber as I gaze at the rag. It seems unlikely that magic, which has been dormant for hundreds of years, would come back to heal *me,* of all people. A liar, a murderer, and a thief doesn't seem like a wise first choice.

My eyes drift to Mirren. Mirren, who is kind and selfless to a fault. Who risked her life to save her brother's then risked it once more to save mine. *She* would be a wise choice to anoint with its power. Because aren't those most suited for power those who will never seek it?

Her gaze meets mine and something stirs in my chest. "Shaw, what does this mean?"

Even though my feet are surefooted on the cave floor, trepidation and excitement flutter within me, as if I teeter atop a precipice. The smallest movement in either direction will have gravity pulling me into something I can't escape. Something that cannot be unfound. Undone.

"If you're right, it means something has awakened."

∽

Mirren

Hours later, I blink up at the inky black that has descended over the cave. I don't remember falling asleep, but it must have been a while ago because night has now decisively fallen. My stomach growls as my eyes finally adjust to the darkness. With a start, I realize Shaw is gone.

I wonder briefly if he's left me now that he's been healed but dismiss the thought as quickly as it comes. Now that I know why Shaw needs me, I'm assured of his continued presence. It's not as if Similian women are easy to come by.

A noise scrapes at the mouth of the cave and cool dread sluices through me. Shaw's bedroll is ruffled, a toppled canteen spilling its contents across the soft fabric. With his usual deliberateness, he never would have left his things this way.

Not unless he was forced.

Something crashes into the dry brush outside, and I grip the dagger I stashed under my pillow. I climb to my feet. The mare chomps happily at a pile of blossoms in the cave corner, paying no attention to me or the commotion outside.

I tense as I creep to the opening, the dagger slick in my hand. Whatever has taken Shaw discounted me as weak, but they are wrong. He's mine now, my ticket to saving Easton's life, and I'll be damned if I let him go without a fight.

I peer around the cave opening and relief washes over me when I spot Shaw. His chest is still bare, agile and gleaming in the moonlight, and he is alone. I walk toward him when he throws a hand out behind him. He clutches his stomach and crouches over the brush, something obviously wrong.

Alarmed, I step toward him. "Shaw..." I call uncertainly.

He shakes his head rapidly and then relieves his stomach of its contents. Our dinner of roots and berries could only be described as paltry at best, but Shaw heaves violently. I hasten toward him, placing my hand on his shoulder gently, the way I would if I were attempting to soothe a frightened animal. With the way Shaw turns toward me, hollow cheeked and fever eyed, I'm not far off. His face is gaunt, as if all his skin is stretched tighter over his bones than usual, and he snarls at me until I remove my hand.

"Are you okay?"

He straightens and swipes at his mouth with his forearm. "I'm fine," his voice is rough, but I don't shy back. Whatever this is, it isn't about me.

"Are you sure? What if you have internal injuries that didn't get healed? Or maybe a head injury—"

"I said I'm fine," he bites out. His face twists into a grin, but it isn't a handsome one. It's humorless and aching.

"And the only thing wrong with my head is something that can't be fixed with magic water."

"What do you—"

He glares at me, his eyes like chips of ice. I almost rear back, but I force myself to stand still. I don't retreat. Not from him. Not anymore. "What's wrong with you?" he demands, his words acerbic. "I'm a monster, aren't I, Mirren?"

My own words, echoed back to me in his voice. But now, they ring false.

"Shouldn't you be happy if I died of internal injuries after everything I've done to you? Why do you even care?"

The question settles in my stomach. "Because of Easton," I answer uncertainly. If Shaw dies, he can't help me find my parents and save Easton. But when I ran to him a moment ago, it wasn't my brother on my mind. Something else drove me to him, something that clutched at my chest.

Shaw laughs mirthlessly. "Well, don't worry. My body is in fine working condition to accompany you across the Dark World."

He turns and retches once more. His body convulses, fighting violently against whatever he's trying to expel. I keep my hand clutched to my side. "Shaw—"

He straightens. His eyes are squeezed tightly shut and his jaw is clenched. And his face is... it is agonized. Like everything that has ever happened in the shadows of the world have come to rest below his skin, tearing at him with their claws. "This just...happens. Sometimes. After a fight," he says quietly, without opening his eyes. Emotion flickers across his face and though I am Similian, I need no tutorage to know this one well. Shame.

Oh. *Oh.*

I think back to every time I've watched Shaw commit

violence, the way he seemed to bask in it as though it were a natural part of him. But I've never seen him afterward, when the threat is gone, and the adrenaline has faded. If I wasn't unconscious, I would have seen the defeated hunch of his shoulders and the lines creasing his face. I would have felt the self-loathing rippling off him in waves.

It's all so recognizable because I've felt it my whole life. Brought by the whispers of my Community and the abandonment of my parents and the restlessness inside me. I have never been able to wash its sticky film from my skin. And here is Shaw—confident, swaggering, infuriating man that he is—drenched in the same acrid feel of it.

When his eyes open, there is no softness in them. "Don't read my weakness as a strength. You should be happy if I die," he says furiously. Anger lines his face and I find that I understand it. It's so much easier to be angry. It swallows the emptiness. "And the next time someone tells you to leave them alone, you should listen. I could have killed you."

"You can't kill me," I tell him softly.

It's the wrong thing to say. He stalks toward me, fury rippling from him. "*Yes*, I can," his voice is low. "The curse doesn't keep Ferusians from killing each other, Lemming. It only demands a sacrifice in return. And if you are willing to pay it, there's no limit to the amount of blood you can spill."

My voice is hollow. "What's the sacrifice?"

But I already know, somewhere deep down.

"Your soul," Shaw growls. "Every kill tears a piece from your soul and takes it wherever the dead go, as payment."

My throat feels dry. "And you have..."

He bares his teeth and I realize he means to scare me. That his shame lies in more than his heart. It is a beast that lashes out at anything that gets too close to him, keeping him safe but forever alone. "I've paid it tenfold, Lemming. Over and over again, until I became this. *A soulless monster.*"

I breathe in deeply, the night air cool in my lungs. "You are not a monster," I tell him and as the words leave me, I realize its truth. A monster, soulless or otherwise, doesn't agonize over every wrong he's committed. I remember the things Shaw has said about himself, behind the aloof curtain and the mask of stone. Somewhere inside of him, there is something that strives to be good. Something he punishes himself with every time he finds himself lacking.

Peace settles within me. I wasn't being naïve when I thought I saw his humanity. I was simply recognizing what is there, believing in what he can't seem to believe for himself.

Shaw shakes his head dismissively and makes to storm back to the cave. Before he can, I reach out and brush his hand with mine. He freezes, his gaze coming to mine, wide and pale. His chest moves with heavy breath as he wars with the need to prove me wrong. And the need to prove me right.

But he doesn't need to prove anything to me. It has already been done. "You are not a monster, Anrai Shaw."

I drop his hand and turn back toward the cave.

~

An absurd part of me hesitates as we prepare to leave. The morning sun has risen, and the sky is clear behind the snow-capped mountains that linger before us. The cave was a shelter not only from the dangers of the outside world, but also from the danger of ourselves. When we leave, the comfortable understanding we came to will be exposed to the open air, molding it into something different.

Be brave, Mirren.

"Good morning, my little hummingbird," I coo at the sleek mare, offering up a few blossoms I picked from the mountainside. She nudges me appreciatively, her silky lips brushing against my palm and curling around the flowers.

Shaw cocks an eyebrow as he secures the last of our supplies to the horse's back. We pilfered what we could from the cave wall, what hadn't been ravaged by time. It isn't much, but it's a good deal more than we had when we got here. "Hummingbird?" he asks skeptically. He tugs on his knots, testing their security.

I shrug, petting her nose gently as she munches. "She flits over the ground so fast, it's impossible to see her feet. Like a hummingbird and its wings."

"I cannot possibly ride a horse named Hummingbird," he scoffs.

"Well, I can't possibly ride an unnamed horse. What would you call her, then?"

Shaw answers immediately. "Dahiitii."

I twist my lips derisively, not caring to admit the name has a certain ring to it. "And I suppose that means something tragically brutal, does it? Something ridiculous like 'flight of death' or 'blood thunder'?"

Shaw wraps his fingers around my waist and my chest flutters as he sets me on Dahiitii with a smile. The one that reveals the hidden dimple on his cheek. "Of course not. It means Hummingbird."

I shift primly in the saddle, secretly pleased. Shaw takes hold of Dahiitii's reins and begins down the rocky path. He moves carefully, his feet soundless. Words have teetered at the edge of my mouth since last night, when he was raw and angry, but I've yet to find the right time to say them. It isn't something that comes easily to me, admitting I was wrong. Admitting I needed help. But in light of what we've been through, of what Shaw has done for me and what he's promised to do in the future, I can swallow my pride, if only for a moment.

"I never said thank you."

"For what?" he replies absently, not bothering to look back. His eyes scan the trees in that restless way of his. As if the forest itself will attack us at any moment. I no longer find the idea is as outlandish as I once did.

"For saving my life."

His shoulders sag slightly, but he doesn't break stride. "There isn't anything to thank me for."

I glare at his back. I should have expected he wouldn't make this easy for me. "I mean, I know I was in the camp in the first place because I was escaping you. But you didn't have to come back. And you did. Thank you."

Shaw stops so abruptly that he startles both Dahiitii and me. He whips around, his eyes flashing. "Don't look at me like that," he barks. His voice is acidic.

I steel myself. We've barely made it ten strides from the cave and already, the solid ground between us is in upheaval, fracturing and colliding on the waves of his ever-changing moods. "Like what?" I shout in bewilderment.

"Like I'm some sort of hero," he glares at me as if I've lobbed the worst insult imaginable at him. My surprise quickly dissolves into irritation.

"I most certainly didn't call you a hero," I inform him pointedly, now glowering back at him. He is always so quick to crawl under my skin and raise the prickliest parts of myself. Parts with no patience, that are better left to the shadows. "But you saved me nonetheless."

He breathes out of his nostrils loudly. "Stop it! I told you last night don't try to see the good in me, Lemming. I was born in the Darkness, and I am the Darkness. And you were well on your way to Shivhai's needle when I arrived. Had I given you a few more minutes, you wouldn't have needed me at all."

"If you'd given me a few more minutes, Shivhai would have raped and murdered me!"

Shaw shakes his head angrily. "*You* freed those slaves, and *you* are the one who stopped Shivhai. You are clever and quick, and you need *no one* to save you," he growls the words so aggressively that it takes me a moment to realize it's a compliment. Or at least, as close to one as Shaw has ever come. "You can save yourself. Anyone that tells you differently is only trying to hurt you."

I stare at him dumbly, unsure whether to be angry or flattered. I decide to be both. "Why do you have to turn everything into an argument? Can't you just say 'you're welcome'? You saved me, you pigheaded bastard, and I'm going to thank you for it whether you like it or not."

Shaw's mouth twists as if he can't decide whether to laugh or lash out. Instead, he whips back around with a muttered curse and tugs on Dahiitii's reins. In a moment, we're moving once more.

I stare daggers into Shaw's back, hoping he can feel every one burning into him. He'd deserve it with the way he insists on throwing my kindness back in my face like it's an abominable weakness. "Where are we going?" I bite out as we reach the bottom of the ravine. "Are we meeting Max and Calloway?"

The mention of his friends tightens something in his jaw. "No. We're too far off track to meet them in Havay now. We'll just have to hope they don't wait for us."

The trees clear and the path grows wider. Shaw swings himself up behind me, moving as if he was never injured. He tucks me in close to his chest, arranging his arms around me as he untangles the reins. He smells wild and I pray he doesn't notice the way my face flushes as so many parts of him brush so many parts of mine. His legs tighten against my thighs and my heart flutters frenetically. If we ride like this all day, I've the absurd notion that it will flutter right out of my chest.

"We're going to Nadjaa," his voice is a hot whisper against my neck, and I suddenly can't remember why I was angry, "the moon city."

CHAPTER
TWENTY-ONE

Mirren

The next few days are a blur of hard travel and cold nights. Dahiitii is strong and we ride fast, only stopping when the moon is highest to get a few hours' sleep. Shaw directs us over meadows with long, amber grasses that sparkle in the sunshine, across rushing streams and in and out of a forest whose trees seem to whisper in recognition of the magic that touched his skin.

After the first few hours of stubborn silence, my curiosity about Ferusa wins out over my need to punish Shaw's unpleasantness. He tells me stories of the old magic, of people flying wherever they wished and building towers that reached the clouds. He tells me of the old gods, a race borne of magic and nature, that spent their time warring with each other and tricking humans. It's too fantastical to be true, but Shaw weaves his words into a comforting and alluring melody, and I find that hours pass easily listening to his stories.

I pepper him with questions, and he answers them all with surprising patience. It's unsettling, at first, to be allowed to ask whatever I wish; to be encouraged for it. Shaw is a willing teacher, if a bit gruff, but as the days pass, I find his candor bolsters my own.

He tells me of Nadjaa, the moon city, so named because of where it sits at the base of the next mountain range. At certain times of the month, the moon hangs so low and large in the sky, Shaw says it looks like the city streets lead straight toward its glowing orb. Like you could walk down any one of them and end up in the sky. He describes Nadjaa's colorful houses and windswept market square; the black waters of the bay that teem with boats and the wild, cerulean waves of a large sea in the distance. My mouth waters when he explains the scents that waft from the eateries, and I spend more time than I care to admit imagining a place where eating is something done for pleasure and not just for nourishment. Where taste is an art, not an afterthought.

I find myself longing for a place I've never seen. Shaw calls it the free city, Denver's dream for the Dark World made real. A place where everyone's voice matters, individual in their tone but melodic in the way they work together. It's where Shaw usually lives, though I notice he avoids calling it home. I wonder if a man like him will ever really be home, or if there will always be another wind, another sky, that pulls at his restless heart.

One evening, after five days of riding, we stop at the base of a mountain pass, hidden in a small outcrop of boulders. Shaw is meticulous in selecting our camps, always opting for somewhere defensible and sheltered. Even as the days pass, I still tense with every odd rustle of the trees, expecting Shivhai will appear to exact his revenge at any moment.

"Nadjaa is on the other side of this pass, but it's steep

and I don't fancy having to cross it in the dark. We'll stop here for the night and reach the city tomorrow afternoon."

I nod my agreement and slide off Dahiitii ungracefully. My feet bounce off the ground and I topple into an unceremonious pile next to her. I'm too tired to care whether Shaw witnesses the display. I drag myself to my feet with a mumbled curse. My thighs and backside ache and the only thing that has kept the blisters manageable is the poultice Shaw mixed for me without comment a few days prior.

"Stay here," he instructs gruffly, "I'm going to find us something to eat, and I don't want to come back to you tied up. Again."

I roll my eyes, his words unnecessary. We've fallen into something of a routine during the course of our travels. Shaw taught me early on to start a fire, a skill he repeatedly admonished me for venturing into Ferusa without. Legs throbbing, I get to the task quickly as he disappears into the woods.

The fire blazes by the time Shaw returns and I've already sidled up to the dancing flames. The warmth seeps into my bones and the ache of the day begins to wash away. Shaw settles across from me and begins skinning a rabbit. It turned my stomach the first few times, but it's become as commonplace as sleeping under the open sky. Still, I'm thankful he has never forced me to learn *that* particular skill.

He skewers the rabbit and after a few minutes, the smell of cooking meat wafts over our camp. My stomach growls loudly and my mouth waters as I inhale. Birds warble from the trees, harmonizing with the clicking of insect wings and the rustle of leaves, and for a moment, I feel my insignificance. The world is so large, and I've only seen such a small corner. The open expanse beckons, promising freedom in its breeze.

Content, if not sore, I ask sleepily, "Is it always like this?"

Shaw glances up from the dagger he sharpens. The firelight reflects in his pale eyes, bathing them in shades of gold. "Like what?"

"Like this? So..." I struggle for the right word, "so wild."

"There is peace in the untamed wilds. Of the world and of the heart," Shaw recites. The words send an electric jolt through me.

"Is that...is that another story?"

"It's a poem. And don't ask me to recite the rest because I read it a long time ago and didn't care for it."

Poem. I try the word out, appreciating the soft way it brushes my lips. Shaw tilts his head and I blush fiercely.

He doesn't mock me, however. Instead, he examines me as if trying to put something together. Finally, he asks, "you don't have books in Similis, do you?"

I shift uncomfortably, feeling defensive. "Of course, we do. I've read every textbook for my year and those for two years above me." It suddenly seems important that he know this; that he believe I'm not a complete imbecile. I may not be adept at the survival skills that come easily to his hands, but I'm capable of doing math and sciences. "It's just that...well, books back home are for teaching you something. They aren't for pleasure."

If possible, Shaw looks more horrified than when I set the yamardu on him. His brows lower and his mouth drops open as if I've announced an intent to dance naked through the metropolis. "*All* books should teach you something, Lemming, but they shouldn't hit you over the head with it and they sure as hell should be pleasurable while doing it. They should teach by making you *feel* something."

I ignore that blatant shiver that washes over me at Shaw's pronouncement of the word 'pleasurable'. A word that conjures decadent, languishing images. I press my teeth into my lip. I most certainly don't care what Shaw finds pleasurable.

He takes my silence as a sign of disagreement, pressing on. "Books are the world's first magic. Stories are our history and culture; our past and our present. If you don't have them, you'd lose who you were and who you strive to be." He shakes his head exasperatedly. "I have a ton of books in Nadjaa. I'll give you some when we get there." He eyes me doubtfully. "You *can* read, right?"

I nod mutinously and pointedly change the subject. "After Nadjaa, how long until we start searching for my parents?"

It's something that has weighed heavily on my mind. I've done the right thing accepting Shaw's help, but it felt counterintuitive to journey farther away from Easton.

Shaw turns the rabbit over the fire. "We'll only stay a few days in Nadjaa. Enough to recover, gather supplies and reconvene with Max and Cal."

Shaw said little about his friends on the way here. As willingly as he answered my questions about Ferusa at large, his answers about himself were always clipped and pointed. He admitted they're his best friends, a fact I'm still trying to work my head around as Shaw doesn't seem like the type to have *any* friends, let alone best ones. He insisted we will need their help both to rescue Denver and find my parents and I'm sure he's right. If I've learned anything, there is safety in numbers in Ferusa. But dread fills me when I imagine reuniting with the two. It doesn't matter how warm Calloway was, the hatred that glinted in Max's eyes was clear. A week or two apart will have done little to temper it.

"The Achijj's territory is only a day's ride from Nadjaa. And if everything goes according to plan, hopefully we'll be in and out before the sun sets."

Does anything ever go according to plan? I keep this thought to myself.

Shaw watches me across the fire. Now that darkness has fallen more fully, the shadows sharpen the planes of his face. "I'm still not sure where to start," he admits thoughtfully, eyeing the coin that still hangs around my neck. I touch it absently. I haven't yet told him it was the catalyst that sent me over the Boundary, but he seems to have guessed it all the same.

Panic rises in my throat, the same that has been threatening to crest over me since I left Similis.

"The world is a big place, Lemming," Shaw says as if I've cast my thoughts into the open air.

"I know that," I bite out. My voice sounds small in the expanse of the forest and my longing for the sweeping adventure of unknown places is overcome by an overwhelming sense of insignificance.

Shaw's face is emotionless. "You've witnessed firsthand the kind of people that lurk outside the Boundary. Lowest of the low, just waiting for easy Lemming targets to be pushed out of the gates," his voice trails off, but he doesn't need to finish his thoughts. He thinks my parents are dead. It's an easy conclusion to come to—*I'd* be dead if it wasn't for Shaw—one that has plagued the depths of my dreams and lined almost every waking moment since I discovered Dark Worlders are capable of killing if they're determined enough.

"They aren't dead," I insist, cringing at the desperate edge of my voice. As if I'm pleading with fate itself. Shaw looks at me sorrowfully and I fight the urge to throw myself at him. How dare he pity me, the boy who is angry and alone, as if *I* am the one in need of it.

I rarely allow myself to think of the last time I saw my father anymore. It's not even really a memory, just a breath of time that has gotten smaller and smaller as the years carry it further away. But I remember his eyes as vividly as if I saw them yesterday. They were—no, *are*—the same shade of green as mine. And the last time I saw him, they twinkled with laughter. We are a muted people, but my father was not. He was vivacious and excited and most importantly, he *dreamed*. He whispered in the darkness of our quarterage, dreams of living and of changing. It's where my voracious appetite for knowledge stems along with my horrendous idea that things can be different than they are. He never took living for granted, even in Similis, and he wouldn't have given up.

"Listen to me," I implore. Shaw straightens at my tone. "I know you don't believe my parents made it very far into Ferusa, but I do. And I will help you save Denver whether or not we find them alive or dead. I just need you to believe that enough to help me in return."

Shaw nods, considering me. "If your parents made it, it was probably as slaves somewhere." His tone is matter of fact, but when he meets me gaze, his face is full of an unassailable intensity that I'm grateful to have on my side. Whatever Shaw's faults, he never retreats. Never surrenders, even when the odds are entirely stacked against him. "But I believe in you, Mirren. And that's enough."

Shaw

Dinner is bland. Food on the road is rarely anything spectacular, but at least when I had my pack, I was able to break up the monotony with a few spices and stale scones. Mirren eats without complaint, as if I've served her a feast. I shudder to think what she eats in Similis that makes unspiced rabbit meat taste so appealing. I resolve to buy her fresh pastries as soon as we arrive in Nadjaa. The kind filled with sugared cream and drizzled in chocolate.

I'm imagining the little sighs of contentment that escape her lips whenever she eats and how much deeper they'd be if chocolate was involved, when a branch snaps to my left. Mirren licks her fingers happily, her pink tongue swirling over the juice, unaware that anything is amiss. But I know the sounds of the woods—had to know, or I never would have survived them—and that sound means one thing. Something, or *someone,* is out there.

I go still and Mirren's eyes widen in dismay. Her fingers fall slowly from her lips as another sound snaps. She is remembering the Ditya wolf and the yamardu, creatures twisted by the Nemoran wood, but we are far enough from that forest a different danger is more likely—one of the human variety.

She moves slowly as to not alert our interloper, but soon enough, her dagger is in her hand. We've trained a little in the few hours we've had along the road, and while it's not nearly enough for her to be competent, it's enough to soothe my raw edge of fear that she will be completely unprotected. After watching her in Cullen's camp, I'm confident she can at least defend herself long enough for me to get to her.

I motion for her to stay still and disappear into the woods, heading in the opposite direction of the commotion. Let whoever it is think I've gone, that Mirren is alone and an easy target, while I circle back and get a good look at who we're dealing with. I was meticulous in covering our tracks, but the Praeceptor's men are resourceful. It's only a matter of time before they hunt us down.

I move silently through the trees, careful of my footfalls against the crunchy leaves, something I do without conscious thought. It was ingrained in me since birth that noise is costly. Deadly. And then reiterated over and over again through blood and fear and pain until I was as silent as a ghost. And as invisible as one.

Another twig snaps. Whoever the intruder, they are either an amateur or confident enough in their skills that the element of surprise isn't needed.

I circle around quickly and peer through the trees. Mirren sits next to the fire, her chestnut mane bathed in flickering gold. All is still. I take a deep breath, allowing the Darkness of the void to flame up inside me until it licks at my fingertips and settles over my mind; hot, pure focus. I slowly withdraw two daggers.

It happens fast. Two of them dart from the trees. Mirren's eyes widen. She stands slowly, slipping her dagger nimbly into the pocket of that gods-awful jumpsuit before her attackers can see. Pride swells in my chest at her fast mind.

"Down on the ground," one of them barks. A man. He holds a standard, low caliber hunting rifle. Not a typical weapon of highwaymen or armed warfare. He shoves Mirren with it and the urge to tear him limb from limb shreds through me. The man is larger than his accomplice, which isn't saying much. Bones protrude from both their bodies in the stark relief only routine hunger brings.

"Please don't hurt me," Mirren whimpers. I almost do a

double take at how easily she slips into that helpless voice. I haven't heard it since before she set the yarmardu on me, this voice that rings with weakness. A character, I now realize, and one she wields with deadly accuracy against those who would underestimate her.

"On the ground," the man says again. It takes me a moment to decipher what's off about his tone. It isn't the voice of a man at all. It's the voice of a frightened boy.

The heat in my veins cools slightly, but I remain wary. I know better than anyone how dangerous a desperate child can be. Mirren lowers herself to the ground with her hands above her head. Her eyes never flick to the trees, never give any indication that I'm somewhere close by.

The boy motions to his accomplice and the smaller one begins to collect our meager supply of belongings. If they're here to rob us, the irony is almost comical; they couldn't have picked worse targets. I'm debating whether or not to simply let them abscond with our meager collection of herbs and bandages when the boy speaks to Mirren once more. "Now your necklace. Give it here."

Her body goes rigid. He means the small strip of fabric tied around her neck, the one that holds a coin worth practically nothing. But in the short time I've known her, Mirren has never taken it off, not even when she was nursing a bruised windpipe. I've watched her fingers drift to it countless times as her mind wandered somewhere far away, as if the touch of its cool metal grounds her. As far as I know, Similians don't make a habit of keeping jewelry —of keeping anything, really. Nothing belongs to them, but the necklace belongs to Mirren. She won't give it up easily.

"Please." Sharpness edges her voice now. Her character is slipping. If the darkness wasn't obstructing my view, I'd see that wild heat flickering in her eyes. "Take anything you want. Just not my necklace."

The boy is harried and anxious. His eyes scan the trees uneasily. He's worried I'll come back. "The necklace!" he snaps and Mirren flinches. For that alone, I'll kill him.

"No."

All lingering traces of Mirren's helplessness dissipates, replaced by that stubborn, fearless edge that sends sparks shooting through my veins. How is it that no one else sees the strong, willful creature that lives inside her? That's been forged in fire and doesn't relent when threatened.

The boy shoves his gun into the back of Mirren's neck and the hair on my arms raises. I prowl closer, as his accomplice dances uncertainly next to him. "Luwei, let's just go. Please."

Her voice is apprehensive. She isn't comfortable with thievery. They aren't professionals. They've probably been driven to this by hunger. But that doesn't discount them. Even the most docile of creatures can be pressed to violence when the life of someone they love is threatened.

"Quiet, Sura. There's nothing else here worth anything." The newly named Luwei presses the shotgun further into Mirren's neck and I vow to shred him apart; to peel the skin from his bones and show him what happens in the Darkness when you leave an ugly mark on something that doesn't belong to you. "Take the necklace off or I'll take it off for you. Your choice."

Maybe it's something like fate that brought Mirren and I together. Maybe it's the old magic, playing with us like puppets on a stage. But I think it's the yawning tempest in us, the storm that never ceases, recognizing itself in one another. Because like whatever lives inside her, I also never relent.

I move like a spring squall over Nadjaa and let my knives fly.

~

Mirren

Shaw's dagger strikes the tree next to Luwei's head. The boy cries out in alarm and twists away from me exactly as Shaw planned. *I do not miss.* By the Covinus, his aim is alarming. Shaw is already on Luwei, one dagger aimed at his throat and another at his spine.

The girl, Sura, screams, all thoughts of robbing us abandoned the moment Luwei is in danger. Luwei struggles, but Shaw only presses the dagger further into his throat until a small trickle of blood spills over his blade. The sight has become disconcertingly familiar in the past few weeks and it's one I hate with my whole being.

Luwei goes still. Sura holds up her own gun, pointing it wildly around the campsite. "Let him go!" Her voice is more of a plea than a demand and I hear something achingly familiar within it. Something that reminds me of Easton. "He doesn't deserve to lose his life!"

Shaw's face twists in a sardonic grin. The pale blue of his eyes sparks with malevolence. "I'm afraid we're in disagreement there." Though he is perfectly still, I know the brutal storm that rages inside him. The one ruthless in its fervor and undeniable in its thirst for justice. "Thieving scum. And probably murderous scum as well if I'd left him to it. I think that's plenty of reasons to forfeit his life."

Luwei's eyes flash and his lower lip trembles. Now that my face is no longer planted in the dirt, I see that he's young. Younger even than I. And terrified.

Sura raises her chin. "Take me if you demand payment."

The way she screamed when Shaw attacked, as if the world would begin and end in Luwei's death, echoes in my heart. The stakes are always so high in Ferusa. For the first time, I realize that the Darkness spoken about isn't part of the curse; it isn't some magical force that twists souls and turns them black—it's the reality of living on the verge of brutal destruction at every moment that shapes people into what they are. And if I grew up here, constantly balanced on the edge of hunger and death, I would be the same.

"It should be my life in forfeit. He only stole because I was starving. Take me."

Sura glances at Luwei and love shines in her eyes. He's her brother, I realize with a start. Doing whatever needed to be done to protect his sister. Surely, even Shaw can respect that.

"He's the one who gave the orders, who threatened our lives. I think we'll see if Luwei here has enough blood to repay what he was trying to steal." Shaw's voice is so casual, it verges on cruel.

"Shaw, no."

His gaze flicks to me and there's nothing of the boy who tended gently to my wounds and lamented the violence he's committed. There is only the cool, unfeeling mask of the man who abducted me with no contrition. He examines me, detached and appraising.

Sura's hood has fallen back, revealing brown skin and high cheek bones and a mouth that would be beautiful if it wasn't wane with malnutrition. "We have some extra from our dinner. Would you like some?" I ask her gently.

She eyes me warily, determining if I'm somehow trying to trick her. The barrel of her gun drops slightly. I motion to the fire where the remainder of our rabbit meat sits, skewered and tender. Sura's tongue darts out, licking her lips, but her eyes flash uncertainly to her brother.

Luwei breathes heavily against Shaw's knife, watching me with wide eyes. My heart cries out for them both, to be so suspicious of an offer of kindness. "Please, you can both eat."

Her worried gaze flicks to Shaw, who hasn't taken his eyes off me. "If they eat, we will go without on the journey tomorrow." His voice is neutral but I've no doubt tomorrow's journey will be filled with a lecture on my naivete. I don't care. I won't let them starve.

I nod. "I know. Let him go."

Shaw doesn't move, a muscle working in his jaw. "He threatened to hurt you. He threatened to shoot you. I won't let him go freely."

I glare at him. "You actually *did* shoot me. Let him go, Shaw."

He's still for so long that I worry he may kill the boy just to spite me. Finally, he purses his lips and removes his knife from Luwei's throat. He shoves the younger boy away from him without taking his eyes off me. Luwei runs to Sura, clasping her to him in a desperate hug. They murmur to each other, tears spilling over cheeks and hands searching faces for any sign of hurt. Longing surges through me. I miss my brother so much and I will never be allowed to show him like that.

Shaw watches the exchange dispassionately before turning back to me. "That heart of yours is going to get us both in trouble someday," he says before stomping toward the fire.

CHAPTER
TWENTY-TWO

Shaw

The mood around the fire is merry, in large part to Mirren's welcoming spirit and appetite for both questions and food. She peppers Luwei and Sura relentlessly with queries about their home and their journey here and they open up to her like petals on a midnight flower. I sit apart, uncomfortable and disquieted against a boulder a few feet from the fire. I begrudgingly admire Mirren for how she turned the siblings so easily to her side, but I can't help but feel unfairly maligned.

We've come a long way from the day I tied her up, but still, she holds her trust out of my reach. I can feel it's edges, the way it dances from my grip every time I reach for it. Are Luwei's crimes against her really less than mine? I answer the thought before it's fully formed. *Of course, they are.* He only threatened them. And judging by the boyish grin that adorns his face now that his belly is full, I'm confident he never would have carried through.

But you will always carry through. For better or worse.

That's the unforgivable thing, the part that Mirren

senses, even if she's never said it. I will always be paying for that viciousness inside me borne of both love and darkness.

"What brings you to Nadjaa?" Mirren asks as Sura licks her fingers clean. The siblings are Xamani, a northern tribe known for their survival skills in the face of some of the harshest winters on the continent. It's odd for members of their tribe to be so far south. They're usually only seen in Nadjaa at the end of summer, looking to trade their furs for supplies. It's far too early in the year for trading and these two are alone.

Luwei's eyes darken. Grief washes over him, so great that I fight the urge to look away. "Our people were attacked. Ambushed. Sura and I only escaped because we were in the pastures with our deer, instead of in the village."

He refers to the deer the Xamani raise as livestock. Solid, like their people, and generally the size of a small house. "Raiders?" I ask the boy gruffly. It would be unusual for a raiding party to venture so far north, but not unheard of. Desperation often pushes people to do things they normally wouldn't.

Luwei meets my eyes and then looks away quickly, shaken by what he sees there. For a moment, I can't hide my surprise. It's the prevailing reaction when people feel my gaze on them, but in the short time I've been with Mirren, who meets my eyes with fire and acid, I've somehow grown unaccustomed to the feeling of being feared.

Luwei shakes his head. "Not like any raiders I've ever seen. They were heavily armed and in uniform. Organized. And they took nothing except for..." His voice trails off.

"Except for people," I finish for him. He stares at the ground and his shoulders sag.

Mirren's eyes find mine in the darkness. Fervor lights them as her mind spins in the same direction as mine. The Praeceptor. His territory borders the Xaman villages. He's never pushed so far north before, deeming it an inhabitable waste of resources, but he always has a strategy. How has he overtaken so many territories without any resistance? And why?

"There were rumors swirling in the villages. Rumors that magic has awoken in the land," Sura says. Mirren looks to her in alarm. "Rumors that someone has uncovered the Dead Prophecy."

"The Dead Prophecy is nonsense," I reply automatically. I've always dismissed rumors of a prophecy that can end the curse as fanciful hopes of the desperate—hope can fill an empty belly almost as surely as food can. But that was before everything. Before Denver was taken and I received a predilection instructing me to find the girl with the sea in her eyes and destroy her. Before that same girl and I witnessed a healing power greater than both our understanding. I would be a fool to write it all off as a coincidence.

Sura shrugs. "It may be nonsense, but the men that attacked our village don't believe it to be."

"What do you mean?"

"They were asking questions," Sura's voice cracks and I understand she means 'interrogating'. "About a visitor to the village a month or so earlier. He was a southerner with an odd accent, and he came to meet with our Kashan," she explains, referring to the Xamani storyteller. Every village has one and they are highly revered, the keeper of history and knowledge. "He was asking questions about the queen's curse. So much of the story has been lost to time, but our Kashanis are meticulous in passing on the legends.

The stranger said the key to discovering the whole of the prophecy was in our stories."

She scrubs at the dirt with her foot. "I don't know if the stranger ever found it, but the men came right after, and they...they tortured our Kashan in front of everyone. They said if...if anyone had any knowledge of the prophecy or the man and didn't bring it forth, they would burn everyone."

"When was your village attacked?" Dread pools in my stomach. I know the answer before Sura speaks it, but it sends a spike of fear through me anyway.

"The day of the full moon. A month ago."

The full moon is a celebratory night in Nadjaa, an easy one to remember. People gather in the streets, eating and dancing and bathing in the lunar light. The bay is a riot of brightly lit boats, all swirling through the reflection of the moon. Denver, as the city's Chancellor, rarely misses a celebration but he missed the last one. He packed for a long journey and only told us it was in regard to an important matter and that he had to go alone.

He never returned.

A southerner with an odd accent—it can only be him and the odd way he speaks, as if he isn't really *from* anywhere. And the prophecy...

I want to throttle myself for not putting it together earlier. Denver's always taken a keen interest in history, but I never imagined it would extend as far as hunting down the words to a lost prophecy. What if he succeeded and has a way to bring magic back? As if in answer, my shoulder throbs.

What if he already succeeded? Was *that* why he was taken?

If magic is brought back, Ferusa will be thrown into turmoil. The warlords won't rest until they claim such power for themselves. Balance may be restored, but at what cost?

My eyes flick to Mirren. Icy fear slides down my spine.

When Denver never returned, I grew desperate for a way to find him. I tore through Ferusa, through cities and farms, but it was as if he'd disappeared from the continent completely. Defeated, I'd gone to Aggie. Depending on who you asked, the old woman was either completely mad or gifted with a power that hasn't been seen since the dead gods. The power of knowledge.

I was a gangly thirteen-year-old when I met her; she'd called me by my full name and asked if I was there to usher her into the Darkness, like she knew exactly who I was. I've been wary of the knowledge she somehow possesses ever since, but Denver's disappearance had me begging her to use it. And that's when her voice grew dark, and her eyes rolled into her head, and she spouted the words that led me to Mirren.

Destroy her. She who captures the sea in her eyes, bound without hate or love. Destroy her and the lost shall be found.

It was the only clue I had to go on. Finding and destroying an innocent girl. It was horrific, but I dipped into the unfeeling mask that kept me alive as a child and pushed all my morality to the bottom of the abyss. Denver saved my life and there was nothing I wouldn't do to repay him, no one I wouldn't sacrifice. And abducting Mirren *had* led me to his location with the information provided by that disgusting Boundary hunter.

But that was before I saw her, knew her. Before I saw the bravery that thrives within her, the heart that beats outside her chest.

And after—after, the thought of it was impossible. I know where Denver is and that has to be enough. I've held onto the idea that we can gain access to Yen Girene and then escape together. That I can keep her safe.

Shivers run up my spine and I get the overwhelming sense we are only pieces on a chessboard; that a game is being played we don't yet understand. If Mirren is the key to some old prophecy, if magic itself led me to finding her, she's in more danger than ever. There's nothing the power hungry of the Dark World won't do to find her and wield her for themselves.

"We're going to Nadjaa to find the southerner," Luwei says. I look to him in alarm. "Sura was training with the Kashan. We're going to help him with the prophecy."

Sura nods emphatically. "What I know is only a fraction of our Kashan's knowledge, but I will do everything I can to honor him. To revive magic and bring balance back to the land."

Balance.

It's what Denver has always talked about. He believes law and freedom are both needed. That the world is off kilter, Similis and Ferusa each pulling in a different direction, and that restoring balance is the only thing that will bring prosperity to all. If the passion with which he speaks wasn't enough for me to believe, the moon city, in all its glory, convinced me beyond a doubt. It's what we've worked for since Denver found me all those years ago. What I still work for now, in my own crude way.

Later, when the soft snores of the others fill the camp, sleep doesn't come to me. Instead, I close my eyes to waking nightmares of burning villages and unrestrained magic. And Mirren, the sea in her eyes, standing in the midst of it all.

Mirren

We bid goodbye to Sura and Luwei the next morning. The siblings have no horse, and we cannot afford to slow, but the farewell aches nonetheless. Sura hugs me before we depart and my heart swells in my chest. It's the first time I can recall being hugged by a friend and when she lets go, it is far too soon. Luwei nods his head with an earnest 'thank you' as Shaw lifts me onto Dahiitii.

"When your journey is over, we'll find you in Nadjaa," Sura promises. I nod, my throat tight. I can't tell her that when this is over, if I'm even alive, I'll be on my way back to Similis. That I won't ever get the chance to enjoy the company of someone who actually seems to enjoy mine in return.

Shaw, who remained willfully silent most of the evening and has continued the trend into the dawn hours, settles himself behind me. He takes the reins, pulling me tight against him, and some of the chill that came with leaving Sura's embrace is sated by his warmth.

"Stay off the roads," he barks at Luwei. The younger man's eyes widen in surprise. It's the first thing Shaw has said to him all morning.

I feel like elbowing him for his gruff manner. The siblings have been through hell and back. They aren't deserving of his sour nature.

"When you get to Nadjaa, go to Evie's boarding house and tell her Shaw sent you. Eat whatever you want and wait there for me. I'll find you in a few weeks." I gape at him in surprise as Shaw clicks his tongue and Dahiitii speeds off.

The mountain pass is a treacherously narrow avenue situated between a rock face and a steep cliff wall. Littered with loose gravel and large boulders that plunge off the ravine, echoing into the unfathomable depths, I can see Shaw's wisdom in waiting until the morning to traverse it. The height is dizzying as I stare down the sheer drop and I resist the urge to squeeze my eyes shut until we're past it.

After a while, the path becomes even more precarious and we hop off Dahiitii, navigating the rest on foot. It's slower going, but I feel steadier on the ground than atop the towering mount.

"Is Denver the man that Sura and Luwei talked about? Is he the southerner?"

Shaw's eyes widen. Something that looks suspiciously like fear flickers across his face so quickly, I can't be sure it's what I've seen. He nods his head. "He fits the description. And he packed for a long journey, though he never said where he was going."

"Is that what you meant when you said he was going to bring light to the Dark World? Magic?"

Shaw lets out a strained laugh. "No, not really. I had no idea Denver was interested in the Dead Prophecy. I was referring to what he's been committed to building in the concrete."

"And what's that?"

Shaw shrugs, but it's clear he isn't as nonchalant as he lets on. That Denver, and his visions for the world, are important to him. "A better world. He's already done it with Nadjaa. When Denver first settled there, it was the same as every other Dark World city. Poor, hungry, plagued with violence. Warlords have fought over it for centuries because of its location and the violence had left its people destitute and the city in ruins. But Denver worked to bring the people together. He gave them a voice in how their city was run. In what laws would govern it and what goals they had for it. He allowed them to choose if they would join the ranks to protect it, and in doing so, created a fiercely loyal guard. It wasn't magic…but it felt like it."

"Ferusians are resistant to it. They're suspicious of anything limiting the freedoms they have, and they're scared of the reactions of the warlords, and rightfully so. It's been a long, grueling process, but he dreams of something greater and it's contagious."

My foot slips, but Shaw's hand steadies me before I even cry out. I flash him a grateful look. "How did you come to be with Denver?"

He's silent so long I don't think he'll answer. He keeps everything about him tightly wrapped in an impenetrable veil. The little I know of him is only a vague combination of clipped words and gut feeling. When he answers, it feels as though I've won a hard-earned battle. "I had a…different sort of life before I met him."

"Different than kidnapping women and storming evil warlord camps, you mean?"

Shaw rolls his eyes. "Okay, so not that different, I guess. But lonelier. I had no one when I met him. Nothing but hunger and the Darkness."

That's why, beneath all his bluster last night, he didn't stop me from feeding Sura and Luwei. Why he swelled in admiration; because he's intimately familiar with the ache of hunger.

"Denver found me and took me in when I was twelve. He educated me, gave me something better to believe in. Something bigger than myself."

"He gave you a home."

Shaw shrugs. "He gave me somewhere to go, at the very least."

Again, he avoids the word *home*. What is it about the word that makes him hold it at such a distance? Almost as if he doesn't deserve to use the term. I'm about to ask when we reach the crest of the trail, and my breath leaves me in a veritable gust. The trail winds down the jagged mountain edge, before flattening out and giving way to a lush green valley. And there, nestled between the next mountain range and the sparkling turquoise waters of the sea, is Nadjaa. The most beautiful place I've ever seen.

A shiver runs over my skin as I realize it *isn't* the first time I've seen it. For the city that sprawls below us is the same imprinted on the coin hanging around my neck.

CHAPTER
TWENTY-THREE

Mirren

I breathe in the abundance of life that teems from Nadjaa's wide streets greedily, as if it's oxygen that's been starved from my lungs. People are everywhere, the different shades of their skin creating a rainbow as enviable as the houses that sprawl across the mountain. Excited chatter and various chords of music spill into the public space from open windows creating an exuberant symphony I'm eager to be a part of. Shaw wraps his cloak around my shoulders and pulls the hood over my head, shadowing my face. He steers Dahiitii away from the clamor, turning instead down a deserted street that leads around the edge of the city.

Disappointment threads through me. "We aren't going to the marketplace?"

On our way down the pass, I glimpsed the way the city threaded itself across the valley and up the mountain. The most bustling section, the market where sailors sell their wares and shops line the cobble stone, hugs the curve of the bay. The Bay of Reflection, Shaw told me, named for the way the entirety of its black waters reflect the moon once a lunar cycle.

"Not with you looking like that."

I peer down dubiously. My jumpsuit is stained with dirt and blood, the slash marks from Shivhai's knife hastily stitched with the same thick thread I used to sew Shaw's skin. And that is without taking into account my bruised face and throat, the cut on my forehead, and the matted state of my hair. Shaw might have a point.

"The fastest way to the manor is across the bay." He gestures to waters below. "We use small boats to traverse the distance. But with Dahiitii and the state we're both in, it'll be better to take the long way around."

I find that even the long way isn't long enough for me to drink my fill of the city. There are no gray quarterages piled atop one another here. Small, well-kept houses, each painted in splashes of bright color, blend together up the mountain in a rainbow sea. Bright green grasses and trees line the clean, white paved streets. Fresh blooms crawl up trellises and dangle from the sides of buildings. A cool sea breeze threads through open windows, carrying with it the scent of baking delicacies.

We cross a bridge that arches over a sparkling river that curls lazily down the mountain. Nadjaa doesn't possess the quiet of Similis, but an ease settles over me anyway. A feeling of contentment. A small sigh of pleasure escapes me, and Shaw stiffens behind me.

"Will you sit still, you menace?" he growls in my ear. It isn't the first time my movement has seemed to cause him discomfort and I push down the urge to laugh. "We're almost there."

We ride for a quarter of an hour, around the southern side of the bay. Hills guard this side of the bay, miniature versions of the ones that surround the city. The houses here are large and spread further apart, hidden by thick foliage. We turn down a small path, marked only by an unlit lantern and climb it until we are nearly at the top of the largest hill on the outcropping.

A house the size of the Education center sits at the top, looking as if it's stood strong against the sea's repeated attempts to claim it as its own. The bright yellow paint of the exterior is chipped in some places and vines crawl up three fourths of its visage, but I can't help feeling it's the most beautiful house I've ever seen. A large, solid looking staircase rises to stain glassed doors. Balconies carved and gilded with spiraling details frame each of the large windows that line the front.

The house might be pretentious, if not for its apparent disrepair. And for the overgrown fruit trees and flowered bushes that crawl unchecked around the property, each a riot of color.

"Is this where you live?" I ask Shaw, unable to keep the awed tone from my voice.

He chuckles behind me. "Sometimes."

I glare at him. He can never just answer a question directly.

Shaw has barely hopped down from Dahiitii when a blur of red hair bursts from the manor door and shoots down the stairs. Calloway hurtles at Shaw, enveloping him in a hug so vigorous that Shaw rocks back on his heels. I hesitate atop the horse, both uncomfortable and intrigued by such a raw display of affection. "When you didn't meet us, we thought...well, we thought the Praeceptor found you somehow."

"Not the Praeceptor, exactly," Shaw edges vaguely, with a look that clearly says it will be discussed another time.

Calloway's bright smile travels to me. "Well, I've seen worse after a journey with Shaw."

I run my hands over my hair, vainly attempting to smooth it down, but its wildness is resistant. "Um, thank you?"

Calloway laughs as I allow him to help me down, just as the manor door bursts open once more. Max's lanky legs prowl the distance between us, and I force myself not to look away. To remember I'm no longer the cowering girl that Max first met. That I have teeth.

She walks right up to me, her coffee eyes running from my head to my toes. Her mouth twists in distaste. "I see the Lemming is still alive," she announces with disappointment.

"I am."

Shaw doesn't move to intervene. Whether it's because he has faith I'm strong enough to handle Max, or because he craves amusement after a long journey, I don't know. I appreciate it all the same. Max will never respect me if I let Shaw fight my battles for me. "And so is he, thanks to this *Lemming*."

If this surprises her at all, she doesn't show it. Her eyes flick from me in pure dismissal. She says to Shaw, "What were you thinking bringing her here? And why did you not meet us in Havay?" Her face is furious, but there is something behind the anger that denotes what she doesn't say. *She thought he was dead.*

To his credit, Shaw doesn't waver in the face of her anger. He only looks slightly bored, that arrogant grin pulling at his mouth. "We've got a lot to talk about, Maxi."

Max stares at him, as if debating whether murdering him right here in the drive would be worth the effort. Then she makes a humming sound of acknowledgement. "Fine.

But it will have to wait until you've both bathed. You're making my eyes water."

Shaw laughs, enveloping Max in a hug. I watch the way her fingers cling to the back of his shirt. An ugly emotion rears inside me, one with beady eyes and a dark soul. I shove it away as Max and Shaw disappear inside the cavernous house, their whispered bickering trailing behind them.

"You might want to give them a good thirty second head start," Calloway says good naturedly. "The yelling can get pretty loud."

As if on cue, Shaw's curse echoes through the open front door. It's followed by Max's shout that sounds suspiciously like 'you godsdamn bastard'.

"Guess they aren't waiting until after a bath?"

Calloway just shrugs, as if to say he told me so. "Since you're no longer spitting or tied up, is it safe to assume you're now here of your own accord? Or this part of your plan to poison us all in our sleep?"

"If Shaw survived my setting him up to be attacked by a yamardu and was excited by my stabbing him, a little thing like poison would probably only spur him on," I remark dryly, not at all kidding.

Calloway bellows. "No wonder he likes you, you vicious little thing," he says, clapping me on the back. "Knew you had it in you."

He throws his hand around my shoulder cheerfully. I hesitate, still unused to the way touch is so freely given here, but it's different than Shaw's. It's pleasant and warm, but it doesn't burn and spark. "Let's show you to your room, then."

I nod gratefully as he steers me inside the house. Exhaustion that has wavered at the edges, staid by adrenaline and determination, now settles with fervor. It sinks into all my nooks and crannies like quicksand. I hope the manor house has some sort of indoor plumbing. I'd probably commit an untold number of heinous acts at the moment to be granted a hot bath.

The foyer is three stories, bordered on each side by large, swirling staircases that meet at the top of the second floor. As worn as the outside of the manor is, the inside sparkles as if every surface has been lovingly tended to. Cheerful daylight pours in through the large windows and what should feel cold, with its ornate details and marble fixtures, instead feels warm and cozy.

Like a home.

A woman bustles in from a side door looking harried, no doubt a result of the shouts that echo from somewhere beyond her, amplified by the cavernous ceilings and cracked marble floors. "Haven't even had a proper meal and they're already fighting like cats in a barn. Mannerless terrors, the lot of you."

In spite of her words, her tone can only be described as admiring. She waves off the shouts and turns an appraising gaze on me. "And who's our guest, Calloway?"

"This is Mirren. She's Shaw's...uh, friend."

A knowing smile spreads across her face, as if she's aware I'm nothing close to Shaw's friend, but she nods. "Nice to meet you, dear. I'm Rhonwen, house manager. Anything you need while you're here, you be sure to let me know."

Rhonwen is similar in age to Farrah, but far more laugh lines fan out from her eyes and mouth. Gray has begun to creep at the temples of her otherwise chestnut colored bun and though she is short in stature, she appears sturdy. Her hazel eyes travel over me and I run my hand once more over my tangled braid. "You're probably just dying for a bath. Calloway, show her to her room and I'll be up with some fresh towels and hot food."

Calloway nods and turns to head up the stairs, just as a large crashing noise reverberates through the hall. Rhonwen shrieks in objection and hauls off toward Max and Shaw. I consider sticking around to bear witness, but my exhaustion wins out and I follow Calloway up the stairs.

"Who all lives here?" I ask as we steadily ascend, "Is it just you three and Rhonwen?"

"It's us and Denver that live here full time, but the manor is always open to whoever needs it. For a day or a month. Or like us, years."

"So, Denver isn't your..."

Calloway raises a brow in surprise but doesn't seem to share Shaw's reticence in speaking about himself. "My father? No. My family died in a skirmish between warlords near Siralene when I was 14." Sadness borne of old wounds clouds his normally cheerful eyes. "No one wants to take in a boy on the verge of manhood, except maybe a workhouse where I was more likely to die than ever pay off my debts. Denver visited Siralene and he caught me trying to pick his pocket. Instead of turning me in, he took me to Nadjaa and gave me a home."

He says the word home guilelessly, the difference between him and Shaw stark. What happened to Shaw that makes the word 'home' die on his lips?

Calloway reaches the top of the third-floor landing and gestures to the right. "Last door on the left. Make yourself at home. I'll make sure there's some desserts on Rhonwen's tray," he wiggles his eyebrows conspiratorially, and I laugh in spite of myself.

My stomach growls loudly at the thought of food, having been unfortunately empty since the rabbit the night before. "Thank you, Cal," I tell him sincerely.

His face crinkles in a smile, pleased at the use of his nickname. He nods once before heading back down the stairs.

∽

Shaw

"What in the world were you thinking bringing that Lemming here? Into our *home*, Shaw?" Max rounds on me before both my feet manage to cross the threshold. I curse loudly. I knew better than to think her happiness to see me alive would temper the sound lashing I was sure to receive, but I did hope she would at least wait until I got Mirren settled.

And maybe had something to eat.

"You are a godsdamn bastard for doing this to us," she shouts as I usher her into the kitchen. Facing Max on an empty stomach is just poor strategy; sparring with her requires anyone to be at their full strength. The kitchen is warm, a fire already roaring in the open hearth. It smells of freshly baked bread, a scent that always makes me wish I could sink into it like a pillow.

Rhonwen tuts from a scrubbed work-table, a plate of half decorated pastries in front of her. "Welcome home, young man," she says firmly, wiping her floured hands on the front of her apron. I grin at her, swiping two of the pastries and stuffing them into my mouth before Max can make her next attack. Rhonwen shakes her head in disapproval, pushing herself off the stool she's perched on. "I take it from all the squawking we have a guest to greet?"

Max's eyes blaze furiously. "Not a guest, Rhonwen, a *Lemming!*"

The older woman only nods matter-of-factly. "Anyone in need of this home is a guest, Maxwell," she chides, and Max has the good sense to look rebuked.

With a wink at me, Rhonwen disappears into the foyer. For a wistful moment, I wish I could follow; to be the one to show Mirren to her room. To study her face and watch the moment she feels safe and warm and cared for. To see the wonder in her eyes bloom as she takes in the plethora of books contained within this manor. As much information as her thirst for knowledge could ever demand.

I steel myself. Those moments are not for me. But Max's ire is, and I'll take it as long as she needs to give it. Max, my first friend in life, who always feels everything so very deeply. Sometimes I suspect she feels too much, sees so much, that she turns it all to ice before it can overtake her. I knew not arriving in Havay would terrify her, especially with the Praeceptor active in those lands, and that her terror would morph into something wholly more violent. Normally, I would have prepared myself for it, but instead, I spent the latter part of the journey distracted by the feel of Mirren's plush curves nestled deliciously between my legs.

I shake my head. Those curves are also not for me.

"What exactly do you think I've done to us, Maxi? She's one girl and we're only going to be here a few days."

Max crosses her arms and eyes me icily. "You bringing her here is not part of the plan. Her being here is only going to make what you have to do harder."

"You didn't even like the plan in the first place," I point out. Neither of my friends had approved of sacrificing an innocent girl on the half assed whim of a prophecy, but Max, in particular, fought ardently against it for reasons entirely warranted and entirely personal. We went around in circles for days, wasting precious time that the old me would never have given up, because I needed reassurance I wouldn't lose her when I did what needed to be done.

When she finally conceded that it was the only way to save Denver, a man who'd shown her kindness and given her a purpose when her sense of self had been destroyed, it was at great personal sacrifice. She hadn't spoken to me the entire journey to the Boundary.

Max narrows her eyes. "I hated the plan. But *you* convinced me it's what needs to be done. And how are you going to do it, Shaw? You're really going to destroy some poor girl after breaking bread with her in your very own house? Give her over to the Achijj and watch her be thrown off a wall?"

"No one is going to be destroyed," I say quietly.

"What?"

"No one is going to be destroyed," I repeat more forcefully. It's the first time I've voiced it out loud, the insanity of my desire. "Not Mirren. Not Denver. I'm going to save them both."

Max's anger is replaced by alarm. I don't blame her. She knows me inside and out. I always choose the path that makes the most tactical sense. The one that will get me what I need in the most efficient way possible. Following Aggie's prophecy and kidnapping Mirren has already led me to Denver's location. If I somehow destroy her, I know now that I'll find Denver.

This isn't efficient. It isn't even smart. It's something else that I can't examine too closely.

"Shaw, the Achijj's fortress is impossible to get into. We spent days trying to find a way. And if it's that hard to get in, just imagine trying to get out. You're the one that convinced me it can't be done."

I had. The night we discovered Denver's whereabouts, we went over every possibility of how to get into Yen Girene ourselves and leave Mirren out of it. Max's gaze softens, like she's trying to let me down gently. But I've had days to go over every possibility. Days to shore up my resolve so that nothing can crumble it, not even a large dose of reality.

"Denver or Mirren will die, Shaw. That's the only way this ends."

I meet her gaze head on. "It's not the only way."

I walk from the kitchen before I can see the way the meaning of my words crash over her like a tidal wave.

～

Mirren

It feels as though I just laid down on the pillowy mattress when morning dawns. Sunlight pours into the room in buttery streaks. I blink against it blearily, taking a few sleepy moments to decipher where I am. A worn armchair sits in one corner, a heavy armoire in another. Through an airy archway is a sunny bathing chamber, the large iron tub I used yesterday positioned on the far side.

Last night, after Rhonwen deposited a fluffy robe and a heaping plate of food on the small table, I sank into the bath with a delighted squeak. After scrubbing a weeks' worth of filth and blood from my skin and hair, I wrapped myself in the robe and proceeded to devour every last morsel of fruit and flaky pastries. Then I promptly passed out on top of the humongous bed without so much as turning the comforter down. It seems I slept all night.

I push myself up, wiping a trail of drool from my cheek.

Shaw never came to me last night and I wonder how his argument with Max ended. It's the longest we've been apart since I set the yamardu on him and I hate to admit how I've grown used to his presence, sullen and brooding as it may be.

I do the quick math in my head, the same as I've done every morning since I crossed the Boundary. How many days Easton has left based on the Healer's projection. It's morbid, but its finite influence steadies me. I still have time. I haven't failed yet. The faster we rescue Denver, the faster I can find my father and be on my way home to him.

As marooned as I feel, stuck between the need to be doing something to save my brother and Shaw's goals, being at the manor feels wonderful. I've never before had the luxury of so many choices, even if they're as small as what to eat and when. I open the door to the hallway to find a plate of baked goods and a large brown parcel. I take them inside, breathing in the succulent scent of chocolate and cream.

I eat the entire plate of pastries, sucking the sweet cream from my fingertips, before I even consider the parcel. They are so delicious that warmth blooms inside me and though I've only been here for a night, I know with certainty that Shaw didn't exaggerate his stories about Nadjaa's food.

After my appetite is sated, I tear into the parcel. It turns out to be new clothes, soft leggings and jewel-colored tunics. And at the bottom, a stunning emerald-green cloak. I drop the robe and pull on the clothes. They fit perfectly and I wonder how Rhonwen found them on such short notice.

After braiding my hair quickly down my back, I set off

down the hall with the equal intent of exploring the vast manor and of finding Shaw and demanding a plan.

I dash down the stairs and almost immediately collide with Max. She looks to be dressed for some sort of training, clad in a matching set of soft pants and shirt. The dark coils of her hair have been braided and hang in thick ropes down her back. A jewel above her belly button winks next to the thick swirls of her tattoos.

I take a breath.

She stares at me appraisingly, her lush lips turned down in a frown. After a long moment, I realize I've been staring at her mutely and she's waiting for me to speak. I try to move my mouth, but all I manage is a strangled, "hi."

Max rolls her eyes impatiently. "Shaw isn't here," she bites out, pushing past me and continuing down the stairs.

"Where did he go?"

"I'm not his keeper."

It shouldn't matter that he's stepped out, but vulnerability yawns wide in my chest. I brush it off as ridiculous. It's not as if Max is going to turn around and attack me in the middle of the hallway just because Shaw isn't here. At the very least, I'm sure Calloway would attempt to stop her.

I follow her down, about to ask after his whereabouts, when she says, "Cal's also gone for the morning."

I hesitate uncertainly behind her. Both of them are gone? What am I supposed to do while they're out? While away the hours uselessly until one of them deems to tell me what our plan is? I've had enough of being useless.

As if Max senses the sudden shift in my resolve, she turns back to me abruptly, her black boots squeaking against the white marble floor. "Look, I've better things to do than babysit a Lemming. The boys will be back by midmorning, so make yourself scarce until then. Just stay on the property. If you get lost or hurt, I'm sure Shaw will think I did it on purpose to spite him."

There is a small amount of care behind her words, a tenderness when she speaks of Shaw that softens me toward her. I can tell the moment Max senses it, her body stiffening warily, ready to devour any point of weakness. "I've done pettier things in my time, Lemming," she says, with a grin so wicked, it's frightening.

She spins on her heel and disappears down the corridor. The idea of being alone in the huge house with absolute freedom both terrifies and thrills me, but it's the latter I allow to guide my feet, pushing them toward satiating my curiosity. Shaw promised me mountains of books on the way here. If he's forgotten, I intend to get them myself.

I begin my search on the bottom floor and come up empty handed. There's a plethora of unused rooms, most furnished much like mine—comfy and functional. A few of the doors I encounter are locked and I wonder if one of them is Shaw's bedroom. He won't like his privacy violated and definitely wouldn't approve of me snooping through his home, but the idea of more words like the ones he quoted to me in the woods is too strong to ignore.

On the second floor, I come across Rhonwen turning down a set of sheets. She gestures me into the room warmly. "Come, come, Mirren. Did you sleep well? Do you have everything you need?"

Rhonwen seems the type to take my comfort level, or lack thereof, as a personal challenge so I assure her repeatedly that everything is wonderful. "Your scones this morning were so lovely," I tell her sincerely, the memory of their warm chocolate still fresh in my mouth.

She looks befuddled before shaking her head. "You mean from last night? Well thank you, dear, but they weren't anything special. Tonight, you'll get to experience the best confections Nadjaa has to offer."

The scones this morning were still steaming, but the mention of *more* of them distracts me. "Tonight?"

"Oh yes, it's the lunar celebration. Half the city usually turns out for it."

Shaw described the celebration on the way here, how the moon perches itself above the mountain and reflects in the bay and Nadjaa's citizens come to eat, dance, and mingle. I remember clearly, because he said that though the Chancellor usually officiates, attendance isn't mandatory, and the celebration is solely for pleasure. I tried to imagine something like that in Similis, gathering not because we were told to but because we *wanted* to with no agenda other than enjoying our Community. The idea seemed preposterous.

"Rhonwen, do you know where I can find books? Shaw mentioned them on the way here and I would like to read one."

The woman has moved to dusting the desk, her focus drifting from me to the work in front of her. "Oh yes, the boy has a ridiculous collection in his room. Just one door over from yours," she replies absently.

I stare at her for a moment, trying to reconcile Shaw being only one door over while I slept. We slept together under the stars for over a week. Why is it that sleeping in separate rooms with a wall dividing us suddenly seems so much more intimate?

I thank Rhonwen and take the last set of stairs two at a time. Shaw's door looks the same as all the others, solid mahogany set with an iron knob. I try it tentatively and it springs open at once. I don't know what I was expecting; maybe for some sort of elaborate trap to spring forth. Or at the very least, a lock. I huff a deep laugh at my own dramatics and step inside.

The room is neat, bordering on obsessive. Though furnished similarly to mine, Shaw's bedsheets are tucked and folded in a manner that is far more ceremonious than what I just witnessed from Rhonwen. Shined boots form a neat line next to the armoire. There are no discarded clothes strewn about, nothing littered on any of the surfaces. Light pours in from the southern facing window, illuminating the clear air and distinct lack of dust.

I follow the light to the opposite wall where a breath I hadn't even realized I was holding pours out of me in a delighted hum.

Books of every size and color, all stacked neatly on shelves that extend from both floor to ceiling and wall to wall. It's hard to imagine someone as tightly coiled as Shaw sitting quietly in a chair and pouring over every one of these. Is such a thing even possible? Is there enough time in one's life?

The idea of trying sends a thrill of excitement through me. I move to the shelves with reverent fingers, running my hands lightly over each cover. Each title beckons more than the last and for the first time I can remember, I feel as though there is something in the world capable of sating the unyielding need in me. The want for knowledge that has burned, consuming in its urgency, no matter how I've tried to push it down in service of my Community.

I pick up one, two, three books and am about to head toward another when the glint of a metal frame catches my eye. It's the only personal touch in the room, aside from the books, small and compact.

Suddenly, it feels as though all the oxygen has been sucked from the room, as though a tempest sweeps through it and it's all I can do to hold on to something solid. Something flutters, and I can't tell whether it's in me or outside of me. The books I've gathered fall to the floor with unceremonious *thwacks.*

Because a younger version of Shaw peers out at me from the frame. Unsmiling, lankier, but just as handsome as he is now. And next to him, eyes crinkled in a happy grin, is my father.

CHAPTER
TWENTY-FOUR

Shaw

By the time the morning sun spills over the mountain and floods Nadjaa's white streets, I've been wandering for hours. The heart blood of the city has just begun to stir, though the bakers began working only a few hours after midnight. Puffs of flour linger outside their shops like odd little clouds in the dawn light.

I stop at Evie's bakery and boarding house. She greets me with a hand on her wide hips and a warm smile, scolding me for appearing so thin and asking after Max and Cal. I tell her about Luwei and Sura and she assures me she'll look after them until I can make my way back to Nadjaa. She asks if I'm attending tonight's celebration and I mumble a noncommittal response, which she accepts as good-naturedly as she accepts everything else. Evie's shop was one of the first places I discovered after Denver brought me here. She's never once treated me as if I were anything other than an ordinary boy, and in return, I've bought more sweets than any one person should eat.

I order some now, to be delivered to Mirren along with a

parcel of clothes I procured from the seamstress. I check in with a few of Denver's investments to be sure all is well in his absence. Their reception of me is colder than Evie's, but it's more familiar, ranging from abject wariness to outright terror.

After, I ride slowly along the shore. It's faster to take a skiff from the manor to the market, but I opted to ride Dahiitii around the bay instead. The air from the Storven Sea is fresh and crisp and the city gleams in the morning light. I ride through the quiet arts district, it's artists still sleeping off the fervor of the night before, and then through the city center, which has begun to bustle with businessmen and women. The city gleams and breathes and I vow to take Mirren on a tour as soon as she wakes. The clang of merchants bartering at the docks, the ring of children's laughter as they race through the grass, the way the buildings themselves seem alive in the southern sun; I know she'll appreciate the vibrancy of it all after a lifetime of monotony.

I breathe it all in slowly, the place where I was remade. The city has grown so much since Denver and I settled here. It was always a bustling port, but was rarely settled permanently. Its access to the Storven Sea, along with the Averitbas and Shadiil mountain passes, made it a target for warlords and mercenaries, a volatile place with a bustling trade in flesh. Until Denver, I thought the only way to establish order was through violence, but I watched him do it with just his words. He was the first to teach me their power, eventually becoming the latent inspiration for my love of books.

I mutter a curse. I should have left Mirren some books.

I pledge to do it as soon as I return. Her lips will part in excitement and that wild curiosity will spread until she glows with it. Her hands will spread across the pages and then, maybe, across my skin...

I'm ripped abruptly from my daydream.

The man is tall; clean cut and dressed in clothes that are expensive enough to fund a Nadjaan family for well over a year, but it isn't him who caught my attention. It's the two children who trail behind him, tattered clothes open to the crisp spring breeze. A boy and a girl, eyes darting nervously. Their shoulders hunch and when the man turns to speak to them, his tone harsh and clipped, shudders run through their frail bodies. Though the words aren't shouted, the little boy squeezes his eyes shut against them as though this will protect him.

It's a practice I know well, a habit learned from a childhood being exploited instead of protected.

Another man appears from the shadows of the alley. I'm already moving. It isn't the killing calm of the abyss that overtakes me; there is no cool planning, no strategy. There is only the flame of a wildfire, raging and consuming every conscious thought—everything except the need to *hurt*.

The man from the alleyway is on the ground with one well aimed blow to the neck. The first man's mouth gapes wide, like the ghastly maw of a river trout, and I drink his fear in like a fine spirit, savoring the sour taste of it. "Go now," I tell the children. I don't need to look to see if they've obeyed. I know they have, the same way I know the man in front of me is terrified of the punishment he's reaped.

"N-n-now, sir, what is it you're after?" he stammers, his hands raised. "I'm sure we can come to some sort of arrangement. I'm a very rich man, with contacts all around Ferusa—"

I cut off his words with a sharp jab to his stomach. As he doubles over, I bring a fist down on the back of his neck and he sprawls out on the ground, face first. I kick him in the ribs and twist my face in disgust as I notice fat tears pouring over his ruddy face. Of course he's a coward. Too weak to take even a fraction of what he's bestowed on others. The fire inside me surges and I no longer feel the individual lick of flames, only the swirling heat of the whole, a hurricane of ash and rage.

I don't stop to think, don't stop to consider where the fine edge of the man's life resides as I let my fists and feet fly. I can no longer make out his face, no longer see that he was ever a person at all. All I see is the terrified face of that little boy. That, and red—of fire and of blood.

∽

Mirren

I dash from Shaw's room as if a yamardu is hot on my heels. I half sprint, half slide down the three flights of stairs and over the marble floor of the foyer. Rhonwen calls to me, but her voice is lost beneath the rush of blood in my ears. I wave my hand dismissively, hoping she takes the gesture to mean everything is fine even though everything is far from it. I shove my feet haphazardly into my boots, which are now shined and devoid of mud, and take off down the drive without bothering to tie them.

It'd probably be faster to take a horse, at least to the small dock at the end of the manor drive, but the thought of stopping, even for a moment to find where the hell the stables are is unthinkable. It's all I can do not to pull my dagger, to be ready to attack Shaw as soon as I see him; to demand he tell me the truth about why my father's picture is in his room. Why my father's lips are curled in a delighted smile and why his eyes, the same green as mine, are twinkling at *Shaw* when they left me cold and alone.

Why, why, why.

The word rings in my head in time to the stomp of my boots and I break into a sprint.

You know why. You know who your father is to Shaw.

I shove the thoughts away. I refuse to name, refuse to acknowledge what threatens to overtake me, until I hear the words come from Shaw's mouth. Until I hear him tell me himself that my father left his life in Similis to come find a new one in the Dark World. He left his children to find replacements here. That the man who saved Shaw is the same man who damned me to a life of ostracism. Who damned Easton's life.

A wave of nausea roils in my stomach and for a moment, I think it might overtake me. Swallowing, I push my feet faster.

As I clear the thick foliage and reach the lantern that marks the beginning of the drive, I hesitate. The Bay of Reflection sparkles in the morning sun and small boats tied to the dock clink together on the soft waves. I have no idea how to handle a boat, so I turn down the path we took yesterday that leads around the bay.

My breathing is labored as I run toward the city center, the rainbow of houses coming into view. I am debating how in Covinus' name I'm possibly going to find that stubborn ass when a horribly familiar noise draws my attention down one of the quiet streets.

The sound of flesh on flesh.

All thoughts of my father dissipate as unease settles over me.

Shaw, usually the depiction of self-containment, is unbridled chaos. His hair is wild and sweat gleams on his forehead. Blood spatters his face and coats his hands like morbid crimson gloves. With horror, I realize he's crouched above a man. His movements are frenzied as he repeatedly brings his fist down. The man's head lolls listlessly; he's obviously lost consciousness.

My feet are moving before I can consider that the man before me is not the Shaw I know. This is not my friend who teases me about books and protects me from the whims of the world. This is someone to be feared—uncontained madness and violent fury. Shaw has always fought with fervor, but he is also sparing. He never unleashes more of himself than required to temper a situation, never renders more force than necessary. But this—this is whatever burns in his eyes, released and unfettered.

I hold out my hand, approaching him as I would a feral animal. If there was anyone else on the street when this began, they've wisely scattered. It's only Shaw, the unconscious man, and me. "Shaw?"

As if he doesn't hear me, Shaw brings his fist down again. The man's head snaps to the side and then grotesquely rolls back, as if connected to a marionette's string. I know nothing of human anatomy, but my gut tells me he can't take much more. And whatever this man has done, I can't let Shaw kill him. "Shaw!" I yell, louder now. I curl my hand around his shoulder slowly, feeling the muscles pull taut beneath my fingers. "Shaw, you're going to kill him!"

At last, he turns to me. Blood, not his own, speckles his brown skin. Every line of his face is hard and sharp, and his eyes—oh Covinus, his eyes. They are otherworldly in the way they burn, a tempest of fire, so hot that for a moment, I feel frozen by them. I swallow roughly, running my hand across his shoulder and down his arm, touching my skin to his.

I don't consider the action, desperation fueling me. Shaw only regards me coldly. If he refuses to relent, what then? Am I prepared to tackle him? Stab him once more? The last time I stabbed him, it only spurred him further and that was when he was fully present. Now...Now, I know I won't be the one to walk away victorious. But I can't leave.

"Shaw, we need to go," I say, my voice steady but gentle.

Another tense moment passes with bated breath, before Shaw's shoulders finally sag. As if whatever raged inside him burned everything away, leaving him empty. His eyes hollow out and his skin is sallow as I weave my fingers through his. He allows me to lead him to Dahiitii, who mills about a few feet away. I consider how I'm possibly going to get him atop the horse, but he swings himself up without argument and waits silently for me to do the same.

I hoist myself up, settling myself between Shaw's legs. His arms come around me, but the movement feels robotic. I take the reins, leading Dahiitii back toward the manor. When the house comes into view, it occurs to me that walking shell shocked and bloody through Rhonwen's sparkling foyer probably isn't the best idea, so I steer the mare around the house. From up here, the sea sparkles and the air is sweet and fresh.

The path is shaded by thick green trees and climbing vines and the thick foliage provides a welcome relief from the growing heat of the morning. Dahiitii slows to a trot, seeming to know where she's headed. After a few moments, the path opens to a large copse of trees. Ancient and gnarled, they lean over a small pond that hangs out over the cliff edge. The sparkling water looks as if it reaches infinitely into the sky, but really, it pours over a hidden edge, the soft sound calming.

Dahiitii stops and I hop down, a little proud of the fact that I keep to my feet. Shaw leaps to the ground nimbly, immediately turning his back. He curls forward, his hand on a tree trunk in support, and heaves. I look away, certain he doesn't wish me to witness his private shame once more. The sound is heart wrenching, like he seeks to physically expel everything he finds unworthy in himself.

I remember the way I ran a hand over his skin, of the way it seemed to calm him and bring him back to himself. I want to do it again.

But I keep my hands at my sides, walking to the pond's edge instead. The morning has grown warm and damp, the air cloying next to the pond. I carefully roll up my leggings and toss my boots aside. Making my way gingerly down the slick obsidian edge, I sit carefully and prod the cool water with my toes. It feels so heavenly that I wish I could submerge my entire body in its brisk depths and feel it's soft waves lap at my hot scalp.

After a few moments, Shaw sits next to me, plunging his legs into the water without bothering to roll up his pants. The color has returned to his face, his brown skin like warm honey once more. He dunks his hands into the pond and scrubs at his face, the other man's blood washing away in spiraling streams. He seems no more inclined to offer answers than usual, a fact that is vastly irritating and oddly comforting. In this, at least, he's back to normal.

"Who was that?"

Shaw doesn't look at me, instead, studying the ripples of the pond water as if they're intensely interesting. "I wondered how long you'd be able to keep your questions at bay. I'm impressed you lasted this long."

I roll my eyes as a grin tugs at the corner of my lips. He knows me too well already and I'm uncertain whether or not I like it. After the display in town, it should probably terrify me. "Shaw, who was that? I've seen you fight before, but that looked…" I search for the word, something to encompass the primal craze I just witnessed, "different. It looked more…personal." The word comes suddenly, and I know it to be true. That kind of emotion, positive or negative, is intimate. "Did you know him? Has he done something to you?"

He's quiet for a moment. "I don't know him, but it was personal."

I wait for him to continue. I'll wait as long as I have to for him to gather his thoughts, to explain what overtook him.

"He had kids."

I look to him uncertainly and he shakes his head. "He was a slaver. He was trafficking kids."

A surprised breath escapes my lips. It's horrible, what the man was doing, but it doesn't explain Shaw's otherworldly rage. "So did the Praeceptor."

"Cullen is a different beast altogether," he mutters, "and deserves more than a beating in an alley. That man in Nadjaa, he targets children. Grooms them to be what his clients want. To be what he needs," Shaw breathes in sharply. "It's all horrible, I know that. But some things are easier to compartmentalize. To put in a box until you can deal with them. But other things…well, other things rear up and attack. Refuse to be ignored. I saw that little boy and I just…I just lost it."

I mull this over, circling my toes in the water and watching the ripples as they fan out across the water. After a long silence, Shaw speaks once more.

"The reason I can do what I do," he stops. Presses his lips together. Tries again. "I have the skills I have in survival and strategy and warfare because I was trained in them when I was a child. When other kids were learning to walk, I learned to fight. Instead of bedtime stories, I was read war time strategy. I could shoot a gun and wield a sword before most kids can even manage their silverware. When other kids were old enough to help around the farm, I was old enough to go on my first mission."

I furrow my brow. "Why?"

Shaw shrugs. "It's best to train early, when your psyche is still developing so you can be shaped into whatever they need you to be. My father needed a child soldier. An assassin."

My eyes widen as the horror of Shaw's words settle over me. "What use would a child be? That's horrendous!"

"It's just good strategy, actually. One that's been used in warfare for millennia. No one suspects an innocent child of being a spy, so no one guards their words around one. And no one guards their bodies around one because children aren't seen as a threat." His tone is pragmatic and detached, as if he isn't speaking of horrors he himself endured. Hatred for Shaw's father rises within me, for jading his son and for stealing parts of his soul he had no claim to.

"I...I did a lot of horrible things, Mirren. Things that would make you run far away from me. You *should* run still, if you've any sense."

I wave him off. "We have a deal and I'm not going anywhere," I tell him resolutely.

At this, he finally looks at me, his face agonized. "Don't say I didn't warn you."

"Shaw, you've been warning me since the first day I met you. Have I ever listened?"

"You do possess a frightening combination of stubbornness paired with an alarming lack of common sense." His mouth twists in a shy grin and I find that I like it so much more than the one he normally arms himself with. I feel myself wanting to smile back, but I purse my lips instead. Waiting.

Shaw huffs a resigned sigh. "My father caught me once, afterward, during my...my episode," his jaw tightens and he clears his throat, "And let's just say, I learned quickly that my aversion to violence was a weakness. And if I was going to survive, I needed to hide it at any cost. I was never what he wanted. Never ruthless enough, never cruel enough. But I tried for so long. Until I turned all that vileness inward. Until I was poisoned with enough self-hatred that I could have died without caring. Maybe even tried to, inadvertently."

I picture Shaw younger and angrier; the one person who by right was supposed to protect him, instead wielding his hurt and trauma as a weapon for his own gain. I want to reach out to that Shaw, to hold him and tell him he isn't alone. I want to do the same with the version sitting next to me.

"And then I met Max. She's from a wealthy family in the southern isles and they had sold her into a marriage alliance to some foreign *legatus*. He brought her to dinner at my father's home and was showing her off like some prized horse. She was only a year older, but she was already so much braver than I was. The *legatus* had her hands and feet shackled and her mouth gagged because he couldn't control her. At thirteen, after everything she'd seen, she still refused to give in to them. Refused to be broken. Watching her was like waking up after years of sleeping. Whoever I was between missions, when shame and loneliness poured into me, that's who woke up. The boy who could still *feel*, even after his soul had been shattered into a million pieces. And I knew then, that boy would die if I stayed with my father any longer."

"Later that night, I went to my father's study. Like there was some naïve chance of reasoning with him, of convincing him I couldn't do it anymore." Shaw laughs bitterly. "When I got there, I heard furniture crashing and muffled screaming. I ran into the study without being invited, something I'd been beaten for before and my father was…he was holding Max by her hair. The pathetic dress she'd worn was ripped and her eyes were watering."

Suddenly, the look on Shaw's face when he arrived at Shivhai's tent makes sense. To him, history was repeating itself before his eyes.

"My father didn't even look at me. Just ordered me to leave so he could enjoy the *present* the *legatus* had given him. Like she wasn't even human. And something snapped in me." Shaw's eyes shine, but his cheeks are dry. "He didn't see Max as a person, and he'd never see me as one. And as long as I was with him, I had no hope for learning to see myself as one either. He'd forced me to give up pieces of my soul, but it took a thirteen-year-old stranger for me to realize that I would never matter to him. I grabbed a dagger and I plunged it into his heart. I still remember the shock in his eyes, as if he couldn't quite believe the weapon he'd created had turned against him. But the emotion of the moment kept me from thinking strategically. Kept me from remembering that my father was always prepared and most definitely always armed. He had a dagger in my chest before I could even move off him. But it didn't matter. I grabbed Max and we ran until I collapsed."

Max's fierce protectiveness of Shaw, borne of terror and

survival. Shaw granted her freedom; of course, she would love him for it.

Shaw swirls his feet in the water, an oddly restless gesture for him. The preternatural control Shaw has over his body—a result of what he was trained to be. An apex predator. A deadly weapon. "I don't remember a lot of the journey. Max got the knife out and stitched the wound, but I lost a lot of blood and infection set in. I was in and out of consciousness for most of it."

"That's when we found Denver. Or he found us. Either way, it seemed like the will of whatever dead magic still lived in the world for us to be together."

Denver's name clangs through me, harsh and prodding. My *father's* name. Or the one he's gone by since he was Outcast. It seems impossible that they can be the same person. How can the man who gave Shaw a place in the world, be the same one who took Easton's and mine?

Shaw doesn't notice me stiffen beside him at the mention of his mentor's name. His gaze is on the sea in the distance, the white caps of waves foaming on top of the sparkling water. "Denver took me in. He educated me beyond military strategy and weapons. He was the first person in my life to show me kindness, even when I didn't deserve it. He never gave up, even when I was hateful and stubborn. He proved to me over and over that the world isn't all dark. That it can be good and so can the people in it," Shaw's voice trails off, thick with emotion.

My heart breaks open at his confession and I see him clearly for what he is—a boy trying desperately to be good in a world that has not been good to him. A man who tries to earn love through self-sacrifice, even when he doesn't think he deserves it. And Denver—my father—is the first one who made him believe his life is worth something.

I hate my father for it in the same breath that I love him for it, the lines of both emotions crossing so fiercely they fuse together in a hot riot. Of course Denver is my father; how was I so blind to it before? It could only be him, with his passion for life and dreams for a better world that are so vivid, they're contagious. I know those same dreams Shaw speaks of, whispered to me in a quarterage a world away. "He loved you," I finish for Shaw, my throat thick.

He swallows roughly and nods. It costs Shaw something to admit that he is loved, in spite of all his faults, and as surely as I know Denver is my father, I also know I can't tell Shaw now. It would feel wrong, like taking a scrap of bread from a starving man. He's had so little love in his life, I can't bear to take away the small amount he's been offered. Can't bear to be the one to twist it or warp it in any way, to cause him to question its scope and validity. *Another time,* I promise silently.

"I'd never known love before. He forgave me for all the horrible things I'd done. He believes so fiercely that I could," he clears his throat and corrects himself, "*can* be a good person that I almost believe it, too, sometimes. When I was 14, I vowed never to take anyone else's life. It will never be enough, never repay what I've already unleashed upon the world, but it felt like something. And I haven't wavered from it. Not once."

The Boundary hunters who pointed guns at us; all those soldiers, the guards, even Shivhai—Shaw never gravely injured any of them. It struck me as odd then, but now I see it is his act of contrition.

"It isn't your fault what you were forced to do as a child. But I think it's brave, to uphold that vow in a world like this."

He shakes his head and meets my eyes. "It's not brave.

It's necessary. Not even because I may actually lose my soul if I take another life, but because I can't bear it. When I told you I couldn't have the responsibility of your blood on my hands, I meant it. Mirren, I can't... Any more blood and I will lose myself completely. I'm just selfishly trying to hang on to what little is left."

I struggle for the words to explain how his soul, bare and battered, creates an aching whirlwind within me that feels decidedly *unselfish,* but the emotions are lost on my tongue. Encapsulating feelings into words, or even deciphering them into something I can define and hold, isn't something I was allowed the luxury of practicing. When it comes to expressing anything, the Similian rigor in me still freezes my tongue.

Shaw doesn't wait for my reply anyway. Instead, he stands abruptly, peeling his shirt off and tossing it to the shore. My face flames as the bare skin of his chest gleams in the sun and I glance away quickly, but not before glimpsing the look of pure delight cross his face. "What are you doing?" I hiss.

He laughs, a real, ringing sound that lights in my chest. "Swimming, Lemming. Aren't you hot?"

I shake my head stubbornly, ignoring the pools of sweat that have begun to gather beneath my shirt. Has the air always been this sweltering? It was never this hot so early in the year in Similis.

"Suit yourself," Shaw replies with a shrug. I yelp as he dives in, dousing me in a curtain of icy droplets. He surfaces a few moments later near the center of the pond, his dark hair plastered to his forehead. His long lashes bead together, framing his pale blue eyes in a way that makes him look almost innocent. Almost. If it weren't marred by the positively wicked grin that rends his glistening face as he glides toward me.

I'm a fraction of a second too slow in realizing his deviousness and my scrambling is useless against the slick granite as he wraps his fingers around my ankle and pulls me from the shore. It's all I can do to hold my breath as I'm plunged into the brisk depths. Water logs in the fabric of my clothes, weighing me down as I kick out frantically. I struggle for purchase on solid ground, panicking as my lungs threaten to expand in want of air. And then a large hand hauls me up under the arm and pulls me to the surface.

I gasp and choke, certain I'm going to go under again, but Shaw's grip is solid. He guides me closer to the shore, my body feeling oddly weightless in his arms. My toes squelch in the sediment. "You ass!" I shout. "I can't swim!"

Shaw's face is a picture of amusement with no sign of remorse. "That seems quite obvious now. Don't they teach you anything useful in Similis?"

I glower at him indignantly, rivulets of water streaming from my soaking hair. "And just how is swimming useful?"

He is gravely serious as he replies, "Well, it is entirely useful to keep oneself from drowning in a manor pond."

I send a wave splashing at him and he makes no move to dodge it. His mouth parts in surprise and he blinks slowly as water streams down his face. He lets out a laugh that sends something warm shooting through my belly, so I try to splash him again, but my feet slip, sending me careening forward toward another potential drowning. Lightning fast, Shaw catches me and pulls me toward him, hauling me upright. Surprise and shock weave through me. I can only imagine how ridiculous I look, flailing around like a drowned rat; or a drowned lemming. A wild peal of laughter escapes my lips.

It feels so good in my chest and in my belly and in my heart. By the Covinus, how long has it been since I *laughed?* Certainly, not since Easton was diagnosed, but I have the feeling it's been much longer than that. Why is laughter against the Keys, when it makes you feel so airy and light, as if actual sunshine expands in your lungs?

I crack open my eyes to find Shaw, still clutching me around the waist, staring down at me in wonderment. "So, you do laugh," he says, his voice low.

And because laughter has rioted through me, consumed me, and made me its worshipper, I smile broadly at him. His gaze drops to my lips with the same sort of hunger that flashed in his eyes when I stabbed him. I almost laugh again; stabbing him is the furthest thing from my mind now. His hand tightens on my waist, so minutely it would probably be imperceptible to any but me. How could I not notice, when every brush of his skin has electrified me since the moment we met, tangled in the woods outside the Boundary?

I'm suddenly aware of the way my sodden clothes cling to every inch of me. Of the way the water droplets gleam on Shaw's bare chest and glide over his rigid muscles. Of that gnarled scar above his heart, a few shades lighter than his buttery copper skin, that I now know was put there by his own father.

By the Covinus, I should *not* be thinking of Shaw's naked chest. I make to pull away, color flushing my face, but he tightens his grip until I'm pressed up against him. Embarrassment floods through me, along with something headier. Something hotter. "I'm sorry, this is...I can't—" I stop talking because I don't even know what I'm trying to say.

The pupils of Shaw's eyes are blown wide, the glacial blue now only a thin ring. "Mirren," he breathes, and I sink into him at the way he wraps my own name around me. "You know that I'm safe right? That I will never again do anything to you that you don't choose."

He watches me until I nod. Because I do know. Have known for a while.

A sinful grin curves his lips, as he says, "but I am not Similian. Don't expect me to act like one."

The words are dangerous, oh so dangerous, because in them, I find a piece of myself. A wild piece I thought I'd successfully killed in service of my Community; the part of me that longs for moon rises and fresh sea air and darkness and *different.*

A small gasp leaves my lips and Shaw's eyes flick to them again with predatory focus. He lowers his head and a thrill of elation shoots through me at the same time as a tremor of terror. I want to run from this pond, from him, back to the safety of the familiar. I want to fling myself at him, burying myself in him until we are so intertwined, I can no longer remember my own name.

Every thought melts from my mind as his lips brush against mine, barely there. So quickly that I wonder if I imagine the spark that lights my blood. If I imagine the deliciously soft feel of him.

"Mirren," he says again, and I am undone. I'd no more run from him than I would my own shadow. *He* is the adventure I've always craved, the darkness I've always longed for, and the desire to plunge into his depths spirals through me hot and potent. Shaw pulls back slowly, and my fingers dig into his chest. I want to cry out, to object to the unacceptable distance between us. To demand that he finish what I didn't know I wanted to start, when a voice rings out across the pond.

"Oh, lovely. I do so enjoy interrupting ill-judged trysts in the middle of the morning. It doesn't make me feel like losing the contents of my breakfast *at all*."

I jump back from Shaw as if burned, sliding my feet ungracefully up the side of the pond until I finally manage to sprawl on the granite shore. Max stands a few feet from us, a hand on her hip and eyebrows raised in abject judgement. "Am I interrupting?" she asks sardonically.

I smooth my hair, which feels like tangled seaweed and futilely attempt to pluck my soaked shirt from my skin. I don't know whether to be angry or relieved by her interruption, but her evaluating gaze makes me wish desperately to sink into the pond silt. Shaw, on the other hand, appears perfectly unruffled aside from his hair, which has begun to curl upward as it dries in an unfairly handsome manner. "Did you need something, Maxi?"

Max purses her lips irritably. "It just figures you'd ask for a favor and then forget you did," she says to him and then rounds on me. "Out! Now we're going to have to start totally from scratch with your hair."

Her eyes rove downward as I stare at her in bewilderment. "And your clothes. And pretty much everything else as well. And we've only got seven hours!"

She glares at me expectantly. I turn to Shaw helplessly, but he only shrugs with a small smile as if to say *good luck.* "Seven hours for what!?"

Max puffs in annoyance and stalks down the embankment like she intends to pull me from the pond herself. I scurry forward hurriedly. Whatever her plans for me, I prefer to walk there of my own accord rather than be dragged bodily. I have *some* dignity.

"To make you look less Similian," she replies as if this is obvious.

I turn to Shaw, a wordless plea in my eyes. But he only watches me, eyes twinkling, an unreadable smile pulling at one side of his mouth. The mouth that only minutes before was close enough for me to taste. To make mine.

"Enjoy it, Lemming. Tonight, you're going to experience Nadjaa at her finest."

CHAPTER
TWENTY-FIVE

Shaw

I blink blearily, the words scrawled across the ancient tome in front of me fading in and out of focus. I roll my shoulders and then my neck, refocusing once more. I've been here for hours and am no closer to a strategy than I was before I left for the Similian border on the vague direction of a prophecy. The Achijj's fortress, aptly named Yen Girene, or 'mighty rock', is impenetrable from both the inside and out.

It doesn't help that every time I try to focus, my mind drifts back to the manor pond. It seems that rigid self-discipline is no match for long, dark tresses trailing over shoulders. Or for rosy lips parted in anticipation. Or water droplets curling their way down curves that demand to be traced by my hand.

Yen Girene. Right.

The gates open twice a day—at dawn and sunset—and only Achijj approved traders are allowed through. The punishment for attempting to gain entrance through falsehoods is being thrown from the wall that surrounds the entire city and stands fifty feet high. Our only way into the fortress remains through Mirren and hoping the Achijj's interest in adding to his harem is great enough.

It's getting out that remains the problem.

The last time I saw the inside of the fortress, I was eleven and there to dispatch a spy that had lost their usefulness to my father. It had been easy then, slipping into the city pretending to be a scrawny, merchant child. I only glimpsed the Achijj, portly belly quivering as he sat at the head of the throne room, surrounded by his wives and concubines. Even then, he'd been an old man. By now, he must be ancient.

His fortress sits atop some of the most profitable gem mines in Ferusa and in terms of Dark World squabbles, he's always been content to remain atop his stash like a drake protecting its hoard. He's never pushed for more territory, as there's been no need. The small bit he controls is every bit as lucrative as territories three times its size. It's why the Boundary hunter's information caught us so off guard.

I suspected the Praeceptor, or perhaps Akari Ilinka, the warlord in Ferusa's southeast region who declares herself a queen. Both, along with a dozen others, are well known for their conquests and interest in Nadjaa's port location. The Achijj hadn't even crossed my mind.

Why now?

The question echoes through my mind for the umpteenth time. It's gnawed at the corner of my brain like a persistent parasite since I discovered the Achijj's involvement, an anomaly that no matter how I contort or bend, I can't make sense of. What if I was wrong to trust Aggie's prophecy? Denver's gained notoriety in Ferusa with his transformation of Nadjaa and the way his ideas that were once viewed as radical have flowed into the mainstream.

There are hundreds of people that could want him dead for that alone.

I press my fingers into my eyelids until splashes of color bloom and am contemplating tossing the book across the room when Calloway peeks in. His cheeks are rosy behind his plastering of freckles, as if he's just been running and his copper hair is damp with sweat. He eyes the pile of books in front of me. "Anything new?"

I glare at him irritably, which he pointedly ignores as he settles himself across from me. He folds his arms across his chest and grins.

"You know there's nothing new," I grumble, "if there was any way to get in and out of Yen Girene, we would have let Mirren go in the Nemoran Wood. And if there were any other leads, we never would have listened to a silly prophecy and gone to the Boundary in the first place."

Still, Cal grins, his white teeth gleaming against his weather-tanned skin. "But then you would have never met Mirren."

I resist the urge to throw the book at him, rather than the wall. "Did you need something? Or are you just here to make unhelpful observations?" I ask, ignoring the way my stomach surges at the mere mention of Mirren's name.

"Seems there have been quite a few unhelpful observations today."

Cal thumbs through the pages of the book with a look so smug I immediately know he's talked to Max. My face blazes and I curse them both for their ridiculous gossip in the midst of a crisis and then curse myself for blushing like some sort of wayward schoolboy.

I slam the book shut with an irritated chuff. "Oh, just get on with it, Calloway!"

His eyes light with victorious mischief, but he cocks his

head innocently. "Get on with what, Anni?" He asks, my nickname light on his tongue.

"You're not here to see if I've made any progress to get to the Achijj, you're here for gossip like a wife at the market."

"Well, I've been called worse," Cal acknowledges with a chuckle. "Moonlit trysts—"

"There was no moonlight!"

"With beautiful Similian girls in sparkling coastal ponds—"

"Now you're just being preposterous," I point out sulkily.

Cal continues, undeterred. "Green eyes wide and innocent and lips pouted just so—"

"Are you writing a romance novel or is there a point to this?"

Cal laughs heartily. "I would write a spectacular romance novel, obviously, but I actually did come to talk to you about the plan for Yen Girene. It's obviously changed since we left the Nemoran Wood. How can I help?"

I feel both shamed and seen. I've been meaning to talk to Cal—and Max, as well, once she calms down—about everything that happened on our journey here. But time seems to slip from my grasp, or more accurately, has been swallowed by another person entirely. Mirren. And not that she's actually stolen my time; it's more the idea of her that has kept me preoccupied since we returned. Thoughts of her consume my waking moments; who she is to the magic of prophecies of the land; how I can possibly keep her safe when the entire country seems to be entrenched in a game I don't even understand the rules of. And in the smaller hours, more intimate thoughts, that involve her lips and her luminescent skin, and those wild curls sprawled across my pillow...

And Cal. I've told him none of this, and still, he knows. And he doesn't judge me, as I judge myself. He only offers himself as if I deserve that sort of loyalty. I swallow roughly and then tell him everything, starting with the morning they left and leaving nothing out. He opens his mouth to speak when I get to the part about Cullen's camp, but I shake my head, unwilling to pause for even a moment. It feels good to let the words pour out of me, to tell someone every selfish, bitter, miraculous feeling I've had since stealing Mirren.

Cal's eyes go wide when I tell him of being healed by the cave stream and wider still when I explain my suspicions about Denver and the Dead Prophecy and Mirren's connection to it all.

"It can't be a coincidence," he says, his face thoughtful, "that Denver is taken while hunting for that prophecy. And it can't be a coincidence that Aggie makes a prophecy about Mirren around the same time. But what I can't figure out is the Achijj's place in it all. Why suddenly decide to enter the fray, and with such a brutal move?"

I nod solemnly, but I feel no relief in Cal's agreement. It'd be simpler if he told me my theory was insane.

"If this is all true, it definitely changes things."

"How so?"

Cal's face falls serious and a lump lodges in my throat. I've known Calloway since he was fourteen when Denver found him on a trip to Siralene. I was still practically feral when we first met, all rage and growling and darkness. But he walked right up to me and enveloped me in a hug as if it was the most natural thing in the world. And indeed, Cal made it feel like it was. In spite of all the horror he's experienced—losing his entire family and the world he thought he belonged to—he's never been jaded. His face is always adorned with an open smile and his arms always open to whoever is in need of them. Even if, like me, they aren't always aware they do.

So if his face is serious, I'm not going to like what comes out of his mouth. "You can't bring Mirren to the Achijj, Anni."

I don't like it. Not at all.

I stare at him, my shock warring with anger. Mirren is the only way into Yen Girene. Is he honestly suggesting I leave Denver there? Give up on the man who gave me something to live for?

"What do you mean?" I reply dumbly.

Cal smiles sadly at me and I consider hitting the pity off his face. I keep my fists balled at my sides.

"I mean, if the Dead Prophecy is the reason why he wants her, there are higher things working here. If magic is really awake and it has chosen Mirren, we can't risk bringing her there. Something's at play here, something we're missing. He may be old, but he isn't going to roll over and let us take Denver and Mirren without a fight. Not if they're both connected to bringing magic back."

"Then I'll give him his fight," I growl menacingly.

Cal shakes his head. "We're missing something here, Shaw. Something important. And until we find out what it is, we can't risk you. And you can't risk Mirren."

I am laid bare in the face of Cal's words. So simple and yet, I haven't been able to even think them to myself. Because they feel like a betrayal and a balm all at once. How can I have grown to care so much for Mirren as to put her safety at the same level as the man who saved me? I owe Denver more than my life—I owe him whatever fragments of my soul still remain. I would give my life for his a thousand times over, but...I won't give Mirren's.

That's what I haven't been able to admit to myself until now.

I meet Cal's understanding gaze, my eyes swimming with humiliation and truth. "I cannot," I admit, my words broken. Ragged.

Cal just nods. "Then let's figure out a new way forward."

∼

Mirren

As it turns out, getting ready really is going to take seven hours. In the face of no electricity, Ferusian girls have discovered creative ways to tame their tresses and all of them take time, especially when someone has such a mass of them, Max insists with a pointed look. I bend over the clawfoot tub obediently, biting my lip as she dumps lukewarm water over my head and then attacks my scalp with a pleasant-smelling soap.

It's easier this way. Without having to look at the distasteful set of her lips, I can pretend she's doing this because we're friends, rather than what we are—a Lemming and a Dark Worlder that can barely stand to be in the same room together. It isn't until Max begins an attempt to untangle my clean hair that I try to speak to her. "What kind of celebration are we attending?"

Max snags the wide toothed comb in a particularly large knot and my eyes water. "It's the lunar celebration," she answers shortly, detangling the knot deftly and far more quickly than I would have managed. "You really need to deep-condition or you aren't ever going to tame this hair," she adds.

I nod, knowing I won't be taking her advice. Once I'm back in Similis, my hair will be braided down my back once more, an afterthought. "What's the celebration for?"

She pours a vial of something into her hands and begins scrunching it into my hair. "It happens once a month when the moon hangs the lowest over the Averitbas mountains and reflects in the bay. They say it started out as a ritual for the old gods a long time ago, something to celebrate the earth's magic and renew it with their faith. But Denver resurrected the practice, mostly as a way to celebrate the community. To just come together and enjoy each other's company."

It's the first time I've heard the word 'community' be spoken so casually. Confidently, like there is no doubt in her mind it's where she belongs. I wonder what it would be like, to be able to choose my community for myself. And if that would make me want to celebrate it.

"Berik proposed to Evie at the last one," Max continues, and I remember Shaw speaking of the baker that also serves as a councilwoman. "It was terribly romantic."

I'm grateful to be staring into the basin of the tub so that Max doesn't see my look of disbelief. Max, with her sharp tongue and iron exterior, doesn't seem to be the type concerned with romance. Then again, I remember the way her fingers curled into Shaw when we returned. The worry and concern she showed when leaving him in the Nemoran wood. Maybe there is more to her hatred of me than I realized.

"Max," I venture timidly as she pulls me to a sitting position and wraps an old tunic around my wet hair, tying it in a neat knot at my temple. She turns and takes a sip from a chipped mug on her nightstand. "Are you and Shaw Bound?"

Max chokes, barely keeping hold of the mug as coffee splashes down her arm. "Dammit," she mutters, setting the cup down and beginning to mop up the spill.

"Is that why you don't like me? Because you're Bound? I never meant to come between you. Shaw and I aren't—"

I want to say 'anything'. *We aren't anything.* But the words stick in my throat.

"We just have an arrangement," I finish weakly. "I'm already Bound to someone else—"

"Oh my gods," Max shouts, throwing up her arms. "Stop saying *Bound.*"

I press my lips together. They call it something different here, but I don't know the words. I meet Max's eyes in the mirror. She knows what I mean.

"If you're asking if Shaw and I are in a relationship, the answer is no," she replies, frowning, "And I'm a feminist. I object to the notion that my hatred for you has anything to do with some sort of societal competition over a *man.*"

"But...you love him, don't you? Isn't that what that means here?"

Max stares at me, her face a mixture of incredulity and pity. Somehow, this is worse than straight dislike. "That word has a lot of meanings here," she says gently. It's the nicest I've heard her speak. "I do love Shaw, but not in a *romantic* way. That's the word you're looking for."

She sets the comb on the nightstand and sighs, settling herself on the bed. She jerks her head, a clear indication I'm to join her. Hesitantly, I sink into the plush mattress, feeling as though I'm positioning myself next to a viper poised to strike.

"Shaw's my best friend in the entire world. We've been through a lot together."

Like escaping Shaw's father. I remember what Shaw told me by the pond. Max is the one who stitched his wound and cared for his infection. Shaw may have saved her life, but she saved his as well. Those soul-deep bargains are not something that can be easily untangled.

"He knows me better than anyone in the world, aside from Cal. I would do anything for him. *That's* why I don't like you."

I furrow my brow. "You don't like me because Shaw's your...friend?"

Max shakes her head and flicks her eyes to the ceiling, as if I'm a great test of patience. "I don't like you because I don't trust you. And I don't like you because you being here puts Shaw in danger and he puts himself in enough danger as it is. He doesn't need a pretty little Similian excuse to be more reckless with his life than he already is and that's exactly what you're going to be."

Max purses her lips and her wide brown eyes turn glassy. "You don't know Shaw like I do, so you don't understand that strong, confident Shaw is just a mask. He has no concern for his own safety because he doesn't think he's worth being concerned about. He acts how he thinks he should."

I don't know Shaw like Max does, but her words ring true. I didn't imagine the look of relief on his face or the way he dropped his arms when Shivhai pressed his sword to his throat as if he were welcoming his own demise.

"How is that?"

"Broken," Max answers, anguish washing over her features. "Like he's worthless. If it comes to your life or his, he will choose yours, no questions asked. And it isn't because of heroics or love, it's because he doesn't think he deserves to keep living. Whatever is really going on with Denver's abduction, you being here makes it even more dangerous. It just gives him another excuse to be a martyr."

Max's eyes are pleading; pleading for me to protect Shaw when he won't protect himself. She is vulnerable and I can feel the fear in her heart as if it's my own. If Shaw dies, Max's world will no longer make sense, the same if Easton leaves me. I want to tell her I will leave Shaw be and not shake her world, but I can no more untangle myself than Shaw can. Too many lives are now woven together. My father's, my brother's, mine, Shaw's.

So instead, I say, "He is not broken. I don't care what's been done to his soul, Shaw is stronger for living through what he has."

Max's eyes light with begrudging approval. We sit in silence for a few moments, but the tension that lined the air between us has eased.

"Max?"

"What?"

"What's a feminist?"

Max laughs. She has a beautiful smile. "I have a lot to teach you."

~

"Well, you don't look terrible," Max announces hours later, as we both stare at my reflection in the mirror. She's painted my lips a soft pink and darkened my lashes. Somehow, she managed to transform my unruly mess of hair into soft ringlets, some gathered at the nape of my neck and some falling softly to frame my face.

I don't look terrible. I look like someone else.

I run my fingers over my hair. "How did you..." I trail off in wonder. Max smiles haughtily.

"Girl, before you leave, I'll teach you not only to take care of those waves, but to worship their very existence." She fluffs up her own shiny coils in demonstration and I smile shyly.

She tosses me a wad of silky fabric. "Put this on."

I stare at it dumbly. "What is it?"

"A dress," she answers with an impatient roll of her eyes. She's painted her own lips a crimson red and her brown eyes shine against the emerald fabric of her slinky dress. The bodice is beaded, and cutouts frame her hips, her dark velvet skin shimmering underneath. She looks ruthlessly beautiful, like an ancient warrior goddess and I have to remind myself not to stare.

"One of yours?" I ask dubiously. I need to play a part in order not to stand out at tonight's celebration, but I don't think I have the courage to dress like Max. It's too far from myself; even whoever I am outside of Similis.

Max laughs. "As if I'd trust a Lemming to pull this off," she says with an elaborate wave toward her own outfit. I sigh in relief. "Shaw got it for you this morning."

Surprise laces through me. Is that what Shaw was doing before he encountered the slavers? Buying me a dress? I try to imagine Shaw in a dressmaker's shop and the image is enough to elicit a short, surprised giggle.

I take the dress and the soft fabric unfurls in my hands. It's a beautiful light green, a color reminiscent of the cliff pond. Will Shaw think of it when he sees the dress once more? Will he remember the way my clothes clung to me, and my laughter rang out across the water?

My skin flushes at the thought and I slip hurriedly out of the robe, intending to pull the dress on without romanticizing it further when the door to Max's room bursts open. I yelp in surprise, shielding what parts of myself I can manage with my hands as Calloway saunters in. He laughs as he takes note of the incensed look on my face.

"Sorry, I keep forgetting your Similian sense of propriety," he says with a flourishing bow that I gather isn't at all serious. "But you can keep hold of your maidenhood, that sort of thing doesn't interest me."

I stare at him in bewilderment, trying to determine the best way to extricate myself from the situation without exposing more skin. If I move my arms to redon the dressing gown, *everything* will be on display.

Max hasn't even spared a look for the door, instead intensely focusing on applying kohl to the lids of her eyes. "What do you want, Cal?" she asks, finishing off the kohl and poking jewels through her ears. To me, with a tone of intense boredom, she says, "he's not attracted to women."

I open my mouth, now realizing what Cal meant by not being interested, but immediately close it. It would be best to wait until I'm fully clothed and have something sensible to say in response.

Cal laughs again at my obvious discomfort and makes a show of turning toward the wall. "I'll count to ten," he informs me cheerfully, "though I assure you, even Similians have nothing new."

Gratefully, I slip the dress over my head and hurriedly shimmy it over my hips. It's more modest than anything Max has donned thus far, but it's a far cry from the khaki jumpsuit I'm used to. The neckline is high, and the silhouette is fitted with long, belled sleeves. Draped silk gathers at my waist, leaving my back mostly exposed and a long slit runs up my thigh. The fabric is plain, but impossibly beautiful and for a moment, all I can do is stare down at it.

"Rhonwen sent me to see how much longer until you're ready. The skiffs are waiting," Calloway says to the wall, his hands stuffed in his pockets. He makes a striking figure in his black dress pants and gray tunic, all tailored to accentuate his lanky frame.

"You can turn around now," I mumble, running my hands across the fabric of the dress self-consciously.

Cal's eyes light on me. "You look lovely, darling," he says with a grin. I grin back awkwardly. "And well done, Max, on making her look Ferusian but not garishly over the top like you insist on dressing."

Max smacks Cal's arm, but she beams, as if 'over the top' is the highest of compliments.

I glance at myself in the mirror and my chest tightens. What would Easton make of me now, so far away from the girl I was sitting with him in our quarterage? Would he even recognize me? Dress and makeup aside; would he recognize eyes that no longer sweep to the floor, pretending to submit? Or the mouth that opens when it wishes, that is heard when it speaks? The thought unsettles me, and I look away from my reflection quickly.

"Shall I be your proper escort?" Cal teases, offering Max and I each an elbow.

"I suspect you've never been a proper anything in your life, Cal," I tell him with a grin.

Calloway guffaws loudly and Max looks wickedly delighted as we make our way down the stairs. "She might be on to us, Cal," Max laughs.

"There's no one better suited to give her a thorough Dark World education in the enjoyment of debauchery than we are."

I laugh, the sound a ballooning warmth in my chest. It is like the water of the cliff pond, refreshing and weightless.

As we circle down the last staircase, my smile fades. All the air vacates the room as my eyes land on the lone figure waiting in the foyer. His back is to us, and with his sweep of dark hair, he appears made of shadows against the crisp, white marble. Shaw.

He turns, nodding in acknowledgement to Max and Cal, but when his eyes find mine, they lock there. I grip Cal's arm to keep from stumbling down the remaining stairs. I've never given much thought to being attractive—vanity is not a quality much doted upon in Similis—but as Shaw's eyes travel downward, skimming over my hips and the slice of bare skin that peeks from the slit of the dress, I understand there is a power to it. His eyes are magnetic, warming every inch of me as they trail from head to toe and images of his hands on my skin and his lips against mine race through my mind.

He is clad in a navy pair of trousers and a crisp white tunic that contrasts beautifully with the deep caramel of his skin. His hair is swept casually across his forehead and a small smile plays at the corner of his lips.

As we reach the bottom of the stairs, I grow self-conscious under his gaze. Is Shaw mocking my attempt to fit into Ferusa? Am I ridiculous for even trying?

Max and Cal, still mercilessly teasing each other, brush past us and out into the night air.

"Is this okay?" I ask uncertainly, smoothing the front of the dress once more, though the fabric lays perfectly. The silk is unblemished, rippling out around me like water from a spring. "Do I look like an average Ferusian?"

Shaw's face is gravely serious as he comes to my side. "No," he replies. My heart sinks. "But you are breathtaking."

The smile at the corner of his mouth breaks out into the open, lighting up his face in such a manner that I immediately smile back. It transforms him from merely handsome to entirely devastating, and I decide that I could happily spend the rest of my life eliciting his smiles.

Shaw offers me an arm and I take it, for once, no thoughts of Easton or Denver or the Achijj clouding my thoughts.

It's only us, stepping into the darkness. Shaw leans over, his whisper a warm caress in my ear, "it's time to see the beauty in the Darkness."

CHAPTER
TWENTY-SIX

Mirren

Shaw didn't exaggerate the beauty of the Moon City. In fact, despite the layered intricacy with which he wove his words, even they couldn't have possibly done Nadjaa justice. As our small skiff streams across the Bay of Reflection, now turned from black to silver, my eyes can't move fast enough.

The moon hangs low in the sky, its iridescent orb so large and bright it looks as if it has fallen from the heavens and come to rest atop the Averitbas mountains. Its light pours into the city's streets, illuminating the white pavers so that they glitter and shine like gemstones. The store fronts of the marketplace and arts district have been draped in shimmering fabrics of brilliant silvers and whites, and the strings of miniature lanterns wrapped around the trees reflect in the large bubbles that float through the air, making the whole world seem effervescent.

And *people.*

So many people.

Notes of laughter ring through the air from groups of skiffs that have gathered in the bay, bawdy and raucous. We stream past, parking at a large dock that wends its way across the length of the marketplace. People shout and hug. They sway to the soft music, the shimmering notes clinging to the air like dew drops. There is so much *life* that it fills me to brimming, as though it might spill out of me at any moment, wild and unfettered. Equal parts exhilarating and terrifying, I decide as soon as I step out of the boat that this is a place I could give my whole heart.

The thought stops me short. This *is* the place my father gave himself to. Left me for.

As I watch it with greedy eyes, I find I can't fault him for it. Not in this moment, anyway.

Max climbs out of the skiff behind me, adjusting her dress and fluffing her hair. Her eyes light on a table laden with sparkling wine and intricately decorated mini cakes. She tugs Calloway toward them with a delighted squeal.

Shaw touches the inside of my arm gently and guilt rolls through my stomach. This may be the city my father gave his heart to, but this is the boy he gave the love that should have been mine by right and by birth. The pale blue of his eyes looks silver in the moonlight, the contrast striking against his dark lashes and brown skin. I should be angry or jealous, but all I can feel is thankful. Grateful there was someone to show Shaw the light in a world that can be so very dark. Someone who gave an abandoned boy a beautiful place like Nadjaa.

I want to reach out and run my fingers down the plane of his cheekbone or the sharp edge of his jaw, but I clasp them in front of me instead.

"You're uncharacteristically quiet," Shaw observes with a roguish grin. "All this and not one question? Not even some scintillating commentary on the lack of manners?"

I shove him playfully. "I've given up on your lack of propriety. You're officially hopeless."

"I'm going to choose to see that as a compliment," he replies with a wicked laugh. "There are a few people I want you to meet tonight. Evie is the councilwoman I told you about," he says gesturing to a quaint little shop painted a vibrant shade of purple.

"What's that?" I ask, gesturing to the wooden arbor that has been erected above the shop's doorway. It looks hand carved, crafted from a deep, richly colored wood. "It's so beautiful."

Shaw follows my gaze. "It's custom after a couple is engaged to leave the arbor over the doorway until the wedding. It's the story of her and Berik's love," he tells me, leaning toward me slightly as he speaks. *Love.* The word elicits a shiver. Because it's against the Keys? Or because it's Shaw's voice that says it? Close enough that I only need to turn my head slightly and I could watch the way it looks on his lips.

"What do you mean?"

"The carvings. One side of the alter is Evie's life before she met Berik. Having her children, losing her first husband, almost losing her life. All the beauty and the pain of it."

Before I'd come to the Dark World, I would never have seen the beauty in any of that, only the tragedy. But now, as I take in the detailed carvings, it is obvious how finely the sweet edge of beauty mingles with the bright sting of pain. How each one defines the other.

"The other side is Berik's story. And the top of the altar is where their stories meet."

Indeed, the top of the altar is the most beautiful of all. The woods of each side, so different in composition and texture, twist around each other delicately. By nature, their differences should repel the other, but instead, they serve to enhance each material's individual beauty. It seems impossible, that the two woods should fit together so perfectly, but they do. So well, that for a moment, a lump forms in my throat. I swallow roughly and tear my gaze away from the arbor, terrified to give way to the knot of emotions in my stomach.

Shaw watches me in that peculiar way of his that feels too close. As if he can read every thought I try to shove down. But instead of mentioning them, he says, "there's someone else I want you to meet, as well. Someone I think can help find your father. She should be here somewhere."

My teeth clench. I almost tell him I have no need of one of his admirers' help and that I know exactly where my father is, thank you very much, when a thought strikes me. "Shaw, have you...does Denver have a wife?"

He eyes me warily. "No. Why do you ask?"

I shake my head, not wanting to arouse his suspicions further. "Just curious whether you'd ever had any sort of mother figure. You never talk about one."

Shaw's brow smooths as he accepts my curiosity as standard issue. "I never met my mother. My father told me she died in childbirth, but I've no way of really knowing. And it's always just been Denver and me. There have been plenty of women who've tried to gain his affections, but he's never shown any interest. Max says it's because he's too focused on Nadjaa, but I don't know."

Disappointment blooms in my chest like thick vines. I've been so caught up in Shaw and the discovery of my father, I haven't allowed my mind to open to the possibility that my mother might very well be in Nadjaa, too. But now, the idea is swallowed as quickly as it formed. If my father didn't arrive with my mother, what happened to her? Did he leave her as he left Easton and I, alone and defenseless on the Boundary?

I open my mouth to demand answers when the oldest woman I've ever seen approaches us. Her dark skin is thin and crumpled like a discarded piece of parchment. Gray spiral curls pour down over her shoulders and hang to her waist, dry and frazzled and glinting in the moonlight. Her eyes stare past us, milky white and unseeing.

"Anrai Shaw," the old woman proclaims, the timbre of her voice odd and rhythmic, like the notes of the music that plays all around us.

I glance at Shaw, startled, both at the fact that the woman knows him without the use of her eyes and at the fact that she knows his full name. I haven't heard anyone call him by it, with the exception of Calloway, and was beginning to think it wasn't something he shared with anyone but me.

"Aggie," he says with the most warmth I've heard him use to anyone, "we were just talking about you." He takes the woman's weathered hands in his. They are gnarled and twisted in comparison with Shaw's smooth, slender fingers and I can't help but stare awkwardly at the affectionate gesture.

Aggie smiles, revealing empty gums and moves her hands to Shaw's face. "Anrai Shaw," she gasps again, her raspy voice rising and falling like a warbled songbird, "I'm glad to see the fire has not yet consumed you. I would be terribly upset if it did before I got another visit."

I glance around, wondering what fire Aggie refers to, but Shaw doesn't seem to share my confusion. He grins almost shyly at the old woman, and she moves her swollen hands to his mouth, running her fingers over his lips perfunctorily.

"You know I'll always come visit, consumed or not, Aggie," he replies with a light laugh.

The old woman cackles happily, removing her hands from Shaw's face and turning to face me as if she knows exactly where I stand. "And you, little bird? Will you come visit after you find what you need, or will you cage yourself forever?"

I gape at her, looking to Shaw for a clue as to how to respond to the strange question, but his face is unreadably pleasant. Damn him. Of course, he'd pick now to take on a manner of polite passivity.

I open my mouth once and then close it again, feeling slightly off balance. Aggie laughs, more of a rasp than anything else and turns to Shaw conspiratorially. "Her wings are not so little, if she will protect them from being clipped," she says matter-of-factly.

"Aggie," Shaw says. He doesn't sound unsettled at all. "This is Mirren."

My eyes widen. We never discussed whether I'd be hiding my true name along with my place of origin tonight, but with the reverence Shaw gives names, it seemed a safe conclusion. Aggie must have done something to earn his complete trust, to possess not only the knowledge of Shaw's true name, but now mine as well.

"Mirren, Mirren, little bird, little bird," she replies, the odd melody of her voice rising and falling.

It's the same thing Shivhai called me before he pinned me to the ground. "It's nice to meet you, Aggie," I manage, uncertain whether or not it truly is.

"It is nice," she declares, the skin around her eyes crinkling even more as she smiles. "I have not had the pleasure of meeting an adventuring Similian in years. Mostly sedentary creatures, you lot."

My mouth drops in horror. A blind old woman has guessed my secret after being in my presence for a matter of minutes. I glance at the merriment of the celebration. How many more people have I given myself away to tonight? How many more potential threats have I just made for myself? How many more obstacles to saving Easton and my father?

"Relax, Lemming," the old arrogance returns to Shaw's voice. "Aggie just knows things. It's why I wanted you to meet her."

I lift an eyebrow, realizing belatedly that Aggie is the friend Shaw wanted me to meet; the one he thinks may know what happened to my parents. I conjured up many images of what Shaw's mysterious friend would look like and none of them were as old and fragile as Aggie.

She tilts her head and though I know she can no longer see, I feel examined. "You have questions for me." She isn't asking.

I manage a nod, before remembering she can't see me, but she doesn't seem to need an answer as she shoos Shaw. "I think Mirren would like some of that cherry wine, Anrai Shaw. Even *you* know it's bad form not to offer your guest a drink."

Shaw nods placatingly. "Yes ma'am," he replies. With a reassuring glance in my direction, he turns and heads toward Max and Cal. I watch his retreating form, dark and tall, and desperately wish to follow him.

Aggie settles into one of the many scattered chairs, a plethora of bangles at her wrists clanking merrily together. Her withered body is wrapped in rich fabrics of aubergine, embroidered at the edges with swirls of gold. I know admittedly little about Nadjaan fashion, but I can tell hers denote respect. Curiosity wars with my sense of wariness. "How... how do you know the things you do?"

Aggie tilts her head. "The same way you healed Anrai Shaw."

"How do you—I mean, I didn't...the water healed Shaw. I had nothing to do with it."

"Well then, I have nothing to do with the things I know."

I furrow my brow and resist the urge to sigh. Why would I have expected a friend of Shaw's to be easy and accommodating? Of course, she'd be infuriatingly mysterious. But I don't have time for any more riddles while the ones I already possess remain unsolved. "Do you know where my parents are?"

Aggie narrows her eyes. "It seems to me, little bird, that *you* know where your parents are."

Heat flames my cheeks and I glance guiltily at the refreshment table, as if there's some way Shaw could have overheard from this distance. He chats animatedly with his friends, paying no attention to our conversation. "I do know where my father is, though I don't know why he was taken. And my mother's whereabouts remain a mystery."

"I knew your mother," Aggie tells me and my heart flies into my throat.

I want to keep her from speaking at the very same time I want to rip the words from her. "Knew?" I repeat weakly.

Aggie nods, her eyes staring off in the direction of Evie's bakery and boarding house. "Knew. The Darkness changes everyone and your parents are no exception. I know her no longer."

"She's...she's dead?"

Aggie doesn't answer me, but her unseeing eyes flick to my face, staring as if they can see what lies beneath my skin. The secrets and the shame and the hungering thoughts I've been having while my brother lays dying a world away. If Shaw's gaze is intense, it is nothing to Aggie's.

"He is the Darkness," she croaks, the sing song quality of her voice gone all at once.

I turn to her, startled. "I—what?"

"The Darkness will change you."

The gray pupil behind the milky white of Aggie's eyes is cratered and colorless. It reminds me of the moon. Not the moon that floods Nadjaa's streets with warmth and light, but the one from Similis that has always seemed so far away, like it belongs somewhere else.

"The Darkness changes all those who enter, but it will touch you especially. Deep down in your soul, deeper than even you know, you will be changed," she pauses, wheezing. Her throat is dry and her voice crackles like wind across fallen leaves. "He is the Darkness. The Darkness is he."

I let out a frustrated sigh through my nostrils. "Changed how? And who are you talking about? What about my mom?"

Her face crinkles into a humorless smile and her gaze leaves mine. "When you decide to hear the earth's whispers and dance in its power, come to me, my little bird," the rising lilt of her voice has returned, and where it once sounded silly, it now sounds ominous. I stare at her, shock and anger mingling furiously.

Before I can give voice to them, Max and Calloway slide into the seats on either side of us. Max pushes a fizzy drink into my hand and wiggles a delicately painted eyebrow at me. "You'll thank me later," she says, clinking her glass with mine and taking a long sip.

I turn to Aggie, to demand she give answers instead of more questions, but she's disappeared. I look around wildly, but there's no sign of the strange old woman. I take a deep swig of the wine, bubbles fluttering in my throat and stomach.

Shaw drops into the seat next to me, raising an eyebrow at the glass already in my hand. I want to laugh at the absurdity of the whole thing: I'm sitting in the most magical place I've ever seen, surrounded by light and laughter and now, all I can think of is darkness.

∽

Shaw

The party is in full swing by the time the moon has fully risen, raucous laughter and merriment echoing across the white cobblestones. The music has evolved from soft and lilting to cheerful and rhythmic, and groups of Nadjaan revelers dance in the soft light, clinking their cherry wine. I sip my own sparingly, having never had a head for spirits, and watch the festivities from the shadows.

Not the festivities. Mirren.

Whatever cloud settled over her while in Aggie's presence has lifted and her face is luminous, her hair a spill of dark waves over her pale shoulder. I watch her greedily, my eyes a consolation for my fingers, running over her skin in their place; over curves hugged in seafoam green silk.

Cal spins her around in time with the music and she laughs, a mellisonant sound that reverberates in my chest. She tilts her head toward him and says something I'm too far away to hear, and for an absurd moment, I feel like taking my friend by his perfectly tailored collar and throwing him against a wall.

"Who is the new curiosity that has enamored Mr. Calloway?" The voice comes from my left, both oily and undoubtedly shrewd in its tone. Jayan.

I curse inwardly, having been too caught up in Mirren to hear the man approaching. If I had, I would have high tailed it in the opposite direction. A member of the People's Council, Jayan has always been a repellant but somewhat necessary evil. The man is undeniably cunning, having used whatever is in his arsenal to be reelected six times in his district, be it campaigning or other, less savory means. It's no secret that his aim is higher than a simple council seat, but a love of power isn't uncommon among politicians and isn't what sets him apart. I've never been able to pinpoint what, exactly, it is about him that sets my teeth on edge, but I know better than anyone what a man can keep hidden.

"A guest," I reply tersely, turning to him irritably. He is shorter than me, coming only to my shoulder, but in spite of his slight stature, he holds himself as if he outmatches me. His watery blue eyes are sharp, and he is dressed as primly as ever, but something in the set of his jaw speaks to ruthlessness.

"Of our esteemed Chancellor? Or of yours Mr. Shaw?" His voice is polite but his eyes flicker with distaste.

Jayan has never hidden his opinion of Denver, nor of me. The former being one of grudging respect and the latter being one of blatant dislike. I've no need of Jayan's approval, but I do need his continued support of Denver. It's one of the reasons I've kept Denver's disappearance quiet. The council grows restless and suspicious in his absences and once word of his abduction reaches their ears, Jayan won't hesitate to vie for power. Denver's vision for Nadjaa will be replaced by a much more brutal one.

"And where is Denver? One would think he wouldn't miss the lunar celebration if he has plans to run for reelection?"

I grit my teeth. *Don't strangle him. Don't grab his scrawny neck and squeeze until his eyes pop.*

I repeat the mantra a few times before I trust myself to speak. "His trip ran long. He'll be back within the week."

Gods, will he though? Is seven days enough time for me to find a way out of Yen Girene with everyone's lives intact? Is seven days enough to outmaneuver whatever the Praeceptor and people like Jayan have planned for Nadjaa's power vacuum? And can I do it quick enough to outrun Shivhai?

An invisible noose tightens around my throat, and I cough. Jayan's eyebrows flick up, startled.

The man settles back into himself. "Wonderful, I shall call a council meeting for then. Much has happened in our fearless leader's tenure abroad."

"Perfect," I growl.

"Where did you say your guest was from? She is quite lovely." The words are harmless enough, but the thought of Jayan's slick gaze on Mirren feels abruptly wrong.

I set my eyes on him, the abyss in my stomach beginning to churn. His eyes widen, but I give him credit—he doesn't stumble back. "If you look at her again, I will pluck your eyes from your head."

My voice is so calm that it takes a beat for him to realize the threat, but I see the moment he does. He sputters and gulps down air. I turn around, not waiting for the rest of his pathetic reaction—we both know I'm fully capable of harming him. And now we both know that perhaps it was only ever Denver's leash that kept me from doing so.

It takes a moment to realize that in leaving Jayan, I am stalking toward Mirren like some sort of animal; unleashed and barely civilized. I stop abruptly, but then her eyes rove in my direction and I am well and truly frozen.

Gods.

The emerald sparkles, accented by the color of her dress and framed by a thick curtain of dark lashes. Her lips twist in a hint of a smile. It's the way I've always imagined her looking at me. With no disgust, no fear, nothing but glowing happiness. How is it that I have bared my soul to her, the terrible things I've done, and still, she looks at me like that?

"Shaw," she says, and with my name on her lips, I forget that I should leave her be. "Have you decided to stop skulking and enjoy the fun?"

"I don't skulk," I retort obstinately. Max roars in laughter and claps me on the back.

"Seems Mirren knows you a little too well, my friend," she says delightedly, her breath smelling of cherry wine. She looks to Mirren. "Shaw doesn't have fun."

I open my mouth to argue but close it upon seeing laughter twinkling in Mirren's eyes. I find I'm willing to be laughed at if she's the one laughing. How strange.

Cal swoops in behind Max, his face flushed from a heady combination of dancing and alcohol. "He might not have fun, but he *is* an excellent dancer. Some might even say better than I am." He places a hand on my back and shepherds me toward Mirren as if I'm a small child. I follow his ministrations with a glower.

Mirren raises an eyebrow. "Do you really dance?" Her eyes run down my body skeptically. It makes me want to grab her and show her exactly what this body is capable of, but instead, I clear my throat.

"It's pretty much the same as fighting. Just fewer weapons."

Cal rolls his eyes as if my very existence plagues him, and right now, I'm sure it does. He would sooner cut off his own arm than compare something as beautiful as dancing to the art of death. Though he's been trained as well as any warrior, he wasn't born with swords in his hands and fire in his lungs. His movements, though skilled, are not innate and he sees no beauty in them, only practicality.

Mirren, however, tilts her head. Weighs my words. "Well then, show me the way, warrior," she says in a low voice.

She threads her fingers through mine, and I feel a foreign tightening in my chest. Her palm is warm, her small hand almost completely enveloped by mine. It's the first time she's touched me when neither of us is under duress, the only time she's reached for me first—unless I count the time she stabbed me, which I twistedly do. It hurt like hell, but it was when I saw the true Mirren. The dark, wild creature beneath what she was conditioned to be.

I see the same beautiful girl now, eyes sparkling with mischief and trepidation. And above all, *want*. Not for me. She's smarter than that. But want for *life* and every beautiful and terrible thing it has to offer.

And I can at least give her that. I lead her to the middle of the street just as the song fades from a frenetic, fast paced beat to one that is smooth and supple. Thousands of candles line the makeshift dance floor, casting everything in a soft glow. I know there are things I should be remembering right now—urgent things, life or death—but my mind has miraculously eddied of everything but her.

She allows me to draw her close. A small sigh escapes her lips as her body settles against mine, a sound that curls low in my stomach. She is soft and slippery and the look of her in a dress that I chose sends a primal urge running through me. *Mine.*

I stiffen as the word clangs through me. *No, not mine. Never mine.*

She gazes up at me with big eyes. Her cheeks are tinged pink, from embarrassment or excitement, or perhaps a combination of both. "I don't know what I'm doing," she explains uncertainly.

Funny, that she can lead a bloodthirsty beast like the yamardu after us, but when faced with a dance floor, she balks. I circle my hand around her small waist and press her hips closer to mine. The melody swirls around us and we sway together in time with the tempo. "Just let the music in. Do what feels natural."

"What feels natural is standing still with my arms crossed," she tells me, a line of consternation appearing between her brows. I let out a surprised laugh.

"I don't believe you," I tell her, running my palm from her hips to her ribs, feeling the way her body loosens at my touch, slowly writhing and twisting to the music. The rhythm mingles in her blood, heating her skin beneath my fingers and lighting her eyes. She watches me shyly but doesn't pull away. A breath hitches at her lips and I have the powerful urge to catch it; to taste something of her, even something dispelled. The moment at the cliff pond wasn't enough.

Maybe it will never be enough.

The thought stops me short and ice pours into my veins. What in the name of Darkness am I doing? Holding her as if I have any right to? It seems the selfish black hole inside me knows no bounds. She deserves someone clean and unbroken, someone worthy of her kindness. Not someone with a fragmented soul and a penchant for kidnap and murder.

"Shaw?" Confusion flickers across her face, followed by what I quickly realize is hurt. She thinks I've rejected her.

I curse and jump back, running a hand raggedly through my hair. I'm hurting her again and I don't even know why I'm surprised. Failing everyone around me is the only thing I've ever been consistently good at. That and killing.

"Look, Mirren. We really shouldn't. I'm...I'm not a good person."

Her eyes harden and she pulls herself up straight, chin raised. A queen readying herself for battle. A thrill blazes through me. She is always ready for me, always strong enough to stand her ground. "I know what kind of person you are."

Gods, you don't. You don't know the depths of blackness inside of me, the lengths I've gone. I've told her the deeds of my past and she forgave them without question. But she doesn't know the deeds of my present. The way I've used her, the plans I had for her.

Suddenly, it seems imperative that she know. That she stop looking at me like I'm a man of worth and begins to see what I really am—a monster. She was right to name me so. Her folly was not believing it. "Mirren, there's something—"

"May I cut in?"

My blood freezes and for a fraction of a second, I contemplate reaching for a dagger. Mirren's eyes are on the man behind me, curiosity glittering. I whirl around, death written in every line of my body. *I will kill him—*

"It took me a moment, Mr. Shaw, because even I never assumed you'd be so bold," Jayan says.

Mirren's eyes flick to me, her brows furrowing in confusion.

"What. Are. You. Talking. About." I grit out. I want to gut the little man and turn back to Mirren. To take her in my arms or push her away, I don't know, but the need is suddenly staggering.

"To hide the Chancellor's abduction from the People's Council. You and your *friends* have put Nadjaa's safety at risk and it must be rectified at once. I'm calling an emergency assembly for tonight!"

Horror and panic war within me. How did Jayan find out about Denver? I force my voice to be calm, slipping into the dispassionate mask that used to come so easily. "There's no need for an emergency meeting, Jayan. We've taken steps to ensure Denver is home within the week."

His lips twist in distaste. "Oh, you mean the prophecy?" His watery eyes move to Mirren and cold dread sluices through me. "*She who captures the sea in her eyes.* I don't know how you intend to destroy her, Mr. Shaw, but the people of Nadjaa can't afford the cost of your games or whatever comes from silly prophecies."

He crosses his arms, a self-satisfied smile on his lips. He thinks he's won, that he'll be able to negotiate Denver's disappearance into taking the Chancellor's seat for himself. There are so many reasons this can't happen, so many things I've done so wrong in all of this. But right now, I can't bring myself to care.

Because now Mirren knows it was her I was after. It wasn't a chance meeting on the Boundary, and it wasn't a half-cocked plan to gain entrance into Yen Girene. I journeyed to Similis. Blew a hole through a wall that has stood for a thousand years. And I would have stormed the city until I found her if she hadn't run to me first.

All to destroy her.

I turn to her, desperation clutching at my throat, but she is already gone.

CHAPTER
TWENTY-SEVEN

Mirren

I tear through dancing Nadjaans frantically, with no thought of where I'm going other than *away*. Away from the small man with the smarmy smile who looks as if he's been victorious in battle. And away from Anrai Shaw, whose entire body is lined with violence and whose lips I imagined on my skin just moments before. *She who captures the sea in her eyes.* Hadn't Shaw said something about my eyes when we first met?

A hot wave of shame rises over me as I burst through a group of harried looking revelers. By the Covinus, I'd wanted so badly for him to kiss me—the man who was perfectly willing to hurt innocent people in order to destroy me.

Is that why he's been so kind to me since that night in the cave? Because he figured out that the best way to destroy me would be to destroy my heart? And like a fool, I've made it so easy for him, practically shoving it into his hands on a silver platter.

I spot Max, slinking up and down a young man who

looks as if he might faint with his good luck. "Max, I need to leave," I tell her breathlessly. Hot tears well in my eyes and I bite my lip to keep them from falling. I will not cry.

She stops dancing immediately and straightens, her eyes assessing me. My gaze is desperate on hers. *Please don't ask me why.*

She doesn't. Dismissing her paramour with a casual wave of her hand, she pulls me toward the docks. "We'll take the skiff. I can bring it back later to pick up..." she hesitates at the dark look on my face, "to pick up Cal."

Max makes quick work of the knots as I climb into the skiff. Shame and anger mingle in my stomach as we set off across the silver water of the bay. I'm grateful Max doesn't press as we make our way to the opposite shore. Despite her mistrust of me, I think she could be something like a friend if we were given enough time.

The skiff stops at the shore, the lantern denoting the manor trail the only light flickering in the darkness on this side of the bay. I climb out of the boat and turn to look at her. "Did you know?"

She doesn't ask for clarification, her face a mixture of resignation and anguish. It is answer enough. I shake my head and turn away.

"Mirren—"

I steel myself, unwilling to hear whatever defense of Shaw she has prepared.

"None of it is okay. Not what Shaw did to you and not what forced him to do it. Just—you have good instincts. Don't let this make you second guess them."

I stare at her. Good instincts? The only good instincts I've ever had were the ones that told me to stab Shaw. That he would only hurt me, and I needed to put an end to it before the pain was irreversible. And now, when my chest has been hollowed out with the edge of a blade, it feels more than irreversible—it feels fatal.

"You're going back to the manor, right? You shouldn't wander alone."

"I need some air. Please don't tell him where I've gone."

Max looks as if she wants to argue but nods her assent. She turns the skiff around and I watch it cut a silent path through the water, back toward the marketplace where the lifeblood of Nadjaa still teems. The celebration, that for a few beautiful moments, I'd felt a part of.

I walk up the path slowly. The manor house is still, only a dim light shining through the entry windows. No doubt lit by Rhonwen before she retired for the evening. Sleep won't come easily and the thought of returning to my room, only to stare at the walls is unbearable, so I head around the manor and down the trail. The Storven Sea crashes against the black cliffs as I make my way down through the foliage.

I welcome the burn in my legs. After a few days rest from traveling, I almost miss the strain in my muscles from a hard day's journey. At least, then, it felt like I was *doing* something. Something that would get me closer to saving my brother's life. I've strayed so far from that in the last week, stagnant and lost. Hiding who my father is from Shaw. Hiding that my mother is most likely dead from myself. Hiding from the fact that I am as helpless to save Easton now as I was in Similis. Helpless and cowardly and naïve.

Before long, I arrive at the cliff pond. Its turquoise waters glisten in the moonlight and the leaves of the protective willows rustle in the soft sea breeze. It should make me angry, seeing the water of the pond and only being able to think of the droplets that ran down Shaw's face. Lower. But instead, it has a calming presence, seeping over my bones like a cooling fire.

I remove my dagger from the leather strap at my thigh. Max insisted it was wise to be armed at all times, even under an evening gown, and now I am thankful, as I line it up the way Shaw taught me. I hold the handle lightly between my fingers and when it feels right, let it fly at the nearest tree. It lands with a thump, handle first against the bark. I jog to pick it up and then realign my stance before letting it fly once more.

Shaw acted so skeptical of prophecies when Sura and Luwei discussed them, but he'd been driven by one himself. One that led him to blow up the Boundary and hurt an innocent man. If I never escaped, would he have lured me out somehow? Dragged me out? There are no limits in his drive to get what he wants. No line uncrossable, no person more important than his goal. How many times has he told me that himself; that he's a monster who is not to be trusted? And how many times did I refuse to listen?

You're going to be very disappointed if you go around thinking everyone has the same heart you do.

He said it to me the first few days I knew him, and by the Covinus, I hate that he was right. I hate that it *is* disappointment that threads through me now instead of hatred. Why, after all Shaw's done to me, does something in him call to me, as if my soul recognizes a kindred spirit? How foolish to think there is anything familiar in a heart so very dark.

He is the Darkness.

I throw my knife harder as Aggie's words drift through my mind. She must have been the one to give Shaw the prophecy, just as she gave me one tonight. I didn't realize it at the time, but it was something otherworldly that spoke through her, something ancient and raw like what lived in that cave stream.

This time, the dagger sticks firmly into the trunk, and I have to level my feet to yank it out.

I throw it over and over again, until I'm panting with exertion and the blade sticks where I intend every time.

I hear him before I see him, a crunch of leaves and a swish of branches. I curse Max for giving me away so soon, but I don't fault her for it. Shaw has earned her loyalty. I haven't.

"I don't want to talk to you," I say over my shoulder, throwing the dagger again. It sticks solidly in the trunk, and I can't help my self-satisfied smile. I hope he sees how much my aim has improved. I hope he knows I'm imagining his face every time I throw it.

A voice, so very different from the rich consonance of Shaw's, rings across the still water. "Talking isn't at all what I had in mind."

*

Shaw

I whip around, rage and grief swirling inside me. Mirren's absence aches like a physical wound, hollow and raw. I can't breathe around it, can't think of anything other than the emptiness. The abyss, which has burned so faithfully my entire life, to my detriment or boon, has gone out. All I feel is cold.

Jayan steels himself as I stalk toward him. If it were another day, I might give him credit for the strength of his backbone. "My personal guards are posted all around," he says, as if this will matter to me at all. He could be surrounded by an electric forcefield straight from the factories of Similis and I would claw my way through it.

My voice is eerily calm. "What, exactly, has Denver told you about me, Jayan?"

The man straightens, opening his mouth to reply, but I silence him with a look.

"Has he told you I was born of the Darkness? That it roils and twists inside me, barely contained? That I have no conscience and would cut you down in front of half of Nadjaa this night without a second thought, before your nearest guard could even draw his sword?" I watch with satisfaction as the color drains from his face. "Ah, so you don't know the entirety of my story. Rather foolish, to make such a bold move without all the information."

Spittle covers Jayan's mouth as he sputters, but his eyes are like chips of ice. The need to go after Mirren burgeons vehemently, pounding through my veins in time with my heartbeat, alongside the urge to spill Jayan's blood. But neither of those things would be prudent. Jayan's knowledge has exposed a fatal weakness, a hole for rot to seep in if I don't staunch it. And quickly.

I clench my fist and then stretch my fingers to keep them from wrapping around his scrawny neck. "Where did you learn of Denver's abduction?"

The sniveling rat has the audacity to smile. I clench my teeth. *He isn't worth your vow. He isn't worth a piece of your soul.*

"It matters not *where* I learned of it, Mr. Shaw. What matters is that the information is now in my possession to do with what I will."

"Where did you learn of Denver's abduction?" I repeat in a menacing growl.

Jayan tilts his head, the moonlight glinting in the slick

of his hair. "Why, Mr. Shaw, could it be that you're questioning the loyalty of your faithful followers? Perhaps it was Calloway, inviting the wrong man to his bed. You know how loose words can be in the throes of passion. Or maybe it was that shrewd little *joveh* Maxwell, desperate and hungry for a piece of power the world has always denied her."

Rage consumes me and I want to sink my fist into his perfectly straight teeth, but I keep still. He is goading me, trying to worm his way between my strongest allies. It's true that Max, Cal, and Aggie are the only ones who know of the prophecy, but unfortunately for Jayan, my faith in my friends is one of the unassailable truths in my life. More enduring than the sun itself, it will never fail.

And no secret is safe in Ferusa. Not when the warlords pay a king's ransom for information. Not when the Darkness itself ferrets them out to wield as weapons.

Jayan glances at his watch. A miniscule movement that most people would miss. A sense of foreboding slithers down my spine. "What was the cost of this information?"

My gaze narrows on the waver of his throat. For the first time, he stutters. "I—I don't know what you mean."

Jayan is nervous. He didn't expect me to guess the truth so quickly, which means his show of strength is calculated. There is a reason he hasn't run from me yet.

My daggers are against his throat before he can speak another word. People around me scream as I shove him against the bricks. Metal scrapes against leather, the sound of his guards drawing their swords from his scabbard. "If anyone moves toward me, I will slit his throat."

They freeze, eyeing me warily.

"The Chancellor has been abducted!" Jayan shouts.

"This man knew and said nothing! He should be arrested for treason!"

A crowd has gathered. Evie pokes her head out of the bakery door, her gray eyes wide. "Shaw! What in godsnames—"

Her voice fades as she takes in the scene.

The hole inside me ices over, hoarfrost crackling in my veins. "I will see you cold in the ground for this," I snarl at Jayan.

Jayan's thin lips curl into a sneer. "No, Shaw. It is I who will trod upon your grave. You have always been only raw, empty violence without any power. You've never understood that if the world is too slow to change, one must be a steward of one's own fate. You and Denver have never had the guts to reach for what is in front of you, and Nadjaa won't suffer from removing such weakness from its seat of power."

I shove a dagger into his shoulder and he screams in pain.

"Shaw! Stop!" Evie cries, running toward me. Her auburn hair is wild around her cherub face, her eyes desperate. "You cannot attack a council member!"

His men are now joined by the City Guard, dressed in their crisp white uniforms and they gather around me, closing me in.

"None of these men will be able to get to me before I gut you here in the middle of the street. Start talking," I snap at Jayan.

He grips his shoulder, his lip wavering in pain. "A stranger gave me the information!" he cries. "Told me to do whatever I wished with it, as long as I told you in front of the girl and kept you talking for ten minutes."

Mirren.

Oh gods. It was all a means to separate us, to get her alone. Is it Shivhai who's caught up to us? Or someone else, someone who's heard whispers of prophecies and magic?

The fire in me sings to life, burning away the ice in my veins and around my heart and spurring me to action. I grab Jayan's neck, viciously going after his pressure point until he slumps over. Cal slides in from behind the alley. He must have climbed over the roof to get between the guards and I, but I don't have time to marvel at his ingenuity. There is so much to explain, but all I manage is, "Mirren."

Cal nods, pulling his sword. "Max was with her," he tells me, his eyes grave.

"Shaw," Evie says evenly, her eyes narrowed on me. I feel an echo of regret. Evie has always been kind to me. She doesn't deserve any of this. "Come with me to the Council House. There is obviously a lot we need to unravel."

I shoot her an apologetic look just as the guards surge toward us and the square descends into chaos. Panicked celebration guests scurry in all directions, their harried screams echoing in my ears as I plow my way through them. Cal is hot on my heels, sword glinting in the moonlight as he covers my back. "You got this?" I shout.

He grins, bringing the flat of the blade against a guard's head. "I thought this party was getting a bit stale."

I sprint toward the docks and spot Max climbing from our skiff. She doesn't seem surprised to see me hurtling toward her at full speed, giving me a perfunctory look as I careen to a stop just before I bowl her over, my shoes sliding across wet wood. "Mirren," I yell, "Where is Mirren?!"

She eyes me distastefully. "She needs a minute. Gods, Shaw, can't you see you just devastated her?"

I know, *I know*. I shake my head and lick my lips. "No, Max, Jayan is—Mirren is—it was a trap!"

I stumble over my words, desperation garbling them together. I am running out of time. Whoever it was that wanted Mirren alone will have acted as soon as she left the gathering. It might already be too late. Gods, what if it's Shivhai that found us? Would he have healed so quickly?

Or worse, has he told the Praeceptor who I am?

I grab Max's shoulders, something I would never do normally. She hates to be touched without warning, something I've always done my best to respect. But the touch has its intended effect and Max's eyes widen in alarm. She studies my face for less than a second before nodding.

"Please tell me you took her back to the manor." The manor, at least, has some semblance of security. Not impossible to get through, but it will buy me some time.

"I dropped her off in the drive. She said she was going for a walk and needed to clear her head."

I curse loudly and open my mouth to explain, to beg for help, to do *something*, but Max waves me off. "Go. It looks like Cal could use a little help. Did you manage to piss off the *entire* city guard?" she asks, sounding slightly impressed.

I don't bother to answer, untying the skiff and rowing toward the manor. The wind of the Bay of Reflection sings in my ears and my heart beats painfully against my ribs, as I pray to gods long dead that I'm not too late.

∽

Mirren

A man appears in the darkness between the trees, and I know immediately it's not Shaw. He would never move so carelessly through the forest. Even on a casual walk, his feet are always silent and this man crunches leaves and twigs loudly beneath his boots.

The stranger examines my dagger with interest before plucking it from the tree. By the Covinus, I wish I'd been able to fit two under this dress. Or taken Max's offer of a jeweled weapons belt. Instead, I only have the small leather sheath, now empty.

"I'm curious who you thought I was?" the stranger asks genially. He steps from the shadows, moonlight illuminating his features. He is young, a few years older than me, but age is no indication of deadliness. Shaw is proof of that.

I glance to the trees. The man stands between me and the path back to the manor house. No matter how upset I was, it was foolish to come here alone in the depths of night.

"My friend," I tell the man, careful to keep my voice confident. *There is always something to use as a weapon.* Normally, Shaw's state of constant vigilance is a source of annoyance, but now the words ground me to my surroundings. The sparkling granite around the pond is full of rocks and branches. I need to keep him distracted long enough to grab one. "He's meeting me here at any moment."

Lie. If Max has even made it back to Nadjaa by now, I'd be surprised. And I didn't even tell her exactly where I was headed. No one is coming to save me. Even if Shaw came after me, there isn't enough time for him to figure out where I've gone. If he even cares enough to do so after I stormed out on him.

The stranger grins, revealing a set of pearly white teeth. His dark hair is shorn close to his head and his dark eyes glint against his pale skin. He knows no one is coming for me. Fear clenches me, but it isn't for myself. What has he done to assure we're alone?

The stranger lunges and I scramble to grab one of the branches. I swing out as hard as I can, but he darts backward, light on his feet. I whirl again, the branch whistling through the air, but the stranger twists out of my reach, a skeletal grin on his face.

He surges toward me. I whip his hand with the branch. If he grabs me, I'll be done for. I can't overpower or outmaneuver him. My only chance lies in moving him out of my path and running like hell toward the manor.

The manor that is empty of people. Of help.

Don't think of that now. You need no one to save you. You can save yourself. Shaw's voice. Calm and calculating. I let it swirl inside me until I, too, am these things. I've survived Boundary hunters and the yarmardu's screams and a bloodthirsty *legatus*. I will survive this, too.

The stranger withdraws his sword. The blade is thin and curved and winks in the moonlight. His murderous gaze glints and I barely have time to throw the branch up as he brings the weapon slicing down. It whistles through the wood as if it's made of air and I'm forced to jump back to keep from being gutted. I dance to the side, praying he follows.

He does, twirling the weapon with deadly skill and striking fast once more. I cry out as his blade comes across my forearm, hot as iron. Blood pours over my fingers, but I force myself to move again. The stranger circles me, watching me bleed with a fervent look, and I get the distinct impression that he is playing with me. If he weren't, I would already be dead.

"I admit, I took this job out of pure curiosity. After all,

what kind of girl requires an assassin of my skill to take care of them? Why not just get her alone and take care of the deed oneself?" The stranger tilts his head, his eyes roving from my hairline to my toes, sizing me up. As if he is trying to peer beneath my skin and examine what lives beneath it.

"I thought perhaps there would be something special about you. Something powerful. But you seem perfectly ordinary." His lips twist in disappointment.

The stranger sighs as if deeply put out, and then adjusts his grip on the pommel of his sword. "I suppose even the wind can be wrong at times," he says softly, before darting forward.

His small movement is all I need. As soon as the heel of his foot leaves the path, I launch myself toward the manor.

∽

Shaw

Where is she, where is she, where is she.

The words run a familiar rhythm through me, and it serves me right. I dragged Mirren into the Dark World, embroiled her in shadows and violence, and my penance is being destined to lose her, over and over. It's deserved. But this knowledge doesn't ease the slimy membrane of fear that coats my heart as I will the skiff to move faster.

My arms burn by the time I reach the dock and I don't bother to tie the boat off before hurtling up the manor path. Where would she go? The wood behind the manor is vast, before giving way to the granite cliffs, and finally the endless Storven Sea. How far did she get?

If only I'd confessed the truth sooner. I should have been brave enough to cut the tip from the weapon of my betrayal so that it could never be used to divide us.

Desperation seeps into my chest as I reach the manor. Whoever orchestrated this has been thorough, watching and gathering information patiently. They will have planned this down to the second. Calculated how long it would take me to extract the truth from Jayan and to ensure the deed was done long before that. And I've already wasted so much time.

If you don't picture victory, you've already lost.

My father's words. Normally, I would battle against them, but now I let them bolster my resolve. Mirren is not dead. I would know. I feel the truth of it in my bones. Her will to live is unmatched. She still breathes. She still fights.

I dip into the abyss and let the fire burn in my stomach and veins, clearing through the fear and leaving only clarity behind. Mirren is too smart to wander the unknown in the dark of night. She would go somewhere familiar. There are only two places on the manor property she's acquainted with. The training grounds, to the left. And the pond, to the right.

The pond, with its sparkling droplets that I brushed from her lips with my own. Her electric touch shooting through me like starlight and crackling through every dark corner of myself.

I think of how that same touch disappeared as soon as Jayan revealed the ugly truth of me. How her eyes glistened, hot and bright, with unshed tears of hurt. She wouldn't go to the pond. She wouldn't go anywhere that reminds her of me.

I steel myself and turn left toward the training grounds.

~

Mirren

I don't make even make it to the last willow when a searing pain rips through the muscles of my calf. I cry out and fall to the ground, the palms of my hands scraped raw, saving my face from a similar fate. My leg burns in agony as I rear up, fighting through the red haze of pain, but the assassin is already on top of me.

He yanks the dagger out mercilessly and a ragged scream erupts from my throat. He flips me over as though I weigh no more than a feather and presses me into the dirt. Another wave of pain rips through me and hot tears spring to my eyes. Oh gods, *oh gods.*

The stranger studies my dagger. Blood coats the blade, running down its intricate hilt and I know it will be the last thing I see before I die. Easton is across the continent and my mother is dead and my father is captured. And Shaw, by the Covinus, Shaw is not coming. I will die alone.

Alone, as I have always been.

I squeeze my eyes shut as the stranger brings my own blade toward my heart.

CHAPTER
TWENTY-EIGHT

Mirren

"Mirren!"

My name, but so far away. As if it has risen through mist and blood and shadows to reach my ears a millennia later.

I shy away from it. I am unmade and my name only serves as a painful reminder of what once was. What can no longer be. What was weakness and loneliness and failure.

Mirren.

My name echoes again and this time, it's not the distant call of an ancient creature. It is intimate and familiar, a soft purr of sonorous syllables.

Shaw.

He shouts my name again, his voice closer this time.

I want to tell him it's too late. I've been alone so long and now, I will die here, too. It's impossible for him to reach me through the thick glass walls the universe has constructed around me. I am destined to die just as I lived; forgotten and uncared for.

But you've never been alone, have you? The voice sounds in my head, both foreign and familiar; a part of me but wholly outside myself. *I have always been here, sleeping in your heart and running through your veins.* The voice is ancient and raw, sounding somewhere halfway between dreams and wakefulness. *I soothe you and empower you, and now, I would save you. If only you'll allow it.*

Everything is so far away, everything but the voice. It is forever, but only a moment as the assassin brings his blade toward my neck.

Truths older than the universe ring through the words, the power of them curling inside me. The part of myself I have always tried to smother, the incurable wildness given form, given life.

You need only open yourself, Mirren.

I know it to be true, but I am so tired. Wouldn't it be easier to just give in? I've gripped the shattered pieces of my heart for so long, desperate to keep them from disintegrating. Wouldn't it be easier to let them go? Let them float away in the Darkness?

Easier, yes.

My soul is relieved at the thought. I can let go of the fear of failure and the pain of abandonment. Let go of the whispers that twist my dark heart. I can be at peace if I choose.

"MIRREN!"

Even through the mist, I can taste the bitterness of Shaw's terror. I feel his panic as my own, as if he lives beneath my skin.

He cannot watch you die.

My own voice now. Whatever Shaw has done, he doesn't deserve this. He will blame himself and give the last pieces of his soul to the Darkness.

He is here and I am here, you are not alone. But you need only yourself to be saved.

I have been fighting against my own power all my life,

refusing to claim it for what it was, to wield its strength. No more.

Living is infinitely harder, but I have the strength for it. I open myself up, allowing the voice to bloom within me. It grows and grows, a soft ripple turned to a crashing tidal wave. It washes through me, filling every crevice with its cool, powerful touch. It laps at my fingertips and crests across my chest. It beats through my heart like a lifeline and fills my lungs until it's the only thing I breathe. I am consumed, swallowed by it, yet a part of it all at once.

When I am drowning in its depths, when it thrums through my veins and my heart and my very soul, I let it all go.

∼

Shaw

I'm halfway to the training site when the abyss inside me flares, an ember proliferated into an all-consuming wildfire. It rages, burning inside my bones and consuming my heart until I'm forced to stop, clutching at my chest, and gasping for air.

I've never felt anything like it, but I don't stop to examine it. Mirren is not at the training site. I know it invariably, somewhere deep, and untouched.

Move, Shaw. Move.

I change directions, racing toward the cliff pond. As if fueled by fire itself, I whip across the moor fast as lightning. Trees and outbuildings blur in my peripheral as I plunge into the moist jungle and down the cliff path.

I allow myself a heartened moment. I don't know why Mirren chose to go back to the place our lips touched for the first time, a place entrenched with my touch and my betrayal, but I pray she uses it. Uses whatever anger lingers in memory to bolster her will to survive. I pray she remembers my eyes when I gazed at her and knows their silent promise to always come for her. To never leave her alone.

Faster.

A scream rends straight through the night and into my heart. My lungs burn with exertion, but I don't slow. I force them to keep expanding, to fly faster through the trees. Over branches and roots, with eyes for nothing but the darkness in front of me. The world suspends around me, as if the entire universe collectively holds its breath with me, until the moment the pond grove comes into view.

As if I've willed its existence into being, the trees of the forest open up, and the willows come into view. The pond sparkles under the night stars, the water cool and calm against the black granite cliff.

But there is no time for relief.

Terror pierces through me, sharp and sour. Mirren is prostrate on the ground, blood pooling around her. The assassin flips her over, lingering above her, Mirren's dagger in his hand. The dagger I gifted her, meant to protect, now poised to take her life.

"Mirren!" I shout, desperation lacing her name. My father would be ashamed of the way my emotions run unchecked, swirling around me like a suffocating shroud. But the sight of Mirren, prone and vulnerable and seconds away from death, has robbed me of all thought. Only the fire remains.

The assassin raises the dagger and *oh gods,* I'm too far. "Mirren!" *Fight. Don't leave me like this.*

I want to scream it, but words don't come. I push

further, harder. My body strains and my breath wheezes and still, I run. But it won't be enough. The assassin doesn't hesitate at the sound of my voice. His movements are smooth and efficient, reminiscent of my own.

"MIRREN!"

Oh gods, oh gods, oh gods. I chant it like a benediction. The Dark World gods are long dead, cut down by the queen's curse. There is no one left to hear my plea, but I pray anyway.

Suddenly, Mirren's eyes shoot open. They are no longer emerald—they swirl and churn, a riot of grays and blues and greens that glow in the moonlight. They writhe like the waves of the Storven Sea itself.

She who captures the sea in her eyes.

It is only then I realize it's begun to rain, though there isn't a cloud in the sky. Droplets speckle her pale skin and I watch in wondered horror as they begin to stream together. Thousands of tiny beads join together in undulating rivulets until a river rages across Mirren's body. It streams across her lips and flows between her breasts before curving across the soft planes of her stomach. The assassin hasn't noticed, the blade making a sure curve toward her throat. Before he can end her, the river jumps from Mirren.

It shoots toward the assassin. It splashes across his face and dives down his throat. The water moves with purpose. Like it's sentient—like it's *alive*.

The dagger falls from his fingers. He claws at his throat as he chokes and sputters. The assassin drowns from the inside out.

Mirren rises. Her hair is wild around her, the glow of her eyes eerie and consuming in the dark. Blood coats her arms and legs. She takes no notice of me as I skid to a stop in front her, huffing raggedly. Her gaze is entirely focused on the assassin, watching him struggle with a foreign detachment, one that is horribly familiar. The man gasps, the sound wet and strained, and falls to the ground.

She's going to kill him, I realize with a vague sort of horror. Mirren, soft and kind, isn't going to stop until the assassin gasps his last breath.

"Mirren!" I cry again, a different sort of desperation ballooning inside of me. It's no longer her life that is threatened. It's her soul.

I try to move toward her, but the water droplets circle around her, an impenetrable forcefield. I thrust my hand forward, but my knuckles crack against it like it's made of pure stone. Whatever is inside her, whether it's part of her or something else entirely, Mirren cannot kill the assassin. He surely deserves it, but Mirren—Mirren will never be able to live with herself or the hole his death will rip in her soul.

I give up trying to break my way through the water and turn, narrowing my eyes on the assassin. If I can't stop the power that rages inside her, I'll have to end his life first.

He isn't worth your vow.

I shove the words away and pick up Mirren's dagger, kneeling before him. His dark eyes are wide and rimmed with red as he gasps for air. His mouth opens and closes and his body twists and seizes. I wonder distantly if I will be giving up the last piece of myself with his death. There's no way to know, really, how many pieces remain, but I don't imagine it's many.

The monster inside me roars for his blood, commands me to take what he was so willing to steal from Mirren, and I give myself over to the beast. No longer ignored, it is a terrifying thing with jagged claws. The assassin's face turns blue, and his eyes roll upward. I have only moments.

I lift the dagger and steel my breath. Just as I give into

the most vicious parts of myself, a voice cries out. From somewhere inside me, it's young and helpless and alone; a child alone their whole life. With this man's death, that child will be no longer. Innocence struck down.

Mirren's soul is pure. You always do what needs to be done. It is your gift and your curse.

I was trained to be ruthless. I can be that now.

Nausea rolls over me. I have never taken a life with my eyes closed, but I squeeze them shut now. I lift my weapon once more.

"Stop."

Her voice is soft, but commanding. I drop the dagger instantly, freezing with my arms in the air. Relief and disappointment war inside my chest. I look back at her. "He deserves to die."

Her eyes have reverted to their natural color and though blood coats her, there is no sign of injury. Her small body trembles, wracked with violent chills and it takes everything in me to stay where I am instead of gathering her close.

The assassin groans and coughs. His body shudders and then goes slack beneath my grip. He's passed out.

"He isn't worth it," Mirren says, her face gravely serious. I wonder whether she is convincing me or herself.

"We can't just let him go, Mirren. He's trained. He won't just say 'thanks' and give up." I know because I wouldn't have. I was caught only once when I was barely ten. The man spared my life because I was a child, the natural inclination of a decent person that my father counted on. Back then, disappointing my father was much more terrifying than turning against a man who showed mercy. I finished the mission while he slept.

I won't give this man the chance to do the same.

Mirren nods, running her hands over her bare arms. The dress I so carefully selected hangs in tatters from her shoulders, matted with blood and pond scum. Her face is pale and wan as if whatever power she held drained and left her diminished.

"We won't let him go. We'll take him back to the manor and question him. We need to know who hired him."

I raise an eyebrow and her mouth lifts in a mocking smile. "What?" she asks blithely. "It's not as if you've never held anyone hostage before."

In spite of everything, I laugh. Another wave of chills ravages Mirren's body and this time, I go to her. I wrap my arms around her, telling myself it's to warm her and alleviate the aftershocks of that power, but it is just as much to soothe my own soul. To reassure myself with the vibrant warmth of life that still runs through her. I was so close to losing her forever.

She allows me to pull her close, her body settling against mine. Her head rests against my chest and I feel her sigh. The electricity that usually rushes through me when I touch her has turned to something softer that runs along my skin and cools the fire still burning in my throat.

My penance may be to lose her over and over again; but in this moment, I allow a treacherous hope to plant itself in my ravaged soul that maybe—just maybe—it will all be worth it to find her once more.

~

Mirren

The power trickles from my veins, my body giving it back to the sky from which it came. I am hollow and I cling to Shaw as if he's the only thing keeping me tethered to the earth. Tears sting my eyes and I make to pull away from him, but he only grips me tighter until I relent and bury my face in his chest.

I admonish myself for letting the tears fall, for not being strong enough to hold them back, but they are unstoppable. It's my own water magic that pours from me now, one borne of pain and trauma. Before long, my sobs are ragged and uncontrollable.

Shaw just holds me. He feels so strong, strong enough to hold my shattered pieces together before I lose them all. His skin is fevered against mine and I savor feeling something outside of myself. Something that is not raw pain. My lungs burn and I gulp down some of the brisk night air. I try to match my breathing to the steadiness of his. His heart beats against his chest, and I focus on its rhythm until my body calms.

I look up at him and he doesn't look away. He is intimately familiar with grief and pain, wearing his own like armor. The power that ran through me will never scare him, never intimidate him—not when he's held the power of death itself in his hands. Not when a curse has rent apart his soul. For the first time, I am innately grateful for who Shaw is. An abandoned child, like me, who doesn't shy away from the ugly parts of life. From the ugly parts of me.

Shaw holds me until I have cried all my tears. Until my breathing calms and the only sound is the soft rippling of the pond and the powerful waves of the sea in the distance.

"Mirren, about what Jayan said—"

I shake my head vehemently and pull away. "I don't want to talk about that now."

I look toward the assassin. Somehow, perhaps by a remnant of the power, I know he still lives. He looks younger than he did when he lingered over me, his face softened by the moonlight. His lips are pouted with sleep and long lashes sweep across his cheek bones. Under different circumstances, he could be handsome. But the world has spoiled him like it spoils everything else.

"Mirren, I have to explain."

I turn back to Shaw, and he falls silent at whatever he sees on my face. Shaw's betrayal still smarts, but it's now buried under a myriad of other emotions, confusion and exhaustion being chief among them. And, by the Covinus, the way Shaw almost sacrificed his vow, sacrificed *himself* —it is too immense. Too encompassing for me to begin to sort through tonight.

"I'm tired, Shaw," I finally say.

He nods and takes my hand, leading me from the cliff pond. "Let's go home," he murmurs.

I don't have the energy to point out the manor is not my home.

~

Cal and Max wait in the foyer when we arrive. Max sports a fresh welt along her jaw and Calloway's once beautiful clothes are torn and dirty. His eyes widen as he takes in my appearance. And Max, *Max*, rushes forward and throws her arms around me.

"I'm so glad you're okay," she whispers into my neck before releasing me.

I nod distantly. Words are entirely beyond me.

"The assassin is still at the pond grove," Shaw tells his friends. "He's...unconscious. I need you to move him here so we can figure out who hired him."

A wave of weariness overcomes me and my legs wobble.

Shaw circles an arm around my waist, keeping me from collapsing in an enervated heap.

"Second man you've held hostage this evening. You're on a roll, brother," Cal says, impressed.

A smile pulls at Shaw's lip but worry shines in his eyes. I consider telling him how unnatural the expression looks on his normally smug face, but I don't have the energy.

"We'll take care of it. Of him," Max says quickly. I must look near death if even she presents no argument.

Shaw steers me up the stairs and into my room. He hesitates awkwardly near the door. "Do you...do you need help bathing or dressing?" He eyes the floorboards as if they've suddenly become extremely interesting. "I can get Max or Rhonwen," he offers.

I shake my head and crawl onto the large bed, with no care for soiling the sheets. I wrap my arms around my chest, gripping my elbows. I only want to sleep; to escape the echoing hollowness. I chose to live, to climb forward everyday no matter how difficult, but I can't bear to think of it now.

Tomorrow.

The light flicks off and I expect Shaw to take his leave. To oversee the transfer of the assassin and begin to dig answers out of him. He won't be able to rest until he ensures everyone is safe.

Instead, he steps into the room and closes the door behind him. I watch him, surprise resonating somewhere remote. He tugs his shirt over his head, its fabric wet from kneeling beside the assassin while the power ravaged him, and it hits the floor with a squelching sound.

The mattress sinks as he climbs in beside me and I note that even his long body is dwarfed by the sheer magnitude of the bed. He circles his arms around me and tucks me into his bare chest, his skin an ember that warms the ice in bones and lights the emptiness.

Shaw holds me until I'm finally claimed by a fitful sleep. And then after—when dreams of Easton and tidal waves of blood crashing across the red square leave me gasping into the darkness.

CHAPTER
TWENTY-NINE

Mirren

The sun is high when I finally wake. Shaw is tangled around me, solid and warm. Turning my head, I realize with no small amount of surprise that he's still asleep. His caramel skin is tinged pink, and half his face is buried in the tangle of my hair.

It's the first time I've ever seen him sleep. His limbs are loose, and his breaths come slowly and for a few moments, I just watch him. Lips lush and pouted, raven hair spilling across his forehead. The sooty sweep of his lashes against his cheekbones, longer even than mine, breaks something open within me and I turn away abruptly.

I told myself I would decide what to do about Shaw today; that I would weigh his betrayal and his sacrifice and decide which matters more. But first, I desperately need a bath. Blood crusts my skin and dress, the iron tang of it nearly overwhelming.

I extricate myself carefully from his arms. He grips the pillow tighter, aware of my absence even through layers of sleep. Padding into the adjoining bathing suite, I pull off what remains of my dress. It settles around my feet in a pool of silky filth. I fill the giant iron tub and sink all the way to my neck with a pleasured sigh. The water is invigorating. It cleanses my skin, but also quenches the ache in my soul.

I scrub at my hair with scented soap before submerging myself completely, feeling weightless and renewed. I stay in the bath until the pads of my fingers prune. Droplets roll off my skin and I watch them intently, wondering at the power that crested inside me last night. It was all encompassing and foreign, but it was more than that—it was like coming home. Like the curve of Easton's shy smile or the ring of Shaw's laughter. Something that is a part of me. Something that *makes* me.

People don't use magic, Lemming.

I didn't understand what Shaw meant at the time, but it's clear now. I didn't use magic last night. I allowed it room to bloom and in turn, it opened up the best and worst parts of myself. The most dangerous parts. The most powerful. It is symbiotic, the power and myself, only capable of growing to our potential when we are intertwined.

Last night, it retreated from me like a wave from a beach, but this morning its presence trickles through me once more. It no longer rages, but laps gently at the corners of my mind. Something that has always been there, but that only now can I name.

I trail my fingers across my calf where the assassin's blade ran me through, hope blazing brightly in my chest. There is no sign of injury, not even the pucker of a scar.

The way you healed Anrai Shaw.

The old woman's words come back to me suddenly and I sit straight up, the water sloshing over the sides of the tub.

If I really am responsible for healing Shaw's injuries, for healing my wound, then Easton—Easton might not need my father at all. I can save him myself. I resolve to find Aggie today and find out everything she knows.

I step out of the tub and wrap a soft robe around myself, tying the fabric securely around my waist. Shaw still lies sprawled across the bed, but his light eyes track me the moment I enter the room. I ignore the muscled expanse of his chest, carved and beautiful, and grab my dagger from where he laid it on the nightstand. I thought the bright sting of betrayal faded with his actions last night, but now it climbs up my throat once more.

Shaw doesn't even flinch as my blade whistles past him, grazing his cheek and sticking into the headboard with a *thump*. His hair is mussed, and his skin is flushed with sleep. That impenetrable mask of his has fallen away and his face is wide open. The anguish, regret, and something like wonder, all written plainly for me to see.

I fling myself on the bed, yanking my dagger from where it protrudes next to his head. He makes no move to stop me as I shove it roughly against his throat. Even sitting, he is so much taller than me that I have to stretch to reach, the thin material of the robe doing little to cushion the way his hard body presses against mine.

His eyes widen, but he doesn't move; only watches me, still as a mountain cat. But he is the predator no longer. If power and strength are Shaw's language, I will speak it clearly until there is no room for misunderstanding.

"Why?"

I don't even know what I'm asking. Why did he have to choose me? Why didn't he tell me the whole truth? Why can't I simply hate him and use him and then be done with him?

"I was ashamed," he murmurs slowly, so as not to brush against the dagger.

My gaze flicks to his in surprise. "You told me you will not feel ashamed for what you do to survive," but even as I say the words, I know they aren't true. Not with the way Shaw's very body rejects violence; how he sacrifices every piece of it whenever needed; the way he spoke of the things he was forced to do as a child and the things he's been forced to do since; shame thrives in Shaw, a poisonous vine that weaves through everything he does.

"You—you look at me like I'm worth something. I was afraid if you saw who I really am, you would never look at me like that again. I was a coward."

"Be brave now, Anrai Shaw."

He swallows roughly against the shining blade. "When Denver was taken, I—I was beside myself. I searched everywhere, but it was like he'd vanished completely. I...well, I'm not proud of who I became. It was like Denver was the one who tethered me to being this person with a soul and when he was gone, I became desperate to get him back. I drove myself crazy trying to find a lead. I interrogated every Dark World scumbag I could find, and everything came up empty. I came back to Nadjaa angry and defeated. And that's when Aggie made her prophecy."

"She's always known things, has always said the earth tells her, but I never really took it seriously. This was different. Her voice changed and it was like something else spoke out of her."

I shiver, having witnessed this exact behavior.

"Destroy her. She who captures the sea in her eyes, bound without hate or love. Destroy her and the lost shall be found. It was obvious that whoever she spoke of was Similian. Everyone knows Similians are quiet, and love is against

their laws. I was so terrified of never seeing Denver again that I traveled to the Similian border. I blew up the Boundary. And before you came running out and I saw your eyes... well, I was going to go in and cut through whoever I needed to in order to find you."

"How did you breach the Boundary when no one else has been able to?" I ask, a question that's plagued me since before I knew the hole was a result of Shaw's actions.

"I'm still not sure. Failure wasn't an option, so I didn't let myself consider what would happen if it didn't work. When I set the explosives, I knew it was my last chance to find Denver. And somehow, it just did."

"And when you found me?"

"When I first saw you running, I really was just trying to save you from the hunters. I've seen what their kind does to young Similians, and I was just trying to keep you from being sold off to some warlord. It wasn't until you opened your eyes the next day that I realized what had stumbled into my hands. It was like every prayer had been answered and the earth had given me exactly who I needed to destroy."

Anger burns in my stomach like acid. It is everything I already knew, but hearing it from Shaw's mouth reopens the wound. I unintentionally grip the dagger until my fingers turn white.

"Are you going to do it, Lemming?"

My eyes widen at his implication. He will make no move to stop me. I can slit his throat and he will bleed out without so much as a fight. Tears spring to my eyes, hot with rage and desperation and something else that feels too wild.

"I deserve it. I will only bring you destruction."

The Darkness will change you. As hesitant as I've been to

admit it, Shaw has already changed me. He tore down the walls of timidity and rebuilt them in confidence and power. Shaw may very well destroy me, but destruction doesn't have to be the end. A forest ravaged by a wildfire grows again as something different. Something renewed. It's my choice whether to rebuild as something stronger.

His eyes flash as I climb on top of him, my legs straddling his bare chest. I press the dagger further into his throat. He has been stripped of the calloused mask of the assassin, now completely vulnerable as I stare down at him through my tears. I wonder how many he's allowed to see him this way, unarmed and entirely bare.

I wipe at my eyes with my free hand and grit my teeth. "There will be no more lies. I will have you unmasked," I press the blade until a tiny spot of blood wells at its tip, "bare," Shaw presses his eyes closed as if he can't bear the word on my lips, "or I will not have you at all."

His eyes fly open at the words, at their implied mercy and the ownership within them. His ice blue irises conflagrate from an ember to an open flame, hungry and consuming. For a moment, I stiffen, waiting for him to disarm me, to pin me to the mattress beneath him and take back his control—uncertain if I'd try to stop him or if I'd revel in the domination—but he leashes himself. Hands pinned beneath my thighs, Anrai Shaw nods his assent.

"I am bared," he says reverently, "only to you."

I let the dagger fall gently to the mattress. A pinprick of blood wells at his throat and I'm both horrified and satiated to have been the one who put it there. Shaw's eyes don't leave mine as I reach out and wipe it away with my fingertip. He holds himself completely still, his way of yielding to me. He won't move unless I ask him to, won't do anything unless I will it. The same way he gave me his name, he now gives me power over his being.

I am prey no longer. The predator now bows to his equal.

I run my finger along his jaw, feeling slightly untethered. My bare thighs tighten around his waist to keep upright, and I feel, more than hear, his breath catch. Hunger, bright and hot, burns in Shaw's eyes and this time, I recognize it for what it is: *desire*. At once, I understand why its expression is against the Keys, for surely something so intoxicating cannot be controlled. It is a different sort of power than what rolled through my veins last night, but it is no less demanding. I drink it like cherry wine, heady and all consuming. Like a twin flame, the same hunger pools deep in my belly.

My eyes rove to Shaw's lips. They part under the heat of my gaze and his pupils blow wide as he realizes, perhaps for the first time, that it is not only power that thrums through me—it is also *want*.

I've spent my whole life wanting, but never having; things danced from my reach for so long that my heart aches for things yet undiscovered. There's always been Easton to think of, or the Community beyond, never just myself. What if I reach out and take something, just for me? Selfishly call something mine for just a moment?

I've never been given a choice in anything, always commanded, or pulled, or swept away. But now, choice sprawls before me like a rushing river, mine to navigate. Mine to take.

So, I do.

I lean down and press my lips to Shaw's. His mouth is warm and gentle against mine and I can feel the effort of his restraint as he allows me to explore. Tentatively at first, much like that first brush of our lips at the cliff pond. I savor the way his breath becomes mine and sparks build beneath my skin as his arms come around me. He runs his fingers down my back, delicious shivers erupting in their wake; over the curve of my hips and back up until he cradles my face between his hands.

I press closer, the ties of my robe straining as I spread my body over his. I plunge into the most primal parts of myself like they are a raging river. I need to be closer, close enough that his fire melds with whatever crashes inside me now, until we are a storm, powerful and electric.

His hands tremble, achingly gentle. But I don't want gentle. I want every piece that he holds back, every bit of him for my own. I run my tongue over his bottom lip, and he opens for me with a groan. *I am bared. Only to you.*

The action unleashes Shaw, the last of his restraint crumbling as a low growl sounds in the back of his throat. I steal it, drink it in and take it for my own. His large palm spreads across the small of my back and his hips grind into mine. I moan as his tongue makes a possessive sweep across my mouth and he spears fingers into my hair. He pulls gently, the tiny licks of pain mingling with the pleasure of his tongue, until I feel as though I will come out of my own skin.

Shaw sits up and I wrap my legs around him. His hands cup my bottom, and his fingertips dig into my flesh, needy and wanting. He's always treated me like I can match whatever he gives me, and I do so now, gripping his shoulders and tangling my tongue with his. He believes I won't break and so I become unbreakable. Waves crest and crash within me and I revel in the feel of him, the current of us.

Mine.

The word echoes like a chime in the wind and I find I

want it desperately. In Similis, nothing is ever really ours. But right now, this beautiful Dark World man with his shattered soul and his loyal heart, can be mine. And in this moment, it feels like enough.

I thread my fingers through his thick hair, and it is every bit as luxurious as I first imagined it to be.

"Mirren," he whispers against my lips, before sweeping his tongue across my mouth. His calloused hands slip beneath the opening of my robe, and I cry out at the friction on the sensitive skin between my breasts. Pressure builds within me, and I grind my hips, needing more, needing everything. "Oh *gods,*" he groans, "I am bare, I am bare," he murmurs against my throat, nipping and licking the sensitive skin.

The words rise up within me and freeze me in place. Tears spring to my eyes. I pull away from him and roll to the other side of the bed, even as my body cries out at the absence. By the Covinus, what is the matter with me?

I demanded bravery and truth between us. I took it from him, soaking in the way he revealed himself to me and giving him nothing in return. I am no better than the warlords that ravage the lands, taking everything. Because though Shaw removed his mask and trusted me with his vulnerability, mine is still firmly in place.

"Mirren?" he asks tentatively, his dark brows furrowed in concern. "Gods, I'm so sorry, I shouldn't have—did I hurt you?"

I shake my head fervently. "No, Covinus, no. That was..." I don't have words for what that was. It was like being awakened.

I pull my robe tighter around me and turn to face him. His hair is wild where I ran my fingers through it and his lips are rose-tinged. Satisfaction threads through me, seeing my mark upon him. "I need to tell you something," I finally say.

Confusion flickers on his face. "Now?" he says weakly, and I almost laugh.

I bite my lip and nod. Dread sinks in my stomach. I don't want to tell him. Not when his face is so tender, and his lips are so thoroughly kiss-worn. But if Shaw, a man who has been devastated by the world around him time and again, has faith in my strength, I must have the same faith in his. Trust in his ability to hold fast to his goodness even when his world is shaken.

Trust that he won't hold it against me. I take a deep breath and spill the secret I've kept from him.

"Denver is my father."

～

Shaw

I stare at Mirren, certain I've misheard. "What?"

"Denver is my father," she repeats, her voice soft but sure.

I sit up straight. Distantly, I realize I still wear my dress pants from the night prior, though now, they're rumpled and stained. I only planned on staying with Mirren until the tremors ceased, but the feel of her tucked into my chest lulled me into a fast sleep. And with everything else this morning, I haven't had time to change.

I frown. Or bathe.

"Denver," I say slowly, "*my* Denver...is your..." I struggle with the word *father*, "...is the man you've been looking for?"

Mirren nods, the story of how she found Denver's picture pouring out of her in a desperate stream. I try to listen, but the words sound fuzzy. Maybe it's because it has caught me off guard in a world where so little does anymore. Or perhaps my mind still hasn't settled from the feel of Mirren's skin on mine, her breath in my mouth and her hands in my hair.

I furrow my brow, trying to focus.

"So, Denver," I hesitate. Can I even call him that anymore? It's certainly not his real name; it isn't Similian in origin. It isn't really *any* origin, which is probably the point. I clear my throat, "so your father was Outcast when you were seven?"

She nods, her eyes wide and glassy. Eyes that are precisely the same shade of green as Denver's. For someone trained to notice details, I certainly failed to see what was right in front of me. Though her lips are fuller, there is something of him in the set of her mouth and the curve of her jaw, now striking in its apparency.

I close my eyes, wishing desperately that we were still tangled together. That I was still watching Mirren tremble with the power I was so willing to cede to her. Gods, she practically glowed with it. Feeling how it heated her, the way my touch brought a needy flush to her skin—I know I'll spend the rest of my life chasing that feeling.

A flame of anger spears through me and I can't even pinpoint exactly why. Because she's on that side of the bed and I'm here alone? Because she kept vital information from me that could have changed everything? Because the man who brought me back to life and sheltered me isn't who he said he was?

Because I risked whatever is left of my humanity for his lie?

Whatever it is, I swallow it down.

"Denver, he...he never talked about his past and I never

pressed him about it." I don't know whether to be ashamed or livid. I poured the darkest parts of myself on to Denver and he accepted them all without demand. Was I selfish for not accepting the same in return? Or was he selfish for not offering it to me?

I rub my palms over my eyes, suddenly feeling exhausted. "Where is your mom?"

Mirren wraps her arms around herself. "I don't know. I was always told they were Outcast together."

Mirren's question about Denver's personal life suddenly becomes clear. Denver never mentioned a partner, but he also never bothered to mention that he left behind two children to fend for themselves. He always stiffens whenever an interested woman approaches him, but I always assumed it was because he shared Cal's preferences for the company of men.

"Gods, Mirren. I don't even know what to say. I don't know how the person who taught me compassion and kindness is the same man who abandoned his children. Who never even tried to get them back."

Mirren swallows roughly, but the tears that line her eyes don't fall. This is something she's already thought about. She's had days to come to terms with this, to align her emotions and present them to me neatly, and I hate the Similian slime of it. I want her as untethered as I am, like the world is unraveling beginning with one untruth.

"Why didn't you tell me?" I ask quietly. Mirren has never been forthcoming with intimate pieces of herself, but neither is she a liar. For the first time since she wrenched herself away from me, I look at her closely. Her hair has begun to partially dry wild around her face and her eyes are red rimmed and agonized. With a start, I realize it isn't worry for herself. It's for me.

She bites her lip, and I can't help but watch the way her teeth worry at the rosy flesh. I dig my fingers into my palm.

"I know what it feels like to have the world you thought you knew upended. I didn't want that for you."

I drop my eyes and shake my head miserably. "My world doesn't matter. I understand why you didn't trust me, but I'm sorry you felt you had to keep it to yourself."

"Shaw," she says quietly. I don't look at her. My world has ended and begun so many times I should be used to the reverberations. I should be the stoic and unaffected assassin my father trained me to be. I should know that it has never mattered how many times the sky rearranges itself, the monster I am will always remain. I am the Darkness, and the Darkness can never be anything else. Even when the moon shines, the Darkness endures.

"Anrai,"

My heart seizes at my name in her mouth. Instantly, I'm reattached to what I am, what I once was, what I still hope to be.

I finally raise my eyes to hers. She meets the fire with a strength of her own—I mistook it when we first met for being a twin flame, but now I recognize it for what it is. It's the strength of the ocean and the calm of a cliff pond. And though its power matches what rages through me, it is entirely her own.

"You deserve the truth," she says so fiercely it doesn't occur to me to argue. "I know I'm not the one who hurt you, but I couldn't bear to lend you anymore pain. It wasn't my choice to make and I'm sorry. I'm sorry I demanded you not hide any part of yourself, while being cowardly myself."

I watch her carefully and try to remember the last time anyone apologized to me. It isn't just my world that is upended by Denver's identity. Instead of spiraling into selfish destruction, instead of directing her hurt outward so that others would feel it too, Mirren tried to contain the fallout. To keep the pain for herself and spare me.

I don't deserve her. I don't deserve to be cared for so meticulously. So selflessly.

"Well. I guess this makes finding him easier," I offer up listlessly.

Her eyes flicker, a wave reminiscent of her power the night before cresting within them. "We're going to save him, Shaw. Together. We'll sort out the rest later."

Tomorrow I will remember that she is not mine.

Today, I reach for her. I run my hands over her skin and wonder at her velvet curves. How is that with every clash of the world, I am made sharper, but somehow, she is made softer?

Tomorrow, I will tell myself to let her go. But today, I hold fast to the only thing in the world that feels true.

CHAPTER
THIRTY

Mirren

The old woman is mad.

When I finally forced myself from the warm cocoon of Shaw's arms, I was determined to find Aggie and discuss my powers. But opening the bedroom door felt like tempting fate; like the room and everything that happened inside it would cease to exist the moment I stepped into the hallway. Like I would step over the threshold and fall headfirst into a black hole of reality.

But it was necessary. The People's Council and half of Nadjaa is demanding Shaw's blood and he needed to go assuage them if we're ever to make it out of the city and to Yen Girene. And I needed to find the one person who might have answers about my magic and my ability to heal Easton.

Now that I've found her, I can't help feeling my time would have been better spent in bed.

Aggie is both barefooted and bare chested. Her long silver hair hangs over her shoulders covering most of her sensitive areas, but as she sways and coils her body, it's an alarming sight, nonetheless.

Calloway, who has just finished tying up our horses, throws his hands over his eyes with a loud curse. "Gods, Aggie," he huffs, his freckles disappearing under a deep shade of crimson, "what in Darkness' name are you doing?"

She doesn't turn toward us. Instead, she moves her body languidly over the grass, her bare skin pressed against the ground as she stretches forward like a snake. "Greeting the moon, Calloway," she replies, as if this is obvious. "Why should she keep shining if no one thanks her for her light?"

Mad. She's entirely mad.

"Maybe this was a mistake," I hiss. Cal looks inclined to agree as he stares at Aggie with abject horror while she brings her naked chest against her knees and spreads her arms across the grass, sinking into a deep bow.

"I'd like to remind you that this was entirely your idea," he mutters through the corner of his mouth.

I shoot him a glare and straighten my shoulders. Mad or not, I need answers and Aggie is the only person who may possess them. "Aggie," I begin tentatively.

She cuts me off with a quick wave of a gnarled hand. "I know why you've come, little bird." She climbs nimbly to her feet.

Cal moves closer behind me as Aggie finally sets her milky eyes on us. Shaw asked him to accompany me and though their conversation was conducted in terse whispers, I gathered it was under the stipulation that Cal act as a sort of bodyguard. Why either of them feel I need protection from a crotchety old woman, I've yet to determine.

"It's why the elements have seen fit to bring you to Nadjaa." Her gaze is uncomfortably invasive.

"It seems it was *you* who orchestrated my coming here,"

I point out. It was Aggie's prophecy that set everything in motion, after all.

"I only speak for the Darkness. I do not control its whims," she says with a cryptic smile. She motions to the small cabin. "I think this calls for tea." She turns toward the house without bothering to wait for our agreement.

I glance at Cal uncertainly. He shrugs as if to say *what's the worst that can happen*. Dread winds tightly in my stomach, but I follow Cal onto the porch and through the threshold.

Though only comprised of one cramped room, Aggie's cabin is an affront to the senses. Every surface is a riot of color. Shelves of all different varieties overflow with books and brightly colored jars. Various knick-knacks line the windowsills and the top of the large iron stove that sits in the corner. Herb bunches hang from the rafters in various stages of drying and a thick perfume of burning incense permeates the air. The few visible patches of drywall have been plastered with paintings of landscapes and graphite portraits of writhing bodies.

Aggie moves through the cramped space with ease, a feat I find impressive as I possess the full use of my sight and still manage to trip over a large cast iron pot that sits by the doorway. Calloway ducks in behind me, his copper hair brushing one of the herb bunches as he stands to his full height. Aggie motions impatiently for us to sit, so we squeeze ourselves awkwardly into the scrubbed wooden seats, the bump of Cal's knees rattling the stacked china.

Aggie hasn't bothered to don a shirt; a fact made more evident by the way Cal decidedly looks everywhere *but* her. She pours the tea into three chipped mugs and slides two of them toward us.

Cal starts to shake his head, eyeing the teacup dubiously. "Thank you, but I'm—"

"Drink, Calloway," Aggie tells him firmly. Cal brings the cup to his lips, looking like a scolded child.

I blow on the tea and take a doubtful sip. It's brown and murky but isn't wholly unpleasant. It tastes of the forest, of herbs and fresh air and a hint of pine. I open my mouth to ask what's in it but fall silent when I feel the weight of Aggie's gaze. She eyes me over her blue teacup, her face revealing nothing of her thoughts.

"Ask me your questions, then," she rasps.

"I have a question," Cal quips immediately. "Is it pertinent to be naked while thanking the moon?"

I shove my elbow into the soft part of his abdomen and he grunts, turning wide eyes on me. "What?" he asks innocently. "If one is thanking the moon, one should be certain to do so properly, don't you think?"

I glance at Aggie apologetically, but she is gazing at Cal with approval. "The rest of the world insists on living in Darkness, but you, Calloway, have always stubbornly shown your light."

Cal furrows his brows, uncertain whether or not he's been paid a compliment. He opens his mouth to retort but I shake my head impatiently and cut him off. "Aggie, I need to ask about what you said to me at the lunar celebration."

"Which part?"

Her white eyes land on me and I take another sip of tea to avoid having to meet them.

Which part, indeed. Am I here because of her comments in her silly sing song voice, alluding to my healing powers? Or am I here to ask after her other comments, darker and wholly more intimate?

You cannot touch the Darkness and remain unchanged.

"I can smell it on you, you know," Aggie says, and I almost leap out of my skin. She can't know that I spent the morning tangled up in Anrai Shaw; can't know that if he is the Darkness, I was changed by him long before she made her prophecy.

"The power," she clarifies with a knowing smile. Calloway quirks an amused grin at my audible sigh of relief, but thankfully, makes no comment. "I sensed something different about you when we first met, but now, little bird, it pours from you like the waves of the sea itself live beneath your skin."

I stare down at my hands. Short nails, slim fingers, pale skin. They look as unremarkably plain as they always have. Could it be true that something greater lives within them, something powerful enough to save my brother's life?

"Where did it come from? Is it...is it mine?"

"It belongs to you as much as you belong to it. It's chosen you and you have claimed it in return. You cannot be parted."

Something bright blooms in my chest that the power can never leave me. That no matter what life brings, I will never again be truly alone.

"As for where it comes from, it comes from the same place all magic comes from. Life itself. Yours is the spirit of the water. The life it gives and the life it takes. The power it exudes and the sacrifice it demands. All that the water contains is yours to wield if you so choose."

"So, I can...I'm able to heal someone? If I learned how...I could heal like I healed Shaw?"

Aggie tilts her head, considering her words. "It is possible," she finally replies.

"Shaw said magic wasn't...isn't...something to be used. But I could use it?"

Aggie makes a rough sound in her throat that I realize is a chuckle. "For a boy that can't find his way out of his own shadow, he is shockingly astute at times. Anrai is correct. It seems that somewhere in time, the lore of magic has been twisted. People now like to think of it as a benign energy source, neither good nor bad. Something that could be formed and wielded according to whoever possessed the power. But the spirits of the elements are just as sentient as you and me, something other but something the same as well."

Cal's face wrinkles in confusion, as if Aggie speaks a language he doesn't understand, but I suddenly feel breathless. Because she has put into words the feeling that crashed through me as the assassin brought down his knife, a feeling that, until now, was indescribable; how something can feel so apart from me but also as if it's intwined with my very soul.

"Do you know what a commenia flower is, little bird?"

I shake my head.

"It's a vine that only grows in the shade of the bayani trees," Cal answers.

Aggie looks pleased. "Yes. Its flowers are arguably the most beautiful in Ferusa and they only thrive in the nutrients of the bayani soil. And in return, the scent of the commenia blooms keeps pests away from the bayani, so that their branches may reach the sky unhindered. Without the other, both would be alive, but they would be sickly and weak, never reaching their full beauty and strength."

She swipes her fingers gently across the table until they find mine. Her hands are calloused and warm as they wrap around mine. "Do you see, little bird? We need magic as much as magic needs us. We have both been slowly dying since its banishment."

I stare at her hand, mulling over her words. "Why did the water magic choose me after being gone for hundreds of years? Why me?"

Aggie studies me. "That is not for me to know. There are good magics and bad, same as people. They are attracted to strong emotions, so I admit it is ironic that this one has chosen a Similian. But I'm not prideful enough to doubt or try to understand its choice."

"Don't you have magic, too? Isn't that how you know the things you do?"

Something like sadness glints in Aggie's eyes. "I do not. I was only blessed with being attuned to the changes of the world, to the sense of change and the whisper of the future. Every so often, a spirit will choose to speak through me as when Anrai searched for Denver and last night when I spoke with you."

My heart sinks. For as much as Aggie knows, she won't be able to train me in the ways of my power. How long will it take for me to figure out how to use it?

"Come back tomorrow," Aggie says, setting her teacup firmly on the table. Her face is pale, and she hunches, as if telling the stories of the world has sapped her energy.

Our chairs scrape against the planked floor as we stand.

"Bring Anrai," she says as we turn toward the door.

"Thank the gods Anni is the one who has to deal with this nonsense tomorrow," Cal mutters under his breath.

"Oh, and Calloway," Aggie says from behind us as we step into the sunlight, "beware brick walls."

∽

Shaw

The hot stink of the council house is unpleasant even in

the best of times. The fact that I spent my morning bathed in Mirren's intoxicating scent makes it seem more untenable than usual as I skirt through a side door. The air inside is hot and heavy, awash with the smell of warm bodies and damp stone. So very at odds with the fresh, flowery aroma that still lingers around me.

The building is the oldest in Nadjaa, built as a stronghold for some ancient warlord. It has since been converted to the city's center. The city guard is now housed in the East wing, barracks and training grounds built up around the expansive courtyard. The sprawling throne rooms have been converted to council meeting centers and the small bedrooms of old now serve as council members' private chambers. Despite the changes to its usefulness, the building still feels ancient and brutal. A fortress made for keeping enemies out, along with fresh breezes.

The only part of the fortress that still serves its intended purpose are the dungeons far below. Built of pure iron and stone, they are just as impenetrable now as they were hundreds of years ago. It is where Jayan is certainly lobbying for me to be kept. I'm sure by now, he's whipped up at least half the council's support in burning me at the stake.

I hold my breath and paste myself against a cold stone wall as two city guards round the corner. The guard is made up entirely of volunteers, men who have a vested interest in keeping the home they love safe, and I've never had a problem with them, until now. Being stuffed in the dungeons while Jayan takes over Nadjaa and leaves it wide open for the Praeceptor isn't an option.

They pay me no mind, focused instead on the punchline of a bawdy joke as they disappear down the opposite hall. I let the breath out slowly and move forward on silent feet. I reach for my daggers out of habit. The feel of them grounds me, even if there will be no use for them. Today is of the diplomatic variety, and I highly doubt Denver will appreciate my stabbing his loyal guardsmen when he returns.

I find the door I seek on the second floor. The dank walls are covered in brightly woven tapestries, an effort to support local artists and brighten the place up. It takes less than a minute for the large oak door to succumb to my small pick and I'm almost disappointed at how easy it is to sneak in. I have no interest in being seen, but a challenge might be a nice way to stretch rarely used muscles.

The council is aware I was previously Denver's ward, but nothing beyond that. I can't afford the questions that will be asked if I'm caught and brought to trial for accosting Jayan. It's better that this remain intimate until I can retrieve Denver. He can sort the rest out and tell them whatever he wishes about me.

Mirren's father.

I shake the words away. They are still abstract, and I have no wish to make them real now. Not when so many lives depend on me being entirely focused. *Later. I will deal with them later.* Even if I know the longer I wait, the more likely they will feel like a dam bursting over me.

The office is small but cozy. A breeze flutters through an open window making it seem much more palatable than the rest of the building. A mahogany desk is piled with neatly stacked papers, a large leather chair sitting behind it. One wall is lined with bookshelves and old habits have me perusing the titles.

A key jingles in the lock outside and the door pops open. A stout woman with orange hair and a no-nonsense mannerism appears. I wait until she has locked us in before making my presence known with a quick clearing of my throat.

The woman startles, throwing a hand to her ample chest and whipping around. Her gray eyes land on me, before they roll straight to the ceiling as if she prays to the old gods. "Shaw," Evie says begrudgingly. "Must you sneak around like a Xamani mountain cat? I'm to be married soon, I don't need to be keeling over of a frozen heart."

"Evie," I say by way of greeting, nodding my head in respect. "I do hope I've purchased enough of your scones to garner an invitation."

She waves me off irritably, rounding the desk and dropping bodily into the chair. "You'd have a better chance if there weren't ten charges of treason against you," she says, leveling her gaze. "The entire city guard has been looking for you. The city is in an uproar that you conspired to kidnap the Chancellor and the council is demanding answers."

"I made no effort to hide," I tell her honestly. "I was at the mansion all night."

Evie eyes me ruefully. "That is *not* what Calloway told me. In fact, he seemed to imply that you'd taken your skiff directly into the Storven Sea, never to return. Something about a life goal to become a pirate?"

I press my lips together to keep from laughing. I can only imagine the joy with which Cal spun that story. He's always had a flair for the dramatics. "Just a miscommunication between friends."

Evie makes a disbelieving sound, a reluctant smile playing at her lips. She is rare, someone who was born on the streets of Nadjaa and then never left. She stayed, working her way up from the slums to be a successful merchant. Though she resides in the Hithe district, the wealthiest part of the city that surrounds the port, she chose to run for office in the Barrow. A small strip of land that protrudes into the Bay of Reflection, where orphans with swollen bellies run the streets and despite all the splendor of Nadjaa, life is still hard. It's where Evie was born and even with everything she has now, she's never forgotten the people that gave her life.

It's this propensity for fairness and kindness that brings me to her now. I will have to answer for my crimes eventually, but I can't do it before Denver returns. There isn't enough time.

"I need you to put the council off."

"I figured this wasn't a friendly visit," she mutters, resigned. She throws her slippered feet on the desk and a few spare papers flutter to the ground. "You attacked a council member in front of half the city. How long do you expect I'll be able to put them off? If Denver were here to speak on your behalf, it might be possible. Has he truly been taken?"

I tug at the collar of my shirt. Before leaving, I exchanged the soothing leather of training clothes for the heavy fabrics favored by the business class. They are suffocating, making my limbs feel glued to my body. I resist the urge to throw my arms up and burst the seams. Once a beast, always a beast.

"He has. The Achijj of Yen Girene abducted him while he was coming home from visiting the Xamani villages."

Evie scrubs at her eyes and a pang of guilt shoots through me at the dark circles there. She most likely spent her night here in the dank walls of the council house dealing with my mess, instead of celebrating the moon with her fiancé.

"To what end?" she asks. It's a fair question, one that

I'm not entirely sure I can answer. It seems unwise to start ranting about prophecies and magic to someone as pragmatic as Evie, even if she's always harbored a soft spot for me.

"I'm not sure. Maybe it's a power grab for the city."

She mulls this over. "There have been rumors that the Praeceptor has been moving against various warlords. Silently overthrowing them and grabbing more land around the Boundary. Do you think this has something to do with it?"

Dread coils in my stomach at the mention of the Praeceptor. I've wondered the same thing in the darkest parts of night. I arrange my face into one of disinterested boredom. "It could," I hedge noncommittally.

She narrows her eyes. "Shaw, we need Denver. Jayan has never approved of the peaceful running of this city and already has half the council whipped into a frenzy, calling for war on whoever's done this. It's just the excuse he needs to wage war on neighboring warlords, to grab for more land and more power. Nadjaa's peace only lasts as long as the people vote for it."

My chest tightens. Nadjaa's peace and law is a novelty in Ferusa and a new one at that. It still has its skeptics, Dark Worlders suspicious of giving up even a bit of freedom for the good of the whole. Everything Denver has worked for teeters on the edge of a cliff. His permanent disappearance will be Nadjaa's death.

"Maybe it would be better to get the city guard involved," Evie muses, "There are men qualified to deal with this sort of thing. There are protocols and procedures the council must adhere to in order to ensure the safety of the city."

I press my lips together and breathe savagely through

my nose. "It is those exact protocols that will keep them from doing what needs to be done. I adhere to no such morals."

Evie regards me sadly. "Shaw, you don't have to do this alone. You're just a boy."

I gaze back stonily. "We both know that I am not just a boy."

I feel cold, having alluded to what Evie has never mentioned. Since I met her, she has never treated me as anything other than another mischievous teen, warm but stern. But if I am to earn her help in holding off the council, she needs to know who I really am.

She removes her feet from her desk and sits straight in the chair, raising herself to her full height. She nods once. "Very well. Five days, Shaw. And then you face the council. I can only hope that when you do, Denver is by your side."

I know better than to argue with the time I've been given, even if the brevity leaves me breathless. Five days to break into an unbreakable fortress and save both Mirren and Denver without getting us all killed. Or worse.

"Go out the way you came," Evie says, a clear dismissal.

I nod. "Thank you, Evie. Truly."

She turns toward the window, staring out at the sprawling expanse of the city. "Don't thank me, Shaw. I fear we are only delaying the inevitable."

CHAPTER
THIRTY-ONE

Mirren

"This isn't a good idea," Anrai says doubtfully.

"You said that already."

"You didn't listen."

"What makes you think I'll start now?" I shoot him a wry grin that he sheepishly returns.

Mastering himself quickly, he furrows his dark brows, eyes intensely focused once more. "Don't get near enough for him to touch you. Don't be bated by anything he says. He will try to rile you, to pit us against each other. It's to weaken us."

His eyes run down the length of my body and a hot wave rolls down my spine. "And put your hair up!" he barks as an irritated afterthought. "I know in books heroines are always running around with their hair blowing in the wind, but it's ridiculously dangerous. It could get in your line of vision at a pivotal moment, or the enemy can grab it—"

"Anrai," I interrupt softly, and he stops short, his eyes softening as they take in my face. *"I know,"* I say, sweeping my hair up into a messy bun. "You've prepared me well. The assassin is tied up and you're going to be with me the entire time."

A muscle in his jaw twitches and he looks as if he wants to argue. Instead, he says, "Do you have your dagger?"

I pat the leather sheath that is now almost always attached to my thigh. I've learned the wisdom of being armed at all times in Ferusa. It only took almost dying numerous times.

Anrai nods approvingly but keeps his body solidly in front of the door. "I don't know why I can't just go question him alone," he says grudgingly, folding his arms over his chest. Though he's changed from the stuffy clothes he wore to meet Evie and is now clad in the supple leather of his everyday gear, his hair is still unnaturally neat. Something, I'm sure, that had to do with Calloway. "I'll be brutal and efficient, and we can move on."

"I need to see his face," I repeat what we've already talked about, but he nods as if he needs to hear it again. "My power is telling me I need to, maybe because it's still in him?" Shaw frowns, as if he doesn't like the idea of anything of mine being in the assassin, but I press on. "I feel a connection and I need to talk to him. I can't explain it more than that."

He nods, lifting his hand as if to caress my face, but seems to think better of it and stops halfway. We both stare at his hand, the air suddenly taut with the promise of his touch. My body awakens at the mere whisper of it. Our interactions since this morning have been honest and shy, if limited and perfunctory. There are more pressing matters than what happened between us, but that hasn't stopped my mind from wandering back there. Repeatedly.

Shaw tucks his hand into his pocket and steps aside with a flourishing bow. "After you, my lady," he says grimly.

I take a deep breath and push through the door.

The assassin is housed on the second floor of the manor in a bedroom similar to mine, except that this one has been stripped of everything but a chamber pot. He springs to his feet nimbly and presses his back to the far wall, his wary eyes locking on me. Color has returned to his skin and my chest relaxes at the visible confirmation that I haven't killed him.

Something sparkles under my skin when I meet his dark eyes as my power recognizes someone it's touched. It begins to trickle inside me like a cool forest spring.

The assassin's hands are bound together with thick coils of rope, in the same manner Shaw bound mine when we first met. Distaste threads through me as the aforementioned scoundrel slinks into the room after me, closing the door with a soft *snick*. This room is no better than an animal's kennel. Or worse, the cage I rescued Asa from.

Emotion rises in my throat. "Shaw, how could you not even give him a proper bed?"

"Are you going to show kindness to everyone who tries to kill you?" He replies sardonically. He doesn't look at me, his pale eyes entirely focused on the man in front of him. There is nothing of Anrai—it is only Shaw now, hard and unyielding. "Tell us, assassin, what would you do with a proper bed?"

The assassin tilts his head as he considers the question. "I suppose it depends on what sort of bed." His voice is deep but rough, most likely an aftereffect of being drowned. His eyes glint in the dim light of the room and his muscles are tightly coiled, as if prepared to fight his way through us at any moment, tied hands be damned.

Shaw grins arrogantly. "Humor her."

The man shrugs. "Take the metal or nails and form it

into a weapon. Sharpen the wood into stakes. Take the thread from the sheets and fashion them into a garrote," he bares his teeth in a humorless grin, "Or maybe I'd simply get a decent night's sleep."

"What's your name?" I ask him.

His eyes rove over me and I determine that they aren't black at all, but a deep shade of brown. His hair has grown in more fully so that his skull no longer gleams through it and though his face is dirty, his skin is smooth and youthful. A large scar runs from his left eyebrow to his ear, as if someone attempted to slice out his eye.

Every scar tells a story. Is every story one of pain?

"That power of yours will be more successful than your kindness if you wish me to talk," the assassin replies, his eyes flicking between Shaw and me. His voice is calm, but fear wavers beneath it.

Of me.

"I have no wish to hurt you," I tell him honestly, taking a step toward him. He presses himself further into the wall and his eyes scan the room restlessly, as if there will be some weapon he's missed. A harsh breeze roars through the window, the pane flinging open and bouncing off the wall with a loud rattle.

"That makes one of us," Shaw growls from behind me. Emotionless brown eyes flick to him. The assassin has seen as much as Shaw has to be able to bear witness to what burns in Shaw's eyes and not rear back. He is comfortable in cruelty and in its familiarity, there are no surprises.

It is my power that chills him. The unknown is always more frightening than the explored places, even if those places were dark and brutal.

Soothe him.

I don't know whether it is my thought or the *other* that

now resides inside me, but I remember what Aggie said about the commenia tree. One cannot thrive without the other. It feels so easy now, to reach where my power once crashed through the assassin, almost like walking a well-worn path. This time, I don't send a raging typhoon, but instead a small, trickling stream.

The assassin visibly stills, his eyes going wide.

"What are...why are you doing that?" Hope and despair mingle on his face.

"Because I saved your life. I don't wish you to live it in pain."

"What do you mean you saved my life?" he asks, nostrils flaring. "As I recall, you tried to drown me on dry land."

"It's true," Shaw says, stepping to my side. I can feel his questioning eyes on me, wondering where I'm going with this, but I don't look at him. He'll have to trust me. "I was going to finish you off and she stayed my hand."

The assassin mulls this over. "So, I owe you a life debt, do I?"

I shrug. "It's not my custom, so the choice would be yours."

The assassin looks momentarily stunned, as if the direction of the evening has taken him entirely by surprise. After a pause, he says, "I will tell you what I can as payment for the debt."

"Wait," Shaw interrupts, "what of those you work for? Are they going to be hunting you down for spilling their secrets and failing your mission? And us, too, for harboring you?"

The assassin looks annoyed. "I work for no one but myself and whoever pays the highest. And I don't believe anyone mentioned anything about *harboring.*" He crumples his face as if the word is distasteful.

Shaw narrows his eyes. "You work for no one? Who trained you then? Or were you born knowing how to split your soul and make men bleed?"

The assassin looks more thoughtful than offended, as if he is reassessing Shaw. "The same person trained me that trained all of us. A bloodthirsty beast that cared for nothing but their own power. Does it matter the name or which particular brand of beast?" He runs his gaze down Shaw, his eyes lingering on the latter's chest. Where, beneath the layers of his shirts, lies the gnarled scar his father gave him.

Shaw snarls, but before he can move, the assassin shifts his attention back to me. "My name is Avedis," he says, bowing as best he can with his hands tied together.

"Mirren," Shaw warns as I move toward Avedis.

Avedis holds up his bound hands, a sign of surrender. "Don't worry, my friend, I have no interest in having sea water shoved into my lungs again. Once was enough for a lifetime. I don't think I'll even be able to step foot in the Storven after this adventure."

Shaw's face turns mutinous at being called 'friend'. I press my lips together to keep from laughing as I slice through the assassin's binds. "I won't apologize for drowning you," I tell him, taking a step back with the dagger still firmly in my grip. "I think you rather deserved it at the time."

He bows his head in agreement. "I'll make no argument there," he concedes. Now that he isn't a snarling monster brandishing a sword, he's downright charming. His tone is polite as though he were raised in a fine house, rather than whatever violent pit actually spawned him. "What is it you wish to know?"

Shaw steps forward and Avedis shakes his head. "Ah, ah. Not you, friend. I owe you nothing except perhaps a sword to the gut as recompense."

"Call me 'friend' one more time and the lady's well pled mercy will be forgotten," Shaw growls, his face twisted in a terrifying sneer.

Avedis tilts his head innocently. "Are we not all friends here? I was under the impression that we're just good chaps, exchanging a bit of Dark World gossip."

I fight the urge to laugh at Shaw facing someone possibly more obnoxiously arrogant than he is, but instead I say his name quietly.

His burning gaze flicks to me and I look at him meaningfully. After a moment, the raging inferno tempers. "Very well," he bites out and goes to stand by the door, crossing his arms and leaning against it in that assured way of his. The one that says even when relaxed, he is fully capable of tearing out your throat.

I turn back to Avedis. "You were hired to kill me." Not a question. Avedis inclines his head in agreement. "Was it Jayan?"

His eyes are so dark, the pupils are practically indistinguishable from the irises. But they are no longer cold, instead seeming insatiably curious as he regards me. "Jayan. Unsavory little man. Power hungry with no actual power to back it up." He states this lightly, as fact rather than conjecture. "No. I used him solely as a means of distraction. I told him of the Chancellor's abduction and the prophecy and knew he would use it to try to seize power. Coups are generally very good distractions."

"How did you know of it?"

"The wind told me," Avedis replies with a deriding smile.

Shaw scoffs loudly. "Who hired you?"

"I never met them. They used various go-betweens, all high born Gireni, and never the same one. Whoever it was did not want to be connected to the job, which isn't uncommon. I was told it was retribution for a political deal gone wrong, but what I'm told isn't always the truth."

"And you accepted?" Shaw spits disgustedly. "You work for yourself and yet possess no qualms about murdering helpless women?"

Avedis' gaze wanders to Shaw. "I don't generally find women to be anymore helpless than the other half of the population," he replies shortly. His eyes trail lazily back to me. "Particularly this one." I blush deeply as he continues, "The client offered quite a sum and it so happened I was in need of it. I admit, curiosity also pushed me to accept. It isn't often a contract is put out on a nameless woman, unless it's by a jilted lover. I never accept those jobs. Too messy. But politics...that intrigued me. Especially since the woman in question didn't seem to be any sort of nobility. She didn't seem to be *anyone*, in fact."

"So, you know nothing then?" Shaw grits out from behind me.

"I did not say that. I am thorough in my business affairs. I did my own research before tracking the lady down."

"What did you discover?"

"That the Achijj has a guest that is not Gireni."

Shaw looks at me imploringly, as if to say, *torturing him would be faster.* I ignore him, telling Avedis, "we knew that."

"Did you know that there is a *second* guest, foreign, but holds a great sway of power anyway. Rumor has it, even over the Achijj. And that this person has been telling someone outside the fortress of the Achijj's capture of the

Chancellor. It is through that channel I was able to garner the information to feed Jayan."

Shaw furrows his brow. "Who is it?"

Avedis shrugs. "That, I couldn't determine. Whoever it is, their presence in Yen Girene has been well guarded. Though I imagine the Achijj would not take kindly to learning his guest is a traitor."

The words light something in me and I turn to Shaw with bright eyes. He nods once impassively, an indication to discuss later, but he has come to the same conclusion I have. We've found our bargaining chip to negotiate the return of my father.

"Now, if that is all," Avedis says, sounding rather bored. He stretches his arms above his head, stifling a yawn. "Might I request a meal and a bed? I will take my leave when the moon is highest."

Shaw shoots him an incredulous look. "You are either stupid or outrageously bold to assume I'd let you sleep under the same roof unattended. What's to keep you from finishing the job while we sleep?"

Avedis smiles slyly, unruffled. "The job is finished, friend. I will not break my life debt by betraying the lady's mercy. And whoever is pulling the strings in Yen Girene wanted to stay far enough away from implication that they won't be pursuing the matter. There is never lack of demand for retribution in Ferusa, so I'm sure I'll find another paying job in no time."

His eyes land on me, that glint of iciness from last night back in them. "Besides, what's to keep the lady from doing the same and drowning me in my sleep?"

I blush once more, unsure whether Avedis' fear of me is repellant or admirable. Fear is wielded as a weapon in the Dark World and worn as a cloak of protection. But I haven't come so far as to appreciate the safety of its womb. I only sense the slick barrier of it that keeps me isolated, just like I have always been.

"Fine," Shaw mutters furiously, opening the door.

I make to follow him when Avedis' cultured voice trails after me. "Might I give a small suggestion?"

I look back. He is bathed in the light of the setting sun through the windows, soft streams of pink and gold. I nod.

"Whatever it is you're planning in Yen Girene, know the danger. Whoever is influencing the Achijj is not someone to be trifled with. There are larger things afoot in the Dark World than the abduction of your Chancellor."

His words send icy dread sluicing through me.

"Make good use of your power, Mirren."

I stare at him. As far as I know, Yen Girene is a walled fortress nowhere near a sea or pond. "How?"

At this, a devilish grin spreads across his scarred face. "Why, the river Timdis runs straight under the city."

˜

Shaw

By the time dinner is served, I'm dead on my feet. Rhonwen has outdone herself, the large oak table practically bowing beneath a multitude of delicious dishes, each mouthwatering in scent and presentation. It's the first meal we've eaten all together since Mirren and I arrived and I should be enjoying it, but I feel as if the rest of the room is bright splashes of color and I remain muddled in shades of gray.

I've been unsettled since our conversation with Avedis, the weight of everything to be done hovering over me along with the feeling of his eyes on my scar. Somehow, he knows who I truly am. It was only a matter of time before someone caught on, but I no longer feel safe in the city I love. I feel vulnerable, like I am standing at the center of an open field and shouting my true name. Everything in me wants to run, to disappear before my enemies find me, but I am as mired here by my circumstances as I am by my heart.

Mirren's colors shine as she talks with Max and Cal; her chestnut hair tinted auburn with the candlelight, her emerald eyes shining with laughter, her fingers stained with the purple jam of one of Rhonwen's many treats. She licks the tips, dancing lightly in her seat as she does, and I can't help the smile that ghosts my lips.

"Rhonwen, that was the best thing I've ever eaten," she exclaims exuberantly as the housekeeper returns from the kitchen bearing another tray of sweets.

"Which part, dear?"

Without hesitation, Mirren declares, "All of it!"

Rhonwen beams and disappears back into the kitchen, laden with empty trays. No matter how many times we've asked her, she always insists on eating separately, a remnant of procedure from whatever house she worked in prior.

I wait until the table has been mostly cleared before beginning, only half empty bottles of wine still strewn about. "We need to talk," I announce grimly.

Three sets of eyes turn to me, Max's only after a dramatic roll. "Can't we have one pleasant dinner?" she whines.

"You know what they say," Cal quips, hiccupping and raising his glass to me, "moody and brooding is best served hot."

A surprised laugh bubbles out of Mirren and I whip my

head toward her. She giggles, eyes innocent. "You are *very* broody."

I scowl, at once feeling light at the sound of Mirren's laughter and justly misunderstood. "I am not broody," I mutter. The sullen tone of my voice seems to imply the exact opposite and the three of them burst into laughter. I flash a conciliatory grin. "Fine, maybe I brood a little. But at least I look good while doing it."

"Here, here!" Cal whoops, thrusting his glass in the air in a mocking toast and then draining the last of its contents.

Max shovels three overlarge bites of chocolate cake into her mouth. "What?" she asks through a mouthful of crumbs when I raise a brow. "I don't want your doom and gloom ruining my dessert."

"I don't think anything could ruin chocolate cake," Mirren sighs reverently. She takes another bite with a contented squeak, a sound that immediately transports me to a bed bathed in morning sun.

Max nods her agreement, smiling broadly at Mirren. Her change of heart is both a surprise and an inevitability. Max does not give her trust easily, but Mirren has proven capable of winning over even the most obstinate of people.

"Alright, Anni," Cal says, sobering his expression to one of resigned appeasement, "let us have it."

"Evie gave me five days to hold off the council. It's a days' ride to Yen Girene and a day back. That leaves us three days." I speak evenly. No one wants a leader whose throat is clogged with fear. Even if that's exactly what I am right now.

"Three days," Cal repeats softly, "to rescue Denver and convince the council that Jayan's plan for Nadjaa is the wrong one."

I nod stiffly. "I know it isn't a lot of time—"

"Shaw, it's impossible," Max interrupts hotly. "We don't even have an escape plan. Even if we somehow manage to find Denver, what then? We'll be trapped inside the city walls."

I explain what took place during our discussion with the assassin and our plan to bargain for Denver's release with the information. I leave out the part where his eyes traveled to my scar. I'm certain I've never laid eyes on Avedis before, so his knowledge of me is particularly troubling. Something I'll be sure to see to before he leaves.

Max stares at the remainder of her cake dubiously, poking it with her fork. "It could work. But if it doesn't? We'll have showed the Achijj our hand with no plan B and no way out."

"Actually," Mirren intercedes shyly, "that's not entirely true."

The room grows warm in anticipation. Max and Cal obviously know *something* odd happened last night, as evidenced by the look of a typhoon having touched ground around the cliff pond though its nowhere close to storm season. But they haven't pressed about it, something I love them for. It isn't my story to tell.

"We looked through Denver's maps after we talked to Avedis."

Max raises a sculpted brow at Mirren's use of the assassin's given name but makes no comment.

"And there's a river that runs directly under Yen Girene. It's the reason they don't have to venture outside their walls. It provides fresh water and a steady supply of fish."

Cal looks skeptical. Max says, "So?"

"So," Mirren says slowly, gathering her strength to

speak what she must out loud, "it means we have an escape route. I can..."

She turns and meets my eyes. Determination lines her face but there is also a question. I answer with a reassuring smile, and it strikes me how easy it comes. Only days ago, I smiled only to further incense my opponents; never because I meant them. Never because I simply *wanted* to.

Mirren searches my face, finding whatever it is she needs. Steeling herself, she turns back to our friends. "I can...do things with water."

Max and Cal are still as they study Mirren, and I can almost see my story of the mountain cave coming back to them, along with all the implications. Of magic and the Dead Prophecy and all of this being about far more than a simple abduction.

"It...the water listens to me. I think if I try hard enough, I could use the river as a distraction to get us out of Yen Girene. If it comes to that."

Tension lines the air and I can't determine whether its Mirren's or my own. What will Max and Cal think of her declaration that magic has returned to Ferusa? Will they embrace her power or fear it? Max hails from a superstitious island, and while Cal doesn't ascribe to a particular belief, he's heard the stories of the nature elements' volatile nature and subsequent downfall.

"Well," Cal says carefully, as if he is digesting Mirren's words like small bites of dinner, "this does explain the seaweed."

Mirren's eyes widen. "I'm sorry—the what?"

"The seaweed," Cal repeats. "There was seaweed all over the path between the manor and the cliff pond, but we're far too high for it to have come from the Storven. Thought it was weird."

Max nods her agreement.

Mirren looks aghast. "Why didn't you say anything?"

Calloway shrugs, but it's Max who answers. She meets Mirren's eyes and for a moment, she's the same girl I saw all those years ago in my father's dining room—regal and strong, sculpted in shades of midnight and brimming with an unassailable sense of honor. "We all have our secrets to bear. We figured we would know yours when they were earned."

Mirren's eyes turn glassy, and she beams at Max. My heart swells with pride and an unabashed sense of privilege, to somehow have found my way through the Darkness to these three. I will never be deserving of their unwavering loyalty and fierce hearts, but I will spend my life trying.

We finish the wine amid peals of laughter and demands for demonstrations of Mirren's magic, which ends with an entire pitcher poured over Cal's head and Max declaring that she, too, has water magic. When the moon rises and Cal's face has turned thoroughly red from an overserving of spirits, I offer to walk Mirren to her room.

Her cheeks are flushed and her lips curve in a small smile as we leave the dining room, Calloway's slurred promise to be up at dawn to accompany us to Aggie's echoing behind us.

"Even if the old loon has given me a permanent tick whenever I'm in hands reach of half the buildings in Nadjaa!" He cries. "*Beware brick walls,* bah!"

Mirren laughs and places her hand tentatively on the inside of my elbow. My heart feels like the inside of a campfire, lit with enough embers that if given enough possibility, could overtake an entire forest.

Touch is not something she gives freely and each time, it feels like a gift. Need balloons inside me to claim more of it, to devour every bit I can before it is ripped away. It wars with the notion of treating it as carefully as a crystal vase, fragile and unspeakably rare.

I settle for enveloping her hand in mine and tucking her body close as we ascend to the upper floors. When we reach her door, we stand awkwardly apart. I stuff my hands in my pockets just to do something with them, an attempt to calm the restlessness of my own skin. Skin that demands hers, has demanded it since I first laid eyes on her.

Braver than me, she is the first to break the silence. "So, Aggie's tomorrow?"

I nod, words stuck thickly to the roof of my mouth.

She nods back, her curls bobbing. I want to reach out and snap one, press its silky coil between the pads of my fingers. "Well, goodnight then, Shaw."

She turns to open her door and fear grips me, hot and slick, that if I let her go through that doorway, I'm letting something go forever. Something I don't even understand.

"Anrai," I blurt out.

Well, damn.

I'd been going for something more eloquent. "I like when you call me Anrai," I clarify, "it makes me feel more like myself. Or a self I haven't been in a very long time." Or maybe one that never existed at all.

A smile curves her mouth, and it isn't small or shy. It is luminous and encompassing and it makes me want to do anything in my power to keep it there forever. "Anrai," she obliges, lightly teasing. I swallow roughly.

"Anrai," she says again, more softly, and something in me unwinds as I watch the truest name I have, the most intimate thing I possess, encircled safely by her perfect mouth. I snake my hands around her waist and pull her to me, pressing my lips against hers. She opens for me with a satisfied noise in her throat, a mingled sound of relief and pleasure as if she, too, suffered for us being apart.

All day. I've wanted this all day. Longer. So much longer.

I thread my fingers through the soft waves of her hair, tilting her head back and sweeping my lips hungrily across hers, taking her taste, her scent, all of her, for my own. Her tongue dances with mine and it is nothing like the tentative exploration of this morning. Now, she demands and takes, powerful and sure. Her small hands dig into the tight muscle of my back, urging me closer.

I run a hand down the smooth line of her throat, feeling the soft hum of her pulse. My lips follow, voracious in their need for more of her sweet skin. She smells of rain and fresh blooms, the scent driving into me with wild force. I need to smell all of her, to consume every bit of her.

She makes a soft gasp of surprise as I bite at the juncture of her neck and shoulder and then soothe the sting with a flick of my tongue. It is a soft exhale of breath that at once undoes me and brings me back to myself. I want to take her up against this door right now, to extract every little sound she possesses. But I remember, rather unwillingly, that we are in the middle of the hallway and Max and Cal are likely to drunkenly traipse up the stairs at any moment.

I remember that Mirren is Similian and doesn't yet know the gravity of what she offers. Or maybe, because of its rarity, she understands it better than I do.

In any case, she deserves more than to be ravaged up against an old door.

I remove my hands, gently skimming her collarbone as I go. I press my lips softly to her bared throat, then her jaw and finally her forehead. I settle back into myself piece by piece. She stares up at me inquiringly, her curls awry where my fingers brushed through them and her eyes bright. Her lips are stained pink.

I force myself to look away from them.

Her cheeks flush as she realizes I'm not going to continue, rejection flitting across her face and settling heavy on her shoulders.

Darkness knows, you really make a mess of everything.

She turns toward her bedroom, embarrassed, and the desperate need to keep her close for even a moment longer has me blurting out, "Books!"

Mirren eyes me over her shoulder, tossing her hair over her back. "What?" I think I imagine the hope that tinges the word.

"I said I'd give you books when we got here. Do you want some?"

"Now?" she asks, bewildered.

Why is it that I can laugh when outnumbered by enemies, but one small girl sends me spiraling into speechlessness?

I clear my throat. "I can never fall asleep. Do you want to come read with me for a while?"

Her eyes light and a smile spreads across her face once more. Her curiosity sparks and it occurs to me how beautiful she is. It was pure folly that I didn't notice it when we tangled outside the Boundary, testament to the way desperation blinded me.

She places her hand in mine, an offering, and an agreement. "I'd love to read with you."

CHAPTER
THIRTY-TWO

Shaw

The assassin's door is unlocked, a sign of confidence or futility, though I suppose even things like doors are no match for the power Mirren wields. I slip in soundlessly. The candles remain unlit, their wicks still white, the only light emanating from Nadjaa's moon filtering through the window. The bed is crisply made, the smell of fresh linen still lingering in the air. Assassin or orphan, Rhonwen practices the same level of hospitality.

Avedis peels himself off the far wall, as if melting from the darkness itself. "I wondered when you'd come see me, friend."

His leathers are now clean, his face freshly scrubbed of dirt and blood. His dark eyes gleam with something like satisfaction as he studies me. "Which statement of mine tugged your curiosity?"

I nod toward the bed, emotionless. "I thought you said you needed a night's rest."

Avedis shrugs, settling himself in an old armchair and

crossing one long leg over the other. "I'm sure you need one as much as I do. That does not mean it comes easily."

I don't need to ask what he means. Nightmares drive me from sleep on a nightly basis, the dark filled with countless faces of horror and the sounds of dying breaths. The names of every soul who has taken a piece of mine.

"What's your name?"

He tilts his head. "I do believe I already told the lady that."

"Your *real* name," I growl, resenting Mirren's presence on his lips, even tangentially.

Avedis laughs, the sound oddly sincere. "And I suppose you'll give me your true name in return?" He chuckles again as if I've made a hilarious joke. "What is it they call you here? Oh yes. *Shaw.*"

I take a step toward him, digging my fingers into my palms. They are restless, longing to pull my blades from their sheaths and extract answers with a brutal slice of flesh. Only the thought of Mirren keeps me from it; I left her curled in my bed, her long lashes swept down over her cheekbones and her breaths deep with sleep. She's seen fit to let the man live, and I won't question her judgement.

Avedis eyes my hands, and a grin pulls across his face. "You can relax. I've had my fill of fighting for the week. Ask me what you wish to know."

I grit my teeth, annoyance surging that he insists I voice my questions even though he seems to know what they are. "How do you know me?"

Avedis mulls this over, as if deciding how much to say. I don't blame him. It would be foolish to give over all your information to an enemy, which is why I'm confident there's more to his knowledge of Yen Girene. And me. "I don't know you. I know *of* you," Avedis clarifies.

Before I can huff in irritation, he continues, "You are correct in your recollection of never having seen me before. I was not trained in your camp, nor have I ever stepped foot there. Probably why I still remain intact."

Unbidden, my eyes go to the thick scar that runs from his eyebrow to his ear. A punishment for seeing something he wasn't meant to. Avedis shrugs. "Mostly intact," he amends, motioning to the scar absently, like it's old news, "a gift from my old master. Not yours."

My breathing quickens and my muscles tense, as if my body prepares to break free from the word itself. Master. Only a word and yet also an iron chain that strangles the air from my lungs the same way it did when I was a child. I force myself to focus. "Then how do you know who I am?"

"There have always been rumors of the boy who stabbed the great warlord. The weapon who turned on its maker," his eyes linger on the scar my father gifted me, now hidden beneath a layer of cotton and a bandolier of daggers. "Rumor also has it that the boy did not escape unscathed," Avedis sighs dramatically, "alas! Tis life!"

While I'm sure Cal would hold great appreciation for the assassin's dramatics, they only serve to irritate me further. "I never showed you my scar. How do you know who I am?"

Avedis' expression sobers, his lighthearted gaze replaced by a glinting intensity. "I have ways that are whispered on the wind," he tells me, and I wonder if I could manage to subdue him without waking everyone in the house.

Subdue, maybe. Speak the truth...that would be invariably louder. If he's trained even half as well as I am, it will take days, if not weeks, to break him and I don't have that kind of time.

"I know because I know. There is nothing you could have done to keep me from the knowledge. That's all I can give you."

It isn't an answer, but his eyes keep me from pressing him further. Something blows behind them, wild and untethered and I feel an unmistakable spark of recognition. It steals my breath and leaves me staring at him, wondering what in godsnames just happened.

"And what are you going to do with this knowledge?" My daggers lay heavy against my chest as the threat in my voice is unveiled. Mirren's mercy not-withstanding, the assassin should know the lengths I'm willing to go to protect what's mine.

Avedis eyes me gravely, the charming smile entirely gone from his face. "Nothing," he says simply, leveling his stare. "I like my life far too much to be the one to tell your father you live. The Praeceptor is not a forgiving man. Even of the messenger."

His gaze travels to the window, to the sparkling city and sprawling mountains outside of it. My father's name draws all the warmth from the room, and I suddenly find myself without words.

"Things begin to stir in the Darkness, things not seen in a millennia. It is no coincidence that your father makes to steal power while the Chancellor has been cut off from his. And it is no coincidence that you and the lady have been brought together. Things are written in the night breezes; things I have no wish to be a part of. I will take my leave before sunrise, and if fate is kind to us all, you will never see me again."

CHAPTER
THIRTY-THREE

Mirren

I curse Aggie under my breath for the thousandth time this morning. Her crinkled face is serene as she admonishes me from where she is perched on the front porch of her cabin, "you must work *with* the magic, not against it."

Whatever that means. Sweat beads on my forehead as I try to concentrate, reaching into myself for *something*. Anything, really. But as I grasp around, I come up just as empty as I have the past forty times. The well water in the can remains stubbornly stationary.

Aggie has spouted off unhelpful nonsense all morning, only moving from the porch once to whack me with her walking stick after I cursed the magic in frustration. She said the power was permanently a part of me, but maybe she was mistaken. Maybe it realized it was foolish to choose a Similian girl who's only real power lies in remaining invisible and abandoned me during the night.

My gaze wanders to Anrai, who leans up against the porch post with his arms crossed, an unreadable look on his face.

My magic wouldn't be the only thing to abandon me in the middle of the night.

I fell asleep curled into him, his arms around me, listening to the soothing tenor of his voice as he read from his favorite novel. The *other* inside me sighed in contentment as we were lost inside the story, its soft waves lapping warmly in my chest as Shaw ran his fingers through my hair.

When I woke, he was gone.

He hadn't bothered returning to his room before breakfast. Max and I were mostly done eating by the time he appeared at the dining table looking distinctly worse for wear and moody as hell. His eyes were rimmed red, and his hair stuck up in the back. He wore the same clothes as the day before, though they now appeared as though he'd rolled through a thorn thicket. He dropped into the seat across from me in silence, glaring at his plate of eggs as if they'd personally wronged him.

Uncertain what happened to the gentle man of the night before, I tentatively asked him if he was still planning on accompanying me to Aggie's. His response was a clipped nod and an indistinguishable grunt. My cheeks heated, embarrassed and inexplicably angry, and neither of us has said a word to the other since.

My anger still simmers in my stomach as I finally cry out in frustration. "It's not working, Aggie," I exclaim, throwing up my hands. Maybe Anrai and my power both realized that I am useless and naïve. Perhaps they went in search of someone more worldly. More well matched.

Aggie appears unruffled by my outburst. She nods slowly, her white eyes twinkling in the morning sun.

"Maybe someone needs to be attacking you for it to work?" Max offers helpfully. Last night's wine had

Calloway declaring this morning that getting out of bed felt akin to getting slammed with a sledgehammer, so Max accompanied us in his stead. I found myself grateful for her presence, because if it weren't for her dry commentary, Anrai and I would have ridden here in complete silence.

"Her life wasn't threatened when she healed me in the cave," Anrai supplies lazily. It's clear he speaks to the audience at large, not to me, and I have the urge to hit him.

"But *yours* was," Max replies with a pithy glare. "Maybe it's a life-or-death thing?"

"Or maybe, it's something none of us understand and we shouldn't be relying on it. Maybe we should be leaving her here," Anrai shoots back, his eyes full of fire as they land on Max.

"It was your idea that she help in the first place," Max retorts, uncoiling her lithe body and standing up straight. Today, her tattoos are covered by a white, linen dress and her hair hangs in thick ropes over her shoulder.

"It was misguided."

My cheeks flush and the anger in my stomach climbs into my throat like flesh eating acid. How *dare* he act as if I'm helpless? He didn't think I was so helpless when I saved him from Shivhai or when I saved myself from Avedis. *I'm* the one who got the information to bargain for my father with and now he suggests I am no more than a liability? I open my mouth, to yell or cry, I have no idea, when Aggie's sing song voice crackles at my shoulder.

I practically leap out of my skin at her sudden appearance behind me, not having noticed she moved from the porch step at all, but she shushes me with a touch of her rough hand on my shoulder. "Use it, little bird."

"I can't," I tell her helplessly. Maybe Anrai's right. Without my water magic, I am no use to anyone.

"You can. Power is attracted to strong emotions. For once in your life, let yourself *feel*. Don't push it down, don't dampen its veracity. Don't pretend to be less than you are. *Feel*. Open yourself and feed your magic with it and in return, it will sustain you."

Feel.

My entire life has conditioned me that emotion is wrong. That feeling too deeply will cause pain; that they are safer packaged away in a neat corner of my mind, never to be analyzed and certainly never to be languished in. I focus on Anrai's face. On the handsome sharpness of its lines and those soft lips twisted into an arrogant sneer, and instead of forcing my emotions down, I let them out.

Anrai turns to me, his pale gaze unreadable. Every ugly and tender thing that has been scratching to get out leaps forth, and suddenly, my *other* is there. It sings beneath my skin and crashes against my lungs, renewed and luscious. Just as Aggie says, it satiates me in return. I feel strong and new, and my mind is clear and sharp as I release all of it at the target of my emotions.

All the water from the bucket leaps up and splashes directly into Anrai's face.

For a moment, everyone is completely silent. Rivulets of water stream from his sodden hair as he stares at me, his face terrifying in its dispassionate affect. He studies me as he would a stranger, no more important than a beetle crossing his footpath.

I stare back, every emotion I liberated still swirling freely. And I let him see it; all the pleasure and pain and confusion and *life* he has wrought, because it's taken an entire lifetime and a journey across the continent for me to realize that emotions have power. They are not to be feared or shied away from, trampled or constrained. They are to be embraced and fed, nurtured and wielded, until they are shining and beautiful.

Max lets out a guffaw of laughter and then clamps her hand over her mouth, her eyes darting between the two of us. But I don't take my eyes off Anrai. Because with the claiming of my power, I have also realized something else— I used to think hatred was the adverse reaction to caring, something equally strong, but it isn't. It is no emotion at all that is affection's opposite. More heartrending than hatred, indifference is what hollows you out and leaves you cold.

Anrai doesn't bother to wipe his face. Water streams behind him as he turns from me and mounts his horse. With a face as impassible as the walls of Yen Girene, he gallops away.

~

Shaw

I slice my dagger through the training bag, then whirl, landing a kick so hard the metal fastening it to the ceiling reverberates with a loud echo. Already moving, I unsheathe my daggers. They land with a satisfying *thump, thump, thump,* each sprouting from the center of the target like morose blooms.

I throw myself back at the bag and though my unwrapped knuckles sing with the force of my strikes, it does nothing to quell the burning hole inside me. It flames, aching with the need for blood; or something else I don't dare name. I strike again and the bag comes loose from its chain. It falls to the floor listlessly.

For an absurd moment, I consider kicking it once more as punishment for its inadequacy when the far door to the training room opens. Calloway saunters in, glaring at me insidiously with red rimmed eyes. "There are people trying to sleep!" he barks, closing the door behind him. He squints at the bright windows as if they've personally offended him.

"It's midday," I reply, turning my back to collect my knives. "Should we all tip toe around because you drank too much?"

"Too much is debatable," he scuffles across the floor as if lifting his feet would require too much concentration, "I drank the perfect amount. It would just seem that my head isn't as fun as the rest of me."

I let another knife fly, but before it even leaves my fingers, I know it will miss. Knife throwing is like walking the edge of a fine blade. It isn't something that can be achieved by rudimentary strength, requiring instead an exact amount of finesse and a precise amount of pressure. Normally, my anger hones my concentration into something deadly, but today it has been blunted into something powerful but useless.

Calloway straightens, the vestiges of his overindulgence disappearing suddenly. He eyes me shrewdly. "A sparring match to take the edge off this headache? Perhaps I need to sweat it out."

I see it for what it is—an offer to temper my aggression. It's one of Cal's many talents, the ability to sense what someone needs without ever having to be told. When Denver first brought him to the manor, all knees and elbows and a mop of copper hair, I was sullen and angry. I rarely spoke, least of all to him. I'd never been around other children before and barely knew how to behave like one myself. But Cal, persistent and kind and seemingly immune to my nastiness, came to this very gym every day. He knew nothing of fighting at the time, but he came anyway.

Every morning at dawn, I would wake up and go through the training exercises that had been drilled into me by my father. It became a compulsive ritual, as if completing them would somehow make up for every other way I failed him. Some days, Cal would sit and watch in silence. Other times, he'd tell stories of his childhood. Of his parents' fields and his sisters' smiles. Even when I told him to leave, he sat, steadfast and cheerful, as if he somehow knew I needed his presence, though I didn't know it myself.

Finally, after months of snarling and glaring, I gave in and asked if he wanted to learn.

I nod gratefully at my friend.

"No knives, though. I may still be seeing double, and I wouldn't want to be held responsible for marring that beautiful face," he says with a cheeky grin.

I roll my eyes and wrap my knuckles in strips of fabric. I wait for him to do the same and then we move to the mat in the center of the room. "Your count," he says lazily, but I am already leaping for him.

He blocks my first blow and responds with a sharp right hook. His fist connects to my jaw with a *crack* and my teeth sing as I duck beneath his next jab, sweeping my legs out to unbalance him. He leaps deftly to the side and throws another punch, this one connecting with my ribs.

My breath shoots out of me as I abandon all pretense of a sophisticated sparring match and tackle him to the ground. Cal has never been able to precisely match me in skill, but in the years since I began training him, he's become a formidable opponent, even in the depths of a hangover. And thank the gods for that, because the abyss roars its approval at the connection of flesh on flesh. My blood rushes through me in a heated whirlwind and for a moment, my mind is blissfully devoid of everything but the most primal parts of myself. Strike, deflect, move.

We scrabble until our breaths come in ragged puffs. Blood streams from my nose and Cal's right eye has begun to swell, but when he smiles, I smile back. Nothing has been solved, but I no longer feel as though jagged pieces of myself are breaking through my skin.

Cal collapses on the mat, resting his hands on his chest as his breathing evens. I lay next to him, staring up at the exposed wood beams. For a moment, it feels like we're both fifteen again.

"You gonna tell me what, exactly, that punching bag did to you?" his voice is teasing, but when I roll my head toward him, his eyes are serious.

I clench my jaw and look back toward the ceiling.

"I take it this morning didn't go well with Aggie? Could Mirren not use her power?"

An image of Mirren flashes in my mind, her green eyes glowing with righteous hurt as she marshalled the strength of herself and sent it splashing into my face. "She can *definitely* use her power."

Can more than use it. Vitality pours from her, almost too beautiful to bear witness to. The magic uncaged the ocean that was locked inside her and now it flows with a life and vibrancy that's contagious.

And when her power touched me...it took everything not to take her in my arms, to run my lips over every shining part of her and taste it for my own.

But that's the problem. Something as beautiful and powerful as she is should not be tainted by the Darkness that stains me. I've ignored it, selfishly lost in her touch, but Avedis' words sent it colliding back with brute force.

I can pretend as much as I want. Pretend I'm worthy of

Mirren, pretend that touching her with blood-soaked hands won't affect her. But none of my pretending changes the truth of the matter. I am Cullen's son, through and through. The Praeceptor's heir by birth and blood.

And also, his truest enemy.

Both terribly dangerous things to be.

And I won't risk Mirren's life for my own happiness. I've always known I live on borrowed time; that one day my father would discover the truth and come for me, a knowledge that has only grown since our encounter with Shivhai. By now, my father surely knows I survived. Cullen's pride is a living thing, terrifying in its inexhaustible zest. Even now, he may be tearing apart the entire continent, uprooting everything that stands in the way of righting the imbalance done to him.

"The assassin knows who I am," I finally tell Cal.

Alarm flashes on his face, replaced quickly by sadness. I don't need to say more; there is no need to explain the darkest places of my heart, because he already knows them. My deepest fears and most desperate hopes, Cal is familiar with them all.

"What's he planning to do with the knowledge?"

I shrug with a nonchalance I don't feel. "Apparently nothing. He says he doesn't want to risk the Praeceptor's wrath."

Cal mulls this over. "Refreshingly wise for a paid blade."

I nod in agreement. My father would never allow the keeper of this information to walk free, able to carelessly spread it. Controlling the spread of information is one of the most basic tenets of warfare.

"If he isn't planning on doing anything with the information, what's changed?"

Nothing. *Everything.*

I tell him Avedis' suspicions about the movements in the Dark World and that they're somehow connected.

"So, you think Cullen is actually behind Denver's kidnapping? Not the Achijj?"

"I don't know. But honestly, it doesn't matter. It's been coming since I left Shivhai alive. It's only a matter of time before the Praeceptor finds me and when he does, he will not play fair. He is ruthless and I am his heir. He sees my betrayal as something to be rectified. He will only be satisfied if I am unassailably under his control once more. And if he can't have that, he will take his payment in blood. He will take everything from me before finally killing me. And I can't..."

I trail off, running my palms roughly over my eyes as if I can clear away the images of my father's ideas of retribution. Cal has heard some of it, but he doesn't know the lengths my father will go. The terrifying monster inside him that he feeds with other's pain. "We need to save Denver and then we need to get Mirren back to Similis. The faster the better. I can't put Mirren in my father's sights. It's bad enough I've already done it to you and Max—" My throat tightens.

Calloway pushes himself up so that he's propped on his elbows. Anger flashes on his face. "You haven't *done* anything to Max or me," he says hotly.

I shake my head and make to push myself up from the ground when he grabs my arm and wrenches me back toward him. "Look at me," he says forcefully, "you can't go around shoving everyone into a protective bubble. Max and I *choose* to be where we are and everything that entails. The good and the bad."

I open my mouth to argue but fall silent at the look on Cal's face. His cheeks are reddened and his mouth presses into a thin white line. It is such a rare occurrence that it takes me a moment to recognize. Cal is not angry. Cal is *furious.*

"You sit there and espouse freedom for Nadjaa, for Ferusa, but when it comes to being brave enough to offer the choice to the people you love, you turn into a Similian. You *can't* protect people from the bad without also keeping them from the good. And you shouldn't try."

"Cal, it's different with Cullen, it's—"

He gets to his feet. "Max never had a say in what happened to her before. I didn't have a say in being forced to leave Siralene, or my parents and sisters being burned alive. *You* had no choice when you were forced to do what you did. We *have* a choice now. You don't get to invalidate them just because you have a martyr complex and think you're the only one allowed to suffer."

Cal meets my eyes and for a moment, I think he might hit me again. But he only shakes his head. "If you respect Mirren, you'll give her a choice, too. Doesn't she deserve that?"

With that, he leaves the gym, the door banging roughly on its hinges as it slams behind him. I stare at it long after it's closed.

CHAPTER
THIRTY-FOUR

Mirren

I spend the next two days entrenched in magic. I wake up with its sweet taste in my mouth and its tangy scent in my nose. I think only of its rushing power and its delicate precision. I cultivate and nourish it with my emotions, feeding it my fear and my love and my loneliness. In return, it spirals through me, invigorating and restorative. For the first time in my life, I don't feel like I am grasping for pieces to make myself whole. I am strong and I'm enough.

I move on from the well bucket to forest streams, calling and shaping the water. It runs over my skin and tangles in my hair, and I wonder how I ever lived without it. My body has never felt stronger, but opening myself to everything I've kept shoved down for so long leaves me exhausted and at the end of each day, I collapse gratefully into sleep.

Aggie is delighted at my progress and her eyes always shine with tears whenever she watches the water move, as if seeing nature's power return home is something she never thought she'd witness. It's her that suggests I try to manipulate the very humidity in the morning mist. "It's water, after all."

I close my eyes, feeling each miniscule droplet, each individual prick of power. I call them to me, and they dance happily over my fingertips and up my arms until I direct them toward Cal, who stands ready, having taken to accompanying me dressed in a cloak and armed with a large umbrella.

I skirt the droplets around the umbrella, and they dive under his collar. He jumps up and down, yelping and cursing, to the great amusement of Max.

The only part of my *other* that remains stubbornly out of reach is the water's healing properties it first showed in the cave. Aggie tells me not to rush, that in time, I will discover the right emotion that opens it to me, but I ignore her warnings. My dreams are filled with Easton gasping for his last breath, Easton crying out for me, forgotten and alone. He doesn't have time to give up to my failings.

Each night, I slice my dagger through my palm and each night, I end up sopping up my blood with a rag, unable to magically staunch the bleeding. As the last evening before we depart for Yen Girene falls, I'm forced to admit that I may not be able to heal Easton on my own. My only way forward is trusting in Anrai and in my own power, and saving my father in time.

Anrai has been noticeably absent from both meal and training times. Max, whose unabashed honesty I've actually come to appreciate, informs me that he's taken to eating in Denver's office, pouring over every snippet of information he can about the Dead Prophecy and how the Achijj might seek to use it. On the rare occasion we run into each other in the candlelit hallways, he never meets my eyes, deliberately skirting around me as if my touch would be unbearable.

Only my pride has kept me from bursting into the study and demanding that he look at me. That he offer some explanation as to why, only days ago, he touched me with reverence, and now the mere sight of me offends him. He is more schooled in the emotional entrapments of the Dark World, but I know enough to know I will never debase myself by begging for his attention. He hasn't argued against my coming to Yen Girene since I splashed him in the face and that's enough for me.

If only my body agreed. There are nights I wake in the dark, my skin feverish and pleading for his touch. I can't decide whether to hate myself for it.

It's during the last meal before we leave—a supper of pasta with peppered sauce and freshly baked bread—that Max asks, "have you talked to Shaw yet?"

His name sends a bolt of electricity through my stomach. I pointedly take another bite of pasta and chew slowly before answering, "no."

"We leave tomorrow," she points out. Rhonwen bustles in and Max looks to her with an appreciative smile. "Thanks for dinner, Rhonwen. It was delicious."

Rhonwen smiles but shoos away Max's thanks as if they are insects in the air. "You'll all need something to stick to your bones while you're on the road," she looks at me with a cheeky grin. "I made that chocolate cake you like for dessert."

I blush, flattered that in the middle of her vigorous workload, she took the time to notice my favorite things. As if I'm the same as any of the others here, cared for and important. "Thank you so much, Rhonwen," my throat tightens. "I...I appreciate everything you've done for me."

She tsks impatiently. "Now, now, none of that. I'll see you in three days' time and there will be plenty more where that came from." Her skirts swirl around her ankles as she hurries back toward the kitchen.

I watch her with a sad smile. Even if everything goes to plan in Yen Girene—if we somehow manage to break into the impenetrable fortress, make a deal with the Achijj, and escape unharmed with my father—there will be no more chocolate cakes for me. I will be on my way back to Similis, Denver at my side. When I originally imagined coming home with the very thing that can save Easton's life, it was a bolstering thought that kept me moving forward, but now it is edged with dread. I will see my brother safe, but it will come at a steep cost. For how am I to fold myself back into the small box I lived in? Am I to take myself apart bit by bit and sort through the pieces, discarding ones the Community has deemed unimportant? Dangerous?

And what of my *other*? Will it thrash around inside me, demanding to be fed? Or will it abandon me when it discovers I am only a shadow of what I once was, capable of only fractions of emotions?

And then there's Anrai.

The man who first colored my gray world, tore me apart and put me back together as something more genuine— something more me. *You cannot touch the Darkness and remain unchanged.* Aggie's words to me, truer than she could possibly know.

I look to Max, who's friendship was hard won and well worth the effort. I've never had a true friend before—or really, a friend at all—but if I were to imagine one for myself, it would be her. Brave and loyal, whose truth streams from her like the power it is. "I know we leave tomorrow," I tell her sadly. As much as I wished for the day to come, for time to move faster, I now want to run from it. I want to stay in this manor forever, listening to Anrai read or Cal and Max argue. Leaving will feel like being torn from a picture I've been painted into, one whose colors and tones align seamlessly with my own and thrust into a new painting—one whose colors clash against mine and whose lines delineate.

"We'll be back in three days," Calloway says from his seat next to Max. Cal, with his boisterous laugh and his mischievous eyes; able to turn even the angriest person into the truest friend.

Max nods, but her eyes are grave. As if she knows it isn't only three days; that after Yen Girene, everything will change. "Do you remember what I said to you before the lunar celebration?"

"That if I don't moisturize my curls, they're going to look like electrocuted straw?"

She laughs, shaking her head. "About Shaw. About how he acts."

He acts how he thinks he should. And how is that? *Broken,* she'd replied.

I nod slowly.

She flicks her eyes back to her plate. "Good."

I stare at the two of them, Anrai's friends, *my* friends. Cal shuffles the food around his plate and Max has returned to shoveling forkfuls into her mouth. They are leaving the decision up to me, I realize. If I decide not to pursue Anrai, to go to Yen Girene with things as they are, the choice is mine.

I am bared. Only to you.

But relationships are more complicated than that. My *other* needs me to nurture it when it is weak, to care for it when it was nothing more than a small trickle beneath me skin. It's powerful, but it needs tending the same as the smallest blade of grass would. And maybe Anrai...maybe he needs the same thing. A reminder that though he is strong, he is never alone.

I stand up abruptly, the feet of the wooden chair scraping loudly against the floor.

My friends look up, Max's eyes gleaming with something close to approval. "He's at the cliff pond," she says simply.

"Tell Rhonwen to save me some cake!" I yell over my shoulder as I take off toward the pond.

∽

Shaw

The forest is quiet tonight, waiting with bated breath for the changing of the seasons. The hot whisper of summer is only days from pouring in off the Storven and there's a soft pang at the reminder that I will miss it. After Yen Girene, I will accompany Mirren and Denver to Similis and by the time I make it back, the summer's heat will be at its full height, baking Nadjaa and the surrounding mountains into a hazy stupor.

And I will be alone once more. The thought is both sobering and comforting. Mirren and Denver will be safely ensconced behind the Boundary, untouchable to the Praeceptor. And to me.

I throw myself down on the granite shore and stretch my legs. The bow I brought to practice with lies abandoned a few feet away. My limbs have burned for days with a restlessness I've been unable to quell. It isn't the same electricity that runs through me before every mission, the one that hones my body and sharpens my mind. This is one sparks unexpectedly, untethering my thoughts and twisting them into a disquieted mess. No amount of training or research has calmed them.

I finally gave up and sprinted to the pond under the guise of bow practice. I almost laugh out loud that I've now started lying even when there's no one else around to hear.

It isn't practice. It's hiding.

I run the blades of shore grass between my fingers, grass that only days before, Mirren's body lay on. Her power drenches the place; the trees, the grass, the water. The very air sparkles with it. The pond grove is now alive the same way she is, shining and radiant.

If avoiding thinking about her is my goal, the pond grove was a terrible idea. Then again, it doesn't seem to matter where I am. She's in everything I touch, every movement of my body, every ray of every sunrise. I've been creeping around the manor like a wraith and still, on the rare occasion that she rounds a corner unexpectedly, the air drags from my lungs and something inside me burns wildly, urging me to touch her, to damn the consequences and take her as mine.

Hiding is better. I only need to survive one more night and then we'll be on the road. Closer to her father and closer to her leaving forever.

"Anrai?"

Shit.

I spring to my feet, heart pounding savagely in my chest. She's there, curls untied, and feet bare as if she sprinted to me unexpectedly. As if I conjured her. She's clad in soft leggings and a sweater, the cloak I bought her thrown haphazardly around her shoulders. Her alabaster skin glows in the moonlight and gods, I want to touch it.

Make her leave. If you want her safe, she needs to be far away from you.

I train my face into one of boredom. "Do you need something?"

Her eyes flash with anger, but its quickly replaced by something akin to determination. "Yes," she says, stepping toward me, "I do need something."

I tense in anticipation and fear and haven't decided which will win out when she steps toward me again. I'm reminded of our first entanglement when I challenged her and she held her ground, refusing to cede a step to the monster that had kidnapped her out of the darkness. The spot where she drove her knife, though healed, still tinges. A reminder of her bravery. "What is it?" I ask coldly.

She doesn't even flinch, meeting my gaze head on. She closes the space between us, and I try to hold my breath, but her scent swirls around me. It is fresh and crisp like a spring rain, and unable to control myself, I fill my lungs with it. I watch, half agony, half hope as she reaches toward me, her intention burning clearly in her eyes.

"Mirren," I warn roughly.

Her gaze doesn't falter as she raises a hand to my face. Her body presses closer to mine as she stretches to reach and her fingers trail lightly over the stubble of my jaw and down the lines of my neck. I should be alarmed at how quickly my body sparks, like the hot snap of flint against steel, but instead I savor it, feeding it until it ignites. My hands find her waist and I pull her toward me until her hips are flush with mine.

Our lips meet and I am satiated, the thirst that has burned for days finally quenched. Her lips are soft and warm beneath mine, and I lose myself in them. My fragmented thoughts come together. It is her, only her, that brings the pieces of myself together. That lights the empty corners and soothes the remaining fractions of my soul.

Her hands never stop moving, exploring the muscles of my back, and then running down my arms. Always insistent, always pulling, *closer, closer, closer*. How did I ever think to live apart from her, drifting aimlessly in my Darkness, overcome by my abyss? She is the beginning and the end, the ocean that washes everything else away.

Her hands drift further up my chest, until they are planted firmly above my heart. On the knot of gnarled scar tissue, a stark reminder of everything at stake. My blood freezes and I leap from her as if I've been scalded.

She is all that matters, and you wish to blacken her with your curse? Get her killed?

I really am my father's child, selfish and evil to the very end.

Mirren's eyes flare and she makes to move back toward me, but I throw up a hand. My chest is tight, the air around the grove suddenly impossibly thin. "Don't come near me," I bite out.

"Why?" she demands, her eyes shining. "What have I done to make you shun me like this?" Her tears brim over, staining her cheeks as she wipes at them furiously.

I dig my nails into my palm, forcing my hand to remain where it is. "Gods, Mirren, please don't cry—"

"Don't you dare pity me!" she shouts furiously. "I'm not crying because I'm heartbroken, I'm crying because I'm pissed off!"

I bite back the absurd urge to laugh at both her mastery of foul language and her complete willingness to yell at me. She has never once cowed to me, not when I held her under threat of her life and not one moment since. It fills me like a new breath, to have found someone so equally matched, who will not back away even from the darkest depths. She is always ready for me. As I am for her.

Mirren glares through her tears. "Tell me the truth," she commands. And then, softer, "you promised to be bare. No more secrets."

She won't be afraid, not even if I tell her everything. She will meet the challenge of my life's mess with a glint in her eye and her head held as high as a queen's. It's what terrifies me; that she is too brave and too loyal to ever leave me in order to keep herself safe. She hardly knew me and threw herself back into my father's camp to save me. It will only be more of the same, more danger and more reasons to risk herself.

"Tell me the truth, Anrai." My name rings in her mouth, a whisper and a command. "Do you want me?" Her voice cracks with vulnerability and it's this, more than anything, that forces me to speak. For how could she possibly think I don't? I've been half in love with her since I watched her clock Eulogious in the head with the butt of that gun, curls flying, lips curled in a fierce snarl.

"Yes," I admit, feeling defeated and victorious at once. It's useless to pretend otherwise, though the truth changes nothing.

"Then come to me," she says softly, her words sliding across my spine like a caress.

"I can't!" I cry out, burying my face in my hands. "Don't you see, Mirren? I will ruin you. And not because of some stupid prophecy. Just because *I am me.*" The first words I remember my father speaking to me: *You are made only to destroy, never to build. Remember that at all costs. Remember when you begin to feel human instead of the weapon that you are. You destroy. You destroy.*

All at once, the words pour out of me like an overwrought dam. "I have made so many enemies in my life, Mirren, and they are well deserved. They won't hesitate to take *everything* from me, and I cannot put you in their path. I won't."

I meet her gaze sorrowfully. Her tears have dried, leaving stained tracks down her cheeks. "I've spent my entire life with no choices," she utters, her voice low, "you were the first to show me that I'm capable. That my judgement can be trusted. That my life and how I live it are my own, for better or worse. You would take that from me now?"

I stare at her, the echo of Calloway's words reverberating between us. *Does she not deserve a choice?* I trust Mirren with my life, why can I not trust her with her own?

My voice is strangled. "I...I'm afraid of breaking apart if something happened to you because of me. Like whatever is left of my soul will crumble to dust."

And therein lies the heart of it. My truest fear. Selfish to its very core.

"I will have you safe," I say to her again, same as the night in the cave.

She steps toward me again, but this time, I don't flinch. "That isn't your choice to make," she says gently. She meets my eyes, the emerald-green cool and soft as the waves of the sea. "I choose how to live. I choose how I feel," I watch with wide eyes as she runs her hands down my chest, hooking her fingers on the hem of my shirt. I lean down, allowing her to tug it over my head.

"I choose what's worth dying for and what's not," she whispers vehemently. Her fingers trail lightly over the ridged planes of my stomach and a blazing fire rises in their wake. She goes slowly, but her movements are intentional as her palms brush up over my pectorals and finally, achingly, come to rest above my heart. "You are worth it," she says fiercely.

I shut my eyes against her words and then gasp loudly as her lips meet my scar. I can barely stand it—something as beautiful as her mouth touching the source of all my shame and poison, as if the contact will twist her, too; warp her into something as wretched as I am. But she doesn't yield. She knows the ugliest parts of me and accepts them as they are.

"You are worth it. I choose it, Anrai," she whispers into my chest.

I open my eyes and meet her gaze, fire to water, feeling at once acutely aware of my entire being and as though I am floating somewhere above us, somewhere light and airy and warm. I vowed never to take Mirren's choices away, never to disrespect her intelligence and instincts again. And while I have nothing to offer but danger and destruction, I can at least give her this—choice.

Because in this moment, I know with undying certainty, that my choice will forever be her. Through fire and darkness, storm and blood, I will always choose her.

I pull her to me, broken and reborn at once.

CHAPTER
THIRTY-FIVE

Mirren

Anrai isn't gentle as he pulls me to him, but I don't want gentle. He's never treated me like I'm breakable; he saw my strength before I saw it myself and that's how he touches me now. With a barely leashed passion that matches my own, he kisses me wildly. One hand tangles in my hair and the other circles around the small of my back, finding the bare skin beneath my sweater. The feel of his calloused fingertips on places that have never been touched has me gasping against his lips.

His skin is fevered beneath my palms as I explore his bare chest, finding every bit of his story and committing it to memory; the large slash of a sword that runs parallel to his spine; the puckered hole of an old bullet wound that dents his sinewed shoulder; the gnarled knife wound that shrouds his heart. I follow my hands with my lips, tracing every place the world has hurt him and rewriting them with something beautiful. Because every mark makes up *him,* so in spite of the pain, I find myself grateful for each one of them.

As I get to the mark made by my own hand, I look up to find him watching me. His pale eyes burn so brightly, he looks almost feral in the moonlight. It would be frightening if the same feeling wasn't coursing through me at the same moment, voraciously heated and all encompassing. He holds his breath as I run my lips lightly over the small silvery sliver above his hip. I don't look away as I flick my tongue across it.

He makes a barely restrained growl and releases whatever hold he has on himself. He scoops me against him and sweeps his tongue across my lips. Hands firmly cupping my bottom, I wrap my legs around his waist. I wiggle closer, pressing my breasts into him, the friction through my shirt deliciously agonizing. His hands cup me through the fabric and heat pools at my center at Anrai's groan of approval. I cry out, alight with pleasure and power.

It's no wonder the Covinus has decreed touch to be dangerous—it is a veritable force in itself, the way Anrai, strong and unyielding, is humbled by the brush of my skin or the sweep of my lips. And in return, the way my being unravels and then weaves itself together as something different at the feel of his hands, his breath; it is an exchange that can shake the very foundations of the world.

We stumble forward, a tangle of limbs and breath and Anrai laughs into my mouth. The taste of it is sweet and luscious and has me scrambling to get closer, to taste more. He works the clasp of my cloak, and it falls from my shoulders, but it isn't enough. The frantic motivation to get more of his skin on mine is no longer a want, but a ravening need.

Anrai pulls his mouth away and I attempt to claw my way back to him, to draw his lips back to mine. He laughs again and the sound, so rare and precious, skitters across my skin. "I just...have you..." Though I am straddling his waist and his hands have thoroughly ravaged me, his voice is suddenly shy. I want to laugh at the absurdity, but the seriousness of his eyes sobers me. "I don't want to do anything you don't want to," he finally says.

My cheeks flame as I realize what he's asking. "I haven't," I profess. A thought occurs to me like a douse of icy water. "Have you?"

He nods. The answer isn't a surprise—such things are revered differently here and Anrai is well above the Binding age, even if he was Similian—but it sends a murderous swell crashing over me nonetheless, like the dark surge of a storm.

Anrai sets me down gently, my body crying out at the absence of him. "I know things are different in Similis and I don't want to take that lightly," he says. His hair is mussed, and his lips are kiss-worn. He looks so torn and so handsome that I want to tackle him, to press my body against his once more until I can no longer feel myself, only the places that are now *us*.

Sex is as regulated as any of our other actions in Similis. It's only for procreation in service of the Community, but at the moment, I can't imagine it as ever being anything other than exultation of each other. Something apart from everything else in the world, only ever ours together.

Anrai bites his lip. "I...gods, Mirren, I kidnapped you. I don't want to do anything ever again that you don't feel comfortable with."

My heart swells and I wonder how I ever thought him careless when it's clear he holds those he cares about in a place that is equal parts fierce and gentle. "I want more," I tell him clearly. My voice is so different than it was only weeks before, but now it is more mine. It speaks my desires with no fear or shame. "I don't...I don't know how much. But I know that I want more."

Anrai's face breaks into a wide smile, beaming with wonder and gratitude. "Slowly, then," he declares, closing the space between us. The air heats once more. "You have me. You control me. You say when it's enough."

He waits until I nod my agreement before leaning down to kiss me. His kiss is slow and sensuous, exploring my mouth until I am breathless, his hands splaying across my back. He hooks his fingers under the hem of my sweater, and he breaks our kiss to pull it over my head. As the cool night air rushes my bare skin, he pulls back and gazes at me, his breath a sharp inhale. It doesn't occur to me to be embarrassed or to cover myself. At the look on his face, wondering and hungry at once, I feel cherished.

"You're beautiful," he rasps.

I don't blush, only stand before him with my chin raised, because in this moment, I am what he says I am. Beautiful and strong, tamer of magic and tormented ex-assassins alike, in charge of my future.

Anrai spreads the cloak across the ground. The fabric is cool against my skin as I stretch myself out on top of it, languishing in the night's freedom, in its power. He sheds his boots and lays next to me, his hands coming to my bare skin, his lips greedily seeking mine. His callouses scrape against my arms, leaving deliciously fevered shivers in their wake. He traces soft circles over my back, maddeningly slow and wicked in their intent.

His body trembles next to mine and I realize with satisfaction that his usual steel self-control is barely contained, that his declaration to take things slow is costing him greatly. A self-satisfied smile settles on my face but as his lips travel to my neck, his tongue flicking over the soft spot behind my ear, the smile is quickly replaced by a gasp of pleasure.

Anrai covers my body with his, the weight of him solid and delicious. His bare chest presses against my breasts, a mirror of the way we lay after I stabbed him. Electricity coursed through me even then, but now, the heat of his skin seeps through mine, warming every part of me and pooling at my core and I writhe beneath him, desperate for more friction.

"What do they teach you about this in that infernal country of yours?" His voice is a wicked breath against my throat and his gaze is scorching as he watches the way my lips part in bliss as he runs a hand between my breasts. I arch my neck, craving more of him.

He pulls away so that his lips linger just beyond my reach, and I realize he's teasing me. He won't continue until I answer him, arrogant ass. Determined to unravel his self-control, to make him as wild as I feel, I press the length of my body closer. His muscles tighten beneath my fingers, and he lets out a soft hiss as I push my hips against his. Heat blazes between us as I feel the effect I have on him, hard and aching. All thoughts eddy from my head and I no longer care who's winning or losing, only that the aching at my core is satiated.

"They teach us..." I begin, breathless and panting, "the mechanics of it."

Anrai smiles against my throat, and I cry out as he nips at the sensitive skin and then soothes it with a swipe of his velvet tongue. "The mechanics," he muses, kissing along my jaw and running his tongue along the edge of my ear. I can feel every muscle of his chest, lean and strongly coiled, and with each of his movements, I feel as though I will leap out of my skin. I squeeze my eyes shut, almost unable to bear the piercing waves of heat that course through me but unwilling to give them up.

"I suppose it's like your books, isn't it?" he says, and I dig my fingers into his back to keep him from pulling away. He moves to the other side of my neck, sucking at the point where it meets my shoulder until I am panting. "All business and no pleasure."

Feverish and wanting, I urge him closer. He obliges with an infernal laugh that skitters down my spine. "It seems your education in pleasure has been left entirely up to me." His hands move down my body, cupping the weight of my breasts in his hands. I moan as he flicks his thumb over one tip, followed by the other. "And since we've already covered literature..."

His mouth replaces his hands and I cry out in pleasure, feeling as though I've come apart. He flicks his tongue over each tip, before sucking them into the warmth of his mouth. Greedy and wanting, I writhe beneath him until we are both gasping. His eyes meet mine with a searing gaze as he kisses his way down the soft swell of my stomach, languishing attention on the rise of my hips. His face reflects mine, frenzied and ablaze, as he swipes his tongue along the waistline of my leggings. "More?" he asks, his guttural voice sweeping across my skin like a lick of flame.

My voice is lost, so I only manage a fervent nod. With deferent hands, Anrai slowly peels the leggings off, first one foot and then the other. I shiver as the prick of the cool night air and the exquisite heat of his touch war with each other over the exposed skin of my legs. *I am bared. Only to you.*

As his reverent gaze sweeps over me, I think how true it is. He knows the least glimpsed parts of me, inside and out, and he accepts them all. He saw me when everyone else wished me invisible, my dark depths and my shallow pools, and never once flinched.

"I've wanted to do this since the first moment I saw you," he says, settling himself between my legs. "I wanted to touch every part of your skin," He runs his hands gently up the length of my thighs, over the curve of my hips. He kisses the backs of my knees, running his tongue over the sensitive skin of my inner thighs until my blood courses like lava and I am whimpering. "But mostly, I wanted to taste you. I've driven myself mad wondering what you taste like."

I twist beneath him, unsure of what I'm even after, only knowing that it's *more*. More touch, more ache, more of *him*. Finally, he settles his lips at my center, the part of me that yearns, soft and blazing. He growls in approval, the sound wicked and delicious. I throw my head back in pleasure, coming apart as he kisses me gently, his lips worshipful and his tongue wanton.

"Gods, your taste," Anrai moans against me, the scratch of his stubble against my thighs and the reverberations of his words almost too much to bear. "you're even more luscious than I imagined." He runs his tongue up the length of me, before circling it around the bundle of nerves at the apex of my thighs.

I moan, thrashing against him brazenly. My magic rises to the surface of my skin, as if Anrai is the one that commands it, the master of both my power and my body. It circles in time with the movements of his masterful tongue, until it is just as heated as we are, with the strength of a summer hurricane.

He sucks me into his hot mouth, drinking from me as if he's been existing in starved agony. Pleasure and power crest within me, threatening to unravel my very being.

But I want to be undone, unmoored, so long as Anrai is the one to do it; to break me apart and piece me back together as something new, something known. With something between a moan and a sob, I am thrown into the center of the storm. Wild and terrible in its beauty, it overcomes me hotter than any flame, deeper than any ocean.

Anrai kisses me reverently as the last waves of pleasure wrack my body. Then he lays beside me, pulling me into the warmth of his chest. I breathe him in, woodsmoke and spice, feeling for the first time, at home in my skin.

～

Later, when the moon is high and we are both tucked beneath his cloak, Anrai asks, "Is that what your power feels like all the time?"

I turn to him, wide eyed. His head is propped on one hand, while the other twists in my hair, twirling the tresses around his fingers. "You could actually feel it? I thought I hallucinated that."

He smirks, and for once, it doesn't embed itself beneath my skin. Tonight, his arrogance is well earned. "Well, I know I'm good, but I'm not sure I'm make-you-hallucinate-good."

I roll my eyes, shoving playfully at his chest. "What did you feel?" I ask curiously.

He grows thoughtful as he pulls another curl and watches it spring back up. "I don't know that I have words for it, really. It felt ancient and deep like an ocean, but also shallow and calm, like this pond. And it...it soothed me. I almost felt..." he trails off, searching for the right word. Finally, he sighs, "extinguished. But in the best way possible. Like I've been burning my whole life and you were my first sip of water."

Odd, that I felt almost the exact opposite at Anrai's touch. Like I could burn forever happily.

"Touching you is the best I've ever felt. And I don't think it was because of your magic." He smiles shyly. I could get used to the rarified humility that adorns his face.

"But you didn't..." I clear my throat, my cheeks flaming. "I mean, we didn't..."

Anrai laughs gently. "It was enough," he says firmly, "whatever you gift me with will always be enough." He buries his face in my hair and inhales deeply. "I've wanted you for so long, I have no intention of rushing. I am going to savor every delicious bit. Slowly." He punctuates each word with a wicked flick of his tongue along my throat and just like that, heat curls low in my stomach once again.

He takes my lips leisurely beneath his, as if he is sipping at a fine wine. My body goes boneless. "I intend to be thorough in your pleasure education," he says, moving his hands down my stomach.

I laugh in his mouth, arching up to meet his deft fingers. "Why do I get the feeling that books are no longer at all what you mean?"

"Maybe we can get creative and do both at the same time," he says with a teasing nip at my shoulder. His eyes light with fresh hunger as his fingers brush the wetness between my legs. "How is it that I just want you more? We could have until the end of the Darkness, and I still don't think it'd be enough time."

I freeze beneath him, a block of ice forming in my chest. Time has never felt like such a looming enemy. We leave for Yen Girene at first light, and after that, I will be gone. For as much as I never want to leave Anrai's arms, I cannot sacrifice Easton. I have to go back. The thought is a wave unearthing the long-buried secrets of the ocean floor and my deepest dreads rise to the surface.

A line of concern appears between Anrai's brows as he senses the shift in my mood. "Hey, what's wrong?" he asks, suddenly wary.

Tears brim, hot and unwelcome. Before coming to the Dark World, I haven't cried since my parents were Outcast and now, my tears are a faucet I can't turn off. "We don't have time."

"Are you worried about Yen Girene?"

I shrug helplessly, the weight of anxiety pressing on my shoulders and making them ache. "And after. Anrai, even if we make it back from Yen Girene with my father, I still...I have to leave. I can't leave Easton to die. I have to go back to Similis."

Back to where my voice is a silent scream in an echo chamber. A tear spills over, running a familiar track down my cheek. Anrai follows it with his finger, before wiping it away along my jaw. There is no sadness in his eyes, only determination. Ever the soldier, he doesn't accept defeat. But this isn't an obstacle he can fight his way out of. The enemy is invisible and ancient and moves with no deference to us.

"I know," he says softly, "you wouldn't be who you are if you didn't go back. But that doesn't mean it's the end. We'll figure something out. There are too many unknowns to worry about it now. Let's get Denver back first."

I nod, knowing he's right. There are far too many unknowns: if we can bargain with the Achijj, if Shivhai catches up with us, if my father is still even alive; and if he is, if the Covinus will allow us back into Similis to save Easton. I bury my face in Anrai's chest, breathing in the warmth of his skin and allowing it to settle in my lungs, soft and soothing.

I listen to his heart beating, strong and sure in his chest, until my eyes flutter closed, and exhaustion overtakes me. Sometime in the night, we reach for each other once more. His lips are a warm welcome from the depths of sleep, and his body wraps around mine like it was made to shield me from the world. I clutch at his fevered skin as his fingers wring pleasure from me, and he devours my cry of ecstasy like they alone are his sustenance.

At the top of my crest, just before I am poised to fall, I realize that home has never been a place. It is a feeling, a sweet breath, a familiar touch, a rasping word. And when I leave for Similis, I will not just be leaving the Dark World behind—I will be leaving home.

CHAPTER
THIRTY-SIX

Shaw

I have always stepped outside myself before a mission. I learned early that emotions are a liability I can't afford, and disassociating is the most prudent way to protect myself. It's a habit that stuck with me long after I left my father, one that has kept me alive on countless occasions.

But today, instead of the mask of a soulless assassin, I am more aware of my body than ever. I feel every piece with acute sharpness, as if I occupy all the spaces and edges—there is no room to pack away the parts of myself that feel, because *all* of me feels. My hands feel Mirren's skin, my mouth is filled with the taste of her and my heart—my godsdamn heart—is twice as large and exposed, as if half of it beats outside my body. A ripe target.

I don't know yet whether to be terrified or amazed and I settle on some combination of both as we ride toward Yen Girene. The fortress lies on the other side of the Girenia range, mountains that sprawl across the land rather than tower over it. It will take all day to reach the foothills where we will camp and prepare to enter in the morning.

Cal and Max ride ahead of Mirren and I, the sounds of their spirited bickering floating back to us on a light breeze. The day has dawned bright and warm, though a cold bite lingers at its edges, the last vestiges of spring. It will only get colder as we go further north, the coastal balm of Nadjaa entirely absent in Yen Girene.

Mirren rides atop Dahiitii and she coos at the mare as we cross a particularly rocky stretch of road. She's tied her hair into two thick plaits that spill over her shoulders and is tucked into her new cloak, the same shade as her eyes. I chose it the first day we arrived in Nadjaa, imagining it would wrap around her in a way I would never be able to. Now that my arms have held her, all I wish to do is tear the stupid cloak off and relish in her lush curves.

Despite my longings, the morning's ride passes quickly. We take turns telling stories and I listen with rapt attention when she speaks, greedy for all parts of her that are unknown to me, hoarding them like supplies going into a long winter. Her eyes sparkle with laughter when I recount the time Cal and I got caught stealing sweets from Evie's window and she guffaws loudly as I describe Cal's screams of terror when Evie chased us. Mirren's laughter is bright in the sunshine, and though I told myself I won't think of it, I wonder if the number of times I will hear it is measured.

We break for a meal at midday in a large grove next to a stream. After we devour a few of Rhonwen's pastries that are, somehow, still deliciously hot, Max and Cal prudently find somewhere else to be. I get down on my knees before Mirren and worship her once more, her taste in my mouth, her power rolling over my skin as she cries out to the open sky.

Later, when the dust of the road has all but swept her scent away from me, the air grows heavy with the weight of tomorrow. Mirren must sense it as well, because after awhile she falls silent, the thunder of horses' hooves and the rush of wind in our ears the only sound. I've prepared as much as I can for what awaits us in Yen Girene—strategized for every variable, researched every angle—but I can't shake the disquieted feeling in my stomach or the echo of Avedis' words. A prophecy brought me to Mirren and led me to Denver's location. It would be foolish to discount that we are being moved like chess pieces on a gameboard by forces we don't entirely understand.

And my father, making a grab for power just as the old magic wakes, cannot be a coincidence. He has not made it to Yen Girene, of that I can at least be sure. The walls of the old fortress haven't been breached since before the curse and it would have echoed across Ferusa if they had been now. But there is no question the Praeceptor now knows I live and that I've been helping Denver build the free city, the antithesis of everything Cullen stands for.

I can only hope that when he makes his move, it's after Denver and Mirren are back in Similis. At least the Boundary can keep them safe.

Until you blew a hole in it.

I shove the thought away. Hole or not, the Boundary is their only chance of escaping my father's wrath.

By the time night falls and we make camp, the uncertainty of the day has me grasping for any small bit of control. I watch the girls head toward the water's edge, to clean and fill the canteens and then pull Cal aside. Even in the middle of nowhere after a hard days' ride, there isn't a hair out of place on his head and I can't help but begrudgingly admire it.

Cal scrutinizes my face, raising his eyebrows. "This

doesn't bode well," he remarks dryly, crossing his arms and spreading his feet apart as if readying himself for an attack.

"Cal, I need you to promise me something before we go in to Yen Girene."

He rubs the back of his neck gingerly. "I don't suppose it's going to be something easy like 'promise to be funny and carelessly handsome, Calloway,' hm?"

"I need you to promise, that no matter what, you will get Mirren out and back to Similis."

The line between his brows deepens and his freckles appear stark in the shadows of the setting sun. "Of course, I'll keep Mirren safe," he assures me as if this is a given. I love him all the more for it.

"I don't mean..." I take a steadying breath. "What I mean is...if something happens tomorrow—if something doesn't go to plan, you leave me when I tell you and get Mirren out of there."

"Anni—" Cal's eyes widen in alarm, but I cut him off with a shake of my head.

"Promise me. Promise you'll leave me if you have to. That you'll make her your priority."

Cal shakes his head forcefully, anger and shock passing over his face in equal measure. "I'm not agreeing to leave you behind, Shaw! You're my best friend, my soul brother. Mirren is strong. She doesn't need your martyr bullshit."

"This isn't...*that*," I snarl, stepping toward him. My stomach is tightly coiled, the terror inside me poised to spring forward at any moment.

To Calloway's credit, he doesn't even flinch. I am known to him, none of my anger or fear or shame unexpected; something that makes me feel both loved and maliciously annoyed. "Then tell me what it is. Tell me it isn't the usual charade of you thinking everyone around you is worth more than you are. Tell me this isn't just another outlet for your death wish."

His words spear me with their truth, piercing the gaping holes in my soul where resentment and self-hatred breed. He's right. Only a month prior, I sacrificed myself in pieces and in wholes, because I didn't feel I deserved to live. But then I met Mirren and she touched the blackest parts of me. They aren't gone—they never will be—but they are brighter, somehow. Cleaner.

I meet his gaze head on. "This isn't about self-sacrifice. It's about self-preservation."

Cal only waits.

"I can't live with myself if something happens to her." And then I tell him the honest truth of it, "there...there won't be anything left."

Cal stares at me, his gaze hard. After a painful pause, he nods reluctantly. "Okay," he agrees, voice rough with grief. It isn't fair, what I've asked him, but he's the only one I trust to protect the most vulnerable parts of myself. Though I love Max, she is too willful. She will die before leaving anyone behind. But Cal, Cal knows there are more important things than being alive.

"Is there something you're not telling me? What do you think is going to happen, Anni?"

I shake my head, disconsolate. "I don't know. I just... something feels wrong, Cal. Like we're going to defeat the dragon in its cave, only to have the entire mountain collapse on us." I roll my shoulders, as if I'll be able to ease the weight of dread that piles down on them. "All the way to Similis," I repeat, glowering at Cal until he nods. "She won't be safe until she's behind the Boundary. Even if we don't manage to rescue Denver and you have to shove her through the gates, get her to Similis. Away from all this."

Away from me.

The words still echo hours later, when I lie tangled with Mirren beneath our thick bed roll, her bare skin warm and tempting. They echo as I kiss every part of her, the rounded lines and soft planes, and they echo as I consume every piece of her power and then gift it back in a rush of crashing waves.

Long after she's fallen asleep, her long lashes a slash of soot against her pale cheeks and her small hands curled against my chest, the words echo like a foretold curse, inescapable and ever looming.

∼

Mirren

"Gods, what a dreary place," Max remarks, her face twisted in distaste as she eyes the expanse of the fortress city, "if depression were a city, it would be here."

She isn't wrong. Yen Girene is Nadjaa's antithesis; where Nadjaa sprawls, flowing and spacious, Yen Girene climbs, severe and stacked. While Nadjaa's bright splashes of color are an affront to the senses sparkling against the dark waters of the Storven Sea, Yen Girene is awash in grays and blacks, lackluster and brutal. The wall surrounding the city is thick and menacing, jutting from the mountain range at a savage angle. It's at least twenty feet wide and hundreds of feet tall, its face sheer and utterly unclimbable. Anrai told us that archers line the top at all hours of the day, trained to shoot first and ask questions later.

I shudder, staring up at the morose expanse of black rock. The only way in is just as he described, through a small gate on the side of the cliff adorned with steel gates that open and close by a lever hidden in a protected room.

Though we're too far away to see, the gate is armed with guards, trained to sniff out even the most elaborate of ruses. No one gets into the city without their say so, and by extension, without the Achijj's.

"Hidden and secure." Calloway appears from the trees where he's been tying the horses. I hate the idea of leaving Dahiitii by herself while we descend into the city, but there's wisdom in keeping our means of escape out of the Achijj's hands. If our horses were to be confiscated, we'd never make it home.

Cal has traded the bright fabrics he usually prefers for the soft black leather of gear. A quiver and bow are strapped to his back and the unadorned sword he had when he attacked the Boundary hunters hangs in a scabbard at his side. Max is similarly armed, with two curved swords strapped in an 'X' across her back and various daggers hidden in what she referred to as 'creative places'.

I pull my cloak tighter and pat my dagger. It is my only weapon, aside from my power. I hope there won't be a reason to use it.

There was little joking between us this morning, as the weight of what we are about to do settled over camp like a thick blanket. Even Cal's ever-present smile has receded into a somber seriousness. My heart thumps wildly and I remind myself that I am not the only one who will lose something if we don't succeed. I will lose my brother, but Max, Cal, and Anrai will lose a father. Nadjaa and Ferusa at large, stand to lose so much more.

Anrai is motionless next to me, but his pale eyes scan every detail of the fortress warily. He is clad in gear, his daggers lining his chest and legs, and a long sword that's too heavy for me to even lift is strapped to his back. There is no fear on his face, only bald determination and I am reminded of the night we first met—ruthless, cunning, and unyielding—but now, I am thankful for the strength of his will. Anrai does not fail. If anyone can find a way to get my father out of here, it's him.

"Let's go," he orders.

The descent to the gate is arduous. The path is steep and craggy, littered with rocks that sparkle in the few slivers of dim morning sun that peek through the fog. "How does any of their trade get through if this is the only path to the city?" I finally ask. Despite the icy chill of the air, sweat beads on my forehead.

"They don't," Cal answers, hopping over a particularly large stone with the grace of a gazelle. "They have everything they need to survive within their walls. They only trade in small amounts, only what can be brought in on horseback. That way, everything can be inspected. They don't trust outsiders."

"That seems like an exhausting way to live. Being so suspicious of the outside world."

Cal exchanges a look with Max. "They say Yen Girene was modeled after Similis," he says carefully.

I process his words, wondering why I failed to notice the parallels. While their Boundary may be made of stone and ours is metal, they were both built to accomplish the same thing—to keep anything different out. Both the good and the bad.

Up ahead, Anrai stops so abruptly that I skid on the gravel to keep from colliding with his back. "Something isn't right," he says, a hand going to the dagger over his heart.

Max turns round eyes on him, her pretty face apprehensive. "What is it?"

His eyes reflect the gray landscape, making them

appear to churn like restless storm clouds. "Listen."

I strain my ears, hearing nothing but the rustle of the long grasses on the southern-most plain of the valley and the distant rush of what I can only assume is the river Timdis.

"I don't hear anything," Cal says after minutes pass and Anrai still hasn't moved.

His gaze flicks to his friend and then back to the towering fortress. "Exactly. We're close enough to the city that we should hear something. Sounds of guards, sounds of the marketplace. But there's nothing. And look," he says gesturing to the enormous black wall, "there are no archers patrolling the top of the wall."

I squint, following the direction of Anrai's hand up to where the top of the wall meets the gunmetal gray sky. Indeed, there is an unsettling lack of movement.

Anrai points to the guards' gate, now only a few hundred feet away. "They're suspicious of outsiders. Someone should have met us by now, threatened us and taken us to the Achijj. Yen Girene is unguarded."

Cal's eyes pop and Max sets her jaw, but it's the way Anrai purposefully avoids my eyes that unsettles me most. He never shies away from the hard truth, but now, it's as if he can't bear to look at me. Guilt has settled onto his shoulders like an iron clamp, and I already know what he'll say before he utters, "we're walking into a trap."

Silence settles over us, thick and stifling.

Cal is the one to break it as he shifts his weight between his boot clad feet. "Okay, so the Achijj knows we're coming. The question is how."

Max scowls. "Do you think this has something to do with that slimy assassin?"

"It wasn't Avedis. He wouldn't betray his life debt like

that," I reply instantly.

Max raises an eyebrow. "You're awfully confident in the honor of someone who kills people for money," her gaze slides to Anrai. "What do you want to do?"

I don't wait for him to answer. "We have to go in."

Anrai's eyes flash as they finally settle on me, his face simmering with potent anger. But I know him well enough now to understand it isn't directed at me. It's fed by fear and his compulsive need to keep those he cares about from being hurt. He blames himself for not sniffing out the trap sooner and keeping us all far away from this place.

I understand him, but it changes nothing. "Even if this is a trap, it's our only lead to Denver. And my brother doesn't have any more time. I have to find him."

Anrai stares at me and I stare back, unwavering. After a moment, he softens, but he doesn't relent. His body remains tense and coiled. He glances at Calloway. "She's right. It is our only lead."

Cal nods once and begins checking over his weapons as if the decision has been made. But Anrai hasn't finished, "but I go in alone."

"Like hell you do!" I shout at the same time Max bursts forward in outrage. She gives me an approving nod.

"Cal," Anrai says, his voice full of a warning that I don't understand. And something else. Pleading.

"Anrai, it makes no strategic sense," the words tumble out of me, imploring and fast. We're wasting time by arguing and the only lead to my father could be slipping farther away with every minute. Being clever and efficient is what Anrai prides himself on, more so than any physical acumen, so it's this I appeal to. "We don't know what we're walking into or what we're up against. We *do* know that there's the Timdis and there's me. My power could be the only thing that protects us from whatever is in there. What if there's an entire army waiting?"

"She's right," Max agrees, glancing at the fortress uneasily. Max, who is so familiar with the horrors the Dark World can bestow, knows well the sort of things that could await us on the other side. "We go together, or no one goes. We'll be quick and smart, but we stick together," she raises a brow at Anrai, her face full of unspoken challenge and I wonder how I ever mistook him for the one in charge. The three of them have always been equals, never one above another. "And if you don't like that, I have no problem knocking your ass out and dragging your body back to Nadjaa."

Anrai straightens as if to argue, but instead, his eyes seek mine. I brace myself, waiting for him to command me to stay. To tell me I'm too weak, that all of this is impossible and wishing it wasn't won't change it. But his body visibly relaxes as he finds something in my eyes. "Okay," he agrees.

And it's settled.

He turns to inspect his weapons and I keep myself from throwing my arms around him. This was never about me. I've never needed to convince Anrai of my worth, my fortitude, because he knew it long before I ever did. This was about him needing to ground himself enough to overcome his own fears. And once again, with a selflessness that breaks my heart, he has put himself aside to champion my strength.

Weapons settled and accounted for, his face is resolute as he turns back toward Yen Girene. "I don't like walking into a trap through the front door, but I suppose it's our only choice. We may have to fight our way inside. Once in, head straight to the palace. Keep your eyes open and your guard up. Always."

Cal grips his bow, an arrow ready. Max palms one of her swords. My dagger sits at my hip, but it isn't the weapon I feel for. I turn inward, allowing the waves to crash over me, absorbing the strength of the sea and the calm of a cool brook. My *other* sings under my skin, awakened and ready.

To save Easton. To see my father again.

We descend on silent feet into the city.

Immediately, we are accosted by a rotting stench so powerful it's a wonder we didn't smell it clear back at the tree line. It can only be a favorable direction of wind that's kept it from us because the reek is so powerful, my eyes begin to water as we climb down the narrow path. The gate yawns like an open maw in the black expanse of wall.

It doesn't take long for the source of the smell to be revealed.

All of Yen Girene's guards lie splayed and motionless across the only road in, their bodies in various states of decomposition. Swords and arrows stick out of their chests and their stomachs have been viciously torn open, whether by enemy or scavenger, it's impossible to tell. Their innards lie in congealed pools, staining the stone road in a watercolor of deep browns and ugly shades of red. Nausea clenches my stomach and I struggle to swallow it down, following Anrai as he strides purposefully past them, already looking forward for unseen threats.

He barely spares the bodies a glance, a stark reminder that he has seen this sort of horror before. Choking on the stench, I hurry past the bloated corpses and into Yen Girene. Max and Cal come up behind me, the latter looking as green as I feel.

As I get my first glimpse of the city, I realize that Yen Girene isn't empty. It is densely populated, and people are all over the streets. But none of them are alive.

CHAPTER
THIRTY-SEVEN

Mirren

In the Education Center, we are shown videos and photographs of the most horrific events in Dark World history. My stomach always rebelled as I sat in the dark cocoon of the classroom, accosted with images of war; of famine; of poverty and disease. In the name of our education, they held nothing back, claiming it was paramount that we know the realities of the world beyond our Boundary.

Those lessons, still as fresh in my head as the first time I saw them, are nothing compared to the carnage that lies in Yen Girene's streets. Bodies are sprawled everywhere, bloated, and rooted to the ground by their own blood. The Girenis have not only been murdered—they've been completely *decimated*. Bile rises in my throat as we pass a pair of crows pecking at the eyes of a head that sits a few feet away from the body it was once attached to.

Anrai picks his way through the destruction on careful feet, the three of us following silently behind. There are no words for what happened here, no sounds except for the cawing of the scavengers. In the distance, I swear I hear the shriek of a yamardu, drawn to the feast.

We come to a market that's been laid to tatters. Wares rot on their purveyor's tables, as if the massacre happened midday.

"There are no children," Max whispers from beside me, her eyes roving over the body of a merchant that's been sliced through, neck to navel. I shudder, wondering at the kind of twisted strength needed to accomplish such a feat. "And the women...there are hardly any women."

I swallow roughly, her meaning clear. Anrai nods, his jaw tight as something of their shared history passes between them. "I know." His voice is devoid of emotion, but when he looks at me, anguish washes over his face. As if he can't quite accept what he sees; or that I am now seeing it, too.

You cannot touch the Darkness and remain unchanged.

The thought strikes at my core, echoing like my body is an empty cavern. I am so far from Similis. So far from Easton.

We make our way gingerly through the marketplace. "These people, they've been dead for at least a week," Calloway observes. His face has markedly paled, his freckles stark.

A week ago today, I was fighting for my life and discovering the power that lived within me. It can't be a coincidence, but I'm lost to what it means. Avedis said there was someone powerful inside Yen Girene; could this be the result of one person's wrath? It's too horrible to fathom that one person could contain this much cruelty, but this massacre isn't efficient and impersonal. It's messy, meant to send a message. But to who? Us?

"Whoever did this, they look to be long gone," Max says with a tinge of relief.

Anrai only shakes his head. "They're not," he says quietly.

"But none of the bodies have been touched. And look at the layer of grime that coats the marketplace. No fresh fingerprints or footprints," Max presses. She shifts her sword from one hand to another and I remember Anrai saying she is an equally strong fighter with both hands. I can only hope her skills aren't required, but judging by Anrai's face, it's a futile one.

He gestures to the largest building inside the wall, an imposing tower made entirely of the same terrible black stone. Instead of shining, it seems to draw what little light the day offers into it, creating a slashing void of darkness against the surrounding mountains. The outside is as smooth as the wall and there are no windows to be seen. I shudder, feeling suffocated from out here.

"They're in there," Anrai says certainly. "The palace was created to withstand siege, even if the city walls are breached. There are enough supplies in there to last a small army at least a year. And according to my maps, the Timdis runs directly underneath it providing fresh water." He looks to me. Whoever awaits us in that fortress, my power will be needed.

"Do you think the Achijj did this?" Cal asks slowly, "that he went mad and slaughtered his own people?"

Anrai shakes his head. "No. He relished his comfortable lifestyle. He wouldn't kill off his work force. There'd be no one to mine his jewels."

"Who then?"

For the first time since stepping through the gate, Anrai hesitates. He shakes his head. "I don't know," The familiar stone mask clamps down over his features like the door to a tomb, "but we're about to find out."

~

Shaw

The door of the tower palace is made of reinforced steel, and I meet no resistance as I push it open. We step into a cavernous room. Despite the overbearing appearance of the exterior, the room is glowing and opulent. Shining granite pillars tower toward a ceiling so high it's impossible to see clearly, gilded with shining red gemstones that twinkle even in the darkness. The marble floor is covered in thick rugs, the kind woven from rare threads in the east. Marble statues and lush paintings line various alcoves and luxurious fabrics curtain the walls. Everything about the room screams opulence, exactly what I would expect from the Achijj, a man known for his rich appetites and even richer treasury.

Except for the fact that it's entirely empty. The last time I was here, the tower palace was brimming with tittering courtiers and harem wives. Music echoed off the towering ceiling and spirits were served around every corner.

Now, dust gathers on the tops of the marble busts and lines the frames of the paintings. The marble stairs that lead up and away are dull and untouched. The lanterns that light the room have long since burned through their oil and the candelabras that line the walls are down to the quick.

But someone is here. My skin hums with their presence, almost as if I can sense the warmth of life somewhere in the bowels of this massive place. Which is ridiculous, but my instincts have kept me alive this long. A morbid accomplishment, to be so good at surviving in the same way rats of the earth are, but here I am.

I motion silently to Cal, and he strings his bow, moving to my left. Mirren and Max follow on silent feet as we advance slowly into the enormous room. Whoever is here took great pains to make the place appear abandoned. A sense of foreboding climbs up my throat. The massacre outside is catastrophic and yet no news of it reached Nadjaa. I know only one person capable of such a feat.

I tell myself I'm being paranoid, that my father is still in the north and even he isn't capable of mobilizing an army so quickly, but dread hangs heavy in my lungs.

"We need to find the way down," I whisper.

According to the old maps, a dungeon system runs beneath the tower palace. Expansive and labyrinthine, thanks to Gireni mining skill, I can only imagine it's grown in the time since the maps were drawn.

Cal and Max nod their agreement, but I don't look to Mirren. I made that mistake as we passed through the carnage of the marketplace and immediately wished I hadn't. Her face was so beautiful, eyes wide and guileless, in direct contrast to the horror around her. It was as if my assassin's mask was ripped from me and I was shoved harshly back into my own body, feeling the sharpness of its fears.

Weapons do not feel. Conquer your emotions or succumb to death.

My father's words, harsh but true. Usually accompanied by the bite of a whip or the sear of a hot iron because I'd failed at it. I won't fail now.

We move through the hallways quietly, each passage wide and comfortable and as lavishly decorated as the entry hall. The tower palace is eerily still, as if even the rodents have gone to ground.

As we round a corner into another antechamber, Mirren's gasp echoes through the stuffy air. The reason is obvious. Pinned to the opposite wall by swords is the Achijj.

The body is pin cushioned with arrows and various knives and the Gireni leader's eyes have been plucked out, leaving his face empty and distorted. His mouth is twisted and gaping, frozen in the final throes of agony. A pool of blood lies beneath his feet, so large that it must contain every last drop that was previously in the Achijj's body.

I've only seen the man once, and even then, it was from a great distance, but there's no doubt in my mind this is him. His crown, fashioned from the same gems that line the entrance pillars, dangles above his head, pinned to the wall in the same fashion as his body. My gaze travels to the floor around him, a pile my eyes previously skipped over. I swallow roughly as I realize it isn't just a heap of fabric—it's a pile of bodies. Judging by the height, at least fifty of them, all in various states of decomposition. The Achijj's harem.

Dread clenches my stomach into a tight fist. I should feel relief that the man who abducted Denver is dead, but there is none to be had. Because whoever killed the Achijj is a thousand times worse and now, we are left with nothing to bargain.

And there were no signs of siege. The front gate was wide open, and the fortress is impeccable aside from the corpses. Which means that the Achijj let the wickedness in through his own front door. Was it his mysterious guest?

"Should we get him down?" Cal asks uncertainly. Even in the face of the heartless warlord who kidnapped our mentor and forced us into abducting Mirren, Cal's need for compassion and humanity wins out.

Unfortunately, we have no time for it. "We keep moving." I thrust past the cloud of apprehension that's settled over the room. Cal only nods, lifting his bow once more. Mirren raises her chin but says nothing as we leave the throne room.

When we find the entrance to the dungeons, I feel as though I'm leading my friends into the mouth of the Darkness itself. I keep moving, determined to outpace my trepidation. I force my feet down the tunnel, convinced that if I pause for even a moment, I'll be stuck here forever. Max strikes a match, lighting a torch, and its dim light reflects off the steeply sloping floor.

The walls here are hewn stone, grittier and without the ornamentation of the floors above. The passageway is only wide enough for us to descend single file and is easily defensible if we're to be attacked. There's no way an entire army lurks down here if this is the only way in.

When we reach the bottom, the river rushes in the distance and the granite beneath our feet is wet, dark pools gathered and gleaming in the dimpled rock. The narrow passage veers off in both directions, no doubt leading to a maze of cells and torture chambers.

I close my eyes momentarily, listening to the sounds of the underground, feeling the prick of heat along my spine. "Toward the river."

There is no dissent. I try not to think of how undeserving I am of their faith, especially if I am leading them into what I expect I am. I should have made them turn back. I should have knocked them out and tied them each to a tree and came myself. Then at least they would be safe.

I push the thought away, burrowing into the abyss and

letting it burn at my fingertips and at the edges of my ruined soul. There is only Shaw now, ruthless and brutal and unyielding. I am a weapon. Weapons do not feel, and they do not fail.

And because Anrai is gone, and with him, fear and love and anything else that is human, I don't even flinch at the sight that lies before me.

The passage opens to a small cavern, roughhewn and dripping. In it are twenty soldiers, armed and hardened, and expecting us. But it's what lies beyond them that focuses my rage, that hones it into something sharp.

There, strung up and chained, is Denver.

His body is unnaturally splayed, his arms and legs stretched impossibly wide between the large iron chains. He's so much thinner than when he bid us goodbye before his journey and his skin is covered in welts and burns.

Red coats my vision as the abyss roars. The sound echoes out of my mouth as I move, cutting down the first soldier. Cal's arrows are already flying and Max spins, lashing out at a man twice her size and bringing him to his knees with a well-aimed blow.

Mirren exhales a breath of surprise and I force myself not to hear the fear that lines the small sound. Because I can't be Anrai now, made vulnerable by a ragged heart and a sense of humanity if I'm to face who holds a blade to Denver's spine.

"It took you long enough." The man's voice is a gruesome whisper, the sound of nightmares. The result of a new scar that glistens an angry red at his windpipe. His eyes light on Mirren, frenzied and hungry. "I've waited so long for you, little bird," Shivhai growls.

CHAPTER
THIRTY-EIGHT

Mirren

The cavern erupts into chaos. With a sound more animal than man, Anrai hurls himself into battle. He takes the first soldier with a blow to the stomach and a swipe across their sword arm, before he drops to his knees and takes the second and third by sliding his blades along the back of their knees.

To his left, Max faces two soldiers at once. Both tower over her, masses of muscle, but only fierce determination lines her face as she outmaneuvers them. Her lithe body twists as she wields her swords. The men fall at her feet, gasping and bleeding, but she pays their pain no attention, already whirling to the next opponent. Calloway follows behind her, notching arrow after arrow, each hitting its mark with a decisive *thwap*. Behind every soldier that falls, another stands ready to take their place, a never-ending hell ride of violence.

My heart beats in my throat and my power writhes as it feeds on the heightened emotions of the dungeon. No matter how much progress I've made throwing knives, I'm next to useless in the heat of battle, so I linger on the outskirts and send my power into the depths of the fight.

I blast a soldier in the face, blinding him until Max can move to finish him. My fingertips tingle and waves crash against my heart as my *other* demands more. As *I* demand more. I sing to the water in the cave, each droplet its own moment in time, its own swirling magic. They dance in rhythm with my heartbeat as I send them smashing into more of the enemy. They don't even have time to cry out; they gasp with wide eyes and gaping mouths as they drown on dry land, their hands clawing desperately at their throats.

And I do not balk from it, do not wonder why I demand their blood. The reason is clear enough as I fight my way toward the other side of the cavern. Toward my father, his mistreated body chained and strung up. His skin is raw and bleeding, and his head has been roughly shaved. The bones of his thin body jut in all the wrong directions. It seems silly now, to have wondered if I would recognize him after all these years. I would know him anywhere. It is ancient and deep, the part of him that is something of myself, something of Easton. It no longer matters that he left me or that I'm angry with him; it only matters that he stays alive to be angry with.

Shivhai has disappeared from his post as jailkeeper. My throat tightens as I realize he's cutting his way toward Anrai. A blood debt to be paid, one that began well before I arrived in the Praeceptor's camp. I feed my fear to my power, and it rises in answer. The droplets freeze to ice as they swarm a large soldier, pelting him with shards sharper than any razor; my fear personified. I don't stop to watch. I dash across the dungeon.

The floor is wet with river water and blood, staining the

stone an odd shade of pink. A soldier makes to grab me, and I imagine the water reaching up and grabbing her ankles, miring her feet and pulling her toward the ground. She falls with a terrified scream.

When I finally make it to my father's chains, bile rises in my throat. From far away, Denver's injuries appeared grievous. Up close, they are nothing short of horrific. He is naked except for a frayed pair of undershorts. His face is unrecognizable beneath a web of slashes and bruising. His legs, no longer able to support his weight, sag listlessly and from the morose way one of his feet points, it's clear at least one of his ankles is broken. The skin of his back and abdomen is mottled with angry red burns and lacerations in different stages of infection. His shoulders are dislocated from the pull of the irons and his head lolls with unconsciousness. I can only be thankful he isn't awake to feel his injuries.

Both his eyes are swollen shut and for a moment, I can only stare at what the Dark World has done to the man from my memories. There are no laugh lines to be found, no twinkling mischief. There is only a broken body. And a pulse.

Relief courses through me, sharpening the edges of my vision. He's alive.

I examine the chains. Made of thick iron and drilled deep into the cavern rock above and below, there are no locks to be picked. The shackles around Denver's wrists and ankles appear to be one complete piece. Cursing, I search for something to leverage but there is nothing on the sparse cavern floor.

Agonized screams echo harshly against the stone walls and then back against my ears. I need to move quickly.

You have the power of the ocean at your fingertips.

The ocean. I have the power of the ocean.

Determination floods me as I close my eyes. I reach out to the cave around me, to the raging river beyond, feeling each pin prick of power and drawing it to me.

I picture the road Anrai and I traveled on, how the forest bided its time until it patiently took back every inch stolen by civilization. The wild of the Darkness has a way of creeping through the smallest of cracks and water is much the same, ancient and steady. Years pass and it wields its power slowly, endlessly carving its way through forests and mountains of rock until streams pour between trees and rivers rage through canyons.

And iron. Water rebels against iron fixtures and bridges built in its path, turning the strong metal to rust. Even if it takes a thousand years, it weakens the iron until it finally crumbles away. Water gives life, but it can also destroy it.

I start with the chains on my father's legs. Wrapping my fingers around the cold metal, I give myself over to my power. It crashes through me, ancient and primal as an ocean and then twists itself against the iron. I feed it everything I have—my love, my anger, my fear—until there is nothing left of me except the *other*. For a moment, the cavern ceases to exist; it is only my power and me, swirling in unexplored depths. Dark, cold and endless, we swirl like an ancient storm, and I push further until finally, *finally*, the manacle corrodes and snaps beneath my fingers.

I fall to my knees, gasping for air as if I've just surfaced from a deep dive. My heart races in my chest as I force myself to stand on shaking legs. I haven't thought much about the limits of my magic and the realization strikes me as severely as a physical blow to the chest. There *are* no limits except that of my own body. My power is greater than the unexplored depths of the Storven Sea and I could fall endlessly into it, swallowed by the dark, the human girl

I am forgotten somewhere on the surface. The pressure is too great at the depths of the sea for anything soft.

My body rebuffs the idea of diving back in, for I know I will have to go further and there is nothing to anchor me to my humanity. I press my lips together and slow my breathing. *Community before self.* I have never embodied the Keys, never saw them beyond what they took from me. But I understand now. Easton is my community. Anrai is my community. Max and Cal and Rhonwen. And the man in front of me, who gave me my dreams and broke my heart; my father is my community. And they are all worth choosing over myself.

I close my eyes and hold onto the chains, the metal biting against my skin.

Come to me. Fall into me, my power calls.

And I do.

~

Shaw

My vision is tinged red, and I see nothing but the next opponent—the next slice of my dagger, the next sweep of my feet, the next obstacle standing between Denver and me. There is no fear in my killing calm, a wave of rage so hot, it burns like ice under my skin. The soldiers are well trained, and after the first wave of surprise dissipates, they don't fall easily.

Water sparkles in the air and dives for the man in front of me, courtesy of Mirren, and I don't hesitate before jabbing him in the solar plexus. He doubles over, wheezing with wide eyes as he swats at the water. I finish him with a knee to the face.

I throw myself further into the fray, ducking under a

sword and side stepping another. I calculate the numbers as I go. We've felled seven. At least thirteen still fight and that doesn't include Shivhai.

A punch to the throat and a slice across the femur.

Make that twelve.

Max and Cal are swept further away as the fighting progresses. The close combat has rendered Cal's bow useless, and he's abandoned it in favor of his sword. He slices it nimbly through the air, disarming a man before he can bring his axe down on Max's neck.

I block a sword edge aimed for my own neck and carve my dagger across the woman's wrist until her hand dangles uselessly and she drops her weapon. I spin around, jamming another dagger into her kidney for good measure. I don't hear her cries of torment as I turn my narrowed gaze on Shivhai. He shoves his way past his own soldiers, murder glinting in his eyes as they find me.

The abyss crows in anticipation. It thrashes and howls, burning up my throat and demanding Shivhai's blood. Ravenous and aching, I pull my sword.

Shivhai knocks the last man out his way, his gray eyes like chips of slate. "He's mine," he growls to his men. He is just as large as I remember, as wide as two Nemoran tree trunks and his face is gnarled by years of savagery. Madness lines every inch of him, from the restless way he holds his sword to the hard press of his jaw, as if his body is incapable of remaining still until he squeezes the life from me.

I grin at him, matching his mania.

He roars and hurtles toward me. The first clash of our swords reverberates up my arm, all the way to my teeth, but I clench down, already swinging on the counterattack. Shivhai is a mountain of muscle, nearly immovable, but he is quicker on his feet than I remember. Probably because he isn't bleeding from his neck this time. He dodges, feinting left before slicing at my right. I move before the blade lands, dancing away from him.

He comes at me again, and I twist, bringing my blade down in a quick arc that Shivhai sees coming. He blocks me with a sneer, our swords ringing. He whirls, lunging forward, his blade a hot iron as it sweeps across my leg. A flesh wound, but one that smarts as I whirl, praying his guard will be lowered by a false sense of victory, but he's too good for that. He deflects my blade, landing a blow to my jaw that sends stars spiraling across my vision.

"You didn't even give my brother the respect of a quick death. Slit his stomach and let him bleed out slowly, like an animal," another blow to the stomach and I'm sent sprawling backward, bile flooding my mouth, "you can be sure I'll give that girl of yours the same treatment after I kill you."

I bare my teeth, lunging and bringing my sword down in a hard arc. He meets me blow for blow, his breath even, his movements efficient. He may be mad with grief, but he is a well-oiled machine, one my father honed for killing. "She isn't anyone's but her own," I bite out, curling around and landing a strike to his shoulder. The wound splits open and blood wells, but Shivhai only snarls and meets my next jab so hard, my teeth vibrate inside my jaw. "And I will tear every bone from your body before you can touch her again."

"Come on, boy! I know your father trained you better than this."

Shivhai knows all about my training because he was trained by the same man. Not with the same intimate cruelty, but with the same careful precision, no doubt. "Where is darling Father?"

"Scared?" Shivhai laughs, his ruined windpipe scraping.

"Don't worry, I'll grant you death long before the Praeceptor gets here. I have no intention of losing my vengeance to his plans."

I wonder briefly what my father thinks of his son abandoning him and then his *legatus*, both driven by something he has always deemed a weakness—emotion. Though different ones forced us down our respective paths, our decisions both driven by something good assassins should never feel, love. Shivhai's all-consuming hatred began with the death of the brother he loved and now he goes after the weapon itself, rather than the one who aimed it.

"My father ordered your brother's death," I tell him, ducking beneath a swing aimed for my head. I bring my sword up just before his blade slices through my spine. I roll over, springing to my feet and then lunge, landing another slash at his side. "He ordered it to be slow. To torture him until your brother begged for death and then refuse to grant it."

Shivhai rushes me with a roar, ducking beneath my guard. I scramble to bring my sword up, but he's too close and I'm forced to resort to a dagger, pulling the small blade just before I'm decapitated. The dagger blade sings, metal against metal, but it won't last long. The blades are made for stealth, not to withstand hard blows.

"Your brother is lucky I was who my father sent, lucky that even at eleven, I could already see what you can't. My father is a monster who metes out judgement on selfish whims and twisted pleasures. Not a leader to be followed."

Shivhai snarls, his lips pulling over his teeth. "You know nothing about what the Praeceptor has done or the lengths he's gone for the Dark World. You're nothing more than an attack dog gone feral."

I bare mine back, the blade growing warm in my hand.

"You should consider your brother lucky for what I gave him. My father would not have been so kind."

The blade shakes in my hand. I'm strong, but I will never be able to overpower Shivhai. The logical move would be to bring my sword hand up, to threaten his side and force his retreat. But he will see it coming. We've been trained the same and though I know my father saved a special part of his cruelty for only me, Shivhai will know how to match almost every move I make.

We will go on and on, blocking and reciprocating until one of us drops dead from exhaustion. And with revenge fueling him and the abyss fueling me, it could be days before one of us relents.

But unlike Shivhai, my father could never quite train me the way he wanted. He was never able to strip me all the way down in order to build me back up in his image. I held parts of myself out of his reach and it was those that saved me and Max on that fateful night. Broken soul notwithstanding, those parts were still wild and fierce, unmalleable. My father has no patience for sentiment, and therefore, was never able to predict the lengths it could lead me to.

And so, I do the exact opposite of my father's training. I leave myself wide open.

I feint left, leaving a hole in my defenses so large, Shivhai's eyebrows rise in surprise and then lower in determination. He knocks the dagger from my hand, victory blazing across his face. My sword skitters across the damp stone, and I meet his eyes as he raises his sword tip to my throat.

I see the moment he realizes his mistake. I watch the moment he knows I allowed him to disarm me to get him close, but it's too late. I slide a dagger between his ribs, and he roars as his blood pours over my hand. He staggers backward and I pounce, throwing my weight at his legs. He topples over, his massive body hitting the ground with a staggering *thud*.

I slice the tendons at his elbows with brutal efficiency and he howls in agony. The abyss roars its approval, demanding *more, more, more*. More of his blood. More of his suffering. *Let him burn with it.* For the way he hurt Mirren. For the myriad of women before her, the daughters that were used and then discarded, tortured and killed. For the sons that will never come home, slaughtered on his orders.

And more than that, for my father—proof to him that I will never be contained, that I will never bow to him. I couldn't take his life, but I took his blood heir and now I will take his *legatus* from him, too. He raised me in blood and torment, to be a weapon, and because of it, he will never know a moment's peace.

Surely, no vow is worth letting Shivhai and my father go unpunished. No soul, especially not mine, is worth more of their reign of terror, more of their sanctioned bloodshed.

And if this kill takes the last piece of my soul with it, so be it. A ruthless heart has always beat inside me, cunning and ambitious. Willing to tear itself, and the world, apart in order to shelter those it beats for.

I raise my dagger, but it is not the weapon. I am. A breath of relief whooshes out of me as I exact my will.

CHAPTER
THIRTY-NINE

Mirren

Though my father's weight is diminished, he's still heavy enough to knock the air from me as we tumble to the ground. The sounds and feelings of the surface come back in soft waves, dragging me up from the chasm inside—the scrape of rough stone against my back, the ring of steel, and there, faintly, the dim plod of my father's heartbeat against my chest.

He's alive, but barely. I'm no healer, but with the extent of his external injuries, it isn't a leap to assume there's damage inside as well. I roll him gently to his side, wincing as his head bounces off the floor. "Dad," the word isn't as strong as I wish it was, "Dad, please wake up."

I call water to me, gently this time, and trickle some into his mouth. "Dad, you have to wake up," I plead as the droplets run over his cracked lips. His breathing hitches painfully and fear ices over my heart. What if he stops breathing and never starts again?

The fight rages closer. I try to shut out the sharp sounds, to focus solely on my dad, but it's like trying to pull my own heart back inside my body. Only feet away, Anrai, Max, and Cal fight for their lives. For mine and Denver's, and Easton's, and my fear for them is a breathing thing.

I trickle more water into my father's destroyed mouth. His skin is so ravaged, I have a hard time finding a place to touch that won't cause him more pain, so I settle for running my fingers gently over his scalp. When I was little and frightened, he would always let me lay my head in his lap and run his fingers through my hair until I fell asleep. It's a memory I haven't allowed myself in a long time, tender and tinged with heartache. But now, it floods me. "Dad!" A curse and a plea.

He spasms beneath my fingers with an anguished groan. His eyelids flutter. "Azurra," he moans. My mother's name.

"Drink, Denver," I tell him, the word 'dad' suddenly too intimate. He was once the most known entity in my world, my entire being wrapped up in one person. But now, the broken man before me is a stranger.

"Shaw," the name is more a gasp than a word.

I swallow roughly. "It's Mirren. I'm here to take you home."

Two fat tears roll from the corners of his eyes. They take on the red tinge of blood as they trail down his cheeks. "Mirri," he cries, his hand grasping jerkily in the air as if trying to find me through total darkness. The sound of my old nickname is like the edge of a sword, but I envelop his hand anyway. "Mirri is gone. Shaw will be lost, too."

"Shaw isn't lost," I tell him gently, "he's right here with us. Fighting for you."

"One more piece," he gasps, gripping my hand roughly. "One more piece and he will be gone!" He slips from my grasp, gesturing wildly. I follow the direction of his hand and my mouth goes dry.

A few feet away, feet that may as well be miles, Anrai hovers over Shivhai. His face is split in a humorless grin and his eyes burn, an uncontrolled maelstrom of anger. He has a dagger poised at Shivhai's throat and the other arcs downward. I've been afraid since the moment I crossed the Boundary—since before, when the Healer declared Easton's life over—but this fear is different. It grips something deep, coating my lungs and heart in hoarfrost. Everything inside me freezes, immovable, as I realize what Denver is trying to tell me.

Anrai is going to kill Shivhai.

The *legatus* deserves death and more for the agony he's inflicted on the world. But if Denver is right, Anrai will surrender the last piece of his soul to the curse and be lost to the Darkness forever. Lost to *me* forever.

You don't know what your morals are, what lines you will cross, until they are tested. And I know there are no lines. His words to me a lifetime ago. At the time, the world as I knew it was painted entirely in crisp blacks and whites. But now, a thousand shades of gray have filled the spaces between.

Anrai was right. There *are* no lines I will not cross to protect those I care about. Even from themselves.

I get to my feet, my legs like jelly beneath me. He has always taken the weight of the world on his shoulders, shredding himself and handing the pieces over to protect those he loves. But this time, he isn't alone.

Community before self. He is my community. He is my home. And that makes my choice so easy.

I send my power flying toward them, the ice shards as cold and sharp as my fear. Anrai leaps up with a shout, turning wide, beautiful eyes on me as the realization of my intent slashes across him like a whip.

"Mirren, NO!" I see the movement of his mouth more than hear his desperate words, but it is too late.

I send the ice flying down Shivhai's throat.

I close my eyes as the shards, sharper even than glass, shred his windpipe and then further—further until I feel the life leave the *legatus* in a small wisp.

It's then I feel the fissure. I gasp, my hands flying to my chest where something cracks, irrevocably broken. The pain burns hotter than any iron, unbearable and unending as it rips through me. Every bone in my body is cracking and I scream as I fall to the ground. It tears and claws me from the inside out and it won't end, it will never end. Because this is what it feels like to lose a piece of your soul.

The fire rages through my body, burning every nerve ending. A gaping abyss opens inside me, darker than the place my power resides, and I fall into it until there is nothing but suffocating darkness.

∼

Shaw

Terror as I have never felt pierces me as Mirren falls to the dungeon floor. Her head bounces off the stone and her hair sprawls, and I think I am screaming as I push myself off Shivhai's lifeless body. The battle around us has ceased, the remaining soldiers surrendering at the point of Max's sword, but I have eyes only for the girl on the ground as I race to her side.

Her eyes are closed, the color leached from her skin. Her mouth is slightly parted, pale and wan. She isn't dead. She is so much worse. Irreparably torn apart. Broken.

No, no, no.

She did this for me. And I do not deserve it, could never deserve the irreversible changing of her soul. The gaping abyss, the one I know so well, is now hers forever. Ugly tears pour down my face. I circle my arms around her and pull her to my chest. I hold her and cry for us both. For her sacrifice and for my rescue. For the gift I'm not worthy of, but she's bestowed upon me anyway.

I feel her stir in my arms and watch her eyelashes flutter against her cheeks. After a moment, her eyes open and she peers up at me, her face awash with relief and something else I won't name—something more powerful than magic and too pure for this dungeon that is drenched in blood and hatred.

"Why is it that I'm always being rendered unconscious around you?" She shifts to sitting, her face breaking into a wry smile. And I can't help it. Despite the enormity of everything, I let out a peel of laughter, loud and joyous.

"I'm told my good looks have that effect on women."

She shoves me playfully, but then her mouth draws down in worry. I want to wipe it away, to never give her cause for consternation again. "Denver," she says, shoving herself to standing. I know better than to offer to help her up. My adopted father's name rings through me with a start, followed by a wave of shame that in the midst of everything, I almost completely forgot him.

"He isn't well, Shaw." I know she doesn't use my name because we aren't safe, but I ache for the sound of it in her voice anyway. Max and Cal, having tied up the few remaining conscious soldiers, run over to us as Mirren kneels beside her father.

Max gasps, throwing a hand over her mouth in horror

as she takes in Denver's state and my own throat is tight as my gaze roves over him.

My gods. What did Shivhai do to him?

I knew Denver was probably being interrogated, but that was when I thought it was only the Achijj behind this. He was methodical, a businessman, but not known for being unduly cruel.

But this. *This.*

It was torture. Not for information. But for the sick enjoyment of it.

There's no way Denver will survive being carried to where our horses wait. I don't even know if he'll survive a few more minutes in this godsforsaken cavern.

Unless...

My eyes shoot to Mirren. "You have to heal him."

She looks to me in shock, her hand smoothing over the patches that remain of Denver's once lush hair, her green eyes stark against her dirty face. "I've tried practicing but I—I've never been able to do it again." Her voice wavers in shame.

Denver's hands are misshapen, his fingers splayed in unnatural directions and the abyss rises inside me, hot and demanding. When I met him, I was dirty, bleeding and half dead and he offered me his hand. His hands weren't callused like the soldiers and assassins I grew up with, but smooth and elegant. As I took it, I thought it was the best thing I'd ever felt. The first hand I'd ever encountered curled to give comfort, not pain.

And now, they are ruined by the same cruelty that ruined me. The Darkness has never spared anyone, but it should have spared him. He has sinned, but he has tried so hard to bring light to Ferusa. To me.

I set my jaw and dig my nails into my palm. "You can do

it, Mirren. You're strong and powerful and both of those things come from your love. Despite what the world has done to you, despite what *he's* done to you, you walked into the Darkness for him. You are so brave and so full that nothing can stop you. That's where your true power comes from, why the magic was drawn to you. Why *I* was drawn to you." I hold her gaze, filling it with everything that lies unsaid between us. "You are strong enough for this."

Her shoulders rise as she takes a deep breath. She places her hands gingerly on his chest and closes her eyes.

For a moment, nothing happens. But then, water begins to peel from the dungeon walls, beads sparkling in the air like a million tiny diamonds. Cal's eyes widen in shock, and he reaches out to touch one of them. It dances away from his fingertips, toward Mirren. Toward Denver.

"I told you that heart of yours was going to get us in trouble," I whisper as I kneel beside her, "but Lemming, it's going to be what saves us all. It saved me. It will save him."

The dungeon looks magical, each droplet glittering in the torchlight as if lit from the inside. The water comes to her, swirling softly before gliding from her skin and onto Denver's. My throat tightens as she starts with his hands and tears fall once more, hers and mine, when the bones slide and the skin knits together until they look just like the day I met him.

Mirren may have broken her soul for me, but she is not shattered. She is still wholly wonderful, wholly herself. Instead of being overcome by the aching presence of the abyss, she fills it with wonder and magic. For the first time since we entered Yen Girene, I feel hope spark in my chest, a small flint in an endless void.

Until everything goes wrong.

I feel it before I see it. The way Mirren's body suddenly

stiffens. The small exhale of breath from her lips. I turn to her but before I can speak, her eyes roll up into her head and she collapses in my arms. "Mirren!" Did the power demand too much of her?

Max and Cal rush to my side. I try to speak, to take charge, but something in the room shifts and there is no more air. I look around wildly, clutching my chest that has suddenly become ice cold, a frozen wasteland. Even the burning of my abyss is gone, replaced by something emptier. As if even my blood has stopped flowing.

Max gapes at me as my mouth moves, but no words come.

Something's wrong, I try to tell her. *Go. Take Mirren and leave.*

When the voice sounds from behind me, I understand the gaping desolation. It is a voice that sucks all warmth from the room, eloquent and cold. A voice that pierces every one of my nightmares like a glacial spire. "I suppose hello is an inadequate greeting after all these years."

Max's face drains of color. I struggle to breathe, clawing at my chest as if it will relieve the frigid cold that grips my lungs. My heart.

Mirren. Oh gods, I need to get her out of here.

But I already know it's too late. I'm frozen in place as I watch a man step into the dungeon. His clothes are exquisitely made and would be out of place in the brutal landscape of a battlefield if it weren't for his face. My features mirrored, but only if they were sharpened with a knife and honed in cruelty.

"But I find I have no other words," the man says, stepping over the unconscious form of a soldier with a look of vague distaste, "so hello, son of mine."

CHAPTER FORTY

Mirren

My throat is too dry to swallow and blinding pain shoots through my skull as I open my eyes. I try to push myself to sitting, but my bones scrape against my skin with every movement. Anrai is next to me, pupils blown wide. He claws at his chest frantically as if trying to tear out his own heart. Mouth drawn in a pained grimace, he drags his body across the floor and positions himself between me and the finely dressed man.

"So hello, son of mine."

The man's voice bounces off the cavern walls so that it sounds like an army instead of one person. I lick my dry lips, trying to think past the pounding in my head. *Son?*

His father is dead. *Isn't he?*

Anrai struggles to stand but falls back to his knees with a groan. I want to reach out to him with my power, but when I grapple inside myself, there is no answer. Just resounding silence.

Where are you? I call to my *other,* my intertwined self.

My voice echoes weakly in the void. Where life and power once rushed, there is only a dry wasteland.

"Hello, Cullen," Anrai bites out furiously.

The man places a hand over his heart. "You wound me, son. I hoped a little thing like trying to murder me wouldn't dampen our family relations."

Abject horror settles over me like a thick mist as the man's name clangs through me. *Cullen*. A name mentioned a lifetime ago, in the little cave beside the stream. Anrai had blanched when I raged that he was no better than the Praeceptor. Only now do I realize how intimate his knowledge of the horrific warlord really was, and what coming into that camp to save me truly cost him.

"If you won't call me Father, you could at least do me the honor of the Praeceptor. I think I've earned it."

With a start, I realize Cullen looks just like Anrai. His skin is several shades lighter, and his cheekbones are not as high, but there is no denying their relation. He's all of Anrai's sharp angles, with none of his handsomeness. As if the pleasing aspects of his face have been carved away by cruelty. His eyes are the same pale blue, but they are flat and dispassionate, even as they settle on his son.

"What...did you do?" Anrai's words come in painful gasps. Whatever Cullen has done to empty my power is affecting him as well. Max and Cal stand still, faces grave as they watch the Praeceptor.

Cullen raises an eyebrow, flicking a piece of lint from his tunic casually. "Oh, you mean the emptiness in your chests?" Something glimmers in his pale eyes as he sets them on me. Something like triumph. "Don't fret, it's only temporary. Your power will come back to you as soon as you cross the threshold of this dungeon. Just a little blood magic learned from a friend. As long as I get what I want, everything will return to normal. And if not," his triumph flattens into something cold, "my men waiting outside these doors will be more than willing to step in."

"What do you want, Cullen?" I gasp.

Cullen's mouth twitches at the name as if the lack of respect physically bothers him. "A lot of things, really. All of which I intend to get in time." His pale eyes, which contrast beautifully against Anrai's dark skin, serve to make Cullen look washed out and colorless, like everything vibrant about him has been carefully scrubbed from his exterior. As they shift to me, they are fathomless. "But I suppose they all come down to *you*."

Anrai shoves himself to his feet. His legs tremble with the exertion but his face is formidable as he faces his father. "Why."

Cullen chuckles. His gait is unhurried as he prowls closer. He appears unarmed above his finely tailored clothes, but I've seen the places one can stash weapons. I burrow into myself, rooting around for any scrap of my power that remains, anything to protect us from Cullen's depravity. He shattered Anrai's soul as a child, he keeps people in cages, and he sanctions someone as evil as Shivhai. He needs to pay. But there is nothing except dust, as if every bit of water inside me has evaporated. Even my blood feels like sludge in my veins.

"It's quite useless. There's nothing left of it, I'm afraid," Cullen tells me, with a pitying smile. "Sorry for the mild discomfort, but I couldn't have you drowning me before I was even able to speak."

Next to me, Anrai's fingers clench into a fist and then stretch, itching to grab a dagger. Rage sharpens the lines of his body, keeping him still. Watching Cullen's every move and waiting for the perfect moment, because if it isn't perfect, Cullen will tear us all apart.

"You did this to Yen Girene," Anrai's voice shakes with barely leashed fury. "You ordered all these people massacred."

Cullen's face curves into a sharp smile. A thick wave of nausea grips me. "The Achijj needed to be taught that I am not a man to be double crossed. I think you'll find he's still ruminating over my lesson in the throne room."

Anrai's jaw tightens as if he's just realized something. "The Achijj was the one who sent the assassin," he mutters more to himself than to his father. He shakes his head and presses his eyes closed, the world rearranging itself in his mind. When he opens them, they're filled with undiluted furor. "The Achijj wanted to keep you from getting her. Why?"

"Why does any leader try to keep something from another? Because of its value, of course. There have been rumblings in the darkest corners of Ferusa, whispers of magic returned. Rumors of the Dead Prophecy coming to pass." Cullen continues his slow progression toward us, his movements unhurried.

"What do you care of the Dead Prophecy? You've never concerned yourself with the occult. You wrote it off as nonsense."

"I would be foolish not to at least look into it. I taught you to shore up your defenses, Shaw. That even one crack can lead to rot and dissension. If you are not vigilant in protecting what is yours, you will end up like the Achijj. A useless lout." He frowns in disgust, his eyes flickering toward Cal and Max. "A return of magic threatens the kingdom I've built so I've made it my mission to learn the enemy."

"You wouldn't believe the sort of things I learned in my studies of the curse this year, things that are beyond even you. But one of the most important was learned from a Kashan I tortured in the north. A man had translated the first line of the prophecy." His eyes settle on me. "Unfortunately, the Kashan was freed from my possession before I was able to ascertain what, exactly, the line said."

I stare at him in horror. *Asa.* Asa was the Kashan who helped my father. It was his village that Cullen decimated.

"It was no matter because I tracked the man down. It seemed like a gift from the old gods when I discovered it was no other than Denver, Chancellor of Nadjaa, the very man who negotiated the Blood Pact years earlier to keep me from gaining more power."

Anrai blanches, looking as sick as I feel. "You were the one who had Denver the entire time."

Cullen nods, amused. "I planned to torture him into giving up what he knew of the prophecy and then kill him. If the information died with him, the balance of the Dark World would remain intact. Words have power and one can never be too careful of them."

"Then how did Denver end up in Yen Girene?" I ask.

"I sent my spies to learn whatever they could about our esteemed Chancellor. I learned he was a lover of peace and had apparently appeared out of nowhere years before, with no homeland or family to speak of. I also learned he was running his own makeshift orphanage for unwanted wretches, turning them into his brainwashed disciples.

Imagine my surprise upon discovering that the leader of his pathetic flock was none other than my own *son*."

Cullen spits the word with disgust, the first emotion that escapes his carefully curated control. "So, my plan evolved. I would use Denver for the prophecy, but I would also use him to get to *you*, Anrai. I made you what you are and there is nothing about you I don't know. You would never come to me willingly, not even if I had your precious mentor, because as well as I know you, you know me the same. You'd know I never had any intention of letting him live. I needed a way to bring you to me, willingly and on your knees."

"The Achijj was the perfect opportunity. Squandering his life away on drink and *jovehs*, he was delighted when I dumped an opportunity for more power in his lap. Alas, when he discovered what he should have known from the beginning, that I would never share the prophecy with him, he was a bit rankled. Though I don't feel I should be persecuted for his naivete."

Cullen stops beside Shivhai's corpse. He toes his shoulder, watching with mild disgust as blood gurgles from the open wound at his throat. His proud *legatus* brought low. "This is the Dark World. There is no place for the weak-minded."

"But Aggie's prophecy..."

Cullen smiles a self-satisfied smile and I want to claw it from his face. "Another small trick of blood magic to fool the witch into believing what she saw. A small leak of information to a certain Boundary hunter and my son was as good as mine. I would bring him home to rule beside me, to mete out my judgement in fire and fury."

By the Covinus. Could Cullen really have orchestrated

everything? How he must have raged when he discovered how close he'd been to having his son when we were in his camp.

"What does any of this have to do with Mirren?" Shaw barks impatiently.

Cullen's eyes light with zeal. Dread coils heavily in my stomach. "Have you not yet guessed?" His lips curl in a snarl. "The man you've sworn your allegiance to is nothing but a weak-minded fool. He begged for his life and then he begged me to end it. It's pathetic that you've shackled yourself to such a coward. Do you think he thought of you at all, Anrai, when he sang his secrets?"

Anrai blanches. My look of horror is mirrored on Cal's face and Max gasps audibly.

Cullen's flat gaze falls on me. "He most certainly cared nothing for you, Mirren, *when he gave me the first line of the prophecy.*" He laughs humorlessly. "Eyes of sea and heart of light will ford the Darkness. So simple and yet, the old gods do play, do they not? The girl of the first line is none other than the first Similian to willingly cross the Boundary. The girl my son was now unknowingly bringing to me. The girl who is none other than the daughter of my enemy."

"Bow before me, Ocean-heart, and I will let you live. I will allow you to stay with my son. To rule my kingdom beside me."

"I will never bend before you," I spit. Pain, bright and sharp like lightning digs under my skin as I scrape the deepest parts of myself. There is always water running beneath the earth, if I can just fight further down.

"Grovel on your knees before me, Anrai, and I will let them all live. Those you *love*," he sneers.

Anrai flinches for the first time and Cullen's lips curve

in victory. "Do not insult me by assuming I don't know all. I know the weakness that lives inside you and how you feed it with those most precious to you. And if you do not surrender to me, I will bathe in their blood and relish every moment of it."

My throat is like sandpaper. I want to scream at the loss of my power, at my inability to defend my friends from the evil that has caused us all so much hurt. Anrai's hand slowly comes to the pommel of his dagger. Beside me, Cal and Max do the same. My friends, so brave and good, will never give in without a fight. I feel for the dagger still strapped to my thigh and shove myself to sitting with a cry of anguish. I may have lost the strength of the sea, but I am not weak.

"Ah, ah, Calloway," Cullen says, his calculating gaze sliding to where Cal has strung his bow. Before I can blink, Cullen flicks his wrist and a dagger sprouts from Cal's chest. He stumbles backward, eyes wide, mouth moving in a silent scream.

I scream in time with Anrai's roar, dragging myself to Calloway's side. I circle my hands around the dagger and press down, desperate to staunch the blood that flows too quickly from him. Max lets out an angry snarl, rising with her sword. A vengeful goddess, face full of fury, she makes for the Praeceptor, but he only regards her calmly. "Don't move unless you wish for more of the same, Maxwell."

Max's eyes widen and her lips part in shock. Cullen smiles, tilting his head. "Did you not think I would bother to learn the name of the slave who beguiled my son into betraying me? *Jovehs* have always been plentiful in my war camps. I've often wondered what it was about you in particular that made him willing to throw his entire life away."

Max freezes, sword still thrust in front of her. Cullen palms another dagger, grinning madly. Anrai lunges toward her, but still mired by Cullen's spell, he isn't fast enough. I open my mouth to scream, but nothing comes out as Max staggers. The dagger protrudes from her stomach, blood splashing across the whorls of her tattoos.

Anrai's eyes flare, anger and agony mingling on his face. I reach for him, tears and blood staining my cheeks, but he doesn't come. The steel mask slices down over his features, and he turns to Cullen, the unaffected assassin once more. When he last faced his father, he left with a dagger in his chest. The irony of his friends' fate has to be unbearable, but his voice is flat and bored as if they don't lie dying feet away from him. As if his beloved mentor's breaths aren't becoming less and less frequent. "I will come."

"NO!" I cry. Anguish pools in the holes my power left, the cracks in my soul taken by Shivhai.

Anrai won't look at me as he says, "but there are conditions."

Cullen raises an amused brow. "Have I not taught you better than this? You are in no position to negotiate. Accept my terms or meet my vengeance."

Anrai grins humorlessly at Cullen, tilting his head with that haughty arrogance I know so well. The disguise, to shield what he loves. "You've taught me there's always something to bargain with, *Praeceptor.*"

Cullen's lips flatten, his eyes on the dagger Anrai now spins idly in his palm. As if he remembers the feel of the blade in his heart.

"You will agree to take only me. You will leave the girl. You will not harm any of them, nor order anyone under your command to do so."

Cullen's jaw twitches. "Two of them are bleeding out as

we speak. And the third betrayed you and won't make it alive from this cavern."

Anrai doesn't waver. He's mastered the pain of Cullen's curse and his body no longer trembles. I try to drag myself toward him, my heart crying for the man who loves so fiercely being forced to hide everything he is under a guise of heartlessness once more. For the man who so willingly pays in blood over and over because he thinks he deserves it.

I try to catch his gaze, to remind him that I know his heart, that he isn't a monster, but he has eyes only for Cullen.

"You will agree to my terms, and I will come willingly."

"And if I don't?"

Anrai smirks. "Then I'll kill us all."

My heart jumps to my throat and I stare at him.

Cullen tilts his head slightly, sharing my confusion. "And why would your deaths bother me in the least?"

"Two reasons," Anrai replies assuredly, "One, I will steal my death from you and your vengeance against me will remain unpaid. And two, you don't know the other lines in the prophecy yet."

Cullen opens his mouth to protest, but Anrai only shakes his head. "You don't. If you did, you would have killed Mirren the moment you set foot in this dungeon. But you can't because you don't know the rest. You can't be sure that her death isn't what will bring magic back. So let my friends go. Allow Mirren to return to Similis. Or I will slit her throat and then my own and you can watch the Dead Prophecy come to life and the kingdom you've built crumble before your eyes."

Cullen's face flashes with rage, and for a moment, I fear

he will fling another dagger at Anrai. But instead, he watches his son. "You're too weak."

Anrai stares at him coldly. "Am I, Father? I am your child, after all." His face is a mask of violence and death, the ruthless assassin that will burn the world down to get what he wants.

Cullen nods. "It's a deal."

"Swear it."

"I swear I will not harm any of them," he affirms.

Anrai only waits.

"And I will command no other to do so. So long as you swear your allegiance to me, the girl may return to Similis."

Anrai nods once. Cullen watches his son stride toward him, a long-sought prize, finally his. His face looks skeletal in the dim cavern light, inhuman and cold, as if he imagines all the possibilities to make his son pay for his betrayal over and over again. To strip everything from him until he is cowering and broken.

"Shaw!" I cry out, scraping my nails against the cavern floor and dragging myself toward him. My nails tear and my fingers bleed, but I will crawl until only nubs remain if I have to.

Shaw opens his mouth, but Cullen shakes his head, a knowing smile cracking his sharp face. "I don't mean to hear your meaningless words. You will swear your soul to me, forevermore."

Cullen gestures to the soldiers that Max and Cal tied up, still huddled against the opposite wall. The Praeceptor's men, forgotten and discarded by their own leader. Until now. "Kill them. Give up the last pieces of your soul and turn yourself over to the Darkness. It is only then you will rule beside me. Give up your humanity and revel in fire and blood. *This* is how you shall pay for your betrayal."

Anrai's eyes flare, hesitation and horror flickering across his face. They are gone as quickly as they appear, replaced by hard pressed lips, a locked jaw, and his fingers curled determinedly around his dagger. He means to give himself up. *All* of him.

I take my hands away from Cal. My bones are frail, but I force them to hold my weight as I shove myself to my feet. My muscles shriek in agony and pain shoots through every limb, blinding hot. But I move forward, toward Anrai. To fight and scream and rage until he knows it is not just his own soul he sacrifices. It is also Cal's and Max's. And mine.

In a world where I have never possessed anything of my own, I know it as surely as anything: Anrai's heart is mine. His soul is mine. And if he cannot defend them, I will.

I fling myself across the dungeon, ignoring the pain that crawls up my bones, the splinters of my heart slicing through my chest. Cullen motions to a soldier at the entrance and he runs toward me, sword drawn. I yank my dagger from its sheath and stab him in the hand. Another comes, and another, their arms as tight as iron manacles around my limbs. Energy blooms within me, fed by something deeper than my power. I claw at flesh, kick at bones until I feel them crumple. My screams of *Anrai, Anrai, Anrai,* echo across the dank cavern.

Anrai stares down sorrowfully at the gagged soldier in front of him.

"Don't do this! It isn't worth your vow!" I thrash and shriek, gouging at a soldier's eye until I feel a pop and squelch. Another wrenches my arm behind my back, but I am already bringing my heel down on the arch of their boot. "I'm not worth your vow!" My feet are swept out from under me, and I'm brought crashing to the ground. My arm cracks. The dust inside me climbs my throat and settles into my mouth, burning my tongue.

Anrai finally raises his eyes to me. "You are," he says fiercely. "You all are." I remember the first time I saw him, enamored and terrified by his pale blue gaze. I was reminded of a glacier, cold and remote. But now I only see his fire; the way it warmed and protected me. How it never stopped burning, never for a moment wavered in nurturing my strength, in enveloping me in his own.

"Anrai, don't do this. We will find another way." My eyes are hot, but I have no tears. Every bit of my water is gone, even the part that longs to weep.

Because after everything, Anrai still does not believe that he is worth saving. He will go to the Darkness believing he is worth nothing but the parts of himself he can sacrifice.

"Heal them, Mirren," he tells me softly and I realize why it must be him; why it must be me that stays behind. "Heal them and heal Easton. And then *live*. You are the only good inside me. And you deserve to live."

I shake my head, thrashing as another set of hands hauls me to standing. I rage and scream and slash, but my body is failing. "I don't care if you swear to him in blood and Darkness, Anrai Shaw, you are mine! Do you hear me?! You can never be his because you are *mine*. Now and forever."

His throat wobbles. He presses his eyes closed for only a moment. When they open again, they are blank. He lowers himself in front of the soldier. The man thrashes against his bindings, lip wavering against his gag as Anrai meets his eyes. Even now, he will not gift himself with anonymity.

He opens the man's throat with one efficient motion.

My screams are lost somewhere in my throat as Anrai's

body seizes. He falls to the ground beside the dead man, his temple cracking against the stone floor. He convulses violently and I gasp as his eyes flash from ice blue to pure black.

Cullen walks to him, purposeful and victorious. He takes his son's hand and with a flash, they disappear while I still crawl.

CHAPTER
FORTY-ONE

Mirren

"Did you hear what I said, Mirren?"

I startle, the manor dining room coming back into sharp focus. Calloway blinks at me with large, russet eyes, his lips curved in concern. I smile at him ruefully. "I'm sorry, what?"

"I said, if Denver is feeling up to it, we can prepare to leave tomorrow. Maybe the day after."

I swallow roughly. I haven't seen my father since we returned to Nadjaa, when he was carried up the manor stairs strung between Cal and Max. I only know he lives because of the tendril of my power that lingers inside him and the small bits of information offered by Cal, even though I've never asked.

It isn't that I don't care—I do. It's just that so much of the ugliness inside me is tangled up in him. I know what happened wasn't Denver's fault, but the black hole that opened inside my chest in that dungeon has enmeshed itself with every ugly feeling I've ever felt. And he is at the root of so many.

But Denver isn't the reason Shaw is gone. I am.

Shaw. Not Anrai. I refuse to think of Anrai, with his viciously loyal and longing heart, beholden to the Praeceptor. Refuse to think of the vulnerable and good parts of him being swallowed up by the Darkness. Thinking about him at all opens a gaping chasm within me, one that scrapes against my skin and tears at my lungs. It has been better not to think at all.

"Have you talked to Denver? About going with you to Similis?" Calloway asks, his voice careful. He speaks to me the way one would speak to an injured animal, and I can't blame him. He was the first one I healed in that dungeon. After Shaw and Cullen disappeared, my magic came back to me in a flood that I wished only to drown in. But when it receded, Shaw's words still lingered. I hauled myself across the floor and pressed my hands to Cal's chest. I poured everything into my magic—my grief, my heartbreak, all the wretched pieces of my soul.

As he studies me now, his face a mixture of pity and sorrow, I wonder if I poured too much. If he can feel the depths that seethe inside me.

When he came to, I was half feral. All the tears I tried to cry when my magic was stifled poured over my cheeks and the only words that came were broken and uneven. He tried to comfort me, but I threw him off, focusing on the only thing my mind could hold onto—*heal them, Mirren.*

I healed Max next, pouring my anger and sorrow into my hands, watching as the magic stitched her insides back together until her abdomen was smooth and unmarred once more. Her demands for the story of Shaw's fate bounced harmlessly off me, as if shouted from a great distance.

Then I knelt beside my father's broken body. His injuries were much more extensive than Max and Calloway's, but I put my hands on him anyway. I fed my power every terrible piece of my anguish. I no longer feared falling too far in the depths; in fact, I hoped for it. I gave every last bit of myself, unleashing every terrifying tendril until the world went dark.

When I woke, I was on Dahiitii's back. That was a week ago.

"No," I answer Cal tersely. I stare at the untouched plate in front of me. It's piled with Rhonwen's cooking, but food turns to ash in my mouth lately.

Shaw's words still echo in my mind. *Heal them, Mirren. Heal Easton.* I still have more to do. My brother still waits for me on the other side of the continent and I have wasted enough time. Talking to my father is no longer a choice.

"I will," I tell Cal.

He looks like he wants to say something more, but I turn away from him. A clear sign there is nothing else to say.

I shove away from the table and leave the dining room in silence. I climb the stairs on weak legs. I have lost too much weight in the past week. I will need to fix that if I'm ever going to make it back to Easton.

I pad down the well-worn hallway, ignoring the room where I held Shaw at knife point and then kissed him. Where I claimed him for mine before I knew what that could cost. Before I understood that if nothing is yours, you have nothing to lose.

I pass Shaw's bedroom, where I've been whiling away the hours rifling through his library and wrapping myself in the blankets of his bed. I breathe his scent like a drug, half-mad, as I pour through story after story. At first, I wondered if anyone would come for his things, or scold me for being in there, but so far, no one has commented.

The door to Denver's study looks the same as every other door in the manor, but it stops me in my tracks anyway. Shame showers me as my cowardice displays itself. I am not ready to face him. I don't know that I ever will be. I thought I would feel victorious and fulfilled when I finally found my father; now, all I feel is numb.

I knock softly and Denver's voice sounds from the other side of the door. I let myself in. The office is lushly appointed, all leather and deep wood and old books. But it is impersonal. No pictures hang on the walls, no artifacts on the shelf. Nothing that hints at the life he leads as the Chancellor of Nadjaa.

Denver looks up at me, his eyes the same green as mine behind a pair of wire rimmed glasses. His chestnut hair has all been shorn to one length and it sticks up from his scalp. On his face, angry red scars still gleam. His internal injuries were so great that I barely managed to knit them together before passing out. His external injuries have been left to heal on their own and he will never again be as handsome as the man in my memories.

"Mirren," he says, his eyebrows jumping up in surprise. He stands at once, leaning on a cane and limping toward me. His arms stretch as if he will hug me, but then, thinking better of it, he stops and lingers awkwardly. "I...I'm so glad you came to see me. I really wished to speak with you but didn't want to press."

How Similian of him.

"I'm not here for me," I tell him brusquely. I want nothing to do with his explanations of why he left Easton and I to the whims of the world. I don't want to hear how he found a broken boy and then lost him once again. I swallow, willing my rising panic to recede. I fear that once I let it out, I will be lost in it.

Denver's face sobers, the hope that lingered there extinguished as quickly as it started. "Of course," he says, nodding, "I know you wouldn't leave your brother and your mother without a good reason. Calloway tells me you weren't Outcast."

I stare at him, my reasons for coming to his study ebbing away as the impact of his words hit me. "My mother?" I ask dumbly, my voice sounding strange, even to me.

Denver nods fervently, rounding his desk once more and settling himself in the plush armchair behind it. His desk is tidy, but sparse. I wonder if it is the Similian in him that keeps him from owning much of anything.

"You may have been young when I left, Mirren, but you've always had a pure heart. You've always loved so fiercely. I know you wouldn't leave them unless you had to."

Black edges my vision. "You know nothing of my heart!" I snarl at him. How dare he speak to me of a pure heart when he is the one who corrupted it? When he is the one who twisted it into the tangled thing it is today? Losing Shaw has wrecked me, but my heart was poisoned long before that. It started with the man sitting in front of me. "Mother isn't in Similis," I throw the words at him like knives, and he recoils exactly as if he's been hit.

Satisfaction and shame thread through me as I watch raw grief color his face. He swallows roughly and tears shine in his eyes and though I know that I should look away, I cannot. For as much as I wanted to hurt him with my revelation, it is now an odd comfort to watch my pain play across someone else's face. It is ugly and familiar and for a moment, my heart twinges with recognition.

"What happened?" Denver finally asks, his voice raw.

I shrug with a casualness I don't feel. "I've always been told she was Outcast with you."

"So, you and Easton...you've been alone this whole time?"

I nod and watch as the consequences of his life choices fall upon him, each one a physical weight.

Denver buries his face in his hands and his shoulders shake. Moments pass and we sit like this—him pretending that he isn't sobbing and me pretending that I don't hear them.

After a long while, he looks up at me with red rimmed eyes. "I'm so sorry, Mirren. If I knew—I thought this whole time..."

I shake my head fiercely, unable to hear his apologies. A week earlier, I was desperate for them but now there is only ringing silence. And Shaw's words. *Heal them, Mirren.* "I'm here for Easton," I interrupt curtly. "He's sick and he needs a parental transplant. That's why I came to find you."

Denver stares at me and I can tell there is so much more he wants to say. Questions he wants to ask and explanations he wants to give. But I have no room for them, so I only stare back at him flatly.

His eyes fall to his hands, hands that a week before had been shattered beyond recognition. Now they are whole and strong, the fingers straight and capable once more. "Are you asking me to come back to Similis with you?" He finally asks softly.

"Easton will die if you don't."

"What kind of sickness?" he asks, his voice suddenly

strangely distant. As if he has shifted from being an apologetic father back to the man who runs this territory.

"Does it matter?" I ask hotly. "He will die if you don't come with me. And I've already been gone so long, we need to go as soon as possible. Cal said we should be able to leave by tomorrow."

Denver watches me with sad eyes. Then he drops his gaze. "I can't go with you to Similis."

The words are spoken so quietly that I think I've misheard.

"What?" I say, dumbfounded.

Now he meets my gaze. The crinkling laughter of the man who tucked me into bed every night is nowhere to be found. Something hard glints in his eyes that sends chills down my spine. *The Darkness changes all it touches.* "I can't go with you to Similis," he says again, the words crisp.

I lick my lips and stalk forward, so that I am leaning over the opposite edge of his desk. "Can't or won't?" I challenge.

"Both, Mirren. I am needed here. With Cullen after the prophecy for himself, it's now become even more imperative that I translate the rest of it. I cannot leave Nadjaa and the rest of the Dark World to his evil whims. I must stop him and restore balance."

Now I understand why the set of his mouth and the glint of his eyes seems familiar. It is reminiscent of Cullen when he spoke of his plans.

"You're going to let Easton die?" My voice is dangerously low. I can feel my power circling the void inside me, a typhoon of antipathy and rage.

Denver shakes his head emphatically and I realize he still thinks he is good. Even after all this time in the Dark World, he hasn't realized that there *are* no good guys. That everyone will cross whatever lines they deem fit and sacrifice whoever they need to in order to achieve their own ends.

"Of course not. You healed me. And Maxwell and Calloway. I'm sure you can heal your brother as well."

"I don't know if my magic will even work in Similis! Are you really willing to risk Easton's life on *ifs*?!"

"I have faith in you, Mirren," he replies, and it is only by digging my fingers into the desk that I restrain from flinging myself across it. From clawing and scratching at him until his wounds reopen and then leaving him to the '*ifs*' of healing. He knows nothing about the nuances of my magical abilities and his faith is only a servant of his goals.

"You sold Shaw and I to Cullen!"

"The pain, Mirren, it was unbearable—"

"Shaw sacrificed himself *for you*. He did it so that you and I could live and that we could save Easton. Are you really going to let his sacrifice be in vain?"

Denver's throat bobs, the only crack in his Chancellor's façade. "What Shaw did was admirable. But I fear it is only one more reason for me to stay in Nadjaa. With Shaw at Cullen's side, he is only more powerful. The savagery that will be unleashed, Mirren, I must be here to—"

I slam my dagger into Denver's desk. Denver shies away, his eyes wide. "Mirren, I—"

"No!" I shout. "You listen. You think you're the good guy, the one that is going to bring balance, but you are exactly the same as Cullen. You abandoned your children to face a cruel world alone and now you're abandoning Shaw. He *loves* you and you're willing to sacrifice his last wishes to keep your seat of power. So let me tell you this, Denver. You don't deserve what he gave you. You never did. And you certainly deserve nothing from Easton and me. I will leave this room and I will save my brother and we will never think of you again."

Denver shakes his head, abashed. I grab my dagger and shove it into the bandolier, an old one of Shaw's I found in his closet. "Once, Mirren, I had a heart like yours and I lost everything because of it. I will not make the same mistake again."

I narrow my eyes. "What do you mean?"

He is silent so long that I turn away in disgust, sure he won't answer. It isn't until I've reached the door that he says, "Love," the word is hushed. Ashamed.

"I was Outcast for falling in love."

~

Max is sitting cross legged on Shaw's bed when I return to the room. Her eyes burn as they follow my movements, watching as I carefully place all Shaw's daggers in his weapons locker. I remove the bandolier, my hands running over the supple leather before storing it as well. Every morning I've been strapping Shaw's weapons to me, a ritual that has kept me tethered, but one that will have to end soon. There will be no need for weapons once I cross the Boundary.

"So it's true," Max spits vehemently. I don't shy away from her animosity as I once would have. Now, I bask in it. It's assuredly deserved. "We're leaving tomorrow to take you to Similis."

I nod without looking at her, stepping out of my boots and placing them neatly next to an old pair of Shaw's. His room has always been obsessively neat, and I can only think he'd approve of my keeping it that way.

"You're just going to leave him to Cullen? He sacrificed everything for you and you're just going to leave him?"

I turn to her, meeting her eyes. Her face is angry and vengeful, but something softer simmers behind it. Pleading. She wants me to tell her that Shaw can be saved. She didn't see his knife slice across that soldier's throat, didn't see the last piece of his soul leave his body. She didn't watch his beautiful eyes turn black, vile Darkness twining itself through every bit of who he was. Who he is no longer.

"He's gone, Max. He sacrificed himself so that we could all live. I'm going to respect his wishes and heal Easton."

She shakes her head vehemently, jumping off the bed. Her face is framed by lengths of fluffy coils, softening her regal features. "I don't accept that," she snarls fiercely, "I don't accept that he's gone. And while you're pampered there behind your Boundary, I hope you know that I will be here doing whatever I can to get my friend back. I hope you're tortured by thoughts of him and how you did nothing to save him."

I swallow roughly and pull Max into a hug. Her body stiffens but after a moment, her arms come around me. Her hands tighten, clinging to my shirt as if it's the only thing keeping her from floating away. I know the feeling.

Her skin is soft against mine and I wish for a moment that the anger and vengeance Max feels could be transferred by touch. I wish so badly to feel outrage, to feel *something*, but all I feel is a swirling void. Numb and icy, like the deepest pits of the sea.

There's a soft knock on the door and Max pulls away from me abruptly, wiping at her eyes. Calloway pokes his head in. "Did you talk to Denver?" he asks.

I nod. My eyes wander to Shaw's shelves, lined with so many unread stories. I wish I could bring them all with me, touching their covers reverently and imagining the man who chose them. But there will be no room for them in Similis. There will be no room for anything I've gained in the Dark World, none of the beauty or the pain. There is only room for gray, for sameness; no space for anything *other*.

"We are going alone. We leave tomorrow."

CHAPTER
FORTY-TWO

Mirren

The Boundary extends as far as the eye can see, a metal monstrosity that snakes through the valley, dividing Similis and Ferusa. On one side, the Dark World sprawls in verdant greens, lush and wild. On the other, everything is neatly trimmed. Nothing grows for beauty, only sustenance.

Dread settles over me, the first feeling to burst through the curtain of numbness that's cloaked me on the journey here. Has the wall always looked so foreboding? And why have I always thought it was built to keep things out, when it was clearly designed to hold things in?

My gaze is drawn to the left of the gate. It has been walled over with bricks, but it seems they weren't able to repair the integrity of the Boundary after all. The hole that led me to the most terrifying and most rewarding times of my life. The path that brought me to myself, that freed everything I kept locked away. The passage Shaw gifted me.

I still don't know how he managed it.

"Why don't you wait until morning, Mirren?" Calloway suggests from his place next to me. His voice is light, but his eyes are worried. The same worry has marred his handsome face for the entire week it's taken us to get here, as if he fears I will crumble away to dust at any moment. I don't know how to tell him there's nothing left to crumble. I am a shell, empty but for one driving force. *Heal Easton.* My body continues to move, to eat and breathe, only because it is necessary to complete Shaw's final request.

Even my power lies dormant and cold inside me, starved and stagnant as the bottom of a bog. Soon, I will have to scrape together enough to feed it in order to heal Easton, but for now, I spend a few more minutes in dissociated silence.

"She shouldn't put off the inevitable," Max snipes. The journey here has not tempered her anger. She wears it as a noblewoman would wear a dress—devastating and beautiful in its power. I can only be thankful for it; thankful that Shaw knew the purity of her and Cal's friendship before his demise. That he was at least granted something beautiful before his world turned to darkness. "If she's going to leave, she should just leave."

Her coffee brown eyes fall on me, daring me to contradict her. I turn away before I can think about the other emotion that glimmers softly. Hope.

"Max," Cal scolds softly, but I shake my head.

"She's right. There's no point in delaying." As I say the words, something in me rears back, revolting against the idea of walking through those gates. From willingly locking myself inside those prisoned walls, away from my friends and my magic, silenced and gray once again.

And away from Shaw. Crossing the Boundary is admitting that he is truly gone forever. Because if he weren't, if there were any way to get him back, I would never be able to leave.

"Do you think they'll just let you back in? It's not as if you were just out for a wandering stroll," Calloway says doubtfully. He eyes the Boundary men in the distance distrustfully.

I remember the way they chased Harlan; the gunshot that rang into the clear night as I ran for freedom. "They won't have a choice. I'll force them to listen," I say with a confidence I don't feel. I imagined that when I came back, I would have my father by my side. But instead, I'm doing this alone.

Cal purses his lips as if to argue, but nods.

With shaking fingers, I unbuckle Shaw's bandolier. My fingers brush the soft leather and longing, hollow and aching, pierces through me. I hand it to Cal. "I can't take these with me," my voice breaks and I can't continue. Can't ask that it be cherished and remembered, just like the man who owned them.

But Calloway knows. He runs his long fingers over the daggers reverently, before fastening them over his own chest. A bow has always been his weapon of choice, but the bandolier fits him well and something loosens slightly in my chest.

I hesitate at my thigh. The weight of the simple sheath has grown familiar, the ridges of the carved blade a comfort, even now. And Shaw's cheeky grin as he pressed it into my hand. *Feel free to use it against me any time, Lemming.*

I unbuckle the sheath and shove it unceremoniously into Max's hands. She frowns, staring down at the knife. Knowing what it means.

"Thank you both for everything you've done for me. You are the only true friends I've ever had, and I will never... never forget how that felt."

Cal's eyes shine as he envelops me in a hug. I savor its

warmth, knowing it will be the last for a long while. Maybe forever. Max stands apart, watching us with shrewd eyes. I don't try to hug her again. Everything between us was said in the lines of our embrace in Shaw's bedroom.

She puts a hand to her heart and extends it straight outward. "*Curae sevilen,*" she murmurs.

I nod and turn away before I do something stupid, like cry.

"We'll stay in the forest until first light," Cal calls from behind me. Tears pool in my eyes and my power stirs, brushing against my skin. Awakened and hungry. I want to shove it away. Being numb is so much easier than the brutal tearing of my heart every moment of every day. But I will need it soon, so I feed it my sorrow and loneliness. My hope and my anguish.

As I emerge from the safety of the trees and down the embankment, I feel impossibly naked. I have nothing to cover my vulnerability—no weapons, no trees, and no friends. But I force myself to keep moving. For Easton. For Shaw.

The moment I'm spotted, the Boundary men are a flurry of activity. Clipped shouts ring out. I walk slowly, my hands raised in the air. I have seen what they do to people who upset the equilibrium. I'll be no help to Easton if I'm dead.

"Halt or we shoot," a familiar voice calls.

I do what I'm told. My magic writhes inside me as if it can feel the pull of the Boundary, its cage growing closer.

The Boundary men run over in a well-formed unit; guns raised high. The sight of the weapons no longer raises a spike of anxiety. I know now they are only cold metal. It isn't the weapons that should be feared, but those who wield them.

"I am Similian," I tell them.

The man in front lowers his weapon, golden eyes wide. "Mirren?" Harlan gasps. "Don't shoot!" he barks at the others.

Hope and shock wash over me. "Harlan? How are you—"

He shakes his head tersely, eyes flashing with warning, and I fall silent. "We have orders to bring her to straight to the Covinus."

My magic swirls, shivering with rage as another of the men handcuffs my wrists. I force myself to hold still. Remind myself that I am choosing this. I soothe my *other*, let it run softly beneath my skin. *No matter where you are, you are not caged, little bird. You have wings.*

Harlan avoids my gaze. Another guard shoves me forward toward the gate.

"I wish to see my brother."

There is no response as they yank me through the gate. When we step across the Similian Boundary, my body jerks suddenly. My face scrapes the cobblestones as I fall to the ground, my arms wrenched behind me. Pain burns through me, hot and sharp and I scream as if hot pokers slice through my heart.

"Mirren!" Harlan cries in alarm. He pushes the other Boundary men away from me, but I can't focus on him.

It is just like before when Cullen stepped into the dungeon. I am left brittle and desolate as every bit of my magic is pulled from my body. I look around wildly, suddenly sure I will see his pale, flat eyes.

I will myself to calm, to swallow despite the sandpaper that coats my throat. Cullen cannot be here. He's miles away in the heart of the Dark World with Shaw. I twist myself to my belly and dig my fingers into the stone. My body screams in agony, pain blurring the edges of my vision until it threatens to go black. But I force myself to move, to drag myself inch by agonizing inch until power and water flood my system once more.

I gasp as I'm revived, fresh breath barreling into my lungs. My *other* swirls in agitated rage.

The Boundary men all stare, wide eyed and fearful as I pull droplets from the depths of the earth. It beads along my skin, renewing every part it touches. It pools over my fingers and the handcuffs break with barely a thought.

It was foolish to think I could save my brother by shoving parts of myself away. I began this journey by trusting the wild in me, the part that would never be molded. I won't abandon it now that it has brought me so far, to the doorstep of my birthplace and the precipice of saving my brother. He is all I have left. I won't fail him.

I stand up, drawing my chin high. Even Harlan has gone still, watching warily as the water swirls around my hands. I glare at the Boundary men. "Bring me my brother." My voice is brave and strong, unrecognizable to any who knew me only a few short months ago.

The man beside Harlan hesitates, his eyes on the power that swirls around me as if it will be unleashed upon him at any moment. "That is the Covinus' decision."

He is trembling, I realize distantly. This is the first time they've witnessed such power and it's at the hands of one of their own.

"Then bring me the Covinus'," I command him. He scurries off.

I watch them all in turn, unafraid. Harlan stares back, something flickering in the depths of his eyes that under normal circumstances, I would be trying to decipher. However he came to be here, however he survived, it doesn't matter now. Nothing matters but healing my brother.

The Boundary man returns, and it occurs to me that the Covinus' was somewhere close, watching the entire exchange. Surely, if they'd been in their office in the heart of the square, it would have taken much longer to reach the gate.

A lone figure follows behind the guard, stopping just before the invisible line that drained me of power. I realize with a start that this must be the Covinus. It is not a chosen group as they've always portrayed themselves to be. It is just a single man.

He is slight in frame and stature. White-blonde hair is combed neatly to one side and his eyes glint black as they study me. "Mirren," he says, his voice oddly warm for addressing someone who has flouted all his rules and is currently threatening his Boundary men with magic. "We hoped you would come home to us."

I stare at him from beneath lowered brows. Suspicion wars within me. "Why?"

"Why?" he repeats blankly, as if the question has never been posed to him. It probably hasn't. "Because you are part of our Community, Mirren," he smiles indulgently, and something crawls up my spine. "Are you prepared to come home?"

The word chafes. *I have no home.*

Easton. *Easton is my home,* I remind myself forcibly.

"I will come after I heal my brother. He is dying and I can't heal him if I'm inside the Boundary."

The Covinus tilts his head, mild curiosity the only emotion on his face. I suddenly wish I didn't choose to do this in front of such a large audience. Maybe if I'd just gone to this mild-mannered man's office, I could have calmly explained what needed to happen rather than display an ugly outburst of emotions that make me appear unstable.

Some things never change.

"How do you intend to heal your brother when our most skilled Healers cannot?" The Covinus' voice is calm, belying no emotion aside from moderate concern. It's the same tone we've been told to emanate our entire lives. Kind and gentle. Robotic.

"Bring him to me and I will show you. And after he is healed, I...I will do whatever you ask of me." The words are so reminiscent of something I said ages ago. *I will give you whatever you want.* A handsome grin and a sardonic reply in return, *what if I want your kidneys?*

Nothing has changed and everything has all at once.

The Covinus makes a small motion with his hand and the Boundary men behind him part. Behind them, lies my brother.

My knees weaken beneath me, and everything screams to run toward him, but I force myself to wait as two guards maneuver him over the Boundary. By the Covinus, he's so thin. His knees, visible beneath his medical gown, look like two balls thrust beneath loose skin. My heart clenches as they lay him gently in front of me. His face is waxen. There is none of his kindness or patience. There is only the same emptiness that has echoed in my heart since the cavern. The emptiness of death.

I fall to my knees and take my little brother's hand in a way he would hate if he were awake. Most of the Boundary men look elsewhere, the contact making them uncomfortable, but Harlan watches us with an unreadable gaze. The Covinus also watches, his black eyes emotionless.

The feel of my brother's skin anchors me back inside myself and the numbness of the past two weeks falls away like a torn curtain. I pour everything of my journey since we last saw each other into him. My terror, my bravery, my hatred. My fear and my courage. And most of all, my love. Tears pour from my eyes, and I use those, too. I dive deep into him, my *other* singing and crying and screaming along with us until it soothes every ache and stitches every hurt.

When I finally open my eyes, my body spent, familiar hazel irises look back at me. Our father's green, ringed by our mother's brown. "Mirren?" Easton blinks slowly.

I thrust my arms around him, burying my sobs in the safety of his neck. He doesn't put his arms around me, but his whispered words soothe me. I don't even know what he says, just that the sound is a gentle susurrus in my ear that eases every jagged piece of me.

"I thought...I thought you'd left me," I tell him, pulling away so I can see his face. Behind the sickness ravaged face is the boy with chubby hands who clung to me at night, who laughed with me in secret.

His lips pull into a gentle smile. "I won't ever leave you, Mirren," he says softly.

He pulls himself to standing, taking in the Boundary men that surround us and the Covinus' odd presence with an even smile. In spite of his diminished strength, he is steady when he offers his hand. "It seems you have a lot to tell me," he says, eyeing the crowd as he helps me to my feet.

"Yes," the Covinus agrees, his voice oddly fervent, "it seems she does."

I will tell them whatever they want to know. I will shred myself apart and give up all the pieces a thousand times over to see my brother smile once again. Shaw once told me that there was no part of himself he wouldn't give for those he loved; that he would do it over and over because it would always be worth it.

Oh Shaw.

I didn't understand then, the worth in something as terrifying and powerful as love. I was afraid to name it, terrified that it would sweep me away if I did. Only now do I realize that in being swept away, in giving all of yourself to another, can you truly know who you are.

Shaw, I wish there had been more to give. I would have given all of it.

I take a deep breath, pain and relief and regret a circling maelstrom. I don't let go of Easton's hand as he leads me back across the Boundary. And this time, when I fall, my brother catches me.

EPILOGUE

Shaw

I am the Darkness, and the Darkness is me.

Everything is black. I fall and I fall, an endless chasm of agony. I am only pieces, jagged and raw and I scream into the void as I try to keep them together. They pierce my skin and I bleed, but they never come together. They crumble to dust, blown away in a howling wind.

I am nothing.

I am void. I am vacuous and empty of anything but pain.

I fall and I fall, my screams echoing off nothing. My throat is in shreds, ragged and useless. Waves of sea green shimmer in the distance and I try to claw my way to them, but I am mired. They only ever get close enough to taunt me.

"Come," a voice commands. I shy away, fearful. But it rips into my mind, tearing through places that were mine and ravaging them until they are his. "Come to me, son of mine."

I scream, fighting my way through Darkness, away from

the voice. But the Darkness bites back. It feeds on my body, my soul, until I sob. Until there is nowhere to go except back toward the voice. That voice of hatred and death.

My eyes fly open with a gasp. My body is naked, but somehow in one piece. I bury my face in my hands, not wanting to look at its hideousness. The outward monster must now resemble the inward one, deformed and wretched. I shiver as cold stone presses into my skin.

"Come now, son," the voice calls. My father's voice. It curls around the empty space where my soul once resided, slimy and beckoning. "Now we can truly begin."

His hands touch the bare skin of my chest, his fingers digging into the scar above my heart. I howl and sob, my body lifting off the stone as it convulses, and then crashing down once more.

Now, I wish for the Darkness.

Because now, there is only unending fire. And I burn, burn, burn.

ACKNOWLEDGMENTS

I've always viewed writing as a solitary endeavor, one I was content to keep contained within the boundaries of my own mind. *Tide of Darkness* completely upended that outlook and is better because of it. This book is the result of the dedication and love of so many people, and I am so grateful.

To Shan, for keeping me from throwing the story in the trash on more occasions than I can count. It's because of you I had the courage to not only share Shaw and Mirren's story, but to stay true to it. To Kirstin and Christin—thank you not only for being willing to wade through the madness of my first drafts, but also, for seeing them as what they could be. To Lindsay, my literary soulmate, thank you for the driveway book clubs and always being willing to dive into the psyche of fictional people with me.

To my editor, Tiarra Blandin, you are as exacting as you are amazing. Thank you for your expertise and guidance, as well as your natural penchant for making daunting things achievable.

Thank you to my mom for acting like the story I submitted to the newspaper in fourth grade about Grover the mouse was the most excellent piece of literature you'd ever read. To Memer, for all the love you've given me—and your excellent taste in paperbacks. To my family, near and far, I love you all.

To Michelle, Jeanine, and Laura, thank for your time

and thoughts. To Sarah Hansen, thank you for the beautiful cover. It's beyond what I could have imagined.

To my husband—thank you for seeing me as a writer before you'd read a word. You are the calm to my wild and your support is the only reason this book exists. You worked, managed children, cleaned and cooked, all so I could write, and never once questioned whether it would be worth it. I love you.

Finally, thank you to every reader who has taken the chance on this new author. I will always strive to be worthy of that faith.

About the Author

Amarah Calderini grew up in the Rocky Mountains, and spent her time imagining magic living in the shadows of the peaks. She writes fantasy imbued with equal parts magic, angst, and steam, featuring strong yet flawed heroines and the fierce-hearted men who love them. When not writing, she can be found soaking up the sun and singing along to the same dramatic songs she's listened to since high school. She currently lives in Colorado Springs, Colorado with her husband, two children, and their geriatric German Shepherd.

Check out my website for my newsletter and up-to-date info about what's next.

www.amarahcalderini.com

- facebook.com/authoramarahcalderini
- twitter.com/amarahcalderini
- instagram.com/amarahcalderiniauthor
- goodreads.com/amarahcalderini
- tiktok.com/amarahcalderiniauthor
- amazon.com/author/amarahcalderini

Printed in Great Britain
by Amazon